About the Author

EVELYN "SLIM" LAMBRIGHT, in her own words, says, "I've been a waitress, a bartender, a go-go dancer, a model, a singer, and a numbers runner, among other things, and am now employed freelance, but the less said about that, the better." She lives in Philadelphia.

THE JUSTUS GIRLS

A NOVEL

SLIM LAMBRIGHT

Perennial

An Imprint of HarperCollinsPublishers

A hardcover edition of this book was published in 2001 by HarperCollins Publishers.

First Perennial edition published 2002.

Designed by The Book Design Group

The Library of Congress has catalogued the hardcover edition as follows:
Lambright, Slim.
    The Justus Girls / Slim Lambright.—1st ed.
        p.   cm.
    ISBN 0-06-018476-0
    1. Afro-American women—Fiction. 2. Female friendship—Fiction. I. Title.
PS3562.A463J87   2001
813'.6—dc21   00-065464

ISBN 0-06-095927-4 (pbk.)

02 03 04 05 06 ❖/RRD 10 9 8 7 6 5 4 3 2 1

To Raleigh and Thelma Johnson, the ones who made me, and Agnes Johnson, the grandmother who taught me to read

ACKNOWLEDGMENTS

This writer gratefully acknowledges the support and assistance of Alice Peck, whose name means magic, Carolyn Marino, my very supportive editor, and, most of all, Victoria Sanders, my kick-ass agent, without whom this book would not be possible.

~ SLIM

THE JUSTUS GIRLS

PHILADELPHIA GLOBE

December 28, 1996

WOMAN, 43, FOUND DEAD ON PORCH

by Nicole Brown,
Staff Writer

Police are questioning neighbors after discovering the body of Priscilla Pearson DeLong, 43, who was found dead on her front porch at 5245 Westmont Street early yesterday morning.

DeLong's body was found lying facedown at around 7 A.M. by a neighbor. There was no one else at home at the time the police arrived, and no signs of a break-in.

Neighbors reported they heard what sounded like a firecracker at around four or five on the morning in question.

"I don't know who would want to do this," said Sheila Brewster, DeLong's next-door neighbor, visibly upset. "Everybody on the block liked her."

Police are seeking DeLong's two daughters, and also her boyfriend, for questioning, although they stress they are not suspects at this time.

PROLOGUE

THE JUSTUS GIRLS WERE THE LAST TO FIND OUT

Red Top knew something was wrong even before she had answered the phone that morning. She hesitated to pick up the receiver, so strong was the taste of ashes in the air around her. In the signs: the dogs howling in the middle of the night, the feeling that her face had been brushed by a spiderweb when she woke up this morning, the dream of blue jays flying through the house.

She didn't really have second sight, but she had always been sensitive to shifts in the wind, changes in the flow of things. She was that way about people, too, quick to size them up, sense what they wanted or needed from her. In her line of work, this was a valuable asset.

Death. She could smell it. She knew the what. She just didn't know the how, the why, or the who. She never figured it would be Ursula's girl, Peaches.

Red Top was still seated in her king-sized recliner where she had remained since she had taken the call from Peaches's neighbor, Sheila. Red sighed, looked out the huge bay window into the spacious yard just below her bedroom. She realized she had calls to make, people to talk to, but somehow, she just couldn't seem to will her sixty-something body to move from the spot.

She reached over, poured herself a neat glass of brandy. She knew it would only raise her sugar, but what the hell. She took a healthy sip, sighed again, and glanced at Daddy, who was lying faceup on the big four-poster bed, snoring softly. She didn't have the heart to wake him with the news. Not yet.

It wasn't quite 8 A.M. She cocked her head and listened for a moment. The house was still asleep.

Let em sleep, she thought to herself, lighting a Lucky Strike. She took a long drag. They'll find out soon enough. Lord have mercy.

She shook her head. She remembered when the child was born, when Ursula had first brought her over for all the girls to see. She was a pretty little thing, Peach was. Red smiled at the memory. That was back in the days, the big-time days. Ursula had been young and fine then, a real moneymaker.

I swear, Red thought to herself, that woman must have had a calculator ticking in her brain. She could move em in and move em out faster than any girl she had ever had working for her. She knew how to get that money, all right. Shame she didn't learn how to save any of it. And Peach. Poor Peach. Life should have been a hell of a lot easier for that girl. It damn sure shouldn't have come to this.

She supposed she would call Puddin and Gigi, Peaches's unofficial godmothers, first. Somebody would have to tell Vaa, the other "godmother." Damn it to hell. "Who done it? Who done it?" she whispered, the liquor beginning to swirl around a little in her brain. She didn't realize she was talking out loud, didn't even realize she was crying until she saw Daddy jump, open his eyes wide, and sit up in the bed.

"Done what? What the hell you talking about, Red? What time is it, anyway?"

As he peppered her with questions, his right hand reached out to the night table for his cigarettes.

"Ursula's baby is dead, DB," Red said in a low, dull voice.

"What? Who's dead?"

He had just lit up and was leaning back against the pillows to enjoy his first smoke of the day. He sat up again.

"Now, who did you say was—"

"Peaches. Ursula's baby."

"What the fuck—who did it? Was it that sorry-ass nigga Griff she been runnin round with down to the Devil? Let me get my pants on."

Daddy slid to the edge of the bed and he was almost about to stand before he remembered he didn't have his legs on. He pitched forward, grabbed the nightstand for balance, and moved back up on the bed again, where he smoked quietly for a few moments.

"Who did it, Red?"

His voice was deep and mellifluous, the same low-toned whiskey voice that had charmed so many women so long ago.

"I don't know, DB. Don't nobody know." Red shook her head slowly. "You know, Sheila, that girl that live next door to her? She called this morning and told me Ursula found her on the porch about a hour ago, shot in the head. She was already dead. The police and all is still over there."

"You call Puddin and Gigi yet?"

"I ain't called nobody yet. I didn't even want to wake you up wit it."

"Well, somebody better start callin somebody round this mothafucka and findin out some answers with the quickness. Somebody gone pay for this shit. That girl never bothered nobody. She always rolled cool. Somebody got to pay," he said. "You know that, don't you, Red?"

Red Top shook her head solemnly in agreement.

"Was she working at the Devil last night?"

"Yeah. Sheila say Peach worked at the bar and walked home. She say she heard Peach talking to somebody outside, but she couldn't tell who it was, even if it was a man or a woman.

"Then she heard Peaches's music come on the hi-fi, she was playin

Aretha, you know how she do, so Sheila say she went on back to bed. Say she heard something that sounded like a car backfiring, just once, no more, and she could still hear the music playing, so she went on back to sleep again.

"That was about five this morning. She looked at the clock. Next thing she know, she heard Ursula screaming and yelling for Peaches to get up." Red was speaking rapidly now, as she always did when she was upset or nervous. Daddy had already taken his Magnum out of the nightstand and it was lying on the bed next to him, a box of bullets beside it.

Red didn't know what he had in mind, but she knew it was useless trying to talk him out of anything. Besides, he was right. Somebody had to pay, and somebody had to do it. She just didn't want it to be him.

"Get one of them girls to draw my bath and lay out my clothes," he said, moving again toward the edge of the bed. "And I'll be wearing my charcoal pinstripe, gray silk tie, and gray fedora."

Red nodded and pressed the in-house intercom.

"Yes, Miz Red," a soft southern voice responded.

"Nettie, draw a bath for DB, please, and lay out his things. You know how he like em." Red repeated the rest of DB's instructions to the maid.

"He'll be ready for his bath in about ten, fifteen minutes. Thanks, Net."

"You welcome, Miz Red."

Red Top stood up and stretched, catching a reflection of her face in her vanity mirror. Still a fine-looking face, if she said so herself.

And after she had bathed and applied her makeup, after she had scented her body with Joy and piled the famous mane of russet red hair atop her head, it usually was a mighty, mighty fine-looking face.

But not today. All the powder, all the perfume, all the makeup in the world wouldn't mask the sagging, the sorrow, and yes, the blood-red rage she wore on that naked face today.

By nightfall, the White Devil Bar and Grill was packed, people three-deep to the bar. Everybody had heard about the murder by now.

The news had raced up and down the strip and in and out of the small surrounding streets like two cops in a car chase.

There was a feeling almost like a mild electric current circulating among the patrons and staff. People who hadn't been to the bar in weeks, months, came by to pay their respects. One of the best barmaids in West Philly was now dead, cut down, gone too soon, and they wanted to be there to toast her memory and pay their respects.

These were the oldheads, the forty- and fifty- and even sixty-something bunch, the ones who had flashed in the fifties, styled in the sixties, and stayed high and fly in the seventies. They had struggled in the eighties when the magic time died, the time when they were new, shiny, and beautiful, when their eyes had glowed and everything seemed possible.

Now, in the nineties, greatly reduced in numbers, they carried themselves like old combat soldiers wearing invisible medals and stars of survival. They no longer turned their faces away from death, as they had when they were younger. They were familiar with it now, recognized it, and gave it its proper respect.

And they enjoyed their triumphs, the winning, the feeling of beating the odds, of standing up to life over and over like undertrained, punch-drunk boxers, still somehow answering the bell, coming out for the next go-round. Still standing.

This impromptu gathering at the White Devil Bar and Grill was really part wake, part family reunion.

Someone had brought in some tapes from the sixties and early seventies: Temptations, Smokey, Otis, Delfonics, Blue Notes, Sam and Dave, Aretha. Their music. Real rock and roll, Black folks' music.

Puddin and Gigi and even China Doll, another of Ursula's old friends, were there.

Red Top and Monsieur Daddy Baby were there, Daddy with his back to the wall as usual, leaning back in his chair at a huge table, nodding and whispering to various visitors, looking for all the world like some seventies movie star Black Godfather, only better. Sheila Brewster, Peaches's neighbor, was there, telling her story again and again to anyone who would listen, thoroughly relishing her big moment in the spotlight.

Red had caught up with Peaches's old friend Vaa earlier at Bebe's House of Beauty, getting his hair done. After hearing the news, he had been too distraught to do anything but go straight home and take to his bed. At first.

Yet, here he was, decked out in black, waving his bejeweled cigarette holder around dramatically, coming dangerously close to setting somebody's hair on fire more than once. He was a vision. A vision of what, no one was quite sure, but that was Vaa, solidly and steadily marching to his own very distant drummer.

As the night grew longer, the music and the conversation grew stronger, feeding off each other.

There was much wine, many tears, bear hugs, and plenty of beer.

There were old wrongs righted, and new loves slighted, as old loves looked new again through the haze of memory, music, and stronger spirits at work. And, of course, death being so close, there were more than a few near fistfights. The usual, when someone they loved passed on.

All in all, it was a hell and a heaven of a night.

Peach would have loved this, Vaa thought, shaking his freshly coiffed head of jet black waves. This was a real home-going ceremony. "This is your night, your people, your party, Miss Peach," he whispered softly to the mirror behind the bar as he lifted his glass. "Precious Lord, take her hand, and lead our baby girl on home."

"More champagne, please," he yelled loudly to the barmaid, Bad Tooth Shirley, waving the glass around in the air. "And don't make me have to come back there and get it myself, ho."

No one had bothered to tell the Justus Girls—Jan, Sally, and Roach—about the gathering until late that afternoon, when Peaches's daughter, Princess, had called Jan from the Medical Examiner's Office, where Peaches's body had been taken. Jan had called Sally Mae, who in turn called Roach.

And that's how it came to be that the Justus Girls finally found out that Priscilla "Peaches" Pearson DeLong, their ace boon-coon, the wild child, midnight mover of their Four Musketeers, was gone.

CHAPTER ONE

THE FUNERAL

Hello, Aunt Sally? It's Princess. We're gettin ready to leave now. Yall are gone ride in the limo with us, right?"

There was a slight tone of anxiety in her voice, a small flutter.

"Sure, baby, we on our way, soon as we pick up Janice. How's everybody holdin up? How's your sister and her kids makin out?"

"Well, so far, so good. Kim's takin it pretty hard, but the kids, they too young to realize what's really goin on."

"Okay, fine. Now, Princess, just in case we don't have too much time alone when I get there, I want you to know I'm here for you. Any problems, just let me know. You know we yo family now, me, Jan, and Roach, don't you?"

"Yes, ma'am, Auntie. Thanks."

"Here she is now. I'm on my way. See you in a minute. Stay calm, baby."

Sally Mae heard a slight sob on the other end of the line, then nothing but the dial tone. Poor babies, she thought, as she set the receiver down. Kim was only twenty-six, and Princess was what, twenty-two, twenty-three? Way too soon to lose their mama. As she grieved for these now-motherless children, the front door opened and in came Omar, her own son.

"Ready, Mom?"

"Yeah, just about. You go head back to the car. Where's my grand-baby?"

"Well—" he hesitated.

"Well, what?" Sal glanced around at him quickly.

"Well, Miss Shirley offered to keep Doll, and I figured that would be best, since she too young to be goin to a funeral, anyway."

"That rotten-tooth cow?"

"Aw, come on, Mom. She is her grandmother, just like you, and I know how busy you and the aunties are gone be." Omar ducked his head, not meeting Sal's eyes.

"Well, I guess one day won't hurt. But know we gone stop and get her after the funeral, now, don't you?"

"Whatever." A quick flash of annoyance passed over Omar's face, then was gone. "You look real nice, Mom."

Sally smiled and finally stopped fidgeting with her hat.

"Thank you, baby. Now, you go head. I be right out."

She brushed her hand across his forehead, tracing the high, deli-cate arch of his eyebrow, so like his father's. Omar leaned down and kissed her cheek.

"Lookin good, Mustang Sally."

"Boy, git on outta here."

Sal blushed in spite of herself. Mustang Sally. Where had that come from? It had to be a coincidence. He couldn't possibly know—She knew she wasn't too shabby for a forty-something ole babe. It was true. Though she had put on a bit of weight in the last few years, she could still squeeze into a size 12. While the face now showed a few more laugh lines than she would have liked, and that pesky frown line between her brows seemed to deepen with each passing year, her breasts were still holding up pretty well, and her waistline was well defined.

The legs, her best feature, were still long, slender, and beautiful. Mustang Sally. She chuckled to herself, shaking her head at the irony of her son teasing her with the nickname she had been tagged with so long ago. If he only knew.

She grabbed the phone before the end of the first ring.

"Sal? It's Rasheeda. Jan's here now. They're out in the car, and I'm on my way. We'll be in our van, and we'll follow you over to Jan's. And Sal?"

"Allah is with us today."

"I sure hope so, Roach. We can use all the help we can git." Though Rasheeda had been using her Muslim name for over a decade, the JGs had never called her anything but "Roach."

After a brief conversation, Sal hung up, grabbed her purse, and took one last look in the mirror.

How could Peaches be dead, God? How could you let her die? She's only six months younger than me.

Oh, Lord.

Fresh tears streamed down her cheeks, ruining her carefully applied makeup. She heard the horn honking somewhere. It dawned on her that it was Roach and them, waiting for her in the car.

Okay, she could do this. She'd just fix her face in the car. She adjusted her hat once more, and went out to the car.

The small procession pulled up in front of Bible Way Baptist Church. This was where Peaches, Jan, and Sal had attended Sunday School, Bible School, and where they had been baptized. Rasheeda sometimes came with them, even though she had gone to Catholic school.

The little church looked even tinier now than it had all those years ago. It stood silent and unforgiving, like a betrayed lover.

Sally Mae stepped out of the limo first, glancing upward to the top of Bible Way's tall spire. She shivered in the cold weather. Janice followed, stepping right into and sharing Jan's memories. The church itself, the very building, seemed to rebuke them, holding Peaches like a hostage, forcing them to return.

They pulled their coats tighter, trying to shield themselves from the deep bone-damp chill that only a Philadelphia winter can bring. Rasheeda stepped out next, standing in between her friends. Sal looked at her and smiled. She was envious of her friend. Islam seemed to have given Rasheeda a calm, centered confidence and sense of peace that Jan herself had once felt at Bible Way, but no longer.

Sal had left the church years ago, disenchanted with the way the membership seemed to turn more inward, insulating itself, even as the problems in the community grew ever larger. Instead of reaching out, Bible Way sat like a lonely outpost in the middle of a war zone. So she had abandoned God's house, and instead of the church, had begun to rely on herself.

As for Jan, once a member in good standing, a strong voice in the choir, the Willing Workers and various other clubs within the Bible Way family, she hadn't been here since Junie, her beloved husband, had passed, and Sal knew she didn't want to be here today.

As for Roach, a former Catholic, she bit her lip, remembering all the times she had snuck out of Mass early to join the others at this very same church, all the while praying that her soul would not be damned to hell for doing so.

One by one, the family exited the flower-covered limousine. First Princess and Kim, Peaches's two daughters, then Pumpkin and Lang Lang, Kim's two children. From the second car came Rasheeda's fourteen-year-old twin sons, accompanied by their father, Hakim, followed by Omar, Sally's only child.

They could see a line of people already entering the church. A few waved or nodded. There was Puddin, Gigi, and China Doll. Tookie and everybody from the White Devil seemed to be there. There was Sheila Brewster, still running her mouth. Even Monsieur Daddy Baby and Red Top were there.

Mr. Daniels, the mortician, nodded. Jan had met with him previously, once with Kim and Princess, to identify the body, and once again with Sally Mae and Rasheeda to attend to the preparations and details of the funeral. Thank God, Peaches had kept her small insurance policy paid up, and even that wasn't quite enough to bury her properly.

The women had all dug into their own pockets to come up with the $1700 more needed to pay the total bill.

Mr. Daniels smilingly assured them that everything was in order.

With that, the women closed ranks around Kim, Princess, and the children, and they all began to walk up the steps and into the church, their own children following closely behind. As they walked in, two by two, the choir, led by Bertha Gray, began singing, "God Will Take Care of You."

Bertha was a shy and awkward girl who didn't say much, but when she sang, ahhh, when she sang, her voice, a sound somewhere between a child's prayer and a sigh from heaven, made the old folks in the church weep and the younger ones grab each other by the hand.

They could see the casket as soon as they entered, all bronze and peach satin. Kim immediately started to break down.

"Mommy, Mommy," she wailed plaintively.

Her broken spirit seemed to flow into Jan, who swayed slightly.

All Rasheeda could think to do was hold on to Kim as tightly as she could.

"Come on, Kim. Come on, baby girl. You have got to do this for your mom. We all have to get through this. Let's just move on down to the front, now," she said slowly, as if speaking to a very young child.

Princess seemed frozen on the spot, staring straight ahead, her eyes locked onto the casket bearing her mother's body.

"Come on, chile, I got you. Aunt Sally got you."

Tenderly, Sally Mae placed her arm around Princess's shoulder and led her down the aisle. Sal and Rasheeda took each of the childrens' hands, while Mr. Daniels stepped in beside Janice, patting her back and speaking to her in soothing tones.

The little group swayed down the aisle, almost in perfect cadence to the song being sung by the choir.

Finally, they reached the front pew and were seated by the ushers. Jan was surprised to see Rome, Peaches's ex-husband, along with his mother and brother, seated in the second row. She nodded, and though his eyes were red rimmed and moist, he managed a grim smile.

"Brothers and Sisters, we come here on this winter morning to say good-bye to our beloved mother, daughter, wife, sister, and friend, Priscilla Pearson DeLong," the new young minister intoned, opening the service.

"Yes, Priscilla was her given name, but most of you knew her as Peaches. And though I didn't personally know this sister, I understand from those who did that if you called her Priscilla, or anything else but Peaches, she would look right past you as if she didn't even know you."

A soft ripple of laughter filled the church.

"And so today, out of respect for those who loved her, especially for you, her family, whom she leaves to mourn her passing and to send her home, this morning, we will call her Peaches."

Well, he wasn't Reverend Fox, but so far, so good, thought Sal. As the minister eulogized Peaches, assisted by facts supplied to him earlier by Jan, Sal, Rasheeda, and the girls, each of the Justus Girls sat lost in her own thoughts about their friend.

They sat suspended in time, ostensibly listening to the service, secretly praying that this was a dream, that the pretty, peach-toned partying girl they knew would suddenly come dancing down the aisle, teasing them all for being silly enough to think she could ever really die, yelling, "Psyche, psyche, psyched your mind," laughing her fool head off.

But this was no dream. This was real. The stiff, waxen figure lying in the coffin with too much orange makeup and the strange page-boy hairstyle really was their friend. The mortician had explained to them that the hairstyle was necessary to conceal the bullet wound in her forehead, but still, her bangs were almost down to her eyes, obscuring almost the entire top half of her narrow, now blood-drained face.

"Oh, shit, oh, shit, it's Ursula." Jan had reached around Princess and was tugging on Roach's arm.

"And she's drunk."

"Aw, hell," Sal whispered, lowering and shaking her head.

Indeed, it was Ursula, Peaches's mother, walking none too steadily down the aisle. Ursula, wearing one of her too-tight red dresses, a big black straw picture hat, FM heels at least six inches high, blood-red lipstick painted way over her natural lip line, eyes glassy and tortured. It was showtime in hell.

"My baby, my baby," she cried out, spreading her arms theatrically. "How am I gone make it without my baby? How am I gone live?" she said, sobbing loudly.

The young minister, who had been reading his sermon, glanced up from his notes, looked at Ursula, and checking out her getup, stopped in midsentence, his mouth open but nothing coming out. He looked over at Jan, Sal, and Rasheeda.

His eyes seemed to be pleading, "Save me, save me."

The Justus Girls looked down at their hands in their laps.

"Aw, hell, the shit is on now," Sal muttered to no one in particular.

The Reverend was still watching them, trying to get a clue as to how to proceed.

Ursula whirled around, following his gaze. "What chu lookin at them hos for? This is my chile, my chile. I birthed this chile. I am the mother." Ursula slurred her words, her lips twisted to one side.

"Ma'am, maybe you would like to have a seat," the minister suggested. He looked quite frightened now.

"I don't need no seat. You have a seat. I don't need no damn seat." Ursula was getting pumped up now. She lurched toward the front, almost losing her balance, pointing a wobbly finger.

"Um-hmn. Yeah. I see all yall up in here, thank yall so damn cute. I am the mother, and yall didn't even bother to come and get me."

By now, she was at the very front of the church, and when she said "me" she pounded on her chest, stumbled a little, and had to hold on to her daughter's casket for support.

"My own granchirren. My own grands. And yall, too, Miss Jan, Miss Sally, and Miss Roach. Thank yall so high and mighty." Ursula spat out the words.

Her eyes were trying to focus on the faces before her.

"And, Rome, I don't know what the hell you and yo family here for, you and yo stuck up mama. Yall downed her when she was alive. What cha come round here now for? Dat's my chile."

"And you, Kim, you really thank you slick, don't you? Sittin up here cryin and carryin on and everything. I know why yall ain't come get me. Cause yall knew I would turn this mothafucka out, dat's why."

She started to move toward them, lost her balance again, and grabbed onto one of the flower displays, which teetered ominously, even as did Ursula's six-inch heels. Kim and Princess started toward her, but both were held back by Sal and Jan.

It happened really fast. One minute, Ursula was standing there cussing everybody out, turning out the joint, the next minute, she was down on the floor, covered with an array of flowers.

In an instant, two male ushers had her by the arms and were calmly but firmly leading her from the room. Her picture hat had fallen off and her long wig was leaning sideways. The mourners, many in tears by now, covered their mouths with their hankies and dropped their heads. No one wanted to laugh out loud. After all, it was a funeral.

All the way down the aisle, Ursula protested, yelling about "all these sorry-ass mothafuckas up in here," but once out in the vestibule, she screamed.

"Oh, God, I'm so sorry. Oh, God, why you take my chile? Why my chile?"

Her voice was wracked and ragged, breaking each heart in the room all over again. She sounded like an animal that had just been shot, stunned and full of pain.

CHAPTER 2

THE WAY WE WERE

As the minister spoke, Jan's mind drifted back to the time when she had first met Peaches. Though most people thought they were cousins, actually, they were no blood relation to each other at all. Jan's late uncle by marriage and Uncle Prez, Peaches's father, had been brothers.

And so it happened that one Thanksgiving when she was about four or five years old, Jan's grandmother had had her customary dinner for the whole family and whoever else showed up. Aunt Liz, her father's sister and wife of the late Harry, had invited Prez to dinner, and he had brought Peaches along with him.

After first eyeing each other warily, Jan invited Peaches to play jacks with her and Peaches accepted.

"Oh, look at the girls. They look almost like sisters. Cousins, at least," someone had remarked, and it was true. Though Peaches had the fairer complexion, while Jan was more of a deep nut brown, the two girls both had the same long legs and arms, same slender necks and high cheekbones.

Jan was shorter than Peaches and a little heavier, but from a distance, they almost looked like sisters.

"Cousins, that's what we are." Peaches smiled, revealing two missing front teeth.

"Okay, cousin." Jan laughed, in turn revealing her own missing tooth, plus showing off her new front tooth to Peaches. They shook hands, intertwining their fingers. This was serious business.

And that's the way it had been ever since.

Eventually, all the kids knew that if you got in a fight with one of them, you would end up having to fight them both. After a while, most kids didn't bother to try them.

Jan lived in an apartment complex with her parents. Her grandmother lived a block away. Both parents worked, so Jan stayed with her grandmother every day after school until one of them picked her up, or sometimes overnight. She was treated by her parents more like a little adult than a child, and spoiled a little, especially by her dad.

Her father was a construction worker and her mother did hair in a beauty salon located halfway between her grandmother's house and the elementary school they both attended. Jan often stopped at the beauty shop to say hello to her mother and the other hairdressers on her way to and from her grandmother's house during lunch periods and after school.

She wore nice clothes to school, got an allowance, and her hair was washed and neatly pressed each week by her mother at the shop. In general, she had a happy and uncomplicated life. On weekends, she would stay over on Friday nights with her grandmother and Aunt Liz, so her mother and father could have what her grandmother called a "vacation" from her.

On Saturday mornings, her father would come for her, and they often spent half the day out together. They went to breakfast, went to the barber shop, the record shop, and even to the neighborhood bar, where Jan would be treated to soda, potato chips, and pretzels, and fussed over by the staff while her dad put in his numbers for the week.

When they finally arrived home, her mother would scold her dad in mock angry tones for keeping her baby out half the day, in dangerous places like bars and number houses, but Jan could tell she was just kidding and was really happy to see them both.

"Yeah, woman, yeah," was all her father would say. But he would scoop her mother off her feet as if she were a feather, spin her around, and give her big kisses.

"Put me down, you crazy man," her mom would scream, but he would just keep spinning her and kissing her. Jan loved to see them like this. Sometimes they would all go to a movie, sometimes to see an event at the Rec Center across the street from her apartment complex, which had typical activities for children as well as for adults: cards, table tennis, Pokeeno nights, checkers, et cetera.

Jan pretty much had taken her relatively fortunate life for granted, until she got to know how Peaches was living. Peaches stayed in an apartment over top the Tip Top Lounge, one block from Jan's grandmother's house, with her mother, Ursula.

Peaches and Jan walked to and from school together, and Jan's mom did Peaches's hair also and gave them both the same hairstyle weekly.

Jan had heard her aunt Liz speaking to her grandmother at the Thanksgiving dinner about Prez and Ursula's poor little girl, that poor child, but it had not registered with her then. Peaches had been well dressed and obviously happy to be with her dad. But Jan learned during their walks to school that Peaches had only once seen her dad since that Thanksgiving dinner and that had been in Family Court, where her father was fighting to gain custody of her.

Peaches's mother was adamantly against her ex-husband getting custody of their daughter, and even though he had visitation rights every other weekend, Ursula would take Peaches and leave the apartment, so that when her father arrived for her, there would be nobody home. They had gone to court many times and each time, her mother would coach Peaches on what to say.

Ursula had convinced Peaches that if she was placed with her father, she would be treated badly by her father's girlfriend, who had two children of her own and one son with Prez. She had also made Peaches believe that without the support money Prez sent every two weeks, she wouldn't be able to afford a place to stay, as she was too ill to work full-time.

So every time they went to court, Peaches and Ursula would put on their little dog-and-pony act.

Ursula would break down and cry, accusing Prez of all kinds of unspeakable acts, and Peaches, on cue, would run to her mother's arms, crying and pleading with the judge not to take her away from her mommy.

Meanwhile, Prez would try his best to convince the judge that he sent support checks every two weeks on time, that he loved his little girl, had never laid a hand on her in an unfatherly way, and that he and his girl-friend would welcome his daughter into their home with open arms.

He would also claim that Ursula was, among other things, a pros-titute, a small-time con artist, a booster, and an unfit mother. He would claim that Ursula left his child alone in the apartment at night, that the few times he did get to see his daughter, she had looked unkempt and uncared for, and that the support money he sent was not being spent on Peaches, but used to support Ursula's fast lifestyle.

He brought witnesses in who swore they had seen Ursula in bars late at night when they knew Peaches was home alone, and other wit-nesses who claimed to have seen Ursula taking strange men, mostly white, into her apartment late at night, when they knew, said the wit-nesses, that Peaches was there. They swore the men were sometimes not seen leaving the apartment until the next day. They testified that Peaches often appeared sitting in front of the apartment on the curb, dressed in dirty clothing, hair undone, while Ursula entertained men upstairs in the apartment.

The fact that all this was true did not help Prez in the least. It was to no avail. Family Court was a lot different back in those days. The courts generally believed children were better off being raised by their mothers.

So over and over, Prez took Ursula to court, Ursula and Peaches performed their little show, Prez took any witnesses he could corner in with him, and over and over, the judge of the day reached the same verdict.

Priscilla was to remain in the custody of her mother.

Seeing her father fighting so hard for her, seeing both of them fight over and over, broke Peaches's heart. Each time after the proceedings were over, she got a chance to say a few words to Prez alone. He usually brought with him a little dress or coat for her and always a toy, usually a doll. She loved getting the dolls, but she loved seeing him even more.

She loved him very much, but she believed what her mother kept telling her, that as soon as she moved in with them, Ms. Earlene, her father's new girlfriend, would treat her badly, that Ms. Earlene was only pretending to like her and want her, that she would treat her own children better.

And besides, she could not, would not leave her mother. Peaches was all she had. Who would be there to take care of her, if Peaches left?

"I have to stay with Mommy, Daddy. She needs me more than you do. You already got a wife and three children. Mommy only got me."

Once she saw his eyes fill with tears, after she had again patiently explained this to him, sounding as if she were reciting a poem she had memorized.

"Don't cry, Daddy. I still love you. I will love you all my life, cross my heart and hope to die." She had placed her tiny right hand over her left breast.

"But Mommy needs me more. Can't you see she needs me more? I'm all she's got. Can't you see that, Daddy."

Her voice had started to rise a little, to get a little shaky. She grabbed her dad's hand, her eyes pleading with him.

"Yeah, Peachface, I guess she does," Prez had answered sadly, and with that, he held her tight, kissed her on the cheek and sat her down again.

He picked up a gift-wrapped box that had been sitting on the floor next to him, placed it in her arms and was gone.

"What he bring you this time?" Ursula walked across the room quickly and grabbed the box. The two of them went over to a bench in the courthouse corridor, sat down, and Ursula opened the box.

"Shit, another damn doll. You got dolls enough already. He could least give you some money. Another damn doll. What we suppose to do wit this one, eat it?"

And that's how it came to be that Peaches had more dolls than she had dresses, more toys than shoes.

Ursula expected Prez to buy the clothes and shoes, while she spent the support check on God knows what. By the time they had walked to school together for about three weeks, Peaches had blurted out the whole sad story to Jan, who was horrified.

Peaches was often left in the apartment alone at night, and the child would be terrified by strange noises. Subsequently, she began breaking out in rashes. First on her legs, then her arms, finally on her neck and around her hairline. She had to go to school wearing thick pink lotion, and of course, kids being kids, she was teased unmercifully and got into fights with her tormentors.

Even though Jan fought by her side, Peaches got to the point where she dreaded going to school, wearing the pink sticky lotion. Once when she came home with a dress torn from fighting and explained what had happened, Ursula had responded by beating her legs with a belt. So then she had welts, a rash, and ugly pink lotion on her legs.

So she simply stopped going. By then, the girls were entering the second grade. When Peaches hadn't shown up for three weeks, Jan walked around to her apartment after school. Peaches was there, sitting out on the steps of the house next door to the Tip Top. She had her dolls all lined up on the steps in rows, and she was playing school, she being the teacher.

"Hey, cuz, how come you haven't been to school? Where you been?" Jan ran up to her, worried but relieved to see her friend was alive and seemed well.

"I ain't going back to that damn school. Them kids tease me about my rash, I get into fights, tear up my clothes, then I get a beatin. I hate it. I hate school."

She tried to hold back the tears but it was too late. Jan was by her side in a second.

"Stop crying, Peach. Stop crying." Jan patted Peaches's back slowly, speaking softly, the way her own mom did with her when she cried.

"Your mother been letting you just stay home?" Jan asked when Peaches had calmed down a little.

"Naw, she don't know. See, I leave the house like I'm goin to school every day, but I go right around into that alley there and just walk around in the backyard and play all day. I sneak my dolls back there, too," Peaches grinned, speaking in a low conspiratorial whisper through her tear-streaked face.

"Girl, you gone get in trouble. Sooner or later, the teacher's gone send the truant officer to your house. You better start coming to school."

Jan was completely stunned. Why, anything could happen to Peaches out in those alleys. She looked at Peach with newfound respect. She must really, really hate school.

"I ain't goin back lessen they come and get me and make them kids leave me alone."

"But, Peach, you know I'm fighting along with you."

"I know, but I'm tired of fighting all the time," Peach had said wearily.

As Jan had predicted, about a week or two later, the truant officer, Mr. Grimes, did show up at Ursula's apartment. Ursula had insisted that she had been sending Peaches to school every day since the beginning of the school term. She called Peaches upstairs.

"This man here say you ain't been to school since the term started. That was almost three weeks ago. I tole him I been sendin you every day. Now, just what the hell is going on here?"

Peaches began to sniffle. Her eyes teared up. Her body trembled and her skinny knees began to knock together.

"I be hidin every day in the alley. Them kids," she said, sobbing, "them kids tease me and pick fights with me just cause I have a rash and just cause I'm scared to stay home at night by— by myself, and I have to wear that nasty ole pink lo-lotion."

With that, she threw herself in front of the truant officer and seemed to pass out. Down to the floor she went.

"Oh, my God, this poor child," said Mr. Grimes, a thin, bespectacled nerdy little white man. "There, there, dear. Don't take on so. I will have a meeting with the principal and your teacher, and we'll put a stop to those kids teasing you. I'll take care of that first thing in the morning." Grimes knelt down beside the girl.

"Mrs. Pearson"—he looked up at Ursula, his voice taking on an officious tone—"perhaps you might come to the meeting also. This child is far too young to be left at home alone under any circumstances."

"But she not, sir. I'm here every day with her. I keep watch on my chile," sputtered Ursula.

"Well, apparently you haven't been keeping watch for the last three weeks, if the child's been right under your nose in the backyard, and you didn't even know she wasn't in school."

His eyes had a hard glint in them. Ursula sized him up, thinking quickly. She walked over to him, a slow, deliberate walk.

What the hell, he was just a man, and if Ursula knew one thing, it was men.

"Look, I'm just a poor, single mother, tryin to raise my chile all by myself. I know we can work this thing out, you and me," she whispered in a low, confidential tone, lowering her eyes to half-mast and pursing her lips so her dimples flashed. She lit a cigarette and stared at him meaningfully.

"Care for a little drink? I got scotch, and I think I got a lil vodka."

Grimes gazed back at her. He had sized up the situation when he first entered the apartment. The tall, beautiful cinnamon-colored woman, now looking a little rough around the edges, the red shimmy dress hanging over the hallway door, the smell of the cheap perfume, the five or six different brands of liquor lined up on the little makeshift bar against the living room wall, the high, high, spiked black patent heels lying on the floor, as if someone had kicked them off and left them where they lay.

Ursula was pulling on the back of her long black wig, hoping she had it on the right way, while at the same time trying her best to strike a seductive pose.

She was wearing a red silk kimono, bare feet, and red nail polish. Nothing else. She pulled the robe tight, so the outline of her breasts and hips showed through.

"So what you say? Come on, honey, give me a break." Her voice was soft. Her lips, full and moist, curved into a slow confident smile. He looked her up and down. Damn, she was sexy as hell, the kind of woman that could probably make a man—

"Oh, please, mister, please. Them kids will tease me again, and I'll get in fights and tear my clothes and get a beatin again and still have to wear that nasty pink lotion," Peaches pleaded, widening her overflowing eyes, and staring up at him in a most pitiful way.

Grimes straightened up immediately, clearing his throat. "Don't worry, Priscilla. After our meeting tomorrow, no one will tease you anymore. I guarantee it. And I expect to see you there, too, Mrs. Pearson, bright and early, nine A.M. sharp, in the principal's office. Good day."

He walked quickly to the front door, turned back once again.

"I'll see you tomorrow, Priscilla. Go and wash your face, honey," he said gently, and left.

Ursula stood silently by the window for a few moments, until she was sure Grimes was gone.

"Why, you lil hussy. Carryin on like that, actin like you were bout to die or somethin. You acted like you were in Family Court or somewhere."

"Yes, Mommy. I did."

Peaches stared right back at her for a moment, slowly and deliberately, then stood up and walked into the bathroom and calmly washed her face. She smiled at her reflection in the mirror, the same confident smile Ursula had just tried to use on the truant officer.

Ursula hooted.

Little heifa learn fast, just like her mama, she said to herself, and with that, she put on her face, slipped into the red dress, stepped into the spikes, wrapped a black feather boa around her arms, and was out the door, going to work.

Hmph. A girl's gotta eat, she thought.

After that day, things did get a little better for Peaches. Ursula did not stay out all night that evening, and the next morning, Peaches and she were in the principal's office at nine sharp. As a result of their meeting, her teacher informed the whole class that anyone teasing any student for rashes, ringworm, stuttering, et cetera, would be suspended from school, on the spot. So that was the end of that.

Janice and Peaches went back to walking to and from school together, and Peach's rash slowly cleared up. Ursula was spending most of her evenings at home now, and even though she was doing business in the apartment she shared with her seven-year-old daughter, at least she was home.

Ursula could be a lot of fun when she was in a good mood. She sometimes would let Peaches and Jan dress up in her glamorous clothes, high heels, and wigs, and she and her working girlfriends would make up the little girls' faces with lipstick, rouge, and false lashes.

"You are going to be beautiful girls one day. Don't blow it," China Doll, Ursula's half-Asian friend would always warn them cryptically.

"Yes, ma'am," they would answer politely, though they had no idea what she was talking about blowing, and she never elaborated, except to warn them to stay in school, get their education, or they'd be sorry.

Of course, they would stay in school. They were only seven years old. What else would they do? In the meantime, they practiced their moves, trying their best to walk, talk, and move like Ursula.

Sometimes Ursula would take Peaches and Jan up on 52nd Street to the drugstore for milkshakes and cheesesteaks, and when Ursula walked down the Strip with her long black wig swaying in the breeze, her full, high hips working, her breasts jutting out against her tight dress, wearing the highest spike heels she could find, well . . .

CHAPTER 3

BACK TO
THE FUNERAL

Jan." Someone was shaking her, pulling her back to the present.

"I'm going to see about Rome. He looks like he's having a hard time." Rasheeda leaned over the children and whispered, tilting her head toward the exit.

Jan nodded.

Peaches's ex-husband, Rome, had suddenly bolted from his seat and up the aisle, a hand covering his eyes. Rasheeda followed.

He looked pretty bad today, she thought to herself as she walked. Hair gone almost white, missing teeth, stooped body, Rome looked a good ten years older than she knew his age to be. She smiled, remembering when Jerome DeLong had been super, super fine, back when Peach thought he'd hung the moon.

"Rome," she said softly, catching up to him in the foyer, placing a hand on his shoulder.

He turned, looked down into her eyes, his own streaming. Rasheeda reached out and grabbed him to her, giving him a long hug. Rome held her tightly, trying to compose himself.

"Rome, I know you're coming back to Jan's house afterward. Don't let Ursula spoil Peach's last day on earth," she whispered, patting his back.

"I'll be there, Roach, I'll be there," he replied gruffly, clearing his throat.

"Roach, what happened to us? You know there was a time when all I could see was Peachie. Never had eyes for nobody else. Just Peachie. What happened to us?" He sighed, shaking his head slowly.

"I don't know, sweetie. All I remember is how crazy she was for you. All we heard about back then was Rome this, Rome that."

Rome nodded, a small smile also playing over his face.

"Nobody knows why things turn out the way they do sometimes. I mean, just look at me and Hakim." Rasheeda smiled up at him.

Rome's eyes lit up. "You ain't lyin, sis. Just look at you. And— Hakim." He smiled, a hint of that old devilish grin still there.

Rasheeda blushed, put her arm through his, and gently led him back into the service.

As she returned to her seat, Rasheeda tried to pay attention to the sermon, but talking to Rome, remembering their first meeting, took her back, way back.

Roach and Peaches were fifteen years old, and she had let Peach talk her into going down to South Philly to play hookey from school. Peaches was going to be with Rome, and Rachael was supposed to talk to this cute boy from their high school named Danny. The hookey party was at Danny's house, as both his parents worked in the daytime.

Rachael had never even been to South Philly before, let alone to a hookey party, but she had seen Danny at a few parties up the way, and though he didn't seem to know she was alive, Peach insisted that Danny had specifically asked her to bring Rachael along.

"He wants me to come?"

"Yeah, child. Said he seen you around, and noticed you givin him the eye," Peach had said, smirking.

"Giving him the eye? I never said two words to that boy."

"I ain't say nothin bout no words. I said the eye."

Rachael was shy, and unsure of herself around boys, who thought she was stuck-up, and said she talked like a white girl.

"He said you, Rachael, Roach, you. Gol-ly." Peach rolled her eyes dramatically.

Peach had nicknamed her "Roach" not long after they met, for no known reason, and the name had stuck.

So the girls met that morning and caught the bus to South Philly. They got off the bus in front of a small corner candy store. They went in, bought sodas, then waited outside. Pretty soon, Rome and another fellow sauntered around the corner and walked right past them, Rome giving Peaches a big stage wink.

"Yo, that's the signal. We supposed to wait till they halfway down the block, and then follow them. We not supposed to look like we're with them." Peach hunched Roach's arm.

They watched as the boys strolled down to the middle of the block, crossed over to the other side, and disappeared between two houses. After a few minutes, the girls did the same. When they reached the backyard, they looked around, saw no one.

"*Pssst!* Up here, up here!" a voice called from above. On the fire escape, on the second-floor landing, there stood Rome, grinning down at them.

"Hurry up!"

Roach and Peach scooted up the stairs quickly, and followed Rome into the building. They found themselves in a bedroom that looked as though it belonged to Danny's parents.

"Come on, everybody's downstairs," Rome whispered.

As he led them out of the bedroom and down the stairs, they could hear voices all over the house and rock and roll music playing softly. Danny was seated on the living room sofa, along with two other boys.

A bottle of vodka and a carton of orange juice sat on the coffee table, directly in front of them.

"Well, hello, ladies, hello. I want yall to make yourselves comfortable. Sit anywhere you like, but you sit with me," he said, pointing to Rachael and pushing the other boy off the sofa.

Roach smiled bashfully, looking down at her shoes.

Peaches nudged her arm lightly, nodding her head in the direction of the dining room. It was then that Rachael noticed there were more people, two other boys and two girls, back in the kitchen, sitting around the table, playing cards.

"Everybody, this is Peaches and Rachael. Peaches is Rome's girl, and Rachael is the one for me," Danny announced, taking Roach by the hand and leading her over to the sofa. She was pleased that he called her by her real name.

Rome walked over to the coffee table and mixed himself a generous drink. "Can I get you one, baby?" He winked at Peach.

"Yeah, but just put a teeny weeny lil bit of vodka in mine."

"Ha," Rome laughed out loud.

"I know your teeny weeny. You must be tryin to impress Roach here, cause you know I know you."

Mixing a full-sized drink, he reached over and handed it to Peaches.

"To us, baby. Young, gifted, and Black." He clicked his glass against hers, fixing her with his smile.

"Love, peace, and hair grease, baby," Peaches replied, laughing. They drained their glasses as if running a race. Rome immediately bent down at the table to make refills.

"Whoa, man, slow your role. Save some for the rest of us," Danny said.

"Aw, man, we got another half gallon. We straight," Rome answered in a dismissive tone, and continued to mix the drinks. Peaches took hers and pulled him over to the love seat by the front window.

The two of them started in giggling and kissing right away. Roach was a little embarrassed, but pretended she was used to such goings-on. She really wanted to make an impression on Danny that she was not some little Catholic school goody-two-shoes girl. She was hip. She was down. So when he made a drink for her, then refreshed his own, she accepted it with a smile and a toss of the head.

"Down the hatch, baby doll?" Danny whispered, his sexy brown eyes narowing in to focus on her.

"Down the hatch." She tried her best to gulp down the vodka all at once, the way Peaches had done it.

She failed. Miserably. Rachael choked, wheezed, and sputtered, tears forming in her eyes from the taste of the liquor. She could not stop coughing.

"Hold on, there, Mama, take it easy. Everybody ain't no alkies like Rome and Peaches, you know." Danny laughed as he patted her back gently. Grabbing a napkin from the coffee table, he proceeded to wipe her mouth.

"Fuck you, man. I heard that," Rome said from across the room.

"Yeah, fuck you, man," Peach echoed. By now, they were up on the floor doing a mean slow drag to Smokey and the Miracles' "Bad Girl." It was a slow dancing, kissing, feeling, grinding motion, all done in perfect time to the music.

Danny turned his attention back to Roach again.

"Don't pay them no mind, Mama. Just make pretend it's just you and me in here today." He patted her hand, motioned to her drink.

"Just sip it slowly and relax. I can tell you not used to it. No big thing. Just relax. We got all day long. Want a smoke?"

He offered her a Kool from the half-full pack on the coffee table.

"Sure. Thanks." Roach smiled, allowing him to light the cigarette for her. She took it from him, sucked in a deep, satisfying drag, then sipped at the drink.

She felt more at ease almost immediately. It wasn't so bad, after all, when you just took a little bit at a time, she thought to herself, feeling very grown up.

Rachael had been smoking cigarettes since she was around thirteen, as had all her girlfriends. They had started out by sneaking them from their parents and smoking them on the way to and from school. Then they graduated to buying their own at Billy's, the neighborhood hangout, where Billy sold them his brand, Camels, no filter, two for a nickel, five for a dime. So much for adult supervision. Pretty soon they were taking their allowances and lunch money and buying their own packs of Kools, Salems, Newports, all the menthols.

After a few more sips of her drink and finishing her cigarette, Rachael noticed she was feeling even better. There was now a warm glow spreading from the pit of her stomach all the way out to her extremities. It was a feeling similar to the way the anesthesia had made her feel when she had had her tonsils removed, just before she went completely under, kind of dreamy, but warmer this time. Her nervousness and inhibitions began to melt away, and her tongue untied itself. She found herself chatting and laughing with Danny as if they were old friends, comfortable and at ease with him.

They sat facing each other, side by side, the music of the Temptations playing in the background.

Roach had always thought Danny was handsome, but now, up close like this, with the music and the vodka, with the touch of his hand on hers and the gentle, teasing tone in his voice, she was just beside herself.

Oh, God, look at his eyes! So pretty. He really does like me, she marveled to herself, closing her own eyes tightly, and opening them again wide, just to make sure she wasn't dreaming.

"Come on, Mama, let's dance." Danny lead Rachael out onto the floor. By this time, Peaches and Rome had disappeared upstairs. They could have gone to Mars, for all Roach cared. All she wanted was to be wrapped in Danny's arms.

Roach was aware that there were still some people back in the kitchen. She could vaguely hear them, and she assumed they were still playing cards.

But as Danny pulled her closer into his lean, hard body, their voices and everything else were drowned out completely by the touch, the feel of him, the very smell of his maleness, and the beautiful falsetto of Eddie Kendricks. If she snuggled in close enough, she could even hear Danny's heartbeat.

"How many have I had now? Two? Three?" She giggled, as he dropped a few ice cubes into her cup.

"Who cares? Have as many as you want. There's more where that came from." Danny winked and drained his cup. He leaned over and kissed her fully, his tongue snaking into her open mouth. Roach pulled back, a bit startled, a feeling of fireworks shooting off inside her head.

"Wow, a French kiss. I've finally been French-kissed." So this was what Peaches and them were talking about. Felt good, real good.

So when, after a few more drinks, a few more dances and a lot more kisses, Danny suggested they go upstairs, she willingly went along. She would have gone anywhere he wanted at this point, as long as he kept kissing her and holding her this way. Danny stopped at the first bedroom, knocked lightly at the door.

"Man, get the fuck outta here," a deep male voice grumbled.

Roach giggled, clapping her hand over her mouth.

"*Shh,* girl, don't make so much noise," Danny cautioned, as he led her to the second bedroom and knocked again.

"Excuse me, somebody's in here," Peaches yelled loudly. They both giggled this time, and walked down the hallway to the third bedroom. Danny knocked.

"Forget about it. We is occupied in here. You got to wait yo turn," answered a male voice.

"Damn! Can't even get a bedroom in my own house."

As they started back down the stairs, Roach noticed that the steps seemed to be rising up to meet her.

"I got you, baby. Hold on to me." Danny grabbed her and and helped her slowly down the steps.

"I feel so—light." Roach lifted her arms. "As if I could fly away."

"Only place you flyin is over here with me."

Danny pulled her across the room, fell back on the sofa, and pulled her down on top of him. Before she could protest, he grabbed the back of her head and covered her mouth with his.

Deep, probing kisses, all over her face, in her ears, on her neck. Her body shivered as if she had just been hit with ice water, but burned at the same time. He flipped her body quickly so that she was now on the bottom and he was on top.

One of his hands went under the top of her school uniform, while the other slid under the bottom, straight to her panties. She couldn't figure out how he had managed to get the top of her jumper down, but somehow, she was all undone. Her bra had been pushed up to her throat. His mouth dropped down from her neck to her left breast. She felt the hot, moist mouth on her titty at the same time she heard the wet, slurping sound his mouth was making.

"Oh Lord," Roach said, groaning. It must be a sin to feel this good. She'd have to make confession next Sunday.

As Danny sucked one breast, then the other, his right hand was between her legs, rubbing up and down, up and down. She felt her body moving to meet his hand, arching up as if it had a mind of its own, bucking and grinding.

"Oh, Mama," he whispered hoarsely. Within seconds, he had his pants down, her panties off, and her legs spread. He was straining mightily, trying to force his long, hard dick into her wet, yet unyielding pussy.

"Oww, Danny, it hurts. Stop." Roach whimpered weakly, and it did. All the hot, yearning pleasure she had felt only a moment ago had vanished, and searing pain had taken its place.

"Please, Danny, it really hurts." Roach was pleading now, and more than a little scared.

"Come on, baby, come on, just relax, just go with it," Danny said harshly. He was pushing harder and harder. His arms and body were clamped down on her in such a way that she could not move, could barely breathe. He was not stopping.

"Oh, man, push it in, man. I want some of that next, man. I'm up for sloppy seconds."

"Me, too, man. Damn! She a virgin!"

Rachael looked up over Danny's shoulder in the direction from where the voices had come.

The two boys from the kitchen were standing over them, staring down at them with glazed expressions.

The taller boy had his hand on his crotch, rubbing it.

The shorter of the two, heavyset, with bad acne, actually had his dick out and was holding on to it, flicking his thumb back and forth across the tip. He grinned at Roach and drooled.

"Hey, man, don't wear her out," he said.

Rachael screamed, and screamed again.

"What the fuck?" Danny froze, midstroke, turned his head, and looked up at the boys.

"Hey, man, git the fuck outta here! Ain't no train goin down here, man. I don't play that shit. Git outta here!"

Danny rose, trying to stuff himself back into his pants, but suddenly, the two boys were pushed to either side, and Roach saw Peaches standing over them, her eyes blazing.

"Da fuck is this shit? Oh, no way. Yall think yall gone pull a train on my roadie? Yall niggahs must be crazy. I don't believe you, Danny. You know better than to try to pull some shit like this," Peaches was yelling at the top of her lungs.

Danny raised his arm in protest, looking embarrassed.

"Damn, Peach. I swear to God, I didn't know they was comin in here."

He gestured toward the two guys, who had slunk away into the dining room, adjusting their pants, then he looked sheepishly at Peaches. He didn't look at Rachael at all.

Peaches dismissed him with a wave of her hand, and a shake of her head.

"Come on, Roach, let me get you to the bathroom," she said softly.

Peach helped Roach fix her clothes, stood her up, and marched her up the stairs and into the bathroom.

Roach moved along behind her, dazed. She felt as if she were somewhere off in the distance, watching this whole scenario happening to someone else. She couldn't quite get her bearings.

Once they got into the bathroom, Peach sat her down on the edge of the tub. She took a washcloth off the rack, rinsed it out, and gingerly began to wash Rachael's face.

"Lissen, girl. I know you go to Catholic school and all, and you not used to boys, like I am. But let me tell you somethin. You can't never, never let no boy get the upper hand on you, like you did today. Girl, don't you know they was gettin ready to pull a train on yo ass? I can't believe that damn Danny. I swear to God, if I knew he was like that, I'da never brought you down here. That lowlife, sneaky, lyin-ass dog."

Rachael opened her mouth to answer her, but instead, started to vomit all over the floor.

"Aw, hell." Peaches reached for the wastebasket and placed it on the floor in front of her friend.

"Just go head and throw up, Roach. You'll feel better." Peach held Roach's head down with one hand and wiped her face and clothing with the other. Roach began to cry.

"It's all right, honey. You ain't done nothin wrong. We might be the same age, but, honey, I'm a whole lot older than you in a lotta ways, and I'm tellin you, you ain't done nothin wrong. You just gotta learn how to get what you want outta boys before they get what they want outta you, that's all."

As bad as Rachael was feeling and as much as her stomach was turning, something made her look up at Peach. She sensed more than knew that what Peaches was saying was true, at least for her, and that when it came to boys, she would never be as old as Peaches.

When the girls went back downstairs, no one was in the living room except Rome. Peaches stared at him stonily and kept on walking.

"I ain't have nothin to do with it, Peachie. I swear. You know I don't play that train shit. Sorry bout that, Roach." He looked first at Peach, then Roach.

"Yeah, well, later, Rome. We splittin," Peach said curtly. By her tone of voice, one couldn't tell if she believed him or not.

"See you tonight, baby?" Rome asked hopefully, as they picked up their books and headed for the door.

"Oh, no. Not tonight. I got something else to do and someplace else to be. Babe." Peach didn't even bother to look back.

Damn, she is so cool, thought Roach. She held her head straight up, imitating Peaches, and the two of them marched out the door.

This lesson in boys, booze, and music would stay with Rachael forever. Of equal importance to her was the knowledge of having a true friend, someone who had your back, who would stand up to a houseful of guys way across town, in the name of friendship. She vowed that day to return the favor, if Peach ever needed her.

"The old man's here," Rome whispered to Roach, leaning forward and patting Kim and Princess on their shoulders.

All the women turned, following Rome's gaze, in time to see three men coming down the aisle, side by side. One was a broad-shouldered white man with a crew cut, the second was a tall, muscular Black man. In the middle was Prez.

The men approached the coffin slowly, Prez looking neither left nor right. As he stared down silently at his only child, his shoulders began to shake violently, and the white man handed him a handkerchief.

The Black man reached an arm over and patted him on the shoulder, revealing the handcuffs linking the two together.

After a while, the three took seats. Prez's eyes were wide and haunted.

"You see that? Don't make no goddamn sense to have both of them bringin him in here like that. He's an old man! Where he gone run to?" Sally Mae whispered loudly. Other family members and friends nodded their heads and grumbled in agreement.

"They ack like he's Public Enemy Number One or somebody. Damn, all the man did was try to sell a lil likka to make ends meet, run a lil card game. So they busted his speak and found some drugs up in there. So what? He wasn't holdin the shit; one of his customers was holdin." Sal was livid.

"Well, at least they brought him, and you know they really didn't even have to do that," said Jan, sighing.

"Praise Allah for small favors." Rasheeda nodded.

"And excuse me, Lord, for cussin in yo house and all, but damn," said Sally.

Jan and Rasheeda suppressed smiles. Sally Mae was going to be Sally Mae, wherever she went.

The service was coming to a close now. The minister gave the benediction, and the final viewing procession began. The choir sang sweetly, just as Jan had requested, "Take My Hand, Precious Lord."

Two by two, the family and friends walked up the aisle to view the body one last time. Everything went smoothly until the mortician offered a small square-shaped cloth to Kim and Princess, so they could cover their mother's face before the coffin was closed.

"No, no." Kim was on her feet, grabbing the man by the arm.

"You can't put that on her face. She won't be able to breathe. Tell them, Auntie. She can't breathe with that on her face. You can't do that."

Kim was screaming and trying to pull the cloth from the man's hands. Sal and Rasheeda had to restrain her, quickly leading her out of the church.

Just as she reached the door, Jan looked back at the pulpit once more, up to the large painting of the Black Christ on the cross that graced the back wall of the church. She turned quickly and hurried to catch up to the others.

On a snow-covered hill in Mt. Lawn Cemetery, on a cold January morning, the homegoing ceremony for Priscilla "Peaches" Pearson DeLong was completed. The minister said a small prayer, the mourners said their amens, the daughters wept and said their good-byes. Rasheeda's husband, Hakim, and Rome embraced tightly.

As the mourners walked back to their respective cars, Janice, Rasheeda, and Sally Mae lingered awhile at the gravesite. Each dropped a personal item down onto the flower-covered casket, then turning together, holding hands, they started back down the hill.

CHAPTER 4

MUSTANG SALLY: BACK HOME

Girl, where the likka at?" Sally Mae whispered to Janice.

"It's in the shed kitchen, Sal. You know I can't put it out yet. And don't be giving nobody none, except family and close friends for about an hour, at least. They can have beer, but only in the white paper cups," Jan instructed. "Don't be leaving beer cans all over the place, so everybody can see."

"Now, you know I know how to ack," Sal tossed over her shoulder, starting for the shed.

"Yall don't need to be drinking already. We just got back from the cemetery. It's only one o'clock in the afternoon. Dag," Rasheeda said, a concerned expression on her face.

"Shut up, Roach," said Sally.

"Shut up, Roach," said Janice. "See, you don't know about the unwritten rules of Black Baptist funeral etiquette, because number one, you came up a Catholic, and number two, you are now a Muslim. But there's certain things you've gotta know about how to put on a decent Black Baptist homegoing."

"Yeah." Sally picked up the ball. "The first thing you gotta know is at a Black funeral, a Black Baptist funeral, especially if the person was a drinker, you gotta have likka. Don't you know if we didn't have no likka up in here today, these people would go outta here and be talkin about us like a dog? Not only us, Peach, too."

"Sure would." Jan nodded her head knowingly.

"It's a serious insult, and we just can't let Peach go out that way."

"Well, why are you hiding it back in the shed kitchen? Why don't you just put it out on the bar, or on the dining room table, and let the guests serve themselves?" Rasheeda asked, looking at both of them.

Sal and Jan looked at each other, then looked at Rasheeda, snickering and shaking their heads.

"You can't do that. You just can't put it out right away. First, you serve the food and desserts, with coffee, tea, and soft drinks, of course. Then after about an hour or so, you can give out the drinks," explained Sal patiently.

"But only beer at first. Then the liquor," added Jan.

"Then you can put it on the table?" asked Rasheeda, still clearly puzzled by all this Black Baptist business.

"No, Roach, you never just put it out on the table. That's real low-class. It's just not done, and I'm not about to start it today, even if Peaches was a barmaid," Jan stated emphatically.

"It's just not done. It's not propa etiquette, don't you know?" mimicked Sally, in a high nasal pseudo-British accent, holding her right pinky up in the air.

They all fell out, laughing, even though Rasheeda didn't quite get the joke, didn't quite understand after all these years some of the more unusual customs of her own people.

"You Black Baptists and your rituals. And yall have the nerve to call our Muslim practices strange," she said, shaking her head.

"Don't feel bad, Aunt Rasheeda. It don't make no sense to me, neither, and we're Baptist, too," piped up Princess.

They were all in Jan's kitchen now, preparing platters of chicken, greens, candied sweets, potato salad, baked macaroni and cheese, corn, roast beef, and potato salad to set out on the dining room table. People had been dropping off pots of food for the last two days, so they had plenty. Janice had set up the coffee and tea servers and iced the sodas before she left for the funeral.

People were arriving at a steady rate, and the women knew they had a busy afternoon ahead of them. It was a wise decision the women had made to receive the guests after the interrment at Jan's house. There was no way Peaches's two-bedroom apartment could have held all these people.

More were coming by the minute, friends of Peach, of the girls, as well as some friends of Ursula's, although Ursula hadn't shown up. Yet. They had already decided that if she showed up acting like she had at the funeral, they would be more than ready to deal with her.

"Ole bitch wouldn't even let Peach die in peace," muttered Sal, sucking her teeth.

"Cool it now, Sal. A little respect, for Peaches's sake," cautioned Rasheeda.

"*Hmph*. She can start that shit if she want. I will step all into her world," Sal responded, narrowing her eyes.

But so far, there was no Ursula, and things were going fine. As soon as they arrived, the women had gone upstairs into Jan's bedroom and taken off all uncomfortable clothing, hats, heels, panty hose, and slipped into something casual, returned downstairs, put on aprons, turned on Gospel music, the old-time kind referred to as spirituals, and began laying the preparations out on the dining room table and sideboard.

They had set up a photo of Peaches on a small table in the dining room, laid with a white starched tablecloth. On the table, they had set a bowl of fruit, a tray of sweets, a small bottle of water, a shot glass filled with rum, a small saucer full of coins, a small saucer of rice, two

green lit candles and two red ones, an ashtray holding a single unlit cigarette. One each side was one of Peach's dolls, covered with jewelry.

They had settled Kim and Princess in one of Jan's guest bedrooms
with the two children. They'd brought them plates of food, soda, and
juice for the kids and tea for the girls. After a short Christian prayer
from Jan, a Muslim prayer from Rasheeda, and a spiritual prayer from
Sally, they had talked softly to the girls for a few minutes, then left
them alone, assuring them again that they would be no further than
downstairs should they be needed.

Now, there really wasn't much left for the women to do, except to
make sure everyone's needs were attended to. Some of the people
from the community center where Sal worked had come over and
pitched in, helping to take peoples' coats and trying to find parking
places for cars, the men doing any heavy lifting that was required.

Jan looked up at one point and was suprised to see Princess downstairs pitching right in, helping out. She figured the girl had to have
something to do to work off nervous energy.

Kim had remained upstairs with the children all afternoon, and
Sally had remarked that the child had seemed remote, distant, was
"actin downright strange," but Roach had scolded her friend gently,
reminding her that everyone had their own way of dealing with grief.

Sally Mae, chastened by her own bouts with loss, had let it go.

Jan smiled, watching Princess moving among the guests, talking,
smiling, hugging. "Looks more like her momma every day," Jan whispered to Sal, nodding over at Princess.

"Yup. And her sister lookin more and more like her daddy," shot
back Sal darkly. Jan put a finger to her lips, giving Sal a silent warning.

"Girl, what you doing down here? You go sit down and rest," Jan
said out loud to Princess.

"I don't mind, Aunt Jan. I want to help. I need to have something
to do," Princess protested.

She grabbed some ice trays from the refrigerator and began to
refill ice buckets. Truth was, Princess liked being in the company of
her mother's oldest and dearest friends, her "aunties," as she had

been taught to call them, and that was the way she thought of them. She had known them all her life, and just being close to them now made her feel her mother's presence.

As they swirled around her in the kitchen preparing platters, refilling bowls, icing cakes and at the same time tossing around words like *honey,* and *chile,* and *daughter,* she could almost hear her mother's voice, her full-throated laughter, mixed in with the voices of her friends.

It was for that very same reason that Kim had remained upstairs most of the afternoon. Each time she looked at them, she was reminded too much of her mother.

"I don't understand why yall do a lot of those things, either. Aunt Rasheeda's not the only one. I don't understand all that stuff about the liquor and all," Princess said. "And why did yall stop the clocks? Why are all the mirrors covered? And what's up with that little table with them candles and food and stuff under my mom's picture?"

Sally and Jan looked over Princess's head at each other, nodding their heads. Somebody would have to sit this child down one day and tell her all about the ways of Black folks, the old ways that her mama should have told her, if someone had told her. She might be over twenty-one, but clearly, she wasn't grown yet.

"You want to tell her?" asked Sal.

"You tell her, Miss Mother Africa. You know it better than me." Janice waved.

"I know it, cause I'm a Geechee girl, straight out the South, where I was raised to know it. Not like yall lil citified girls with yo citified fancy ways," Sally sniffed, fluttering her lashes and pantomiming an exaggerated stiff-legged walk, what the boys used to call a white girl walk. "I tell you what. Later on, we'll tell you and Kim, and then you can tell Kim's kids and yo kids, when you have em. It's stuff every Black woman oughta know."

"Well, I don't know. When are you going to tell me?" said Rasheeda, pouting.

"Later on tonight, Roach, after all these folks leave," Jan answered.

"Yeah, cause we got some talkin to do tonight anyhow." Sal nodded. "Now pass me a drink, Jan, scotch and ice. I'll mix in the soda myself. And put it in one of them lil white cups."

"You know, I think I'll have a beer myself," Jan said as she poured.

"I'll have some apple juice," Rasheeda piped up.

"Oh, for Christ's sake, Roach," said Sal.

"Don't even start, Sally Mae. You know perfectly well I'm Muslim now, and I can't be drinking no liquor."

"*Ahh,* but there was a time . . ." Jan's voice trailed off as she looked skyward.

"Shut up, Jan." Rasheeda smiled.

Princess looked at the three of them. She shook her head, smiling, too.

The rest of the day went without incident.

Rome, his mother, sister, and his little son by his girlfriend came by and were very nice. He talked to Kim and Princess for a long time upstairs.

The staff, as well as many of the patrons from the White Devil, stopped by and presented Princess with a beautiful card and $300 and change they had collected.

Rome and his family had put up over $500 toward the funeral expenses.

Even Red Top and Monsieur Daddy Baby made an appearance, Red Top decked out all in red, as usual.

Daddy Baby, slim and elegant as ever, flashing gold, gave the girls another $500. Actually, he put the money into Sally's hand.

"This is for the children, Sally Mae," he said simply, thrusting an envelope at her.

"Why, thank you." Sal took the envelope, surprised that he was even there. She knew they were friends of Peaches's mother, Ursula, but she herself only had a nodding acquaintance with this mysterious man, the onetime biggest pimp in the hood. She was surprised that he even knew her name.

He stood there staring at her for a few minutes.

"Can I get you something?" Sal asked, remembering her manners.

"No, I'm fine. Red's taking care of me."

Sal followed his gaze across the room to where Red Top stood talking with some of the Devil's regulars. Turning back, he cocked his head, staring at her again.

"You know who I am, don't you?" he said finally.

"Sure, I know who you are. I just don't know you. I'm surprised you know who I am."

"I make it my business to know everything and everybody round here, and everything that's goin on. And I'm a make it my business to find out who killed that lil gal, too."

Sal looked at him, not quite knowing what to say.

"Have yall heard anything?"

"No, not a damn thing," she answered truthfully.

No one seemed to know anything about Peaches's murder. Nobody could think of anyone who would harm her. She had been so well liked.

"Yeah." Monsieur Daddy Baby shook his head. "If this was back in the day, I could maybe understand it. But that gal had settled down these last few years. I already checked out her old man, that Griff dude. He got a solid alibi."

Sal nodded. She had heard about Peaches and Griff, about them supposedly being in love, going together for about the last six months, and from what Princess said, even talking about marriage.

"Well, if you do hear anything, you will let me know, won't you, Sally Mae?"

"I sure will, and thank you for coming."

There was something vaguely familiar about the man. She couldn't put her finger on it, but whatever it was, it made her uneasy, uncomfortable.

She moved on to hand the envelope over to Jan, who put it up with the rest of the donations that had been coming in all afternoon. Even Prez was there. The prison had allowed him to take a furlough for the funeral, but he had to be back that night.

The corrections officers who had accompanied him were very courteous and discreet. From the way they acted, one would never guess they were on duty, guarding a federal prisoner.

Kim and Princess were happy to see their Pop-Pop, and he was delighted finally to see his two great-granddaughters. But Prez was now a broken man, a person who seemed to drift in and out of the here and now involuntarily. When he first saw Jan, he didn't recognize her.

"I'm Jan, Uncle Prez, Roy and Lila's girl."

"Oh, my God, lil Jan." His eyes had filled with tears as he took her face in his hands and kissed her on the forehead, the same way he used to do Peaches.

He pulled her close.

"Jan, what happened to my lil girl, what happened to my baby?" he whispered. "Jan, I know you know. She used to tell you everything. What happened to my lil girl?"

His eyes were pleading with hers for an answer that she didn't have.

"I don't know, Uncle Prez, I don't know."

She blinked back fresh tears as she hugged him tightly, wishing she wouldn't have to look into those eyes again. "Don't worry. Whoever did it will pay."

Prez nodded slowly, smiled, then seemed to drift off again. Emotionally, he had left the room.

Please, God, please don't let Ursula show up while he's here, prayed Jan, gazing heavenward.

After about an hour or so, supper, the cake, pie, and coffee had been served, most of the older folks began to leave and the gathering became less formal. The old-time spirituals were replaced by more contemporary gospel and inspirational music: Kirk Franklin, Sounds of Blackness, and the Winans filled the air.

The coffee and tea servers were whisked away, the beer was removed from the ice chest in the shed kitchen and stacked in the refrigerator. The liquor was placed openly on the kitchen table.

"And that's as far as it goes, too," harrumphed Jan, who still thought it was a bit early to be setting it out in the first place.

"Oh, Jan, lighten up. This is the nineties, you know. Just about everybody in here has a drink in they hand by now," chided Sally.

"Not everybody." Rasheeda smiled. "I'm still drinking Martinelli's, and don't even say it, don't even go there."

"Go where?" Sally laughed.

"Shut up, Sally. Shut up, Jan."

"Yo. Did you spike her cider or somethin, Jan?" Sally asked.

Jan shook her head. "I don't know who you laughin at. You know, I'd stay away from that potato salad if I was you, Miss Thang," she said, rolling her eyes down in the direction of Sal's hips. "The ole girl's putting on a bit of spread back there, ain't she, Roach?"

"Probably from sitting up in that Devil night after night. If you don't use it, it starts to grow on you, you know." Rasheeda winked at Sal.

"Speaking of sittin on it, when's the last time you had any, Jan?" Sal asked, still laughing.

"Nineteen ninety?"

"Now Sal, you know Jan don't roll like that. Probably in nineteen eighty." Rasheeda knocked her juice on her lap, she was laughing so hard.

"Ha. Serves you right. My hips are not spreading. It's just the way this dress is made. It's a little too tight in the hips, that's all," Sal said, placing the bowl of potato salad down on the table and trying self-consciously to smooth the dress down on her hips.

"Well, as far as my love life is concerned, it was the best, even if I am speaking mostly from memory," Jan retorted.

"Mostly? Mostly?" Sal was doubled over now, slapping Rasheeda across the back.

"How about all the way from memory? How about history?"

Jan laughed in spite of herself. They had been teasing her so much now about not having a man in her life that she was getting used to it. She sat back down at the table and helped herself to another serving of potato salad.

It was now around eight o'clock and most of the guests had finally left. The women quickly cleaned up the living and dining rooms, washed and dried the dishes, and settled down at the kitchen table, having their own meal. Princess was in the living room talking to friends of hers who had dropped by. Kim and the kids were still upstairs.

"Aw, Jan, you know we was just teasing you, girl." Rasheeda reached over and patted Sal's hand. "We only do it cause we love you and want you to be happy."

"I am happy, Dr. Ruth. Thank you very much," Jan said between bites of chicken.

"She means happy with a guy, Jan," Sal said dryly. "Remember guys? You know, those good-lookin things with the deep voices and hair on they faces and chests? The ones with the third legs? Come on, girl, think, think hard. It will come back to you." Sal was waving a soda straw back and forth in front of Jan's face as if it were a wand.

"Very funny, Miss Freedom Rider. Everybody can't just love em and leave em like you, you know." Jan smirked.

"Okay, ladies, break it up, break it up, show's over," Rasheeda said, spreading her arms like a boxing referee. "I swear, I don't know what yall would do without me around to mediate all the time."

"Don't say that, Roach." Sal dropped her gaze to her plate, suddenly serious. They ate silently for a few minutes.

After all these years, the Justus Girls had immediately fallen back into their old teasing routines, as if they had never been apart, only now, they all sensed the absence of Peaches.

As they finished eating, the conversation turned from the food, the dessert, the people at the funeral, who stepped through wearing what (Girl, did you see Cynthia Johnson, still wearin that blue Queen of the Nile eye shadow, ever since 1969?), the new minister (who had given Jan the eye), the mortician (who had come by and eaten three helpings of food and had the nerve to take two platters home with him), even the undertaker.

They talked about everything except their reason for being there.

Presently, Jan rose and swiftly cleared their plates from the table, stacked the dishes in the dishwasher, and wiped down the table.

"Just sit tight, ladies. I've got just the thing." She smiled mischievously and disappeared into the shed kitchen. She was back in a minute with a large paper bag. She winked, walked over to the cabinet and produced three large brandy glasses and a can opener.

"Look what I got, look what I got, just for us," she said excitedly, pulling out a magnum of moderately priced champagne and a large can of chilled cling peaches.

"Git the hell outta here," cried Sal.

"The JG's main taste."

"Sure was, sure was." Rasheeda grinned.

"Now, look, Roach. I know you abstain nowadays because you're into Islam and all, and I still got plenty of apple cider left, but if you want to go off the wagon for just this one night, we won't tell, will we, Sally Mae?" Jan winked over at Sally.

"Indeed not, chile. It's our world." Each woman poured herself a generous drink.

"To Peach," Sal started off, holding up her glass.

"And to life," Rasheeda added.

"From Jazzy Janice, Rockin Roach, and Mustang Sally," declared Jan.

Laughing out loud, the JGs clicked their glasses together and took long swallows, Sally Mae draining her glass. "Damn, that's good. Do me again, Jan."

"At your service, girlfriend." Jan refilled the glasses.

"You know, this is almost like old times, when we used to sit around each other's houses, sneaking beers when our parents were out, smoking cigarettes, and pretending we were grown," mused Rasheeda.

"Yeah, we was somethin back then, girl." Jan's speech was slowly sliding back from the usual standard English to the hood slang, the Black talk, the full-tilt Ebonics, as the champagne relaxed the tension she had been feeling all day.

"Like the kids say, we was the bomb." Sal laughed, feeling better every minute.

"We was the shit, babeee," bragged Jan.

"We was the JGs. Member how we used to come struttin down the street, side by side, telling everybody our rap?"

The JGs nodded, smiling and tasting.

"Shoot, we was rappin before it was happenin," Rasheeda spoke up.

The JGs looked at each other and, as if on cue, they all stood, moved out onto the floor, and lined up side by side.

"You know, you know, you know, you know, we are, oh, yeah, The Justus Girls, oh, yeah, We looking fine, oh, yeah, Our hair's in curls, oh yeah.

We get big play, oh, yeah, We outta sight, oh, yeah, The boys all say, oh, yeah, We do it right, oh, yeah, We in your face, oh, yeah.

We talk that talk, oh, yeah, You know we rock it, baby. We walk that walk, oh, yeah.

And when we step, oh, yeah. You better sit, oh, yeah. The Justus Girls, oh, yeah. Don't take no shit, oh, no. Don't take no shit, oh, no. DON'T TAKE NO SHIT!

They slapped high-fives and fell back into their chairs, marveling that they could still remember the words to the chant they had made up over thirty years ago. They were so tickled that they didn't even notice Princess and Kim standing in the kitchen doorway.

"The Justus Girls? What is that?" asked Princess.

"You mean you don't know who the Justus Girls are?" Sal was up again. "Jan, she don't know who the Justus Girls are."

"Oh, no," Jan said, moving out next to Sal. "The JGs? You don't know about the JGs? Hold on a minute." Jan ran out of the kitchen and up the stairs.

Roach jumped to her feet and they were at it again, really on this time, pumping their arms in the air, sliding across the floor, swiveling their hips. Jan returned and joined right in. Princess, Kim, and several of their friends crowded into the doorway watching.

"Waaay strange," Princess whispered to Kim.

"They're doin one of them strange dances like Mommy used to do." The girls nodded to each other in agreement, but found themselves inexplicably shuffling their feet and moving their heads in time to the JGs' beat.

The JGs finished their second go-round and took their seats again, now winded, fanning their faces and wiping sweat from their brows.

"That's the JGs." Jan handed Kim a large, tattered black-and-white photo of ten young girls dressed in white-and-gold drill team uniforms, standing at attention. Princess, Kim, and their friends oohed and aaahed, looking from the picture of the JGs as they were then, to Jan, Sal, and Rasheeda as they were now.

"The Justus Girls. The JGs. All for one and one for all." Sal was wiping the sweat off her forehead. "Now, whose hips was yall talkin bout? Cause yall know Mustang Sally can still kick it out when she want to."

"You're gone be reaching for your blood pressure pills in the next half hour," Jan remarked dryly.

"No way." Sal dismissed her with a wave. "These hips can still rock it." She patted her ample behind.

The girls were still studying the photo. "Wait a minute. I remember that. The JGs. I remember when I was little, yall used to come over and do that, playing all those old sixties records." Kim was shaking her head. "Yeah, Aunt Sal. I remember they used to call you Mustang Sally. You were the best dancer around then. Wow. Seems like a long time ago."

Kim and Princess were five years apart. A lot had gone on that she could remember.

"I remember my mom would be right up there with yall, doin that dance, doin that rap."

By now, Kim and Princess's friends were squeezing into the kitchen, begging the women to do the chant again.

"If we must perform, ladies, let's take it to the living room," Sal stated in her mock British voice again.

"Yes, yes. You must give us room to work."

Rasheeda headed toward the doorway, waving the girls out of the way, Sal following behind. "Bring the likka, Jan," she yelled over her shoulder.

"You got it, girl. You know I know what to do." Jan gathered the bottle, the peaches, and the ice bucket up and headed for the living room.

Rasheeda had already beaten the others to the stereo and was busy pulling records and tapes from the shelves.

"Come on, one more time now, aunties. Yall promised." Egged on by the girls, the JGs performed what the women called the Justus Girls rap again, then fell on the carpeted floor laughing. They felt wonderful, like the girls they once were.

"And yall were all real tight back then, weren't you?" asked Princess.

"Tighter than tight. We were like sisters. We had each other's backs. If you did something to one of us, you did it to all of us, and that's the way we took it. Even the boys knew," Rasheeda declared emphatically.

"Damn straight," yelled Jan.

"Fuckin A," chimed in Sal. "Oh, excuse my French, girls. It's just the pagne talkin. This was our drink back in the day, peaches and pagne. Bring on the pagne. That's all we used to drink."

"Except when we were broke, and it was, bring on the beer," said Jan.

"Ain't that the truth. But you knew, sooner or later, somebody was gone come through and spend that money and buy us that pagne."

"Yeah, but that was when we was young and fine and used to wear miniskirts, fishnets, and fringes. Everybody was spendin back then. Hell, you could walk down the Strip without a dime in your purse, cause before the night was done, somebody was definitely gone be your sponsor." Sally was nodding. "Of course, we never did nothin like that," Sal said quickly, but she couldn't quite wipe the smirk from her face.

"Yeah, right, Aunt Sally. Yall never did nothin like that," Kim mimicked, truly smiling for the first time that evening. "But you know," Kim continued, "sometimes I wish I had come up back then. Those days seemed like more fun than now, in a way."

"You better believe it, honey. When I look around at the old neighborhood now, I could cry."

Rasheeda nodded sadly.

"Well, can't live in the past, got to move forward." Sal shrugged.

"Yes, well, I guess. But speaking of moving forward, Kim, Princess, yall go on with your friends. Yall don't have to sit up here with a bunch of old broads reminiscing about the old days. The kids are already asleep. They can stay with me tonight. I'll call yall in the morning," Jan announced, waving away their protests.

She knew about being young. She knew when you were young, you believed you would live forever, and all thoughts of death were put on hold. No, they did not want to dwell on death, the young, even if it was their own mother's. They'd have plenty of time to grieve. Jan understood.

So the girls left and the ladies stayed, and played, and sang, and danced, and talked. All night long.

They started with Smokey Robinson, then went on to the Four Tops, then of course, the Tempting Temptations.

They did the cha-cha to Mary Wells's "You Beat Me to the Punch." They shimmied to the Contours' "Do you Love Me." They hitchhiked to Marvin's "Hitchhike." They bopped all over the floor to "Please Mr. Postman," the great Marvelettes' tune.

And of course, no party would be complete without the Sounds of Philadelphia. They screamed to the Delfonics' "Didn't I Blow Your Mind This Time," swooned to the Stylistics' "You Made Me Feel Brand New," and sighed to the Intruders' "I Want to Know Your Name."

They were more than ready for Teddy's "Turn Out the Lights," screaming "Teddy, Teddy, Teddy" so loudly, it's a wonder they didn't wake up the children.

They sold their hearts to the junkman with Patti LaBelle and her

Bluebells, and they rounded out their impromptu concert with a mean impression of Tina Turner and the Ikettes, Sal, pulling off her half-slip, placing it over her hair, and swinging her head around and around, in imitation of the great Tina, really getting into the spirit of the thing, backed up by Jan and Rasheeda, as the Ikettes.

"Yeah, girl, all I needed was my long black wig and my FM heels, and I'da done it right," Sally said, puffing, as the last strains of the bass line to "Proud Mary" faded in the background.

The JGs fell to the sofa, exhausted, giggling, then weeping.

"How can she not be here? How can she really be gone?" Rasheeda whispered.

"I know, honey, I know." Sal sniffled. Jan said nothing. Just then, as if in answer, "Forever" by the Marvelettes, one of Peaches's favorite songs, began to play. The JGs listened in silence.

"Maybe she's not," Rasheeda said quietly. "Maybe she doesn't have to be."

Sal and Jan turned to Rasheeda.

"What?" Jan said tonelessly.

"Uh, Roach, I think you better stick to that apple juice from here on in," Sally said, giving Rasheeda one of her are-you-on-drugs looks.

"I mean, I know she's dead, but there must be some meaning to it, to her life as well as her death," Rasheeda spoke carefully. "I don't know about yall, but I've been feeling very guilty about this. I can't help it. If I would have only kept in closer touch with her, maybe I could have been there for her, you know? I just feel I owe her, that's all."

"You? How do you think I feel?" Jan asked. " Everybody knows Peach and I were barely speaking for almost the past six months. You must know I can't even sleep because of this. I always looked out for her, and where was I? Sitting here on my ass with my nose stuck up in the air." It was as if a dam had burst in Jan. Words poured from her mouth like rain. "She was a grown woman. She was living her life the way she wanted. What right did I have to be judgmental? Who am I to disapprove of somebody? I should have been watching out for her. I should have—" Jan broke down, her body heaving with sobs.

"Okay, okay, now, stop it, Jan. Stop it right now," Rasheeda broke in.

"Don't even go there. Don't even start. You always did watch out for her. You always had her back. Like you said, she was a grown woman. She had to live her own life. You had to pull away the crutch."

> *An altar for Peaches: fruit—something to eat on the journey home. Sweets and rum—to please the spirits, who have a sweet tooth and are known to be partial to rum. Water—to quench her thirst. Coins—for traveling money. Rice—for continued procreation of the family line. Green candles—for luck. Cigarette— to soothe the soul. Red candles—for the heart's sake. Photos, dolls, and jewelry—for the spirits, who adore beautiful things.*

CHAPTER 5

MUSTANG SALLY:
COMING OF AGE

The Justus Girls.

That's what they called themselves, all right, in the summer of '59. First it was Janice and Rachael. Then Peaches came to live with Janice, then they all met Sally Mae. The four of them had been to the annual Elks parade that spring. They had been very impressed with the drill teams, some of them teenagers from their own neighborhood.

They had loved the drums, the precision in the movement of the marchers, their splendid gold-braided uniforms sparkling in the sun. They had especially loved the white, tasseled boots the team members wore, their military stance, and the air of discipline they projected.

So they had decided to form their own drill team.

They recruited Bertha Gray, with the beautiful voice, who was in the Sunday School choir, Carolyn and Sylvia Miller from around on

Osage Avenue, Dodi and Di, the Gaines twins, also from Osage, and Ruthie Bolton from over on Delancey, whose older sister Esther was a member of the Elks. An even ten.

Their first meeting was held one September afternoon in the Stanton Elementary School playground.

It was just them, no grown-ups. They had already tried to join the Elks but had been turned away, the Elks telling them they were too young. They didn't think so.

They couldn't find any adult to take charge of them, so they took charge of themselves. After they had decided on practice times, meeting schedules, dues, and so forth, they set to work, marching, mostly copying what they had seen the Elks teams doing.

Ruthie had picked up a few steps from Esther, which she shared with the group. Peaches and Jan had done a little drilling with the Peewees, the team at the rec center in their old neighborhood, so they taught the other girls what they knew. All in all, it went pretty well.

A few people had gathered in the corner of the schoolyard to see what they were up to, mostly the boys, yelling catcalls at them and make silly breaking wind noises, just being boys, as usual. The girls made faces at them or pretended to ignore them, but were secretly pleased at the attention.

"So who yall think yall supposed to be?"

The mocking voice came from Bad Tooth Shirley, standing near the boys, one hand on her hip, her already rotting teeth exposed by her open mouth.

The boys laughed. The girls ignored her.

"I hope yall don't think yall no Elks or somethin. Yall ain't hardly no damn Elks, you know."

The boys laughed louder. Shirley, emboldened by the boys' raucous laughter, sashayed over to the girls. (Sashaying even then.)

"Ain't nobody say we was the Elks, Shirley," Peaches said, stepping out of the line.

"Then I guess yall must be the moose, huh?" Shirley screamed, clasping her hands together in delight at her joke.

By then the boys had doubled over, punching each other in the arm, falling out all on the ground, pretending to wipe away tears. "The moose, the moose, the moose is loose. The cows, the Pine Street heifas." They began to make animal noises, howling and mooing.

That did it. In a shot, Sally Mae had run over and knocked Shirley to the ground. She stood over her, fists up and ready.

"What you call me, you bald-head, bad-tooth hussy? What you say?" Shirley lay there, clearly praying someone would intercede. Rachael and Janice quickly and mercifully did, grabbing Sal by each arm, pulling her away from Shirley, who hastily scrambled to her feet and ran back over to the schoolyard gate.

"And you better not tell my grandma, either, or I'll really whip yo lil dusty butt," Sal yelled after her.

"We ain't no damn Elks, either, Shirley. You just mad cause you ain't in it," Peaches spat the words out.

"Aw, you just shut up, Peaches. Everybody know yo mama ain't nothin but a whore, and Sally, you ain't even got no mama, wit yo Black, country, nappy-headed self. My mama say yo mama went crazy and you ain't got no daddy, neither, and that's the onliest reason you up here in the first place. Everybody know that. Think yall so damn cute. I don't want to be in—"

Sal and Peaches were racing across the schoolyard before Shirley could finish her last sentence.

"Fight, fight, fight!" The boys were beside themselves now, anticipating a knockdown, drag-out rumble among the girls.

Shirley took off down the street, Peach and Sal in hot pursuit. The only thing that saved her was Miss Mabel, who happened to be standing at the door of her candy store. Peach and Sal backed off. If Miss Mabel saw them whipping Shirley's butt, she would tell on both of them, and it just wasn't worth the trouble. They headed on back to the schoolyard.

"Well, what's the name of yall, then?" one of the boys, the one they called Chicken Wing, yelled over at them.

"I don't know. It's just us," Peaches answered, shrugging her shoulders.

"Hey, that's boss, Peach," Jan said, smiling.

"That sounds cool. Just us. The Just Us Girls," she said slowly, looking around at the rest of the girls, who all smiled and nodded their heads in affirmation.

"We's the Justus Girls, you dumb ass, for yo information," Peaches shouted at the boys, tossing her head and shaking her behind at them, grinning. Each of the Justus Girls did the same. They put their hands on their hips, they rolled their eyes, they tossed their heads, and they shook their narrow behinds at the boys, grinning.

The summer of '59. That was how it started. They practiced nearly every day, weather permitting. They stole steps from dancers or made them up on the spot.

They got better and better. The boys still teased them brutally, calling them the Pine Street pigs or the Stanton School skanks, but they didn't care. They practiced each step over and over until they got it right. And eventually they did.

They became a tight, disciplined unit of girls who moved as one in lockstep precision. If someone had asked them why the team was so important to them, why getting it just right meant so much, they probably wouldn't have been able to answer.

These were not the children of privilege, not the children of the onward and upward burgeoning Black middle class that one always read about. These were the daughters of the blue-collar workers: the sanitation men, the porters, the truck and cab drivers, the maids, the cooks, the seamstresses, and the factory workers. The people who took the early bus.

Most of their parents had never gone beyond the eighth grade, if that far, having been forced to forgo education. They had had to go to work to keep a roof over their families' heads. Their highest goals for their children were that they finish high school, and for the girls, there was a tacit understanding that many of them wouldn't even make it that far.

If a young man could manage to get himself hired on the docks, driving a truck, at the steel mills, or, have mercy, a good post office job, he'd be set for life. If a girl could manage to capture one of these lucky young men, she'd make out just fine. Just fine.

It wasn't that these parents loved their children any less than the middle class, the upper class, or anyone else. It was just that they themselves were the children of parents who had climbed up from the deep bottom. They were the first generation of Blacks to migrate north, sons and daughter of sharecroppers, people who really knew poverty, knew what it was like not to have enough to eat, to be cold to the point of frostbite.

They had been beaten down so much that they had grown afraid to expect too much.

So they realistically didn't see the sense in pushing their kids too far, education-wise. What was the use? Nobody had any money for college, anyway, and even if one of their children made it that far, what good would it do them? Hell, they had people in their own neighborhoods who had gone to college, working right in the post office or driving trucks, living right alongside them.

They knew white people weren't hardly going to let their kids into the game, so why get their hopes up?

It would only make them crazy. These were not the children of the house Negroes; these were the field hands' kids, and survival was their first priority.

A "clean job" was the most they allowed themselves to dream for their bright-eyed boys and girls, a job where one could put on clean clothes every day, maybe even a suit or a dress, catch the bus downtown, and work with their brains instead of their backs. A clean government job was even better. Security. Set for life.

Mind numbed and work weary, it was the most they dared to dream for their little ones.

Growing up that way, without that crystal-clear, eyes-on-the-prize vision that only parents can provide, these girls had no true goals of rising any farther than their parents had. So the drill team had become their goal. They worked harder at it than at anything they had ever encountered in their young lives. All winter long they practiced, in the cold, in the snow, often down in Jan or Roach's basement.

Come the following spring, the Stanton School held their annual May Day program out in the schoolyard.

There were games, cotton candy, and hot dogs. There was singing and recitals and dancing by the children of the various grade levels.

And there was the first public performance of the Justus Girls. Rachael and the Miller girls had been given special permission to perform, since they attended Catholic school. The music class had allowed their best drummers to accompany the team. The Girls were nervous wrecks.

Carolyn Miller had been out of school for three months with rheumatic fever, and had only returned a month ago. They were worried that she would forget the routines, among other things. Bertha forgot her socks. Ruthie only had one glove and had to race back home and get the other. Their white blouses and red skirts, white gloves and red berets looked nice, but they couldn't afford the fancy white marching boots they so adored, and had had to make do with white sneakers and bobby socks with red pom-poms attached.

They held on to each other, whispering words of encouragement like prayers. Some of them actually did pray.

And they stole the show.

From the moment the drummers started drumming, from the moment the principal, Mrs. Detweiler, announced over the microphone from the podium, "And now, a special treat. Ladies and gentlemen, I bring you the Justus Girls," they knew they owned it.

Resplendent in their red-and-white attire, they entered the schoolyard from around the side of the building at a running trot, arms pumping, adrenaline flowing, eyes forward, and hearts beating hard, not stopping until they were in front of the podium, where they came to a halt at once, on Janice's, their captain's, command. The drummers and cymbalists had worked out well with them and anticipated their every move.

The JGs executed each routine flawlessly, each maneuver perfectly. Carolyn Miller didn't miss a step, not a step. They were sensational. People started rushing forward to take their picture, folks stood up in the bleachers to get a better look. Even some of the midday drinkers from the Strip walked out of the bars and over to the schoolyard to see what all the commotion was about.

All eyes on them, they moved like queens, each one. The applause lasted a full five minutes, and the crowd yelled for more. They were stars for the rest of the afternoon. Their brothers and sisters bragged about them, neighbors posed for photos with them, even the principal asked for a group shot. Girls from all over approached them, asking if they could join.

And the boys, the same boys who had tormented them all winter long, who had called them mooses and cows and heifas and skanks, now smiled sheepishly and hung their heads. Wing, the bold one who had laughed the loudest, slid over behind them.

"Yall did good. Yall did real good. Specially you, Peach." He smiled shyly.

"Git outta my face, chump. Don't be tryin to be my friend *now*." Peach tossed her head at him, but could not hide the smile playing across her face.

A week later, their group pictures had appeared in the *Tribune*, Philadelphia's premiere Black newspaper, along with their names, and the name of their team.

Unbeknownst to them, the principal, Mrs. Detweiler, had asked one of the paper's photographers to be at the May Day show, and he had snapped their photo.

They performed at block parties and playgrounds all that summer, and on Labor Day, the Justus Girls Drill Team finally marched in the streets of Philadelphia with the Elks, fronting their annual parade, gold-braided white uniforms, fancy white-tasseled boots, and everything.

They had even appeared on local television.

No one could believe they did not have a sponsor or coach, that ten poor Black city girls, aged nine, ten, and eleven years old, could have put together such a crack drill team by themselves.

But they had done it. And they continued to march for the next four years, under the sponsorship of the Elks, who showcased them everywhere, until the old Elks home was torn down. Although Sal, Rasheeda, Peaches, and Jan had remained close through their coming-of-age years, the rest of the JGs had drifted apart after the team disbanded.

But that team and those four years, particularly the first year, had been a lesson they should never have forgotten: that victory will surely come to the unbeaten, unbroken spirit, that the will to rise was the strongest force on earth.

Rasheeda had had to remind them as well as herself about the JGs, about how they had shone like gold that afternoon. Sometimes Black women tend to forget that they once were queens.

CHAPTER 6

AFTER THE FUNERAL

Don't even start tryin to blame yourself, Jan," Sal said defensively. "Hell, I wish I had known more about what was going on with her myself. I wish I had tipped down to that Devil more often. Maybe I'd know what was goin down."

"See, that's what I mean, Sal. That's what I'm talking about. We all just lost touch."

"Oh, right, Roach. You gone go down to the Devil with all that Muslim stuff on. I'd pay to see that." Sal chuckled.

"No, no, that's not it. I'm talking about none of us have a clue what was going on in Peaches's life, and now that she's dead, we don't even know where to start." Roach stretched her arms, palms up.

"Shit, probably can start with that rowdy-ass, dope-selling bar." Jan snorted, wrinkling her nose in disgust. "I remember when that used to be a nice place to go on the weekends, even some weeknights or after work. Used to have live bands, jazz, blues, and rock and roll. Rags and them used to play there all the time. Remember?" Jan was on a roll. "Used to sell good food, too. Now, you got to pass through an army of young boys selling crack right outside the damn door to get in the place, and after you're in, you don't even know hardly nobody in there. They scared all the nice folks away."

"Now, see, Jan? That's exactly what I mean. All that stuff you're talking about the Devil, that's old news. That problem was taken care of months ago. And you didn't even know about it. That's what I mean by losing touch," Rasheeda said, a bit smugly.

"What you mean, taken care of? Who took care of it?"

"We did, that's who," Sally spoke up.

"We? Who is we?"

"We is me, some of the people from the community center, some of the neighbors, and Hakim and some of the Muslim brothers. Indeed so, chile." Sal warmed to the subject. "We did some good old-time activism. You don't see nobody hangin on that corner now, do you? You don't see no drug dealin, no drug takin, no pissin in people's bushes and things goin on down there now, do you?"

"Well, now that you mention it, I haven't seen that kinda thing goin on lately." Jan felt a little shamed now, because the truth was, she hadn't even bothered to notice what was going on down at the White Devil, or anywhere else, for that matter.

"Yeah, and you won't. We stepped to Tookie. We talked to the brother first, and when that didn't work, we started callin the cops every night, makin a nuisance out of ourselves, then we got together and stood outside of that joint one Friday night and threatened to close that motha down. And you know, once Tookie seen them Muslim brothers step up, it was all over. Now, they workin together to keep that corner clean. Girl, you shoulda seen Hakim get all up in Tookie's face, ready to rock his world." Sally laughed.

Rasheeda blushed. Oh, yeah, her man sure had taken care of business that night. "But that's what I'm talking about, Jan," she said aloud. "I didn't even know about the protest until Hakim came home one night and told me Sally and them were standing out there in front of the bar, talking about hurtin somebody." Rasheeda and Jan laughed.

"Hell, we had to do somethin," Sal said. "We warned Tookie we was goin to the po-lice if he didn't clean up that corner. But he was scared of them young boys, too. Claimed he stopped em from sellin inside the bar. But they was still on that corner, night after night. We started scopin on that place six months ago. We even called the Mayor's Action Committee and the TV stations. No response. But you just let some violence go down round here, I bet they be out there then. When George Johnson was shot six times out there, I bet they all came out then. Mothafuckas," she snapped, shaking her head in disgust.

"This is what I'm trying to say." Roach spoke up again. "We don't even know what Peaches was about lately. Maybe we could have saved her if we had known what was going on in her life, maybe not. All I know is it's too late now. But look at the three of us. We don't even know what we're about these days." Rasheeda picked up the ball. "Oh, we pass each other on the street now and then, see each other on the Strip from time to time, but do we really know about each other's lives right now, today? Me, for example. I'm going through some serious changes right now, and if I died tomorrow, yall wouldn't know anything about it. I'm not accustomed to talking to anybody outside of my family and the sisters in the Masjid these days, but, you know, they don't really know me like yall do. And for all I know, you two might be having your own problems. But see, we don't discuss . . ." Rasheeda's voice trailed off. She was really getting fired up now.

"What I'm sayin is, it didn't used to be like this. That's all I'm saying. Yall know it. When I told those girls tonight that we used to be tighter than tight, I really meant it. Kim was right. It was better then. We all used to look out for each other, the four of us, and all the JGs. For that matter, the whole neighborhood did. You remember how it was then."

Sal and Jan both nodded.

"Not to cut you short, girlfriend, but what's your point? I mean, we all grown now. The past is the past. Like I say, look ahead, not back. We can't do nothin bout the past," Sal stated bluntly.

"You're right, Sal, we can't. But if we had kept in touch, maybe, just maybe we wouldn't have had to bury our sister today. The past is gone, just as dead as Peaches is, lying out there in the ground. But we can do something about right now. We can at least try to make it like it was, if only the three of us. Just us." Rasheeda laughed. "Just us? Get it? As in the Justus Girls?"

Sal and Jan groaned at Rasheeda's corny play on words, but liked the sound of her message.

"We can band together like we did back then. I know we can't hang out together every day or anything like that, but we can make a commitment to get together, oh, I don't know, maybe once a month or so, to share problems, come up with solutions. We can show these young sisters by example how it's done, what real friends are, instead of just telling them about it. We're too late for Peach. But we can at least try to be on time for ourselves. Not to mention those two daughters and grandbabies she left behind. If not us, who?"

Rasheeda took a deep breath. There. Said it.

It had been on her mind all day, from the time she met up with Sal and Jan. She hated to sound preachy, but she felt so strongly about this that she didn't care. These were her friends. She looked first at Jan, and Jan was smiling at her, nodding her head slowly.

"Honey, you are so right. That's exactly what we can do. You're not the only one with problems. It's just that I'm so used to doing everything by myself, I don't even know how to ask anybody for help anymore."

This was true. It had been so long since Jan had shared anything with anybody. They just didn't know. She was always good at keeping up a good front, but now her facade was falling, and she knew it.

Rasheeda and Jan turned to Sal. She stared back at them for a moment. Then she grinned, threw up both arms, made two fists, thrust them up in the air and shouted, "Action time! The Justus Girls ride again."

"Right on!" yelled Rasheeda, fist up.

"Seize the time!" cried Jan, pumping the air.

The women spent the rest of the night sharing secrets, tears, and fears, while the music soothed their tired souls. As they talked on into the night, they knew in their hearts they would do this. For themselves, yes, but also for Peach, for the JGs, for Kim and Princess, for the hood. It would work. It had to.

And so, just before first light, dazed by death, remembrance, and resurrection, soothed by sixties soul and sparkling wine, they folded on the floor like midnight flowers, sleeping where they lay.

CHAPTER 7

URSULA AND PEACH GO TO SCHOOL

You really done it this time, god damn you, you little hussy. You really done it. Get yo bony ass up," Ursula muttered through clenched teeth. She marched out of the principal's office, grabbed Peaches roughly by the arm, and pulled her off the bench.

"Did what, Mommy?" protested Peaches, as she was dragged along down the hall toward the school's exit doors by a livid Ursula. She was walking so quickly, Peaches had to struggle to keep up with her.

"Just wait till we get outside. You and yo damn big mouth," snapped Ursula. "Wait till the last week of school and then start actin up."

"But, Mommy, I didn't tell them anything bad," Peaches whispered anxiously.

"Just shut up, shut up."

Ursula pulled her along roughly. It wasn't until they had left the building, walked up the entire block, and turned the corner, out of sight of the school, that Ursula slowed her pace. She still had Peaches firmly in her grasp, however. She stopped abruptly, jerking the girl around in front of her.

"Just what the hell did you tell them people, girl? What did you tell em?" she shouted, shaking Peaches by the shoulders.

"No-no-nothin, Mommy," Peaches whined weakly, her large eyes searching her mother's face as if for some hidden dangerous clue. "I didn't tell em nothin."

"You just come on, girl, and just remember, whatever happens is all yo fault. You the one started this shit in the first place, hookeyin school. Stupid ass," Ursula said meanly, as she proceeded to drag Peaches by the arm again.

But even as she spoke, Ursula sensed the girl was telling the truth. She even sensed, deep down, that this was not Peaches's fault; it was her own, for neglecting the child, though she would never consciously admit it.

True, after the truant officer's visit and the subsequent meeting with the principal, Ursula had made sure Peaches went back to school. But her attendance was poor. Out of a full year, from September to June, the child had missed 78 days out of 180. And then, just two weeks before the summer recess, Ursula had been sent a notice in the mail to meet with the principal again.

What the hell am I gone do now? Ursula was thinking hard as they moved through the summertime city streets. It had been made clear to her in the letter that this was no ordinary little parent-teacher chat. In addition to the principal, the truant officer, Mr. Grimes, the school nurse, and a social worker would be present.

"We've been investigating this matter for some time now, Mrs. Pearson," Miss Delaney had begun the meeting after they had first talked to Peaches alone, and then showed Ursula back into the room alone.

"We are aware of the poor parenting example you have set for your daughter. We know all about the late and irregular hours you keep, the men you entertain, the barhopping. And we know even more." Miss Delaney had stared at Ursula meaningfully then.

"Me? I don't know what you investigatin me fo. I ain't suppose to have no life just cause I got a kid?" said Ursula sharply, glaring at the social worker.

Hmph. Dried-up ole bitch just jealous, Ursula thought to herself.

"I'm still young," she said aloud. "I ain't gone be sitting at home alla time like no damn house pet."

"We are not suggesting that you should, Mrs. Pearson." Mr. Foster, the principal, intervened.

"It's just that once you have a child, you have a duty to see that that child is taken care of properly. And it just doesn't seem to us that Priscilla is being cared for properly."

"For Christ's sake, woman. You've only got one kid, and you can't even get her to school every day," Grimes, the truant officer, said with a sneer.

Ursula glared at him. *Horny little toad,* she thought, narrowing her eyes. Grimes's face flushed pink, his gaze traveled downward, checking out Ursula's cleavage, then, catching himself, he turned his head swiftly and looked out the window.

Ursula was really getting ticked off now. Just who in hell did these folks think they were? Fuck em. She flicked the long hair in her wig back over one shoulder.

They stared silently at her for almost a full minute. Miss Delaney leaned forward and looked straight into Ursula's face.

"You see, Mrs. Pearson, we were wondering if perhaps Priscilla's father would be willing to take her. Or if not, we could place her in foster care, where she could be cared for properly. Of course, you could always visit her. We just don't see you as a suitable parent for her at this time."

Ursula's mouth dropped open, closed, then opened again, the reality of the situation striking her like a brick to the side of her head. She couldn't breathe for a moment.

Take Peach away. These mothafuckas is settin up here talkin bout takin my baby away, settin up here talkin just as normal, like they was talkin bout the weather or somethin.

She had to think fast. She couldn't let it happen. With Peach gone, the check from Prez would stop.

She couldn't make it without that check. She couldn't make it without her child, either. She had to stall them. They hadn't contacted Prez yet. There was still time.

"Look, give me two weeks, that's all I'm askin for. I'll make some kind of arrangements. Just two weeks. I'm begging you people, please don't take my chile away from me." She searched each face and rested on the principal's kind eyes. "Please don't get my husband involved. Please, brother."

The principal knew how things were in the neighborhood. He had been poor. He had to give her at least one more chance. Grimes and Delaney didn't give a damn about breaking up Negro families, but Foster did. He knew the odds were about fifty-fifty that Peaches would end up in a good home.

"All right, two weeks. No more. You are to report back to me in two weeks, and if you don't, we'll contact your husband and Miss Delaney, and it will be in the hands of the Department of Children's Services," he said to Ursula gruffly.

"Oh, thank you, thank you so much, Mr. Foster. I'll take care of everything. You'll see. I'll be back in two weeks," said a beaming Ursula, rising to leave.

"And, Mrs. Pearson?"

"Yes, sir?"

"Don't let me down," Mr. Foster said, the softness back in his voice.

"I won't, sir. You'll see. Bye." Ursula waved, hurrying out the door.

As for Peach, she was truly mystified.

Everyone had been kind to her at the meeting, especially Mr. Foster. They had spoken to her in soft voices when they questioned her about her home life, and why she didn't come to school on a more regular basis. She had patiently explained how Ursula sometimes forgot to set the alarm clock to wake her up, and how sometimes her mommy didn't feel so hot in the mornings, and how she would have to bring her coffee and toast and run her a tub of bath water, how sometimes after doing all that, it would be so late that she wouldn't feel like going to school, so her mommy would just let her take the day off. She would fix herself some cold cereal, climb up into her mommy's big bed with her, and together they would talk and watch television for the rest of the day.

These were the times Peaches loved her mother the most. They would seem almost like sisters, talking, laughing, teasing each other.

Peach didn't even tell them about Ursula often being too hungover to get out of bed, and how she would have to push the trash can over to the bed so her mother could lean over and vomit into it, and how she would then have to take it into the bathroom and rinse it out.

And of course, she didn't tell them about the men, mostly white, who would sometimes spend the night with her mommy, and then give the child quarters and fifty-cent pieces, once even a whole dollar bill.

When they got back to the apartment, Ursula went straight to her bedroom and pulled out her phone and address book. Other than instructing Peaches to fix herself some lunch, she said nothing. Though she had closed her door, Peaches could hear her dialing the phone, making a series of calls. Once when Peaches picked up the phone to call Jan's, Ursula yelled at her to get off and stay off.

This went on for about a week. Peaches returned to school, went every day, but when she returned, the apartment was unusually quiet. There were no hot dates during this time, no boyfriends coming to the house at all. Whenever Puddin, Gigi, or China came by, they were immediately ushered into Ursula's bedroom, and Peach could only detect low whispering coming through the closed door.

Ursula herself was unusually quiet, pensive.

Peaches often caught her mother staring at her when she thought the girl wasn't looking. Ursula would then quickly turn away. Once Peach even thought she saw Ursula crying.

"What's wrong, Mommy?" Peach had run over to her, touching her face. The child was truly alarmed. Ursula never, ever cried. Cursed, stomped, screamed, yes. Cried, no.

"Nothing, baby, nothing. Just go on outside and play," Ursula had brushed Peaches's hand away, turning her head. "It's just this music. Sometimes it gets to me. I remember when I was yo age and my own mama used to play it all the time." Ursula closed her eyes and nodded in cadence with the song on the radio, a Mahalia Jackson spiritual. And that was another thing. All of a sudden, Ursula seemed to be listening to the gospel station every day now, all day long.

Before this week, she had only turned on gospel on Sunday mornings or when somebody died. Peach couldn't figure it out for the life of her.

On the following Saturday, early in the day, well, early for Ursula, which was around elevenish, Ursula was up and about, chattering a mile a minute, something about them going to see Uncle Elmo today.

"Who's Uncle Elmo, Mommy?" Peach had never heard of him.

"Oh, you probably don't member him and Aunt Liddy. You haven't seen em in such a long time. He Mommy's cousin. Don't you member him? He a cop. I took you over there befo, and Aunt Liddy gave you a bunch of candy. Don't you member?"

Ursula was talking and walking, setting one of Peaches's good outfits on the bed and trying to do something with the girl's thick hair at the same time.

Peach knew this to be a sign of nervousness.

"I don't remember. How old was I when we went there?"

"Oh, bout two or three." Ursula averted her eyes.

It took Ursula and Peach two buses to get to Uncle Elmo's house. Soon they were walking down a large, beautiful tree-lined street with houses on one side and a huge park on the other. Peaches saw plenty of children playing in the park and more riding bikes up and down the street. Ursula came to a stop directly in front of a large red-and-white brick house, with a white wrought-iron gate in front. There was white outdoor furniture set on the porch with plastic cushions and pink cement flamingo birds on the small lawn.

"Well, one thing you can say for Elmo. He really keep his place lookin nice," said Ursula, admiringly.

Just as she was about to open the little gate door, a loud voice startled them both.

"Well, as I live and breathe, Miss One. The bitch is back. Tie down yo men and lock up yo sons, the bitch is back, and wearing black."

This declaration was followed by mischievous throaty laughter, loud, but quite pleasant. Ursula shaded her eyes, following the direction the voice had come from, somewhere up the street.

Walking, sashaying rather, down the street toward them was a golden tan, handsome man, tall, sleekly built, with very large, diamond black eyes.

"Vaa! Damn, it's Vaa!" Ursula cried out with delight. As she reached out to hug him, he picked her up and twirled her around, laughing.

"What you doin round here, chile?" she asked, after he had released her and she had a moment to catch her breath.

"What do you mean, what am *I* doing around here? I happen to live here, hon," the man explained, pointing to the house next to the one they were now standing in front of. "The question Mother wants to know is what are *you* doing here? What are you even doing outside in the daytime?" he said, chuckling. "And who is this exquisite little creature here?" He looked down at Peaches, smiled, and winked.

The little girl blushed, bashful now. Ursula introduced them.

"Why, I do declare. You are about as pretty as a Georgia peach. You've got the right name, honey." He bowed grandly, and spoke in a mock southern accent. "Miss Ursula, would yall permit me the honor of escorting Miss Peaches to the Ku Klux Klan Harvest Ball?"

Peaches decided right then and there that she liked him, although she was a bit puzzled by his appearance. He was obviously a man. He was slim, yet muscular, he had a deep throaty voice, and here in the bright afternoon sunlight, she could detect the hint of a mustache and beard beginning to sprout on his otherwise smooth and handsome face.

Somehow, he reminded her of her mother and Puddin, Gigi, and China Doll. He had on tight black pants, made of some sort of stretch material, and they stopped just below his calves. Over this, he wore a white shirt, a man's shirt, only he had a woman's stretch belt over the shirt, cinching his waistline, and he had cut the sleeves completely off the shirt, revealing hard, well-curved biceps. He was wearing loafers, but he had walked on the backs of them, turning them into what her mother called slides. He wore red ruby-stone earrings in both ears, and his eyebrows appeared to have been plucked or waxed.

In his left hand, he held a long black rhinestone-encrusted cigarette holder with a lit cigarette attached. When he spoke, he made grand and sweeping gestures, which reminded Peaches of the actress Bette Davis, whom she and Ursula sometimes watched on the late show on television. His hair was covered by a black scarf, what everybody called a doo rag, but she could see that underneath the scarf, he had pink hair rollers in his hair.

Hair rollers. On a man's head. He was something else. But he had a nice wide smile and seemed like a good friend of her mommy's. It was like him and my mommy and Puddin and Gigi and China were all in some kind of secret club, she thought to herself, as she listened to them ramble on.

Peaches wondered why she had never seen him before. She had been standing there only half listening to their conversation, so captivated was she by Vaa's very presence, that when his voice suddenly rose in pitch, she actually jumped in alarm.

"Oh, God no. Oh, honey, you can't mean it, Ursula, you just can't. Don't you know what a prick he is, what a bastard he is? Oh, no, my dear, you simply cannot do this, you—"

Ursula looked at him, then quickly down at Peaches.

"Here, Peach," she said, fishing a fifty-cent piece out of her bag. "You go on down to that lil store there on the corner and get yourself somethin. Don't you want some ice cream?" She handed Peach the money. "It's right there on the corner, darlin. They've got all kinds of candy and stuff. You'll love it."

Vaa pointed out the store to her with a wave of his cigarette holder. On each finger of his left hand, she noticed there was a ring. Peaches was fascinated.

"Go ahead now, Peach. Mommy be right here when you get back." Ursula waved in the direction of the store, already turning her attention back to Vaa.

Peach knew she was being gotten rid of so she wouldn't hear whatever they were talking about, but she didn't care. Fifty cents was a lot of money to her. She could buy all kinds of stuff, as Vaa said, and if there was any change left, she knew her mommy would probably forget to even ask for it.

She bought a soda, a Popsicle, and some candy, and her favorites, Squirrel Nuts and Mary Janes. She got thirty cents in change. Hot dog. She took her time walking back to her mom and Vaa, slowly savoring her Popsicle and clutching her small brown bag of candy and soda.

She could see from the corner that another man had joined them, a taller man than Vaa. Then she saw the tall man put both hands on his hips and step in closer to Vaa. She saw her mom move in between the two men quickly, as if to separate them. She couldn't hear what was being said, but she didn't like the looks of things.

She quickened her pace.

By the time she reached them, Vaa had placed both hands on his hips, too, his eyes narrowed to black slits of coal. There seemed to be some type of staring contest going on.

"Oh, here's Peaches, Elmo. Here's my daughter now," Ursula said too brightly.

"Peaches, this your uncle Elmo." Ursula pushed Peaches in front of her.

The tall man stared at Vaa a few seconds longer, then dropped his gaze down to the girl's level.

"She look like both you and Prez, but she sho nuff got Prez's eyes, don't she?" he said, nodding his head.

"Sho do now, Elmo. Everybody say that. Look just like the bastard." Ursula laughed nervously. "But she gone be built just like me."

The tall man looked Peaches up and down.

"Maybe. We'll see. Yall come on in the house now. It's too damn hot to be out here in public, with everybody gettin all in yo business and whatnot." He stared pointedly at Vaa, and then moved toward the gate, opening it for Ursula and Peaches. They trailed behind him slowly, Ursula still joking with Vaa.

"Ursula, I said, I got better things to do than stand out here fussin with no lowlife faggot."

"Who you calling lowlife, you damn hypocrite? You don't want me to have to read you in front of your family out here, do you? Don't make me start." Vaa yelled after him, still gesturing wildly with the cigarette holder.

"Please, Vaa, let it go," Ursula pleaded under her breath.

"Ursula, you know I will cut that bastard's ass too short to shit between two shoes."

"I'll stop by and see you later, okay honey? Be good," Ursula said in a louder tone, simultaneously waving him away and pulling Peaches up the porch steps behind her.

Uncle Elmo didn't even bother to look back. He had entered his house and was holding the screen door open for them. They both disappeared into the house behind him. Vaa stood on the sidewalk a bit longer, watching the door. Then he shook his head and went into his own house.

Inside Elmo's house, it was dark and cool. The furniture was nice, but covered with plastic, even the lamps. There was something old and kind of musty about it, a museum-like quality.

"You two have a seat. I'll just go up and see how Liddy doin, and I be right back down," said Uncle Elmo, gesturing toward the sofa. He quickly took the stairs to the second floor.

"This a nice house, ain't it, Peach?" Ursula said, as soon as Elmo left. Peaches looked around, her eyes taking in all the little knick-knacks on the coffee table and mantel, the starched doilies pinned to the arms of the plastic, and the extreme tidyness of the living room.

"Yeah, Mommy, it's nice," she answered, almost whispering.

Something about this house made her not want to speak out loud. She shivered, though it wasn't at all cold. "It's nice, I guess, just so—"

"So what?"

"It's just so neat. Like, you know, it's nothin outta place in here."

"Girl, I swear, you say the craziest mess. It's a nice house. It's sho nicer than ours," Ursula said sharply.

Before Peaches could reply, Uncle Elmo walked back down the steps. He sat in the large armchair next to the mantel.

"Liddy asked me to say hi to yall. You know, I told you she ain't been feelin too good these days. She back and forth to the doctor all the time, but it don't seem to be doin her no good. Sometimes she can't even keep her food down."

Elmo paused and looked at his hands. He seemed genuinely upset. "Anyhow, she said for me to feed yall some lunch first, then bring yall up to see her."

"Oh, that's all right, Elmo. We don't want you to go to no trouble," Ursula protested.

"Ain't no trouble. It's already made." He rose and started toward the dining room. "I got some of the women from the church to come by and do the cookin for us and the cleanin, since Liddy got sick."

Ursula and Peaches followed Elmo into the dining room.

"Have a seat, and I'll get the food."

"Oh, Elmo, don't be foolish. I'll help you," Ursula insisted, following him into the kitchen. "You sit down at the table, Peach."

Peach sat at the dining room table, looking around. Here again, everything was very nice, but just too tidy. The matching dining room set, the dish-filled china closet, the silver tea service on the buffet table, resting atop still another starched doily. So neat. So unlived-in. No music on, no TV playing, no nothing, she thought to herself.

Elmo and Ursula returned from the kitchen, their arms laden with food and dishes, Elmo still talking about how much he had to depend on the ladies from the church to do things around the house, ever since Liddy got the sickness, as he referred to it. In fact, the topic of

Liddy's sickness and the inconvenience it was causing him dominated the conversation at lunch, an otherwise pleasant meal that consisted of ham-and-cheese sandwiches, potato salad, and iced tea. Elmo had started to take a tray of soup and tea up to Liddy, but Ursula had insisted on taking it up herself.

"It will give us a chance for a lil girl talk." She smiled at Elmo.

While Ursula was upstairs with Liddy, Peaches glanced shyly over at Elmo. He was staring directly at her, his deep cloudy eyes shaded by large bushy eyebrows.

Why was her mother acting so nicey-nice to this man she didn't even remember?

"So you gettin ready to have a birthday, huh, girl?" He chewed his food quickly, still staring.

"Yes, sir. I'll be eight years old."

"Eight? Do tell. Well, eight is almost halfway grown, you know." He smiled for the first time, revealing a mouthful of gold and yellow teeth. "Yup, halfway grown," Elmo said, grinning.

He said nothing else. As Peaches ate her meal, she studied him out of the corner of her eye. He really wasn't a bad-looking man, though he was kind of mean-looking. And old. Though Elmo was just shy of sixty, to Peaches, he seemed ancient.

She was glad when Ursula came back down and rejoined them.

"Oh, Elmo, you po man. I can see what you mean." Ursula shook her head at him sympathetically. "Poor Liddy. I got a little soup down her and she drank the whole glass of tea. But she really is looking po'ly. She want me to bring Peach up after lunch, but I know she just took her pain pill, so if she sleep, I won't wake her up. She got plenty of time to see her."

"Speaking of which . . ." Elmo cleared his throat.

"Yes?"

Ursula looked up from her sandwich at him expectantly, almost childlike.

"I got somethin a lil stronger than that tea. You still drank scotch and soda, right?"

"Right." Ursula nodded, flashing Elmo the phoniest smile Peach had seen in a long time.

After lunch, Elmo produced a fifth of J&B Scotch from the buffet. He went into the kitchen and came back with a tray containing ice, glasses, and a large bottle of Coca-Cola. He and Ursula repaired to the living room, while Peaches was sent out to the porch with her candy and soda.

Peach sat swinging back and forth on the large white glider on the porch, eating her candy. She watched the children playing in the park across the street. She felt full and sleepy. It was a warm day, and having stuffed herself full of lunch, along with the candy and soda, she could hardly stay awake. As she began to drift off, she could just make out the sound of music, blues, softly playing inside the house.

"Peach, come on, baby, wake up. Time to go."

Ursula was shaking her awake. The sun was almost gone. Peaches couldn't tell how long she had been sleeping. Her mother was pulling her gently to her feet.

"Say bye to Uncle Elmo," Ursula instructed, as she led her daughter to the front steps.

"Bye, uh, Uncle Elmo. I had a nice time," Peaches recited automatically, waving toward the door.

"Anytime, sweetie. Anytime." Elmo waved back, smiling. But the smile never reached his eyes. The hard stare remained, and there was something else, too. She just couldn't figure out what.

"Let's go, Mommy." Peaches ran down the steps, out the gate, and joined her mother on the sidewalk. That man gave her the heebie-jeebies. "What about Aunt Liddy, Mommy? Why didn't I get to meet her, too?"

Peaches had waited until they were safely on the bus before asking this question. She didn't want Ursula dragging her back to that house again.

"Oh, Aunt Liddy took some medicine that put her to sleep, and I didn't want to wake her up, honey. You'll get to meet her next time." Ursula was glancing out of the bus window, watching the streets whiz by. "So, how did you like the house? You should have seen the back-yard. They got a real big tree back there. And the bathroom got a real shower."

"It's all right, I guess. But it's too quiet in there. It's like somebody died."

"Well, how did you like Uncle Elmo?" Ursula pressed.

"Mommy, I'm sorry, but he is creepy." Peaches shook her head, laughing.

SMACK!

Peach never saw the hand coming. Her head bumped against the metal on the back of the bus seat behind her, and she cried out before she even knew it.

"Don't you never let me hear you say nothin like that again, you ungrateful lil bitch," Ursula hissed into her ear. "You don't preciate nothin."

Peach could smell the alcohol on Ursula's breath. People on the bus were staring at them now, the flamboyant, cheaply dressed but beautiful woman and her pretty little long-legged girl. The women passengers shook their heads disdainfully, and sucked their teeth in disgust.

"And just what in the hell is yall hincty heifas lookin at? Like yall ain't never chastised yo kids before. All yall can kiss my Black ass," Ursula snarled, staring each woman in the face. The women turned away, still shaking their heads.

The next morning, Ursula acted as if nothing had happened the evening before. She was already up and had had her breakfast by the time Peaches stumbled sleepily into the kitchen.

"Something to eat, honeybun? I cooked bacon and eggs," Ursula asked in her kindest voice. Peaches immediately cocked her head suspiciously. She wondered what was up now?

"No, I'm a just fix me some cereal," Peach answered warily, sneaking glances at her mother out of the corner of her eye.

"Suit yourself. I'm goin shoppin with Puddin and Gigi. There's lunch meat and Kool-Aid in the fridge." Ursula walked across the room to her quickly, lifted her face by the chin, and kissed her fore-head. "Later, baby. I'll bring you somethin back."

Ursula kissed her once more, ruffled her hair, and was gone, leaving Peaches staring behind her.

The remainder of the week went by uneventfully.

Peaches rose each day, washed quickly, had a bowl of cereal, then headed off to school. Ursula would go out in the late afternoons, but she was usually in by early evening, except for maybe an hour or two downstairs at the Tip Top, and she would stay in for the rest of the night.

Peaches loved going to the playground after school with Jan. There were plenty of kids to play with, a lot whom she knew from school or around the neighborhood, and there was always lots to do. Mrs. Birch, the rec center supervisor, made it her business to know all the kids by name, and she knew most of their parents also.

"Hi, Peaches." Mrs. Birch would smile cheerfully in greeting each time she saw her. Peaches liked that Mrs. Birch didn't call her Priscilla, like most other grown-ups.

Peaches began to eagerly anticipate the long, carefree days of summer, as only a child can. Three more days to go, then two, then one, and finally, freedom at last.

Even though Peaches wasn't registered formally in the rec center's day camp program, she was given lunch and snacks each day and allowed to participate fully in all camp activities along with the other children. She knew this was Mrs. Birch's doing. In camp, each day, the children did something different. There were jump-rope competitions, jacks, hopscotch, and table tennis. They had potato-sack and relay races. There was story time, music time, art and dance lessons, and you didn't even have to take a nap, either. Best of all, her cousin Jan was there, the two of them thick as thieves.

By the end of the first week, her skin had already begun to turn a tawny, golden color. Peaches was aware that her mother had called the school and spoken to the principal, but when she questioned Ursula about it, she was told not to worry, that everything had been taken care of. So she had put it out of her mind. This was summer, and she was enjoying just being a kid.

On the Friday afternoon of her third week in camp, Mrs. Birch came over to her group as they sat making collages and asked all the children to please wear something special the next afternoon, as there was going to be a surprise party at the playground.

"Party for who?" the children squealed.

Peaches knew it wasn't for her. She had just celebrated her birthday almost ten days before.

"Can't tell. It's a surprise. Just be here."

Mrs. Birch winked and smiled at her. When Peaches arrived home that afternoon, she discovered that Mrs. Birch had already called Ursula and informed her about the party being held the next day.

"I know all about it." Ursula waved her away. "Go in your room. I think there's somethin on yo bed for you."

Peaches ran into her bedroom and excitedly tore the cover off the large box lying atop her bed. She squealed with delight.

"Oh, Mommy! Oh, thank you, thank you, thank you!"

Peaches ran through the apartment, holding the new party dress up in front of her. The dress was a mass of pale orange chiffon, adorned with ruffles and small white rosebuds. There was a large crinoline slip that was to be worn underneath. It complemented Peaches's complexion perfectly.

She finally settled down long enough to give her mom a hug and a huge sloppy kiss on the cheek.

"Can I try it on now?"

"Yeah, I guess so. Just don't get it dirty. That's for you to wear . . ." Ursula's words trailed off.

Peaches had whirled around and tore back down the hallway to her bedroom, ready to try on her new dress.

". . . tomorrow," Ursula said softly, her eyes cloudy.

The next afternoon, after helping Peaches to dress for the surprise party and doing her hair, Ursula surprised her daughter by announcing she was going to the party with her.

"I just want to take some pictures of you and yo lil friends. You look so cute in yo dress and you growin so fast, you probably won't be able to wear it in another year or two. See, I got Gigi's camera and three rolls of film."

So off they went, hand in hand, the two short blocks to the playground.

"Surprise!"

When Peaches and her mom entered the large indoor room where her group met, there was loud applause. Everyone was beaming at her.

"Happy birthday to you!" The children started singing. Peach stepped back, stunned, and looked up at her mother.

"But, Mommy, it's not my birthday," she protested weakly, ducking behind Ursula shyly. By then, Mrs. Birch had joined them by the doorway.

"Peaches, we know you recently had a birthday," she announced in her loud, clear voice. The room quieted down immediately. "But because you are so very special to all of us, and your mommy told us you have never had a birthday party before, we wanted to give you a special belated birthday party today."

Mrs. Birch reached from behind her and produced a beautiful, brown-skinned doll, which she placed in Peaches's arms. "Happy birthday, honey." She leaned down and kissed Peaches on the cheek.

"Happy birthday, baby," Ursula said, hugging Peach to her, seeming on the verge of tears.

The children clapped and cheered.

"Well, time to get this party rolling. Start the music, please," shouted Mrs. Birch.

And party they did. There was ice cream, candy, potato chips, and pretzels, even a large cake with Peaches's name spelled out on it in orange icing. Ursula ran around taking picture after picture. There were photos taken of Peaches with Mrs. Birch, with the kids, with the camp counselors, with the cake. Mrs. Birch even took a couple of Peaches and Ursula together, smiling and laughing. And of course, there was one of Peach and Jan. Peaches had never been so happy.

It was true. She had never had a real birthday party before, and she would never, ever forget this one.

Ursula left after about an hour or so, first talking with Mrs. Birch and assuring her she would be back later that afternoon to help Peaches with her cake and other small gifts given to her by the children and staff. The party rolled on. The children played games, ate everything in sight, and pretty much ran themselves ragged.

After a while, it was time to go. Mrs. Birch reminded Peaches that she was to be picked up later, so she remained seated at a little table beside her cake, her new doll, and her birthday presents, as the other children bid her good-bye.

SNAP!

She blinked in the light and turned toward it, thinking it was her mother back again, taking still another snapshot. But instead of Ursula, Puddin and Gigi were smiling down at her.

"Hey, munchkin. My, don't we look pretty today," exclaimed Puddin, walking over to Peaches.

Gigi waved, but stayed where she was, talking to Mrs. Birch.

"Hi, Aunt Puddin. Where's my mommy?" Peaches sat up and stretched, peering around the room for Ursula.

"Oh, she asked us to pick you up, since I got a car and all, Munch. Would yall look at all this stuff you got here. You sure cleaned up, kid." Puddin laughed.

Peaches laughed, too. She sure had cleaned up. She had plenty of loot, enough candy to last her a week, and a big hunk of the birthday cake that was left over.

"Ready to go, sweetie?" Gigi, smiling, walked over to help Puddin gather up all Peaches's things.

"Yeah, I'm ready, Aunt Gigi. Thank you for comin to get me."

"No problem. Looks like somebody's ready to meet the sandman early tonight," Gigi said, as Peaches yawned and stretched.

"Yes, ma'am, sure am."

Peaches was tired. She walked over and said good-bye to Mrs. Birch and the staff and thanked them for the party.

"Why, you're welcome, honey." Mrs. Birch hugged her again.

"See y'all tomorrow," Peaches yawned, following Puddin and Gigi out the door.

"Good-bye, Priscilla." Mrs. Birch waved back.

She was not smiling.

Outside, Puddin had packed all Peaches's things in the trunk of her big red Cadillac convertible.

"You gone leave the top down, Aunt Puddin?" Peach asked.

"Sure am, Munchkin."

In no time at all, she was stretched out in the backseat, one arm clutching the newly christened Sarah, fast asleep. Presently, she was dimly aware of being lifted out of the car. She heard her mother's voice, felt Ursula's arms around her as she was carried up the stairs and placed faceup on the bed.

"Hold still, baby. I gotta get you out of this dress," Ursula whispered as she removed Peaches's party dress.

Peaches sleepily did as she was told, allowing Ursula to get her ready for bed. All she wanted to do was lie down again. By now, she couldn't even keep her eyes open.

"Night, night, baby." Ursula's soft kiss on her cheek tickled her.

"Night, night, Mommy." She giggled, lazily drifting down into dreams of ice cream, candy hearts, and red Cadillacs.

But there was no ice cream, no candy, no Cadillac car to greet her in the morning. There was also no Ursula. All there was was Uncle Elmo, sitting on the side of her bed.

CHAPTER 8

JAN'S DREAM

Jan could bring Junie back just about any time she wanted to now. All she had to do was sit at the little altar she had raised on a small table in her bedroom. Her altar held candles, a cactus plant, small trays of candy and loose change, pennies, mostly, and pictures of June Bug and her now-deceased parents and grandparents.

She would light her candles, offer up a small prayer, think of Junie while staring at his picture, and meditate, accompanied by the Dells' old hit, "The Love We Had Stays on My Mind," playing softly in the background.

Then she would go straight to bed. Before long, as she drifted down, down, and just before succumbing to sleep, she would begin to feel a soothing, almost liquid warmth spreading through her, as if the sun were on her ceiling, beaming down on her, baptizing her body in pure light.

Then the tingling would start. Her entire body would begin to vibrate, to tense and tingle as if she had been struck by a spiritual tuning fork, starting at the tips of her toes and slowly working its way up to the very top of her head. Her body would then seem to rise up, her arms and legs extending, sensing its way like radar, love-directed, seeking communion, reunion with the spirit of a long-dead lover.

And what a splendid spirit he was. He was everything she had ever wanted him to be in life and had made him out to be in death. Strong, yet tender, firm, yet compassionate, a wonderful lover, achingly masculine, yet sweet as the juice from a purple plum on a summer day.

He took her breath away. Even now. He was often with her these days whether she was asleep or awake. He was just there, totally unbidden. She talked to him all the time. Jan was a woman who sometimes, even on winter nights, stepped out the back door and stared up at the stars, so drawn was she to the beauty of the night sky. She was a woman truly in thrall to the pull of the moon, though she would be at pains to explain why.

"Oh, Junie, I wish you could see it, it's so beautiful," she would whisper on those particular evenings when the sky seemed like a lush velvet carpet and the stars like holes in heaven's floor.

"And oh, the moon—it's all yours, baby, all yours." She giggled out loud, remembering the night when Junie had reached up, standing on the very top step of her house, framed the moon with his long tapered fingers, then placed them in front of her laughing face.

"Miss Janice Jackson, I now present you with the moon. Now, if this ain't enough, I'll make you a deal. Marry me, and I'll give you the stars. Now, it might take a lil time, but I'll chase those suckers down just for you. Every one of them."

"Is that a promise? Every one?" she had asked, laughing.

"Baby, that's a bet. Deal?" he had replied, extending his hand.

"Deal," Jan had repeated, sealing it with a kiss. And that was it. They had been together from that day on.

Spending her nights with June Bug was far more comforting and enjoyable than facing her now anxiety-filled days, ducking bill collectors and ignoring the telephone when it rang. Her nighttime dreams were becoming more and more her real world, her daytime life more a never-ending nightmare.

Thoughts of suicide were never far away these days, and recurred with odd regularity. What did she really have to live for, after all? The only man she had ever known, ever loved, was dead. Her home, once filled with laughter, love, dogs, sunshine, and flowers, now functioned only as a museum for her cobwebbed memories.

Most days, her faithful German shepherd, Shaft, was the only living creature she saw all day long. She had found Shaft whimpering in her backyard one cold night, shortly after Junie's death. She had taken the starving pup in and bottle-fed him back to health, and now he was spoiled rotten, her baby.

Something to care for. She believed him to be a gift from her husband.

Her once-promising home-based business, her pride and joy for which she had mortgaged everything and gone for broke, now lay in ruins, gone, yet another mocking memory. How much easier it would be to simply surrender, to let go, to be with June Bug again, far away from the dull pain and growing uncertainty of her empty, walking-dead life.

Her home had always been the one place where she found peace, the warm, safe cocoon from which she butterflied daily out to face the world. And now, they were taking that away, too. So why even fight it?

Why fight anything anymore?

She had begun to feel with each day that passed by that she was only going through the motions, merely existing, with one foot in this world and the other in the next. She never left her house anymore unless it was absolutely necessary.

She did her grocery shopping late at night, hoping not to run into anyone she knew, and if she did, if she saw them first, she would quickly detour her shopping cart and head in the opposite direction. If she hadn't moved quickly enough, or if they saw her first and spoke, she would force herself to acknowledge their greeting and make brief, wooden conversation, feeling like an untalented, unprepared actor, suddenly thrust out onto a stage in the lead role.

She was aware that she was behaving oddly, but she couldn't seem to help herself, and truthfully, she didn't much care what people thought of her. As far as she was concerned, she wasn't much longer for this cold world anyway.

Even household tasks she had once diligently performed now seemed like drudgery, grunt work. She was too tired, too weary. Her plants were all dead, her prized green thumb now having reverted back to basic brown. She hadn't tended to or watered them in what seemed like ages, hadn't even bothered to throw them out when they died.

Her house was now filled with clutter. Old newspapers, magazines, and dust bunnies shared the same space indiscriminately. She never washed the dishes until she had used up every clean plate, fork, and spoon in her cabinet. Same with the laundry. Not until she was down to her last set of sheets, her last pair of panties, did she bother to turn on her washer. Her bedroom looked as if a hurricane had passed through it, with the exception of the altar.

Only the living and dining rooms still retained a halfway decent appearance, just in case she had unexpected guests. But no one came by. She had turned down invitations and made herself unavailable so many times that no one bothered to call or visit anymore.

And that was just fine with her. She didn't want to see anybody, anyway. It was enough for her to just get herself out of bed most days, drag herself to the bathroom, brush her teeth, and wash her face. She had even let that go a few times, simply going straight from bed down into the always messy kitchen, making herself a pot of tea and two slices of toast, bringing her breakfast tray upstairs and crawling back into bed, spending half the day sleeping and the other half watching soaps and silly sitcoms.

She didn't have much of an appetite. She ate only to keep hunger pangs away. She chain-smoked constantly. She lived in jeans and old sweats and wore her hair pulled back in braids, so she wouldn't have to be bothered with it. Too much trouble. Everything was too much trouble.

And Junie knew that. He understood. He was always with her when she needed him to be, concerned and sympathetic. She much preferred her nightly living to her daily dying.

It was in this state of mind that Janice Jackson Shephard pondered whether or not she should actually meet with Sally Mae and Rasheeda over at Rasheeda's shop on this chilly winter evening, one week after Peaches's funeral.

The speed with which she had pulled herself together for the funeral had astounded her. As soon as she had received the call from Kim, calling from the morgue to tell her Peaches had been pronounced DOA, her body had gone into action, with a mind of its own. She had grabbed her pocketbook, dashed out the door, and jumped into her battered Crown Vic, praying all the way that she had enough gas to make the trip.

She was living pretty much hand-to-mouth these days, her small widow's pension from Junie's military service not even beginning to cover her expenses, so she rarely put gas in her ten-year-old car unless she had a specific destination. The needle was set at just over a quarter tank. She figured she could just make it down there and back.

Once at the Medical Examiner's Office, she had quickly sized up the situation and immediately taken control. Ursula and Princess were weeping uncontrollably. Kim was arguing with a clerk, trying to get information as to what should be done next. Jan spoke quickly with Kim, who seemed more in control of herself. She got coffee and sodas from the vending machines for them and gave them all aspirin, which she carried in her oversized pocketbook.

It wasn't much, but at least it temporarily distracted their distress, and they began to calm down.

She then approached the clerk, a hard-faced, overbleached blond, thirty-something white woman with a smug, I-am-the-head-bitch-in-charge-here manner.

The clerk glanced up over her black rhinestone-studded reading glasses at Jan and gave her a bored once-over. Jan sat down on a hard plastic chair and produced from her pocketbook her glasses, a small notebook, and a pen. She crossed her legs, and in a firm, business-like manner, asked the woman for her name as well as her immediate superior's name, which she proceeded to write down in the notebook.

She then leaned forward slightly, giving Miss Rhinestones a cold, fixed stare, a look that said, "Don't play with me. I might be just another Black woman in sweats, but then again, I might be a judge's wife, so you better get your po-white, bad-skin, Kmart elastic-waist-pants-wearin ass in gear."

It took about two, maybe three seconds for the message to register telepathically with the gum-snapping clerk, for her to either play or fold.

She folded. Within ten minutes, having gotten all the forms and pertinent information needed as far as arrangements to pick up the body, insurance, and so forth were concerned, Jan and Peaches's family were on their way to Peaches's apartment.

Anyone who knew her would have sworn that the person who had taken charge in the morgue that day was the same old Janice, as forceful and in control as ever.

Only she knew how difficult it had been. She had been so beaten down recently that she had almost forgotten how to stand up for herself, let alone anyone else.

But it had come back. The rage against unfairness, the will to go toe-to-toe with anyone who dared commit any wrong against her or those she loved, had come reflexively roaring back. The feeling had surprised and excited her.

Maybe it could work, she mused, thinking back on that terrible morning. Three heads were better than one, and God knows, it couldn't get any worse. Then she checked that thought. Yeah. It could. It could get much worse. She could be out on her ass in forty-five days, her house sold at a sheriff's auction.

Her things would be put in storage somewhere.

All the lovely treasures and mementoes she had saved over a lifetime, which in cold dollars and cents might not amount to much in the eyes of a stranger, but meant everything to her. Things that had belonged to her mother and father, her grandmother, to Junie, were lovingly packed and stored in her basement.

If she lost her house, she knew she would die.

But wasn't that what she wanted? Truly? Because to live would mean to fight, and she wasn't at all sure she had much fight left in her. And yet on that day at the morgue, it had come from somewhere. That natural instinct she had always possessed to fight back, to take it to the mat, had welled up inside her like a flash fire.

She picked up her purse, turned off the lights, and walked quickly out the door, before she could change her mind.

CHAPTER 9

PEACHES AND ELMO

Time to get up, girl," Elmo ordered when he saw that she was awake.

Peaches sat up quickly. She looked around the small bedroom and then back at Elmo. "Where's my mommy?" she demanded, suddenly wide awake and afraid, hastily trying to cover her whole body up with the sheet.

"Yo mommy's gone home. You gone stay here with us now, with me and yo aunt Liddy," he whispered, his lips stretching across his teeth in a grim imitation of a smile.

"Now, come on now. Stop that cryin. You got to meet yo aunt Liddy."

"I ain't stayin wit you. I ain't stayin here no such a thing. Where's my mommy?" Peaches's voice rose with each word she uttered. She skittered across to the other side of the bed, over near the wall, and tried to slide down to the bottom, but he was too fast for her. He grabbed her roughly by her arm and pulled her clear across the bed.

Elmo leaned in, holding her by both arms now, until they were face-to-face. "Now, you lissen, girl. I'm doin yall a favor, you know. I'm doin yo tramp-ass mama a favor, takin you in. If you don't like it here, yo little sorry ass can go straight to a foster home, for all I care. I don't give a good goddamn. But if you stay here, you gon do what I say, when I say it.

"Now, if you cain't do that, the hell wit you and yo sorry-ass mama." Elmo relaxed his grip on her slightly, still looking into her eyes. That was all the slack Peaches needed. Like a shot, she was out of his arms, off the bed, and running out of the bedroom, into the dim hallway.

She looked down at herself. All she was wearing was a pair of jammies. She didn't even have any shoes on. Where would she go? She didn't know, but she sure as hell was getting outta here. Down the steps she bounded, straight for the door. She turned the screen door lock, hesitated for a moment, and looked back up the stairs.

Elmo was standing at the top, hands on his hips. "Ha! You be back. You be back. Where you gone go, huh?" He laughed softly, though it came out more like a snort.

Peach bolted out the door. Once on the porch, she hesitated again. Where would she go? She blinked and adjusted her eyes to the Saturday morning sun. Something real bad must have happened to Mommy, she thought. She would never have left Peaches here with this smelly old man if something hadn't happened to her.

Peaches had no money; she was scared. She was a just-turned-eight-year-old child, standing on the porch of a stranger on a Saturday morning, shaking in her nightclothes. She started to cry softly. People passed by on their way to work, or shopping, or just going about the business of living. Some slowed down and stared curiously at the crying child, but no one stopped. No one asked what the matter was. They just kept on walking by.

"Well, I declare, is that the Georgia pea— Child, what's wrong?"

Vaa leaned over the porch railing, his handsome face an outline of concern.

Just hearing his kind words and seeing his friendly face made Peaches start bawling for real now. "My mom-mommy ain't here. She left me here with that mean old ma-man."

"What? You come on over here this instant. I have Ursula's number. I'll call her right now and straighten this mess out." Vaa reached over, took hold of Peaches's hands, and led her around to his porch. "Come on in, lady. We'll see about this," Vaa stated with a dramatic wave of his hand, for once without the cigarette holder.

Vaa motioned Peaches to a chair in the living room and was thumbing through his address book. Before doing so, he had given Peaches a large glass of lemonade and a sticky bun. He had also stroked her hair and quieted her tears, promising to set Ursula straight for leaving her with Elmo, the sick bastard, as he referred to him.

He then absented himself to the dining room telephone, keeping one eye on Peaches.

"Ursula? Hi, Doll Baby, this is Vaa. Yeah, you, too. Listen, sweetie, you know I wouldn't tell you nothing wrong but— She's over here now, wearing nothing but her pajamas. Ursula, she is terrified. You simply cannot—"

Peaches strained to hear, but could only pick up bits and pieces of the conversation.

"No, I will not!" Vaa was practically screaming now.

"If you want to speak to her, you bring your sorry whoring ass self over here and tell her to her face. Don't try to make me clean up your mess."

Vaa dropped his voice a bit, realizing Peaches could hear him, and was back in the living room in a few minutes. He also had a sticky bun and had made himself a cup of tea. He offered Peaches seconds, but she declined. She hadn't finished the first pastry. She was too nervous to eat.

"Is my mommy coming to get me?"

"She's on her way, Miss Peach," he answered, his glance not meeting her eyes.

"Want to watch some TV? I think there's cartoons on." Vaa switched on the television in the corner. Peaches drank her lemonade and watched Bugs Bunny silently, sneaking sidelong glances at Vaa.

In the harsh morning light, his face had a decidedly masculine appearance, and there was a definite five-o'clock shadow on his cheeks and above his upper lip. He appeared to be wearing nothing but a silk bathrobe and fuzzy slippers, and she could see the faint outline of hair on the exposed upper portion of his chest.

A Yellow Cab screeched to a stop in front of Vaa's house. Peaches and Vaa both raced to the front window, in time to see Ursula exit the vehicle, say a few words to the driver, and quickly walk up on the porch, her high heels clicking against the pavement.

Vaa was standing with the door opened before she could ring the bell. "Well, good morning, Miss Thing," he said sarcastically.

"Good mornin, Vaa. Where is my chile?" Ursula answered in a curt tone.

"Mommy, here, I'm in here," Peaches yelled from the parlor.

Smack! Smack! Smack!

"The hell is wrong wit you, girl? Elmo told me you just ran outta his house in your jammies wit no shoes on." Ursula berated Peaches in between smacks. "Do you know how much I had to low-rate myself just to get him to let you stay there?" *Smack!*

Peaches managed to duck the full force of the blows Ursula rained down on her face and head. But she was in shock. What was her mother talking about? She thought Ursula was here to pick her up, to take her home.

"Ursula! Ursula! Stop striking that child this minute." Vaa moved across the room quickly, grabbing Ursula by the wrists. The tone of his voice was commanding, authoritative, and brooked no nonsense.

Ursula crumpled into his arms like a deflated toy doll, while Peaches slid down to the floor.

"Vaa, you just don't know. What else could I do? Huh? What else could I do? You think I want to leave my baby there?" Ursula had turned her body around in Vaa's arms and rested her head against his shoulder. She was sobbing. Peaches sat on the floor, looking up at both of them, rubbing her still-stinging face.

"Go watch your cartoons, Miss Peach. Your mother and I are going to have a little chat in the kitchen. Okay?" Vaa led Ursula toward the back. He looked at Peach and winked.

"Okay."

Vaa took Ursula to the table in the large, cheery yellow kitchen, poured her a cup of tea, and sat a plate of sticky buns down in the center of the table. They spoke for a while.

He left the kitchen once to pay the taxi driver and send him on his way.

After a while, Vaa stormed out of the kitchen and ran upstairs. Peaches could hear Ursula on the phone, talking, but she couldn't make out the conversation. Ursula then hung up the telephone, came into the parlor, and sat beside her daughter.

"Peaches, turn off the television. I have something to tell you."

Peaches walked over, clicked off the set, then sat back down beside her mother.

"Baby, what Uncle Elmo said is true. He told you the truth. You gone have to stay with him and Aunt Liddy for a little while, but—"

Peaches was already wailing.

"Shut that noise up now, girl. It's yo own fault. If you had showed up at school stead of playin hookey alla time, this wouldn't be happenin."

Peaches wailed even more.

"Look, I ain't got no time for none of yo shit now. It won't be long. It's just for a lil while. I just got to get you outta that damn school," Ursula said, her voice alternating between pleading and threatening. "If you stay in that school, they might take you away from Mommy and put you in a foster home. You don't want to go to no foster home now, do you?"

"I don't want to go to that stinkin ole house and that mean Uncle Elmo's neither. I'm scared of him, Mama."

"Well, Peach, this is the only thing I can do right now, till I can find us another place to live and put you in a new school," snapped Ursula.

It was a rational explanation, the same one she had given Vaa earlier. But it was not a complete explanation. Ursula had conveniently left out the fact that it really wasn't necessary to move Peaches from her home at all, that the very thought of losing the monthly support check from Prez had so panicked her that the quickest and easiest solution she could come up with had been to send her daughter to live with Elmo and Liddy, and to tell the principal and the social worker that both her and Peaches were moving there, thereby getting Peaches out of the school district and away from their scrutiny.

She had begged Elmo to go along with the scheme, explaining that Peaches could work for her keep.

She could do some of the housework, as well as acting as an on-call nursemaid for Liddy. She had had to do considerably more than beg to get Elmo to agree, but he had finally come around with the added provision that she also turn over half the food she received from welfare each month to him.

"Shit, it ain't like it was gone be forever, just till I can get myself together, get another place. That's all."

So Peaches was delivered over to Uncle Elmo.

Ursula called Vaa downstairs and thanked him for looking after Peaches. He rolled his eyes at her and sucked his teeth in reply. But as they headed toward the front door, he grabbed Peaches by the shoulders and turned her around to face him. He knelt in front of her so his face was level with hers.

"You take care of yourself, Miss Peach, and if you have any trouble with that bastard, I've got your back. You hear me? You ring my bell anytime you want. You hear?"

"Yes, Mr. Vaa." Peaches sniffed.

"Just Vaa, dear. No mister. Now, don't forget what I said."

"Yes, Vaa," answered Peaches, grinning a little.

"Shut up, Vaa. She ain't gone have no trouble. Stop putting that kind of shit in her head," Ursula scolded.

But Peaches did have trouble. It began almost immediately after Ursula left. They had crossed over to Elmo's porch and Ursula knocked on the screen door.

Uncle Elmo answered, greeting Ursula with a smile, and led them into the living room as if the earlier incident between him and Peaches had never taken place. He was polite and solicitous, offering Kool-Aid to Peaches and a beer to Ursula.

All of Peaches's clothes, toys, and personal possessions had been moved there and hung up and placed into dresser drawers the day before, while Peaches was at her surprise birthday party, so there was really nothing for Ursula to do.

"Has Peach met Liddy yet?" she asked Elmo.

"No, she didn't. She left so quick this morning, I didn't get a chance to introduce em," Elmo said with the same grimacing smile he had shown Peaches that morning.

"Well, I'll take her up now," Ursula said, jumping up quickly, glad to have something to do.

As she and Ursula started up the staircase, Peaches figured Aunt Liddy just couldn't be any scarier than Uncle Elmo.

But she was. If Uncle Elmo was scary, Aunt Liddy was just downright creepy. The first thing that caught Peaches's attention when she and Ursula entered the front bedroom was the smell. It was sickening, almost sweet, and heavy, like the odor of a wet dog.

"Liddy, you up? Hi, it's me, Ursula," her mother called out in her bright, fake cheerful voice, as they entered the room. "And look who I brung wit me. Come on, Peach."

She pulled Peaches closer to the large bed. The girl hung back, trying to adjust her eyes to the gloom. The thick shades on the window were pulled halfway down, covered by drapes that looked like midnight maroon velvet. The furnishings were large, heavy, and seemed to come from another time period. There was a TV set perched on one of the end tables, the only modern convenience in the room. The sound was turned way down.

On the other end table, there was a dimly lit lamp, the glow outlining a small thin figure lying in the very center of a large four-poster bed, surrounded by pillows on all sides.

"Well, how do, Ursula. Let me just set up a little, so I can see you." A tiny, weak voice came from the figure on the bed.

"Here, let me help you up." Ursula plumped up the pillows, lifted the sparrowlike figure, and leaned her against the pillows at the headboard.

"Come on over here, Peach, and say hi to yo aunt Liddy."

Peaches stepped all the way up to the bed, where she could finally see by the lamplight that this was a tiny, gray-haired woman with a small, completely round and wrinkled face. Her hair was fine and sparse, her mouth, toothless, thin, and caved in. Although Liddy was exactly the same age as Elmo, the ravages of her illness had made her look almost twenty years older.

"Well, how do, Peaches," the woman said, again, extending a weak, trembling arm.

"Hi, Miss— I mean, Aunt Liddy." Aunt Liddy's hand felt like a dry brown paper bag when Peaches shook it gingerly. The woman reminded her of a stuffed and mummified monkey she had once seen on a class trip to the Museum of Natural History. Really frightening.

Though no one spoke the word out loud, it was common knowledge that Aunt Liddy had cancer—was, in fact, dying. "The sickness" was all Uncle Elmo had ever called it. Peaches didn't know what to call it, but she sure could see it and smell it, too.

Death was here in this space, swirling and sweeping around her. Peaches didn't know if she wanted to run or vomit first. She did neither.

Aunt Liddy told her how happy she was that Peaches was coming to stay for a little while to help her out, told her what a pretty child she was, and what a brave girl she was for not crying or acting like a baby. She even offered Peaches a peppermint from a jar on the nightstand beside the pills.

"No, thank you," Peaches declined quickly.

"I'm only gone be here for a little while, though. Just till my mommy finds us a new place to live. Right, Mommy?" Despite her fear, Peaches kind of liked the little old lady, and didn't want her to get her hopes up too high.

"Right, baby, right."

They chatted a while more, until Aunt Liddy began to tire. Ursula repositioned her in the bed again to her liking. She waved them away, falling asleep, even as she said good-bye, and they went back downstairs.

Ursula spoke to Elmo once again, this time in the kitchen, where he had prepared a salad for their lunch. Peaches sat in the dining room. After a while, the doorbell rang.

"Taxi," a voice called from the porch. Taxi?

Peaches panicked. The taxi was going to take her mommy away and leave her here with these stinkin ole people.

Her calm, grown-up facade dissolved. She began to cry again, loudly. Ursula ran from the kitchen.

"Taxi? Okay, just a minute. Be right out," she yelled to the driver, at the same time grabbing her purse and sunglasses from the telephone table where she had laid them. "You not gone start this shit again, girl, you hear?"

Peaches jumped up from the dining room table and and circled Ursula's waist with her thin arms.

"Please, Mama. Please don't leave me here. Please. I'll be good. I'll go to school every day. I promise. Please don't leave me here."

Ursula turned to walk away, but Peaches was holding on to her so tightly that she was actually dragging the girl behind her across the room.

"Stop it, stop it, now. Git off me. Git off." Ursula threw Peaches to the floor. "It's yo own damn fault. Yo fault," Ursula screamed, running from the house. She jumped into the cab, which quickly sped away.

Uncle Elmo had been standing in the dining room watching this whole scenario unfold. Now, he slowly walked across the room to where Peaches still lay on the floor crying.

"I told you you would be back, didn't I, you lil hussy. Now stop that cryin and get up off the floor. And take yo little skinny ass to the bathroom and wash yo face, fore I really give you somethin to cry about," he whispered into her ear.

Thus began Peaches's life with Uncle Elmo and Aunt Liddy. If there was a particular hell for eight-year-old girls, this was it. Elmo worked Peaches all the time. In the mornings, she had to get up, get herself washed and dressed, then go and empty Aunt Liddy's Porta-Potti.

Then she had to take Aunt Liddy's soiled bedding down to the basement and place it in the washer to soak, then go back upstairs to help Uncle Elmo wash and dress Aunt Liddy, after he changed her adult diaper.

Then she had to dispose of that and brush Aunt Liddy's hair, then comb her own hair.

Finally, she went down to breakfast, toast and tea or cold cereal, which she made for herself. Then back up to Aunt Liddy with toast, tea or hot cereal, oatmeal or baby food on a tray, which she also made.

Then she had to put Aunt Liddy on the bedpan, then empty and rinse that out. Again. And so it went for the last six weeks of summer. On the day after Labor Day, Ursula showed up bright and early to register Peach in her new school. Oh, she came with new dresses, new sneakers, black patent leather shoes, new leotards, and a jazzy Mickey Mouse book bag. Peaches thanked her mother curtly for the new things.

"Well, what's wrong wit you? Why you got yo mouth poked out, after I done bought you all this nice stuff?" Ursula seemed miffed.

"This is the first time you been to see me since you left me here, Mommy. All this stuff is nice, but I'd rather have you," Peaches replied.

Ursula said nothing.

At last, she could escape to school. After school, same thing all over again. In addition to feeding, washing, and caring for Aunt Liddy, she also had to dust the furniture and knickknacks during the week.

On the weekends, one of the two ladies from the Willing Workers at the church came by and cleaned the place thoroughly, and cooked a number of dinners for the week. Peaches thanked God for them. Elmo probably would have made her do all the cooking, too, but the Willing Workers warned him that she was too young, and might set the house on fire.

Once school started, Ursula dutifully showed up every week for about the first month or two, then dropped down to about every other week. On each visit, she brought fresh, clean dresses for Peach to wear to school, and took the dirty ones home to launder. She brought shoes, socks, coats, gloves, and whatever else Peaches needed.

Each time she came, Peaches would ask when she would be going home, and each time, Ursula changed the subject. Eventually, Peach stopped asking. But she did get to go home with Ursula at least one weekend a month.

Home was a lot different than she remembered it, but she was happy to be there all the same. She and Ursula would stay up late, watching old movies, eating popcorn and Chinese food, just like in the old days, if there was such a thing as old days for an eight-year-old.

She was almost nine and had been at Elmo's not yet a full year when the touchy-feely stuff first started. She had been half asleep in her bed one night, clutching Sarah and surrounded by her other babies, when she felt something on her leg. She changed position, but the something moved from her knee on up to her thigh.

Then she smelled liquor and that other peculiar smell, that man smell. She lay rigid, still, narrowing her eyes to slits, and there he was.

Ugly Uncle Elmo, his hand inching up higher and higher on her thigh. She attempted to kick his hand away from her, but he grabbed her thigh hard, digging his fingers in. She looked up at him then.

"You keep yo mouth shut, or I'll make sure you wind up in an orphanage, a bad girls' school, and you really won't see yo mama no more," he whispered harshly.

Peaches remained still, shut her eyes tightly so she wouldn't have to look at him.

His hand was under the sheet now, stroking first her thighs, then up to her privates. He hiked her thin legs up and apart. His breath was coming in ragged gulps as he rubbed her with one hand and masturbated himself with the other.

"You likes it, don't you? You know you likes it. Just like yo mama, ain't you?"

He could hardly manage to get the words out, he was rubbing and pulling so fast. Finally, he cried out, then threw up her gown and buried his head on her small chest, kissing her and slobbering all over her stomach.

Peaches choked back salty tears. Why was he doing this nasty stuff to her? Why was he talking about her mommy like that? How could she leave her here with this horrid man? She knew what she would do. She would tell her mother. Her mother would cuss Uncle Elmo out, and take her home. She would tell.

Elmo lay on her stomach for a moment, breathing hard, then sat up and straightened his pants. "I swear fore God, girl, you better not tell nobody, or you know what's gone happen to you," he whispered to her in the dark, then tiptoed silently out of the bedroom.

The next morning, he acted as if nothing had happened the night before. He was his usual, mean self, barking orders and grunting replies. Peaches thought about burning down the house, and she would have done it, too, if it weren't for her bedridden aunt Liddy. She liked Aunt Liddy, even though she hated acting as her nurse and cleaning her dirty stinkin sheets and potty.

The way she figured, Aunt Liddy and she had something in common. Liddy was a prisoner of her dying body, and she, Peaches, was a prisoner of this horrible house. Aunt Liddy couldn't help her situation any more than Peaches could help the situation in which she found herself. It never occurred to Peaches to place blame on Ursula for putting her in harm's way. She never even told her mother about Uncle Elmo molesting her.

The last time she had gone home, Ursula had warned her that she had better behave at Uncle Elmo's, because if she didn't, he would call her old school, and they would have Ursula put in jail and Peaches placed in foster care. Foster care sounded scary, but not as frightening as the thought of her mother being in jail. No, she wouldn't tell.

On the afternoon following the first night he had violated her, Peaches found herself standing at Vaa's door. As she raised her hand to ring the bell, the front door swung open, and standing there in the doorway, swathed head to toe in white satin and rhinestones, was a tall, caramel-colored woman beautiful enough to give even her mother serious competition.

"Why, hello. And what can we do for you today?"

"I— I come to see Vaa."

"Vaa, darling. This beautiful child is here to see you. She's not one of yours, I trust," the lady teased, as she led Peaches into the very center of the creative storm, the dining room-cum-showroom.

"Stuff it, Foxy," Vaa said, laughing.

"But, daahling, I already have. The problem is keeping it stuffed," Foxy laughed again and suddenly, just like that, pulled what looked like her breasts out from under her gown and threw them across the room at Vaa, hitting him on the side of the head.

Peaches's mouth dropped open. This was no lady.

"Just too much to stuff, I guess, girl," said Vaa, patting his curls down.

"Come on over here to me, Miss Peaches. About time. Ladies and gentle— Well, ladies. I would like to introduce yall to my friend who I wish was my daughter, the Georgia Peach." He beamed at her, pulling her close and placing a small rhinestone tiara on her head. The place was swarming with activity. There were gay men there, Black, white, and everything in between. But there were also actual women in attendance. All seemed to be in various stages of undress, either trying on, being fitted for, or being shown selections from smart business suits to casual pants to full evening gowns.

Everyone oohed and ahhhed and proceeded to spoil Peach to

death. She loved all the attention. It was almost like being home with Mommy, Puddin, China Doll, and Gigi. From that day on, she had become a regular fixture at Vaa's.

After arriving home from school, she would first check in on Aunt Liddy, do her chores, then sneak out to the backyard and climb over the small fence separating Elmo's home from Vaa's. After banging on the back door, she would be let in by whoever happened to be in the kitchen on any given day, always being careful to get back home before Uncle Elmo came home from work. She knew he hated Vaa almost as much as Vaa hated him.

Vaa's friends were a whole different breed of animal. He was, by profession, a tailor, but he was really a designer, and a gifted one. He specialized at going in as a sort of dress doctor to some of the white downtown designers, never getting credit for his work, but getting paid a little better than most for his discretion. He whined and bitched about his talent being exploited, but he was also a realist.

How far could a Black designer go, really, in the world of fashion in those days? Even being gay didn't help. He took the money and ran. Besides, the money he made from the white designers allowed him to pursue his true passion. The balls.

Vaa had been one of the founding members of the group of gay men who had originated the fabulous drag queen balls, a sort of underground Miss America contest that was held each year in New York, after preliminary events had been held in major East Coast cities, Philadelphia being one of them.

The biggest, grandest ball of all was held each year on Halloween night in Harlem, New York City, and Vaa prepared each year for it just as if it were the real Miss America pageant. For him, it was. So it was not unusual to walk into his house on any afternoon and become lost in a maze of rhinestones, feather boas, chiffon gowns, queens and ladies, who knew of his expertise with fabric and thread, and came straight to the master.

Peaches didn't even tell Ursula what a good friend Vaa had become to her. She somehow sensed her mother wouldn't like it. She had become Vaa's unofficial assistant, helping out in the showroom, pouring drinks, champagne, of course, for visitors, picking up leftover materials and placing them in bags for later use. Vaa would give her twenty-five cents, sometimes fifty cents a week, whenever she helped out. He didn't know it, but that was the only money she ever had for herself, except when Ursula came by.

Whenever Vaa tried to ask her about her life next door, however, she would give him a short answer, or change the subject. She couldn't tell him. He was, after all, a man. If she couldn't tell her mother, she sure couldn't tell a man.

The sexual abuse continued, approximately once a week, week in, week out. It got so she could almost tell when it was going to happen. She would catch Elmo staring at her for no reason and Oh, God, he gone come in my room tonight. She had tried wearing three or four layers of underpants to bed as a way of discouraging him.

One night she had even deliberately wet the bed.

He had slapped her face hard, warning her that she had "better not try that shit again."

But he had left her alone that night. On her way to school the next day, she walked slowly, dragging her feet, wondering which was worse, being molested weekly or lying in her own cold wet urine. She hadn't even realized her face was wet with tears.

"What you cryin about, girl?"

A low voice to her left startled her. She wiped her face quickly, then turned toward the voice.

"What?"

"I said, what you cryin about?"

This time the voice was even lower, barely a whisper. It was Dorothy, one of her classmates. Even through her tears, Peaches could see her friendly wide smile, accentuated by deep dimples.

"I ain't cryin." Peach sniffed defensively. She wiped her face rapidly. Her arm was beginning to itch. She thought maybe her rash was trying to come back. "Good. Maybe then that ole bastard will leave me alone," she said out loud. She scratched her arm vigorously.

"What ole bastard? Listen, Priscilla, you can tell me. I can keep a secret."

Peach looked at her sideways. Dorothy was kind of a tough girl, cursed a lot, but she had always been nice to Peaches, had even taken up for her when she was the new girl and some of the others had wanted to try her.

"My uncle does nasty stuff to me."

There. She had blurted it out for the first time. It wasn't her doing it; it was her uncle. Dorothy was silent for a moment.

"He touch you between yo legs?" Dorothy asked calmly, as if Peaches had simply commented on the homework assignment.

"Yeah."

"He kiss you down there?"

"Yeah."

"He make you pull on his dick?"

"He try to, but I won't do it."

"He make you kiss it, put it in yo mouth?"

"No. But he want me to. I'm scared he's gone make me do it."

"How much you get?"

"What?"

"How much? How much money you get?"

"What? No-no-nothing." Peaches was incredulous. What was this girl talking about, how much.

"You mean he don't give you no money?" Dorothy asked, wide-eyed.

"No, he don't give me no money."

"He buy you nice clothes, then, huh? I see all them pretty clothes you be wearin." Dorothy shook her head knowingly.

"No, he don't. My mommy buys me all my clothes," Peaches declared.

"No lie?" Dorothy gave her a cockeyed look.

"No lie." Peaches sighed.

"Well, I don't understand you, girl. If you ain't gittin no money from him and you ain't gittin no nice clothes or nothin, why don't you just tell on him?"

"I can't." Peaches shook her head slowly.

"Oh, yeah, you can. Just tell that mothafucka to leave you alone, or you gone tell yo mama," said Dorothy emphatically.

"I can't, Dorothy. I just can't." Peaches hung her head. She began to sniffle again.

"Hush, girl, don't cry." Dorothy reached over and awkwardly patted Peaches on the shoulder.

Peaches, in a slow, halting voice, proceeded to explain to Dorothy all the reasons she just could not tell anyone, about her mom saving for their new house, about the mean ole school people being after them, about how she might have to end up in a foster home or a home for bad girls if she told, how she would just have to stick it out, no matter what, and do what she was told.

Dorothy listened to all this in silence. She thought about it for a moment, pondered it.

"Bullshit," she finally said.

"What you mean, bullshit?" Peaches liked the sound of the bad word on her tongue.

"I mean bullshit. You might haf to do what the bastard say, but at least you can be gittin somethin out of it."

"Gittin what?"

"Gittin money, gittin clothes, gittin earrings, gittin candy, gittin whatever you want, girl, cause no matter what he tell you, he just tryin to scare you. He don't want nobody to know what he doin, chile. They never do."

"How you know so much about it?" This girl sure was strange, Peach thought to herself. She only nine, but she sound like a grown woman.

"How you think I know? How you think I be dressin so fine and always be having money in my pocket?" She winked at Peach.

"It happened to you, too?" Peaches said suddenly, clapping her hand over her mouth, pointing to Dorothy.

"It's still happenin to me," said Dorothy. "My mother's boyfriend, chile. I just learned how to get somethin out of it, that's all, just like she gets somethin out of him. And you got to learn how to, too. No wonder you don't never have no lunch money or milk money half the time. No wonder you don't go on no class trips. Girl, you don't know how to make no damn money." She chortled, shoving Peaches playfully.

"Dorothy, I think I see what you gittin at," Peach said slowly, "I just don't think I could—"

"Oh, hell, yeah, you could," snapped Dorothy impatiently, cutting her off. "And I'm a teach you how to do it." She laughed impishly.

Dorothy and Peaches had their heads together the rest of that day, and the next, and the day after that. They became fast and inseparable friends. When they weren't in school together, Peach would wait for her uncle to go out after dinner, then rush and call Dorothy on the phone. Fast friends with a secret.

Peaches listened to everything Dorothy had to tell her and learned her lessons as though they were school assignments. She began to feel much better.

She bided her time, and the next time Uncle Elmo started that staring at her, she stared right back at him, and as she did, she suddenly remembered Mr. Grimes, the truant officer, and the performance she had put on that long-ago afternoon. It was just playacting, that's all. She squared her narrow shoulders and took a deep breath.

"Uncle Elmo," she began, staring at him, holding his gaze. "My class is going to the zoo next week. I need you to sign my permission slip, and I'm gone to need some money."

His eyes widened, then narrowed.

"I ain't got no money for no trip. You wanna go on a trip, you better ask yo mama. I already give you room and board."

"I want you to give me the money for the trip. I don't want to bother my mother about it," Peaches said slowly, never taking her eyes away from his.

His mind was racing.

"Yeah, well, maybe," he said finally, "What's this foolishness gone cost me, anyway?"

He had blinked. Peach smiled and walked away.

Later that night, before she went to bed, Peaches went downstairs to the china closet where Uncle Elmo kept the liquor. She grabbed a bottle of vodka, put it to her mouth and took a large swig. Dorothy had said to use the vodka, cause it had no smell. Man, it burned going down. She had to force herself to take two more swallows, not so big this time. Her eyes were burning as it was.

She replaced the bottle, hurried upstairs and brushed her teeth. Then she went into her bedroom and stuffed her mouth with spearmint gum drops. She turned on the small radio Ursula had given her, found some music, and lay down in bed. Waiting.

By the time Uncle Elmo came into her room that night, as she knew he would, she was feeling pretty relaxed. The vodka and music had done their work. She lay on her side, facing the wall. As soon as she felt his hand under the covers on her thigh, she turned over and sat up in the bed.

"Hi, Uncle Elmo." She smiled. She was a little high now.

"What? Be quiet, girl. You tryin to wake up your aunt?" It was the only thing he could think of to say. He was completely unnerved at the sight of her. She didn't seem nervous or scared or anything, as she usually was. He opened his mouth again, then closed it.

"No, I don't want to wake Aunt Liddy. But I want you to sign my permission slip and give me the money for the zoo trip."

She took the permission slip from her night table and threw it in his face, still smiling.

"Look, okay, I'll sign it. I'll give you the damn money, just as soon as, as we—" He hesitated.

"As soon as we what?"

"Aw, you know. I give it to you first thing in the mornin," he said, looking away.

"But I want it *now*, Uncle. I want it *now*." She smiled, narrowing her eyes.

Elmo was shocked. Was this lil bitch flirtin with him? He wondered.

"Well, why you gotta have it now? Why cain't it just wait till the mornin?"

"Cause I want it now," she answered softly, eyes like slits.

And she got it. The money and the permission slip, signed. Right then and there. She was not quite ten years old yet.

Life became relatively better for Peach after that night, *relatively* being the operative word. She now had plenty of money in her pockets, and as much candy as she wanted. She went on all the class trips, always had lunch money, and Elmo had even brought in a nurse to take care of Aunt Liddy part-time.

She now had her own record player, and was allowed outside after school to join in the games of double Dutch, jacks, and hopscotch with the other little girls in the neighborhood. She delighted in sharing her newfound largesse with the children not as fortunate, for lack of a better word, and often sprang for treats all around.

But there was something decidedly different about her. Even her teachers had noticed it. Where there had once been a shy, friendly child, who moved like a born ballerina and painted pictures of lovely pink-and-yellow houses surrounded by blue-green grass, orange, apple, and lemon trees, and of a mommy and her little girl standing in front of every one, there was now a bolder, more aggressive child who laughed a little too loud, snapped her fingers and wiggled her behind when she danced, and no longer painted a mommy and a little girl.

Indeed, who no longer painted houses or mommies at all. There was now only the little girl, and her smile had gone away. Oh, she was still friendly. Everyone liked her. But her once wide-eyed wonder seemed to have been replaced by knowing hard-eyed cynicism, a kind of doubting attitude that seemed to size everything and everyone up, searching for the scam, looking for the lie.

Those were the days when sexual abuse of children, or even child abuse in general, was considered a family problem, and rarely mentioned outside of family circles. Her teachers, not being trained to recognize the symptoms of child sexual abuse, had no clue as to what was going on. Whenever they tried to reach out to Peaches, asking if there was a problem, she swiftly changed the subject, effectively shutting them out.

So they watched her sadly, missing the child they remembered. A nine-year-old with an old woman's soul, murmured her art teacher, shaking her head. Just like Dorothy, replied the music teacher, missing yet another one.

Peaches pretty much had a handle on things for a while. Between hanging out with Dorothy at school, playing with the neighborhood girls after school, and sitting around Vaa's where she was still pampered and spoiled by him and his customers, her days were pretty easy.

The nights were something else again. Uncle Elmo, who had taken to acting like some kind of love-struck teenager, was becoming more and more difficult to deal with. He wanted to come into her room all the time now. He wanted to take her out, show her off to all his friends, his pretty little niece, as he called her.

Silly ole fool. Peaches sucked her teeth at the very thought of him. But these were small things.

What she couldn't handle was the abuse. It was getting harder and harder to hold him off now. He wanted her to do more and more. He wanted to do more and more to her.

If it hadn't been for the vodka, she didn't know how she could have stood it.

"No matter what, just don't let him put his dick in you. Just don't let him put it in." She closed her eyes, remembering Dorothy's words, shuddering. She vowed she would never let that happen.

But one night, it just went too far. Either he had had too much to drink or she hadn't had enough.

Whatever. One minute, he was doing his usual masturbation, touchy-feely act, slobbering all over her chest, and the next, he had jumped on her, with the full weight of his body pinning her down. Peaches couldn't breathe. She gasped for air, clawing at his face. She felt something pushing at the opening of her privates, which she knew was his thing, hot, and hard like a pipe.

"Stop it, Uncle Elmo! Get off me!" she cried out. He kept pushing, she kept resisting, trying to clamp her legs shut. The pain was unbearable. She was screaming now. "Stop it, stop it, damn it!"

The first punch glanced off the side of her head, the second hit her dead in the mouth. Peach fell back, her mouth bleeding, banging the back of her head against the backboard.

"Who's there? Elmo? Peaches? Who is it?"

It was Aunt Liddy. Elmo froze, clamping his large hand across Peaches's bloody mouth. Aunt Liddy called out again in her weak, raspy voice. "Elmo? I say, Elmo? Who is that?"

Elmo relaxed his grip on Peach. She scooted out from under him in that split second, ran down the stairs, out the door, and straight over to Vaa's. Leaning on the doorbell, barefoot, and wearing nothing but a nightgown. Again. Only this time, there was more.

Her left eye swollen shut, her mouth a bleeding, gaping hole, her head spinning from pain, blood dripping down her face, staining the front of her white gown red, Vaa took one look at her, picked her up, and carried her inside.

He took her straight upstairs to the bathroom, gave her hot washcloths, ran her a tub of water, and called the police. Then he called Ursula.

CHAPTER 10

RASHEEDA

Rasheeda was really pushing it now. It was already 6:30 P.M., and she was taking a brief time-out before rejoining the others downstairs in the Oasis, which had a lively crowd this evening. It always did during Ramadan, the holy month for all Muslims, during which all members must fast from one hour before sunrise until the sun set.

Members were also expected to reread the Holy Qur'an, a practice that Rasheeda religiously followed.

Jilani and Jibari, her fourteen-year-old twin sons, were downstairs helping out Sister Safia, and her five-month-old, Jamilla, was asleep on the sofa. The family hadn't eaten dinner and made Salat (prayer) until six o'clock that evening. Hakim had been unable to get away from the job until then, and Rasheeda firmly believed in the family breaking the fast and praying together as a family whenever possible.

She had sent the boys downstairs immediately afterward and Hakim had gone straight back to the docks, to pull another shift.

"Don't work too hard, baby. It will still be there tomorrow," she had told him before he left, bussing his cheek lightly.

"Don't you work too hard," he had answered, kissing her full on the mouth.

"As long as the boys are finished with their homework, they can take up the slack for a lil while," she said.

"Any phone calls today?" he questioned her pointedly, turning to leave.

"No, no, nothing." She wrapped her arms around him and gave him a full, hard kiss.

"Now, get on out of here, if you are going, before you make me forget it's Ramadan," she said huskily, with a mischievous smile.

"Well, it is sundown, you know. Technically, we wouldn't be in violation." He grinned, leering down at her.

"Just kidding. See you, baby."

She had made herself another cup of herbal tea just after he left and now sat sipping it slowly, rocking in her favorite chair and watching her baby girl sleeping. Five months old. My goodness, how time flies when you're having fun.

Rasheeda had been so busy, she had almost forgotten about the meeting with Sally and Janice, set for 7:30 tonight. Well, a promise was a promise, and since she was the one who had suggested the whole idea of the JGs reuniting in the first place, she was certainly not going to back out now. Hakim hadn't seemed totally pleased with the idea when she had first broached it to him following Peaches's funeral. After all, Muslim women usually kept among themselves and tended not to discuss their personal lives with nonbelievers, outsiders, as some referred to them.

But the particular Muslim community to which they belonged had a more liberal and enlightened attitude toward such things and even encouraged some interaction in performance of Dawau, or facilitating understanding of Islam in everyday life, speech, thought, and action.

Besides, she had reminded him, if she were to leave Islam today or tomorrow, not that she ever would, of course, but if for some reason she simply had to, these women would be there for her and she knew it, and he did, too. She had seen the wrinkle of concern crease his forehead when she had made that last remark, and it had hurt her to see it, but there it was, and that's the way it was.

"You're a grown woman, Rasheeda. You do what you have to do," he had replied, then quickly excused himself to go to their prayer room. She shook her head but didn't call him back.

How could he not know by now that all she wanted to do was be with him forever? How could he not know that being with him and the children, sharing their modest home and growing their own small business was the happiest she had ever been? He couldn't possibly think she wanted more. How could he?

She had been there, done that, and moved on. It seemed like so long ago. And it wasn't the money. It never had been about money or material things for Rasheeda. Even as a child, friendship, love, and loyalty had always come first with her. Always would.

When she had first started dating James Wade, her first husband, back at Temple University, everyone was so impressed that he, the big man on campus, was spending time with her, a mere cashier in the campus bookstore, not even a real full-time student, no social connections, and definitely not the kind of girl a brother like him was usually interested in.

James was going somewhere, definitely someone to be watched. He was a charming, good-looking senior.

He excelled in his coursework, and he had an affinity for computer science, which in the late sixties was still a fledgling industry. While still in his senior year, he had been approached by at least ten major companies.

Some had even made firm offers. He was on his way and he knew it. Men found him personable, and whites found him non threatening, with his persimmon-colored skin and lack of facial hair. And with his wide smile and dimples deep enough to stick dimes into, women found him damned fine.

He had his pick of the girls, Black, white, and brown, and had never lacked an invitation to the ball, the party, the dinner, or the dance. But he had fallen for Rachael. Small, curvy, rounded, and lovely Rachael. Perhaps it was her quiet spiritual nature, her calming influence on him.

He was a comer, that one, a man on a mission, a man with fire in the belly. And the times were just right for him. He was the first in his family to go to college, the first, for that matter, to even finish high school. Not that it was much of a family, anyway.

He'd told Rachael that one of his earliest memories was of him and his older sister, Dottie, finding their mother's body one morning lying on the living room floor of the projects they had lived in, framed in a pool of blood. His sister was screaming and trying to lift their mom's head up from the floor but it had just kept flopping back down, hitting the floor with a dull thud, splattering the blood onto his clothes. He had been about four years old then, his sister about six, but even now, whenever he thought of his mother, it was that sound, that thudding sound of her head hitting the floor again and again that filled his mind, he said. That and the blood.

Altogether, by the time he reached the age of sixteen, James had been in four different foster homes. He was not physically or sexually abused. He never went to bed hungry. There were no horror stories, except for the daily, dull horror of a little Black boy and girl growing up with no real mama, no real dad, no "that's-my-boy" when he hit the ball over the wall, no soft mommy kisses tucking him into bed at night, no tender touch. Other than that, everything was just fine.

To plug the gap left by an absence of love, Dottie went to the streets, easy prey for the first set of masculine arms to hold her, hug her, the first male voice to whisper that he loved her, that she was so pretty, so fine.

Reaching out, grabbing for the love she should have gotten uncon-ditionally from her absent father, she fell instead into the unformed, immature arms of the gangly seventeen-year-old teenager down the block, and was pregnant and married at fifteen.

It being the fifties, in those days, they didn't play around. If you broke it, you bought it. If you knocked it up, you married it. Especially, when it came to a fifteen-year-old ward of the state, and the state wouldn't hesitate to prosecute a seventeen-year-old for statutory rape.

So the shotgun marriage was the way to go.

James, devastated by the abandonment, as he saw it, by his sister, filled himself with books. He had always been an intelligent child, and on the day of Dot's thrown-together wedding, he made a vow to himself to study hard, to some way get to college so he could find a good job and to someday buy himself a big beautiful house, like the ones he saw on television, far, far away, anywhere but here.

He would have a pretty wife and pretty kids and a pretty car, and nobody would take any of it away, ever, because it would be his, truly his. And study he did.

He volunteered for extra-credit work in school and sometimes stayed in the library until closing. He made the National Honor Society in high school, as well as being named a National Merit Scholar.

He was the class valedictorian. Upon graduation, he received a full four-year academic scholarship to college, including room and board. In the summers, he worked as a caddy at an exclusive country club in the suburbs of Pennsylvania, after telling the college dean he had nowhere to go in the summers, since he had aged out of the foster care system at eighteen.

He cultivated the right friendships, joined the right fraternities and clubs. He never discussed his background and, in his presence, neither did anyone else, for just beneath the easy charm, the show of affability, one sensed a strong, almost desperate determination to make it, whatever the cost.

James had plotted his life with methodical devotion. He had dated the pretty girls as well as the homely ones with social status, checking each one out with an attitude similar to that of one trying on new shoes, looking for the best fit, the one that would go with everything in his wardrobe, the ones that would give him the best bang for the buck. Which one had the best grades, whose father had the most money, which one had the best connections to get him ahead. One date with Rachael had blown them all away. All his careful planning, all for nought. He fell hard. That was it. She was the one.

So when everybody told her how lucky she was, Rachael was very flattered, but very puzzled. Why her? she thought. Why would he want her, when he could have anyone he wanted. She decided he must be after her for sex, figuring she was so dumb and unsophisticated, she would be easily flattered into his bed.

But he didn't know Miss Rachael, oh, no. She had never forgotten that hooky party with Danny, how easily led she had been by passion. If they had been in one of the bedrooms instead of on the living room sofa, if Peaches hadn't come charging to the rescue, only God knows what would have happened, because Rachael sure didn't.

Rachael had decided that very day that she wasn't giving up a damn thing until the day she was married. Peaches and them could have this sixties free-love thing all they wanted, but not her. No way. The Girls had laughed out loud when she made this announcement, especially Peach, but she didn't care.

And she had stuck to it. James, at first, couldn't believe she didn't "put out," thought she was trying to play hard to get. So one night after pizza, after a movie, after sharing a six-pack of Miller's and in the middle of a hot and steamy necking session in his old raggedy Ford, while parked up on George's Hill in Fairmount Park, he had finally lost his cool.

"Woman, what is your game? How long are you gonna do me like this?" He was breathing hard.

"James, I told you I'm not into sleeping around."

"I don't want to hear that shit. This is my last semester. I've only got four more months. Then I don't know where I'll be going. We've been together now for over six months. How much longer are you gonna play hard to get?"

"James," Rachael said quietly, sitting up in her seat and adjusting her clothing. "I'm sorry if you feel that way, but I didn't lead you on. I told you from the start. I'm not playing hard to get. I'm playing impossible to get. That's just the way it is. So if that's too hard for you to take, we might as well shake hands now and part friends."

She turned toward him and extended her hand.

James graduated that May. He had accepted a position with IBM as one of their first Black computer programmer trainees in the New York office.

Approximately six weeks later, on June eighteenth, he and Rachael were married.

"Oh, yeah," Rasheeda murmured aloud, "I have definitely been there." She got up, moved to the kitchen, refilled her teacup, returned to the living room, and smiled into Jamilla's sleeping face once more before sitting down in her rocker again.

New York. The company had secured an apartment for them in the upper west seventies, furnished, so it was simply a matter of packing up their belongings into a moving van, picking up his somewhat overwhelmed bride, and riding off into the sunrise of their future, the bright sunrise of New York City.

To say it took awhile for Rachael to make the adjustment would be an understatement. After all, here was a nice Catholic girl who, except for sleepovers at the JGs' homes, and yearly two-week-long visits to her grandparents in Baltimore, had never been out of Philadelphia in her life, unless one counted daytime bus excursions to Atlantic City and Coney Island. It was all a bit too much, too fast.

"Get used to it, baby. This is the big time, the only way to live," James said.

Rachael resolved in her mind that she would get used to it, get acclimated to her new life. Their honeymoon days were their best. They bought tourist guidebooks and rode the trains all over town, marveling at the underground subway city below a city, with what seemed like hundreds of train lines, compared to Philly's two.

They visited Central Park, the Bronx Zoo, the Empire State Building, the Schomberg Library, and all the happening nightspots in Harlem. They checked out Greenwich Village for jazz, rode the Staten Island Ferry, and even rode the train to Coney Island. They couldn't believe they could actually catch a train to the beach.

Then there was Broadway and off Broadway, where one could catch first-rate plays and musicals, starring first-rate talent at bargain prices. The now-famous Negro Ensemble Company was in its infancy then, and it was thrilling to Rachael to be able to see all the young and veteran Black talent on display.

Their nights were spent getting to really know each other and making love. Well, at least the former.

James finally opened up to her, revealing the sad circumstances of his early life. She hadn't even known he had a sister until about a week before their wedding, when he had casually mentioned that he had invited her to the wedding.

And if he hadn't introduced them a few weeks before the actual ceremony, Rachael would have never picked Dot out as his sister. Now twenty-three and long separated from her husband, Dot had three children. They lived in the Mill Creek Projects, not very far from Rachael's West Philadelphia neighborhood. Yet James had never mentioned them.

They were as different as night and day, James and Dottie. Where James was soft-spoken and polite, Dot was loud, coarse. Where James wore tasteful, almost too-conservative clothes for such a young man, Dot was all dyed red-blond hair, bangles, bright beads, and too-tight dresses. James was too little; Dottie, too much.

"I know you. You live up round the Strip, right?"

"That's right," Rachael had responded quizzically, wondering where in the world she could have known this hot-to-trot mama from, but Dot only smiled and nodded knowingly. "Yeah. I seen you around."

Since the woman offered nothing more in the way of explanation, Roach had let it go.

"You seem like a nice girl, Rachael." She had smiled the night they met. They were sitting across from each other at her small kitchen table, drinking from a bottle of Sangria Dot had set out on the table when Rachael and James first arrived. Later, when James had excused himself to go to the bathroom, Dot leaned toward Rachael, lowering her voice, still smiling. "But my baby brother is all I got that I can really count on in this world, and if you do him wrong, I will personally fuck yo lil skinny ass up."

Rachael's mouth had popped open in suprise, but before she could think of a reply, James was back in the kitchen.

"You girls getting along all right?"

"Jus fine, baby boy. Just having ourselves a lil girl talk is all." Dot had winked at Rachael and glanced up at James, flashing the same deep dimples, same gap-toothed smile.

Lord have mercy, Rachael thought.

At the wedding, Rachael, Jan, and Sal had been surprised to learn that Dot and Peaches already knew each other, had attended elementary school together.

"Oh, yeah, me and Peaches go way back," Dorothy had said, winking at Peach. Peach had winked back, but neither woman said anything more about it.

The two had sat in a corner whispering together for a long time, seemingly oblivious to anyone else.

Hmmm, strange, Roach had thought at the time.

James and Rachel's nights were something else again. Rachael had expected it to hurt a little and had even been prepared by the laughing JGs, her bridesmaids, of course, on how to make first-time sex easier on herself.

"Now, I know you a virgin and all, Roach, but just what are we talkin about here size-wise? I know you at least seen it by now," Sally Mae had teased.

"Well, ah, no, not really," Rachael had stammered.

"Never even seen it? Oh, Lord, Roach!" Peach yelled, incredulous. The JGs roared. Rachael lowered her head, blushing profusely.

"Well, you did touch it before, didn't you? You did feel it?" Jan whispered, covering her mouth with her hand to keep from laughing.

"Yes, of course I did."

"Well?" asked Sal.

"Well?" echoed Peach.

"Well, what?"

"How big is it?" the JGs had yelled in unison, falling all over themselves, screaming hysterically.

After a few more minutes of good-natured ribbing, the JGs got down to the business of advising their fellow sister on the act of being deflowered gracefully.

"Pack you some Vaseline," offered Jan.

"No, K-Y Jelly is better," argued Sal.

"What the heck is K-Y Jelly?" Roach had asked innocently.

"Have plenty of likka in you, plenty likka. After the first time, you won't feel a thang," advised Peaches.

"Well, damn, Peach, we want the girl to feel something, don't we?" hooted Jan.

"All depends. Like we said, how big is it? Listen, if all else fails, take these." Peaches handed Roach about fifteen small tablets she had removed from a small pill container in her purse.

"And just what are these?" Roach held one of the pills up to the light.

"Oh, girl, please, it's just Valium. Nerve pills, that's all. You get em from the doctor. Just pop one or two of those babies and gulp down a couple of glasses of hooch, and you'll be ready for Freddy."

"She don't want to be ready for no damn Freddy. She want to be ready for James," Sally said.

"Fuck a Freddy."

"No, girl, you got it wrong. It's James she's got to fuck," Peach screamed. They all fell out again, even Rachael this time, despite her nervousness.

"But look, honey. If nothing else does it for you, try these." Sally reached into her wallet this time and pulled out three joints. "Straight, pure marijuana, a natural sedative grown from God's own green earth. No chemicals. Guaranteed to make you high, horny, and hungry, though not necessarily in that order."

Rachael took everything, stuck it all in what the JGs called her big D throwdown kit, marched solemnly over to her large suitcase as if she had just received the Holy Grail, crammed the kit inside, raised her head and arms in mock reference and chanted: "I, Rachael, now do offer and sacrifice myself to the, to the—"

"To the big D, girl," the JGs chanted in unison, wiping tears from their eyes.

The big D throwdown kit certainly did come in handy. By the end of the honeymoon, Rachael had tried, used, smoked, and swallowed everything in it. She had desperately wanted to please James, especially after he had waited so long.

And like the girls had warned her, it had hurt like holy hell the first time, even after smoking a joint. The second and third times were no better. But by the fourth time they did it, the pain was finally gone.

Only—only, she sensed James wanted to please her, but it just wasn't happening for her. No stars. No earth moving. Just a big, big buildup, and then—nothing. Things would start off on the right foot. The hot tender kisses, the electric touching, the warm, syrupy feeling, the fingers playing across her nipples, her nipples hardening with desire. Her breath would start coming faster and faster, her lower jaw would drop open, she could feel her wetness, the juices starting to flow down from her insides.

Her body would begin to shudder and tingle involuntarily and move along in rhythm with James. There was a push, another push, then another. Then it was in.

Then out, then in, out, in, out, in, out, all the way in.

Then over.

What the hell, she thought to herself in quiet alarm. What the hell was wrong with her?

"Oh, baby, that was so good. I gotta tell you, the first couple nights, I was kind of worried that we might not be compatible. But, baby, you sure got the hang of it fast. We fit like a glove." James was smiling down at her. "If I hadn't been the one to bust your cherry, I would swear you had done this before, the way you move that body around." He kissed her, sighed contentedly, rolled over, and went to sleep. And that's the way it went, night after night. Every night.

She would lie quietly, listening to him snore, silent tears running down her face. *Something is wrong with me. It must be me, cause he comes every time, and I don't feel a thing.*

As soon as she was sure James was in a deep deep sleep, Rachael snuck out of bed, reached into her bedside table, and removed her throwdown kit. She tiptoed into the bathroom, popped a Valium, and lit up a joint. She sat down on the closed toilet lid, leaned her head back, and eventually felt her tightly wound muscles and nerves begin to smooth out.

The frustration of her unreleased desire began to melt away. *Damn,* she reflected, *now I know what they mean by faking it. I've just gotten started, and I'm faking it already.*

She closed her eyes and started to drift. She finished the joint, brushed her teeth, and went back to bed. And just before she surrendered to sleep, her mind wandered back to the same memory she had been having since her wedding night.

Danny, Danny's wild hands and moist tongue on her body that long-ago day on the sofa. She shut her eyes tightly and willed the hot fresh desire welling up between her thighs away. Tears filled her eyes.

Something must be wrong with her.

James and Rachael Wade's marriage lasted eleven years, and in all those years, Rachael faked it every time.

Aside from this, their marriage looked like the kind one sees in profiles in *Ebony* magazine. James received promotion after promotion, they had a grand apartment on the Upper East Side, they attended the opera, the theater, were symphony season ticket-holders.

They threw lavish parties, to which they invited a mix of old-guard rich white businessmen and their wives, young up-and-comers like James, and a few people from the arts and entertainment world, thrown in for spice.

Rachael was always stylish and tasteful, a good conversationalist, and a great hostess. She had turned out to be a wonderful professional helpmate to James, for she had always had a natural empathy and curiosity toward people, and her charm and easy manner often closed a business deal for him, without her even being aware of it.

It was an amiable marriage in the sense that they were comfortable with each other, and in most things, they fit well together. She had taken the pill for the first six years of their marriage. James had insisted they would be financially ready before bringing children into the world. Remembering his sad childhood, she had agreed. But Rachael had secretly pined for children. Her childhood, unlike James's, had been full of love and family.

She had a brother she loved dearly, and a mom and dad that she never doubted for an instant would fly to her aid at the hint of a missed heartbeat from her. James had never had that sense of security. So she went along with him. However, after she had been off the pill for more than a year and still nothing happened, she had put her foot down.

Reluctantly, he had let himself be dragged by her to a fertility counselor. And after almost two years of pills, shots, counting off her fertile days and the like, they had finally become the proud parents of twin sons, Jilani and Jibari.

This was Rachael's first step, then unknown to her, toward a new beginning. Rachael had delivered her boys by cesarean section, and was in quite a bit of discomfort. Her tight-tummied, well-exercised body had felt torn apart, even though she had stopped all pill taking and joint smoking during the pregnancy. She craved it now, if only to relieve the pain.

On her second day in her semiprivate room, another woman was wheeled in and placed in the next bed. The woman was still asleep, and Rachael really couldn't see her face from where she lay. Rachael had just finished nursing her sons, and they had been taken back to the nursery. She lapsed in and out of a fitful sleep.

Presently, three women dressed in Muslim garb came into the

room and stood around the newcomer's bed. They spoke softly for a few moments, then commenced to pray for the woman. Rachael couldn't understand the words, but presently she began to calm down under the hypnotic chanting. She felt her body relaxing itself, almost the way it did under the influence of marijuana. The women's voices, almost musical, rose and fell in soft whispers, filling her with a sense of peace.

When they had finished, Rachael called them over and told them how much their prayers had helped her.

"I'm so glad to hear it, sister. I'm Sharifa," one of the women said, extending her hand to Rachael. "This is my sister-in-law, Kareema. She just had a C-section." The woman motioned toward the bed.

"Oh, tell me about it. I just had one, too," Rachael commiserated.

"If you enjoyed our prayer, sister, let me leave you with these." She pulled two small handbooks from somewhere in the folds of her habit and handed them over to Rachael.

"Oh, that's all right. I'm not very religious these days and, besides, I'm Catholic," Rachael had protested.

"Well, since you are not religious, anyway, they can't hurt you and it just might help." The woman smiled, leaving the books on Rachael's bed, within her grasp.

"If our sister wakes, please tell her we'll be back later." With that, the women nodded, smiled, and seemed to float out of the room.

Well, what the hell. It wouldn't do any harm to just look through them. She didn't want to hurt the woman's feelings, Rachael decided, fingering the books gingerly.

When Rachael Wade picked up those two books, she had opened the first chapter in her new life.

CHAPTER 11

TEAM MEETING

R*ing!*

What in the name of? Rasheeda sat upright.

Ring!

"Mom? Yo, Mom." It was the intercom.

Goodness, what time was it? Rasheeda had fallen asleep. She got up and looked down at Jamilla, who'd slept right through the noise.

"Mom? Yeah, it's Jibari. Mom, what you doing? Miss Sally Mae is down here. You are supposed to be meeting with her tonight at seven o'clock. Mom, it's seven twenty-five."

"Tell her I'll be right down, Jibari. I fell asleep. How's business down there?"

"Busy, Mom. Folks all over the place."

"Yeah, yeah, I get the hint. You're working so hard. Be right down." She laughed as she hung up the receiver.

"Come on, sweetenin," she crooned to Jamilla as she wrapped her swiftly in a huge blanket after pulling on her socks and shoes. "Girl's gone be up all night," Rasheeda mumbled to herself, snuggling her face into the baby's warm smell. Her gift from Allah.

She checked the apartment quickly, then went down the back stairway from their upstairs living quarters to the Oasis on the first floor.

The sight that greeted her was like a combination African marketplace and open-air bazaar. There were people everywhere, all kinds of folks. The Oasis was her and Hakim's baby, like Jamilla, grown from a seed, and just like Jamilla, a lively, bouncing healthy product of their love. It was a take-out, an eat-in restaurant, a grocery, a butcher shop, a book, record, and tape store, as well as an unofficial community meeting place.

In its three years of operations, the Oasis had grown from a small butcher shop and eatery to a local landmark for Muslims and non-Muslims alike of Philadelphia, the burbs, and even south Jersey. Their clientele were African, African-American, Asian, Indian, Latino, and even a few whites.

They always got busy around 5 P.M., catering to the after-work crowd, but because this was Ramadan, there were even more people than usual in the store. That, plus the fact that one of the customs of the Rashad family, in following the doing of good deeds during Ramadan, was to feed all customers at sundown, breaking the fast for Muslims, and simply as a goodwill gesture to everyone.

So every customer that came in after sundown during Ramadan received a cup of chicken soup, or curry, maybe a few dates. As a result, Jilani and Jibari, her twins, and Sister Safia, her new part-time employee, were working hard to accommodate all the folks. Even Sally Mae had been pressed into service. Tying an apron around her waist, she had gone to work, filling cup after cup with the hot, nourishing soup, served from large kettles resting on the restaurant-type stoves.

"I can't believe we haven't run out yet," said Rasheeda, handing the baby over to Jibari, as she tried to shoo Sal out of the small kitchen area. "Sal, sit down. You're supposed to be a guest. Sorry I'm late. I just dozed off."

"Uh-oh. Sound like somebody might be expectin again," whispered Sal into Rasheeda's ear, chuckling as she walked over to the counter to take a seat. "Bring that baby over here, Jibari. Ooh, she's gettin so big," Sal exclaimed as she took the baby from her brother, settling Jamilla down into her lap.

"I know, girl. I think she's going to be tall, like her father," Rasheeda replied, as she went about stacking the dishes and pans, preparing to close up for the night.

The crowd was thinning out now, but there were still a few stragglers, which the boys, at the signal from Rasheeda, were gently trying to usher toward the door.

"No, I know I'm not pregnant. It's just with Ramadan, you know, abstaining from food all day, can put you into a very spiritual, almost mystical place, where one minute you're daydreaming, and the next, you're asleep, without even knowing how you got there."

"*Umm,* sounds like a good stick of ganga to me. Does the same thing, all year around, and I don't have to starve myself. Of course, I don't lose no weight neither." Sal snickered.

"Sally, *shhh,*" Rasheeda whispered, glancing quickly at the boys, who appeared not to have heard Sally's remark, but Rasheeda knew they had.

As the last customers were being let out of the shop, Janice ducked in quickly.

"Well, it's about time," Rasheeda said, bringing a tray of soup, bread, and a pot of tea and mugs over to the table where Sally Mae sat holding Jamilla.

By now, they had tidied the place up and the boys were ready to take the baby upstairs and put her down for the night. Safia was still puttering around in the kitchen, doing heaven knows what.

Spying, thought Rasheeda to herself.

"Sorry I'm late." Jan smiled sheepishly, taking a seat at the table with Sally.

"Don't worry about it. Just come on back here and get yourself warmed up and comfortable." Rasheeda took Jan's coat and hung it up with Sally's.

Jan gratefully accepted the soup and tea. Rasheeda extricated Jamilla from Sally's arms, after Jan had oohed and awwed over her for a few minutes, then handed her over to the boys.

After both boys, handsome and deep dimpled like their father, with the same gap-toothed smile, said good night and went upstairs for the evening, Rasheeda sat down and stretched her arms lazily.

My, Roach has never looked more content, thought Janice, watching her old friend. Sally Mae was thinking the same thing. They winked at each other and smiled, happy for their buddy's happiness, even a little jealous. The smile of a satisfied woman was truly a radiant sight.

"Well, here we are, the Justus Girls, together again. What's up?" said Sally Mae, breaking the spell.

"Anybody heard anything about what happened to Peach?"

Peaches had been dead a little over a month now, and so far, the police hadn't gotten anywhere. Janice had kept in touch with Kim and Princess, calling them once or twice a week, but no one could think of any motive for the killing. Peaches had been well-liked by everyone. The police admitted they were stumped.

"Well, you know how it is. Just another poor Black woman killed. Who gives a shit, really?" Janice said, her voice dripping with sarcasm.

As the women grumbled and sucked their teeth over this outrage, Sister Safia, who had been silently eavesdropping all this time, now joined in and began to offer her own observations.

"Well, if you ask me, that woman probably got what she deserved. I mean, what did she expect, working in bars, walking the streets all hours of the night?"

Failing to read the clear and distinct body language given off by the three women seated before her, Safia boldly continued. "And I heard she wasn't nothing but a drunk, anyhow, and her mother—"

"Who the fuck you think you talkin about, bitch?" Janice was out of her chair, around the counter and up in Safia's face before she could finish her sentence. Safia backed away quickly from the wild-eyed woman before her, standing legs apart, hands on hips.

Jan was so mad, she was visibly trembling. "One more word, hear, and I'll stomp yo ass to the ground."

Rasheeda and Sally Mae ran around the counter and grabbed Jan by the arms, pulling her back, allowing the shocked Safia an escape from the kitchen area. They led Janice back to her chair and sat her down, all the while patting her shoulders, trying to calm her down.

"Yall hear what she said about Peach? Yall hear that? Why she want to talk about my cousin like that?" Jan was crying now, great racking sobs shaking her body. She dropped her head into her hands, unable to stop the flow of tears. As soon as she could, Rasheeda left Jan in the care of Sally and walked over to Safia, who was now putting on her coat and moving toward the front door.

"Listen, sister, Peaches was a very good friend of ours, and I don't appreciate you disrespecting her in my place. In fact, I really don't appreciate you disrespecting her, period." Rasheeda spoke in a low quick voice, struggling to keep her anger under control.

"Friend? I didn't know she was no friend of yours. You supposed to be a good Muslim woman. You don't need no friend like that. Everybody know what she was," Safia, said defiantly, a little bolder now, since she was standing near the front door.

"I don't care what she was, she was my friend, my good friend, and if you don't like it, sister, you can step." Rasheeda hurriedly took the locks off and flung the door open wide. She looked at Safia.

"Oh, so it's like that?" Safia stashed back, her weight resting on the heels of her feet, cocking her head to the side.

"It's exactly like that," Rasheeda countered, pushing the woman out the door and slamming it behind her.

"Yo, go ahead, Roach! Did you hear her, Jan? Sounded like she did back in the day." Sally Mae laughed and playfully pushed Jan's arm, trying to cheer her up a little.

Jan managed a small smile through her tears. "You go, Roach."

"Now, you know this girl can still snap back when she want to," Rasheeda said, giggling. "Forget her. I never really liked the sister, anyway, always hanging around listening in on everything that goes on around here. We only hired her because we really needed help, and she's a member of our Masjid. You know how we are. Help each other out when we can. I'll pray for the sister, but I have got to leave it to Allah to help that one out."

"Hell, I wish somebody would have helped me out before I made such a mess of everything," Jan blurted out, eyes cast downward, as if she were talking to herself. The tears had started up again, rolling down her cheeks, silently falling to the table.

Sal turned Janice toward her and held her by both shoulders. She forced Jan's head up, looking into her eyes.

"Okay Jan. It's just you, me, and Roach now. Tell us what it is. What's the problem?"

Sally's voice echoed concern, but it was the touch that did it. When Sally Mae and Rasheeda had placed their arms around her and led her back to the table, Janice realized that this was the first time she had been physically touched, held, comforted by another human being in so long that she couldn't even remember just how long it had been. And now they were touching her again, Rasheeda leaning over, patting her tears away with a napkin.

It was the touch, the laying on of hands, as her grandma used to say. So she opened up and told them everything.

They already knew she had left her city government job of ten years as a secretary to start her own secretarial and word-processing business some time ago. They remembered her mentioning that at Junie's funeral. What they didn't know was that the only way she had been able to open the business in the first place was by convincing certain government officials that she could perform the services cheaper than it would cost them to hire new staff. She had sized up the situation for months in advance and taken a small-business course before approaching them with her business plan.

Jan had been ecstatic when they accepted her proposal. She had promptly resigned her position, set up a home office in the spare bedroom, and bought another computer, and secondhand office furniture. For the first year, this arrangement had worked wonderfully, for it allowed her to be home with Junie for the last year and a half of his life.

She was at his beck and call, exactly where she wanted to be. She couldn't bear the thought of leaving him with someone else. Her contract for the second year was automatically renewed and was almost twice as large as the original. She found herself jammed with work, especially as June Bug's condition had started to rapidly take a downward turn. She ended up hiring a staff of three and renting a small downtown office, which she supplied with leased, state-of-the-art equipment, using the city contract as collateral.

After Junie's death, she had thrown herself into her work. The business was humming along. She had even picked up a few more accounts, though 75 percent of her revenue was still derived from the city contract.

Then, without warning, the bottom dropped out.

It started when John Webber, the city official she normally dealt with, suddenly retired, and just as suddenly was replaced by Bob Milligan, a former subordinate of Webber's. She had met Milligan only once before, and she had disliked him instantly, disliked the way his small piglike eyes had traveled up and down the length of her body in a suggestive, almost insolent, manner.

Jan had been polite but formal, her usual manner, and excused herself from his company as soon as possible. Milligan had called Janice and asked for a meeting about a month into his new job, ostensibly to talk about the future direction of the city contract.

When she arrived, he shook her hand, ushered her into his office, and showed her a chair. Jan had been pleased by the invitation. She had wanted to see what this new guy was all about. Milligan leaned forward at his desk, looked into her eyes, and smiled.

"Mrs. Shephard, I'm afraid there have been a number of complaints concerning the quality of your work. It seems you have missed two deadlines, at least, and our superiors aren't happy with you at all."

He was still smiling as he said this. Jan's mouth dropped open. She began to think back frantically. As far as she could remember, she had missed only one deadline by one day, due to Junie's hospitalization, and another because of a bureaucratic mix-up. There had been a few late deliveries because of snow days on the city's part, when she had delivered work and there was no one there to receive it, but other than that, she knew her work was on a par with that of other office work contractors the city employed.

As she started to explain all this to Milligan, he leaned back in his chair, shaking his head from side to side, the smug smile still on his face.

"I'm sorry, Mrs. Shephard. I'm afraid that won't do," he said in a matter-of-fact tone.

"Just what are you saying, Mr. Milligan?" Jan asked in a tight voice.

"I am saying, as of today, we are terminating your contract with the city, Mrs. Shephard."

He was openly grinning now, as if delighted to be giving her this news. Jan's sense of calm was collapsing. Fear was feeding on her brain now, overtaking her carefully constructed professional demeanor. She shook her head, trying to get it back, trying to get her cool back.

"How— how can you do this? You can't do this. This is the second month of the contract. I am in debt because of this contract. You just can't do this with no warning, without—"

"I assure you I can, and I have, Mrs. Shephard. All I have to find is just cause to terminate any city contract under my authority, so the contract is terminated." Milligan laid his palms down flat on the top of his desk.

"But how am I supposed to pay off all these creditors if I don't have the contract? My husband just passed, I have hospital bills, and—"

"You should have turned your work in on time. That's all I can say."

By now, there was a wildness showing in Jan's eyes, the kind one sees in horses right before they rear up on their hind legs and bolt. Her nostrils were flaring, her normally full lips now pulled back tight against her teeth. She rose slowly and started for the door.

"Uh—Mrs. Shephard?"

"What?"

Milligan swiveled his chair around to face her as she stood by the door. "I was just thinking. Perhaps there is a way we can arrange for you to keep the contract, at least until the fiscal year is out," he said in a low voice.

Jan stood where she was.

"Come and sit back down, Janice." He was smiling again.

Jan walked woodenly back to the chair, body braced, as if she expected to be struck. Milligan leaned forward at the desk again. Janice was still standing by the chair. His eyes traveled from hers, down her body to her full breasts, lingering there. He spoke in a very low voice. "If we could meet, maybe Friday night, for drinks and, well, ah, a little fun, maybe then I could see my way clear to over-looking your past poor performance."

His gaze swept quickly down the rest of her body, then looked straight into her face. Okay. It was out there. Jan shut her eyes, then opened them wide.

She glared.

"Where, and what time?" she asked, her voice barely audible.

Jan was to meet Milligan that Friday night in the cocktail lounge of the Windrift Motel, on Admiral Wilson Boulevard, just over the Walt Whitman Bridge, in New Jersey. About two hours before their arranged rendezvous, set for 9:30 P.M. that evening, Jan stopped at the Gold Post, a Center City bar that catered to a Black clientele. She had been to the Post a few times before when she had worked in Center City, but never in the evening, and she saw no one she knew.

She put a five in the jukebox, played some tunes, and hopped up onto a bar stool. There was a nice crowd in the bar. People drank, danced, and partied hearty. Jan ordered a vodka double. She knew she had to be at least halfway high to get through this, and champagne, her usual, just wouldn't get her there fast enough. She fished a cigarette out of her pack of Marlboros and lit up, placing the pack on the bar in front of her. She silently smoked and sipped her drink, trying not to think too hard about what she had to do later.

She had taken out a third mortgage on her house, the house that had belonged to her mother and father, to get the new equipment for the business. She had spent most of her personal savings. She was in debt up to her very neck. So there was really nothing to think about. No question. She had to do it. That was that.

After the second vodka double, she was nodding her head in time with the music, something about the morning paper by Prince, and starting to feel a little better. By the third vodka double, she was tapping her foot, snapping her fingers, and feeling just fine, singing along lustily with Boyz II Men's "End of the Road."

The bartender, a tall, lean, bronze god who had been flirting with her from the time she had come in, began to look more and more like Wesley Snipes with each drink she imbibed. Jan flirted back.

Damn, bro looks good, she thought. By now, the jukebox was turned off, a DJ had come on board, playing oldies, and the Gold Post really began to rock. Jan danced with quite a few of the unattached brothers, kicking up her shapely legs and twirling her well-dressed, graceful body across the tiny dance floor.

She was having fun, singing and dancing and having a ball. At least, that was the last thing she remembered before waking up in the hospital.

"In the hospital?" Sally Mae echoed.

"In the hospital." Jan nodded, hanging her head in embarrassment. "This guy that looked just like Laurence Fishburne was standing over me, telling me I had passed out in the bar," she added in a tiny voice, face flushing with shame.

"Wait a minute, wait a minute. First, you said Wesley Snipes. How did Laurence Fishburne get in this?" Rasheeda asked, eyes wide as a child's.

"No, Roach. See, the bartender that looked like Wesley Snipes, or somebody, had called the police, and they came and took me to the hospital. The only reason I know all this is because of the guy that looked like Laurence Fishburne, who was standing over my bed when I woke up. I have no memory of it at all."

"So who was he, the doctor or what?"

"I don't know who the hell he was. I never saw him again, or Wesley, either, for that matter."

"Oh, no, you didn't, girl?" Rasheeda said, incredulous.

"Oh, no, not Jan, not Miss Always-in-Control, not passing out in a bar?"

"Oh, yes, I did. I hadn't had anything to eat since that morning. I was too nervous, wondering if I could really go through with it. I guess I was just drinking too fast, and I'm not really used to vodka," Jan offered lamely in the way of explanation.

"Golly." Rasheeda shook her head.

"Git the fuck outta here." Sal began to laugh, followed by Rasheeda. "I'm sorry, Jan, but it's just too funny. Girl, I would have given anything to have seen that," she gasped, wiping her eyes.

"Golly," Rasheeda yelled, roaring with laughter.

"Well, you can imagine how I felt, waking up in the emergency ward with a catheter stuck between my legs," Janice muttered, shaking her head.

"Better than wakin up in that no-tell motel with a fat lil peckerwood stuck between yo legs," hooted Sally Mae.

They were all laughing, now, even Jan.

"Ain't that the same place we had to go over to and rescue Peaches from that night that guy handcuffed her to the bed and left her there?"

"Same place." Jan nodded, smiling at the memory of Peach, naked, hungover, indignant, and cuffed to the bedpost in the wee hours of the morning, with no memory at all of how she got there.

"Well, what happened next?" Rasheeda asked anxiously.

"What happened with the Laurence Fishburne guy?"

"I don't know what happened. First, he was there, and then he was gone. Then the nurse came, and she was really nice, and I spent the night there. The next day, I caught a cab and picked up my car. That thing like to scared me to death, chile. No shit. There's really not much to tell after that," Jan continued, as Rasheeda refilled their tea mugs.

"All I knew was the contract was over, and since the contract was seventy-five percent of the business, the business was over. The equipment was repossessed, my house was put into foreclosure, and my staff and I were out of work. I got very depressed. I just shut down. I was afraid to apply for work after that because of what that bastard might say, as far as a reference. I finally did apply at one place with a temp agency, and the city, just like I thought, gave me a very bad reference. I didn't even try anymore after that. Now, here I am, and my house is going to be sold out from under me in two weeks, my mama and daddy's house." Her eyes started to well up again.

"Oh, fuck, no, it ain't," Sal said with assurance. "That just ain't gone happen. You can be sure of that. All you have to do is file for bankruptcy. We help people with that all the time, down to the community center. Haven't you looked into that yet?"

"Sal, I haven't looked into nothing. I told you, I just shut down. If it wasn't for Peaches's funeral, I would still be shut down. But now, I'm scared."

"Well, fuck that. This is what we gone do. If you have any money, we'll hire a lawyer to do it. If you don't, we'll go to Legal Aid, that's all." Sal continued to pat Jan's shoulder, but her face was full of real concern as she looked over Jan's head at Rasheeda.

This was not at all the Janice Jackson they knew. Passing out in bars. Letting her house go into foreclosure without a fight. Oh, no. Jan had always been the control freak of the crew, the one who insisted on planning just about every little thing carefully.

Rasheeda shrugged as her eyes met Sally's. She had been discreetly sizing Jan up since she had arrived and had noticed something was definitely off. The hair, for one thing. Jan's hair needed serious rebraiding.

The plaits hung limp and dry, and there were visible split ends all over her head. Her skin had a dry, dead-leaf kind of dullness to it, and her trench coat and sweater could definitely stand a good laundering. There were even a few buttons missing from the coat. She appeared thin and drawn, nervous. Rasheeda shook her head sadly as she gazed over at Sally Mae.

This was not their Jan. Not the always-together, well-coiffed *Essence* model look-alike they knew. They had to get girlfriend together.

Jan went on to explain that the only income she had was the small pension from Junie's military disability and pension, which came to just about enough to pay the utilities and food, certainly not enough for the enormous stack of bills she had accumulated.

"Well, if you want to make a little money, you can come on in here tomorrow and work with me. Safia is out. That's it. I'm shorthanded, especially during the day, when the boys are in school, and I've got the baby all by myself. And you see how the evening rush is. I can't pay much over minimum wage, but I sure could use you, girl," Rasheeda said.

"But what about Hakim? I mean, I don't want to get in your business or anything, but I was wondering, you know, where is he?" Jan asked.

Sally Mae had been wondering the same thing, but before Rasheeda could answer, there was a knock on the door.

"Oh, what now? Can't they see we're closed?" Rasheeda reached the front door in time to see a piece of paper being slid in through the mail slot. She grabbed the paper, opened it, and read quickly. "Damn him, damn him to hell. He just won't stop. Just won't stop." She crumpled up the paper and threw it to the floor disgustedly.

"What's up, Roach?" Jan and Sal had come running to the front as soon as they heard the sudden outburst from Rasheeda, who never, ever swore. Well, hardly ever. Rasheeda had flung open the front door and, seeing no one, slammed it shut again. She was now pacing back and forth in the small front area of the shop.

Janice bent over, picked up the discarded piece of paper, scanned it for a moment. "It's a subpoena for you to come to Family Court," she announced, as if Rasheeda were illiterate.

"I know what it says, Jan," Rasheeda answered sharply.

"Go to Family Court for what?" Jan asked, her voice still shaky.

"Yall wanted to know why Hakim's not here. That's why Hakim's not here. He had to take a job down at a warehouse so we can pay the lawyer who is supposed to be taking care of this." Rasheeda bit off her words as she spoke, still pacing, the wide-sheathed sleeves of her Muslim habit waving in the air as she gestured wildly.

"It's that damn James, trying to take my boys away. You understand me? He's trying to take my boys."

This time, it was Sally Mae and Janice leading a distraught Rasheeda back to the table, and Sally Mae pouring the tea.

This time, it was Sal and Jan patting Rasheeda's arm as she blew her nose and told them all about James, how out of the blue, he had shown up one afternoon at the shop, demanding to see the twins, how after years of only seeing them once or twice a year, all of a sudden, he couldn't bear to be without them, had sued her for joint custody, which she had gone along with, and now was petitioning the court for full custody. In a matter of a few months, he had turned all their lives upside down.

"And the worst thing is, he's got a real good chance of winning. He makes big money, you know that. He lives in a real good New York neighborhood, way, way better than this one, he's got a new fiancée, matching his-and-hers Lexuses, slick New York lawyers." Rasheeda shook her head miserably.

"Compared to him, we look like trailer parkers. We've already spent almost all the money we had saved to open our new shop to pay the lawyer to fight him off. We don't spend a dime of the child support money for the boys, except on the boys. But James has plenty of money, and he won't stop. He won't stop. Now, he's claiming he doesn't want the kids with me because of our religion. He never gave a damn about religion before, but now—" She shrugged and held out both hands, palms up.

"Who's the judge?" Janice asked. From her years with the city, Jan knew nearly all the judges in the Family Court system.

"Califano, I think his name is. Something like that," replied Rasheeda.

"Oh, hell, Califano. Italian Catholic. Oh, yeah, I know him." Jan wrinkled her nose in distaste. "Thinks he's hot shit. From South Philly."

All the women groaned.

"Califano, from South Philly, huh? Spell his name for me, Jan," Sal asked, taking out her small notebook. Jan spelled the name, Sal wrote it down. Jan and Rasheeda stared at Sal quizzically.

"Why are you writing down his name?" Rasheeda asked.

Sal smiled, closed the notebook.

"Don't worry about it. I just might have to get my mojo working." She laughed.

"Oh, hell. There she go with that roots shit." Janice chuckled.

"Don't knock it, ladies. You know you talkin to a straight-up Georgia girl here. I grew up playin the mojo hand, raised that way from a baby. I know how the thang go," Sal said, a secret smile playing across her face. It's about settin things right, and ladies, I can see we got a lotta work to do." Sal leaned forward, reached across the table, and grabbed Jan and Rasheeda each by the hand. She bowed her head. "In the name of the Holy Spirit, in the name of all the ancestors who came before us, we ask that you look down on us, your daughters, and help us in what we are about to accomplish, to walk with us, guide us, and show us the right way to go."

Jan and Rasheeda nodded, smiled, and were silent. When Sally Mae started talking about the mojo, they were usually not quite sure if she was serious or not. This time, they knew she was.

"All praises due to Allah," Rasheeda murmured softly.

"Praise the Lord," whispered Jan.

"And hail, High John de Conquerer," shouted Sal, fist in the air.

"Now, ladies, since we got all that business covered, I suggest we have another cup of tea and start makin our plan."

And putting their heads together, that is what the Justus Girls commenced to do.

It was only after Jan had put her key in her front door, and only after Rasheeda had finally put her baby down for the night that the two of them had the same thought, almost simultaneously.

Sally Mae hadn't given up anything about herself. She had been a compassionate and sympathetic listener, had blotted tears, patted backs, and shared sorrows with them. But they knew no more about her state of being, about what was really going on with her these days, than they had before the funeral in December.

CHAPTER 12

THE WANDERING STAR

She's never settled in one place; this one was born to roam, in any town, and anyplace she lays her head is home. As sure as the wanderer loves his ways, as straight as the sunflower stands each day, a path will surely make a way for our restless, yearning, ever-burning wild and wandering star.

"Yo, Shirley, do me again."

Shirley took her own sweet time sashaying down the bar to where Sal sat.

"I just know this one's on the house, right?"

"Now, Sally Mae, don't start. You know I cain't be givin out no freebies," Shirley said with a wicked smile.

"Same ole Shirley, huh? Still spittin in yo tater chips to keep from givin anybody any." Sally sucked her teeth in disgust.

"Now, you know it ain't me, Sal. It's Tookie's policy. No freebies on beer. I don't own the place. I just work—"

"All right, all right. Damn. You know what, then? Give me a split of pagne, OJ on the side, rocks."

Shirley smiled, revealing a row of gorgeous, perfect teeth. "You sound just like Peach. Yall the only people I know call champagne pagne."

Hell, we probably the only people you know who drink it, you raggedy-mouth ho, Sal thought to herself, saying nothing. Shirley had been wearing full dentures for years now, but somehow that childhood name, Bad Tooth Shirley, still managed to stick in the minds of the people who remembered her when.

"So how's them kids of Peaches gettin along?"

Sal pretended not to hear her. She didn't want any conversation with Shirley. She didn't like the woman, never had. And she knew the only reason Shirley was trying to be friendly was she was afraid Sal might set up another picket line outside and threaten to close down the bar, like her and the community group had done six months ago, but no.

No more young boys congregated outside the bar, frightening off would-be customers. No more crack vials and beer bottles littering the sidewalks. No more urinating in the nearby bushes and trees.

So when Tookie had invited her to stop by some night, she had taken him up on the offer. So far, so good. As Sal mixed her champagne and orange juice, she grinned, thinking about how Peach used to yell out, "More pagne, more pagne," whenever they went out to the clubs, how she herself now used the same phrase whenever she drank it.

And ole Bad Tooth Shirley had been there when she had first met Peaches, too. Damn.

Sally Mae Washington, then an awkward girl of ten, straight up from Augusta, Georgia, had been sitting on her front steps playing jacks when she looked up and saw a skinny long-legged girl with hair of many colors, but mostly red, coming down the street from Miss Mabel's, the corner candy store.

The girl was licking on a Popsicle and holding a small paper bag. She walked directly up to Sal and stopped.

"You the new girl?"

"Yeah."

"What's your name?"

"Sally Mae Washington."

"Sally Mae? Umph, that sure is a country-ass name." The red-haired girl made a face.

"Well, I'm from the country." Sal had set her jaw, balled up her fists. She had been through this before with these smart-ass city kids making fun of her name. "And what's yo name?"

"Peaches."

"Peaches? That's not a girl's name. That's the name of some fruit."

"Well, I ain't no damn fruit," Peaches shot back, laughing.

"And I ain't in the country no mo." Sal laughed, too. She liked this girl.

"You talk kind of funny. Where you from?"

"From the South, Augusta, G.A. And you talk funny to me, too.

"Augusta, G.A." Peach repeated it over and over, liking the sound of it, liking the sound of this serious-looking girl's voice, the way it rolled and stretched the vowels out, the way it purred. She sounded like the old ladies in church who called you honey and sweetie and baby all the time, like they were your mama.

"Wanna play jacks?" Sal asked, hopefully.

"Okay. Want half my Popsicle?"

At that moment, Shirley had come walking down her steps, carrying a large bag of L&G Barbeque Potato Chips. Sal didn't like this one at all. Shirley was the first kid she had beat up for making fun of her accent.

"Watch this." Peaches had winked at Sal. "Yo, Shirley, come on over. Give me some of them chips, girl," Peaches said, smiling.

Shirley walked over to Peach and Sal. "I already spit in em."

"You did what?"

"I already spit in em," said the girl again, flashing a mouthful of rotting teeth.

"You hear that, Sally? She so stingy, she spits in her food so nobody won't ask for none. You's bout one *nasty* heifa, I swear to God." Peaches wrinkled her face in disgust.

"*Eyeeww*, that's real nasty," Sal mimicked Peaches, wrinkling her own face and looking down at Shirley like she was the most disgusting person on the planet.

"Now, get the hell away from us, you lil nasty-ass, bad-tooth bitch," Peaches said in a low voice. She made a motion as if she was going to hit Shirley. Shirley stomped her foot and took off back into her house, Peaches and Sally's high, ringing laughter following behind her.

From that day on, they were fast friends.

Sally Mae had only been in Philadelphia for about two months. She and her grandmother had come to live with her aunt and uncle after her grandfather had died of a sudden stroke.

Gram was the only real mom Sal had ever had.

She had never known her father, who had "run off and caught the first thing smokin," was how her grandma described him, and her mother had died when she was only six.

"Yo granddaddy would have killed dat polecat, too, or me one."

"Stomach sickness," was what Sal was told by her grandmother when she would ask about her mother's death, but Sal had heard the gossip, in snatches and whispers, that her mother had been "fixed," that she had been messing around with some woman's husband that lived over on one of the islands, that the woman had warned her mother to stay away from her man, and when her mother wouldn't listen, the woman had worked some of those sea island roots, and Sally's mother had been fixed good.

"Couldn't even go cross the bridge without gettin sick," was what they said. Her memories of her mother were vague, came in bits and pieces. Wild, thick hair, strong life-loving laugh, a warm womanly smell, but young and natural, not old, like Gram's musty glycerine-and-rosewater scent.

Vibrant, fresh, with lips that kissed her all over her face and arms that swooped her into the air, swung her around, then held her close enough so she could hear their two hearts beating together.

She had one small photo of her mother, taken by a passing photographer, but the face wasn't clear enough for Sal to tell if she looked like her or not. Her grandma said she did, a little bit.

"But you really look like *him,* look like he spit you out, the devil." And that's all the old woman would say about it.

Spit you out. Sal would sometimes as a child imagine a man who looked like her, spitting her out of his mouth. Other times, she would imagine him showing up one day in a big beautiful car to claim her, his child, to beg her forgiveness, to tell her he had meant to come back for her and her mama all along, but he had gone to the Army and had got shot in the head by a bullet and had forgotten about them, and he had just been cured. Or something.

Sometimes she even dreamed, or imagined she could hear him, see his smile, hear his voice, whispering, "I'll give you a million dollars for that million-dollar smile." Or something.

Meanwhile, she had her Pop Pop. Big Joe Washington was the best moonshiner in the county, and everybody knew it. People came from miles away, even whole counties away, to buy his corn. His clientele included businessmen, farmers, politicians, even the sheriff and his deputies. He had had an arrangement with the local law enforcement, though every now and then, mostly around election time, he would have to be taken down to the county jail, booked, and held for a few weeks, just to make it look good.

"Make what look good?" Gram would snort. "Everybody and they dog know what's goin on."

Her grandfather was pretty philosophical about the whole thing. He viewed these short trips away sort of as vacations. Gram would cook up a big batch of food for him, load up the pickup, and she and Sal would drive down to the county jail to deliver it. She would pack his checkers and marbles and playing cards, knowing he would make a little money, even in jail, with these tools.

When he came home, it was back to business as usual. The sheriff would even send a deputy to warn him whenever federal agents or IRS were coming into the area.

Joe Washington could break down a still and set one up again faster than any two men working together.

So Sally's life had been fairly happy, living in the country. She had her grandparents, her school, her church, her friends. Then one night after supper, Pop Pop went out on the porch, sat in his rocker, lit his pipe, and keeled over onto the floor. Just like that. Just like her mama had gone, swift and sudden.

So now, the only mainstay in her young life was her gram, who couldn't bear to sleep in that bed nor stay in that house without her Joe. And now, here they were in a strange city, in a strange house, living with her aunt Tamar and her uncle Buddy.

Tamar was her mother's sister, and she and Buddy were nice enough to her, but she really didn't know them. She had only seen them for two weeks each summer, when they came south to visit. Pop Pop and Gram would often tease them for their citified ways then, and they had no children, which was really strange to everybody.

And now, here she was being teased for her country ways.

What the hell they expect? Where they think she was from, China?

Ever since her grandfather died, Sally Mae had taken to talking more and more like him, swearing out loud when no adults were around. But she really admired the mouth on Peaches, cursing up a storm like she was a grown woman.

Sally Mae practiced rolling her eyes, tossing her neck the way she saw Peaches do. And Peaches had helped her get her city act together. She had shown Sally Mae how to make sure her clothes matched, not to wear stripes with plaids, and not to wear sneakers in the winter.

Peaches had styled Sally's thick, kinky hair into a French twist, the way all the girls were wearing theirs, and Peach, Jan, and Roach refused to be seen anywhere in public with her if she wore anklet socks.

They didn't have to teach her about loyalty, and they certainly didn't have to teach her how to fight.

Not this tough, yet tender, hands-on-hips-walking, country-talking Georgia girl.

Sal rounded out and complemented their crew, and *they* were the crew. Inseparable. The JGs. They liked the same clothes, same dances, same songs, same boys. But there was a difference.

Coming of age in the sixties, all the JGs were affected by the civil rights struggle. Each Sunday in church, they gave a separate donation to be sent to the Freedom Riders. They watched on television as Black people were beaten, hosed with water, set upon with dogs and cattle prods, simply for standing up to vote.

They had watched Daisy Bates and the Little Rock Nine walking through throngs of hateful white faces screaming curses in the late fifties. And now they watched James Meredith trying to enter "Ole Miss" and being attacked by more hateful faces. The Justus Girls sat in their living rooms transfixed, urging the Freedom Riders to march on.

They knew all about the four little girls burned alive in the southern church, girls the same ages as the JGs. It had weighed heavily on their young hearts, and they sometimes felt a little guilty because their own lives seemed so normal and ordinary by comparison.

But it was Ruby Bridges that did it for Sally Mae. The little girl with the big bright ribbons in her hair, escorted by a phalanx of federal marshals, bravely walking up the steps to a school where she was the only student in the classroom. Sal prayed for all the students each night, but Ruby Bridges held her heart with both hands. So small. So all alone.

"You just walk on, Ruby, walk on. Don't look at em, don't even look at they devilish faces. Just look straight in front of you, Ruby." Sal would talk out loud to Ruby, yelling at the television, praying that her words would somehow reach the small brown girl with the big bright ribbons. If there had been a way she could have willed her body to Ruby's side, she would have.

So the JGs knew about racism. It touched the lives of their parents daily, and their own by extension.

It was just that Sally Mae knew a little bit more about it than the others. Being a southern girl, it was more real to her than it was to them. It was more than the pictures on the six-o'clock news, more than the sermons they heard at Bibleway.

Joe Washington's father, Sal's great-grandfather, had been lynched in Georgia at the beginning of the twentieth century. Her grandmother's first cousin had been shot and thrown into the river in the thirties. Sally Mae had grown up surrounded by stories like this, told late in the night, stories told in soft voices, in painful detail, after the adults thought she was sleeping.

She had been taught as a small child how to behave around white people, to try not to look them in the eye, to move off the sidewalks in town and let them pass.

So the Freedom Ride was more than a romantic illusion for her, the sorrows of the south more than campfire tales. She knew what these people were capable of. She had begged her grandmother and aunt to let her go to the March on Washington with Miss Mabel and her church group, but was told she was too young.

They were concerned for her safety, as well as the safety of everyone else. They were, after all, still southerners in their souls. But she knew her time would come, she just knew it.

By the time she was in high school, Sal was involved in a number of civil rights causes, and was once even suspended from high school for reading *The Autobiography of Malcolm X* in study hall, but it had been worth it.

Reading Malcolm had changed her life. She began wearing her hair natural and raiding the public library for anything and everything she could find relating to African-Americans. She started attending protest marches, helping to write and carry picket signs, planning further actions at strategy meetings. By the time she began attending classes part-time at the community college, she knew just about everyone in the local movement. She was working full-time at a community recreation center in South Philly then, but she managed to make it to meetings and demos whenever she could.

And so it happened that one late fall Saturday afternoon found her walking a picket line to desegregate Stephen Girard College, a boarding school located smack dab in the heart of the North Philadelphia Black community. Girard, a penniless orphan who had grown up to become a pirate and looter, had achieved enormous wealth. He later founded the college, and left a vast fortune in his will, earmarked for the education of "fatherless White boys."

Sal was tired, cold, and hungry (as usual). She hadn't dressed warmly enough, and the people who were supposed to be bringing the sandwiches and coffee that day hadn't shown. She decided to take a break, find something to eat down on Ridge Avenue. As she moved to step out of line, someone bumped into her back, knocking her to the ground.

"Hey! Yo, sis, I'm sorr—"

"What the hell? Can't you watch where you walkin?"

She was really irritated now. Struggling to rise and trying to rescue her sign before it was trampled on, she was aware of two strong arms helping her to her feet, and a scent, a mixture of sandalwood and cloves, she thought.

Sal looked up into the most striking pair of eyes she had ever seen. Brown, hazel, really, with just a glint of gold. Tiger eyes, eyes she wanted to snatch from their sockets, jam in her pockets, and run all the way home.

Oh, my, she thought, one hand going up to her hair.

He smiled. Beautiful boyish face, large Afro, the beginnings of a mustache, all framed by a strong, masculine jawline. About six feet one, slim, long legs, large hands.

Oh, my. Just the way she liked em. Sal knew she probably looked silly, but for once, she couldn't think of a thing to say.

He grinned, showing a mouthful of even, white teeth, and, taking her by the arm, led her across the street to the corner of Ridge. Then he turned the full force of the tiger eyes on her again.

"I've seen you around before, sista—"

"Sally Mae."

"Yeah, Sally Mae. From Georgia, right?"

"From Augusta, G.A., as a matter of fact. Now, how you know where I'm from?"

"Like I said, I've seen you around. My name is Kenny Roker, but everybody calls me Kenyatta. Now, you tell me something, Miss Sally Mae, from Augusta, G.A. Do you belong to anybody?"

"Belong? What you mean, 'belong'?"

"You know. Are you anybody's girl or anything?"

"Oh. Yeah." Sally grinned. "I'm my grandmama's girl."

He grinned back, holding his palms upward.

"Solid, solid. All right. I deserved that one. Now, Sista Sally Mae, can I buy you a cup of coffee or something to make up to you for being so clumsy?"

"Well, yeah, a cup of coffee would be nice. I wouldn't mind a fried chicken leg sandwich, neither." This time Sal treated him to the force of her smile.

"Dag! You mean I got to buy you lunch, now?" He clutched his chest in mock alarm, eyes glowing gold.

"Well, you asked."

He laughed as he led her through the crowd gathered around Girard College, past the news vans, police barricades, and patrol cars.

That's the way it began, and that's the way it was with Sal and Kenny. He led, she followed. He was her man. They protested, planned, marched side by side. They were arrested for civil disobedience together. They gave speeches on local college campuses and at community gatherings together, trying to draw support to the movement.

They attended concerts featuring Gil Scott-Heron, War, Carlos Santana, The Last Poets, Nina, together. They read all the Black authors: African-American, African, French, etc. They filled themselves with the philosophy of Black Pride and Power.

They fed themselves with Black love.

But they were impatient. They wanted the revolution to happen now, and felt the citizens of Philadelphia were far too conservative to suit their tastes. So on the day after Martin was killed, Sally Mae was heavily grieving when her aunt called her to the telephone. It was Kenny.

"Hi, baby," Sal answered, sniffling.

"Yo, babe. Look, here's the deal." Kenny spoke in a low, excited voice. "You know I talked to Cinque last night, and he wants me to come out there with him. They got a heavy thing goin down, Blacks and whites workin together. No more of this hat-in-hand, Uncle Tom, nonviolent bullshit. The brothers out there are ready to throw down. They ready to seize the time."

Kenny's cousin Cinque lived in Los Angeles, California. He was a dedicated movement man, a college student like Kenny, with the exception being that he had given up on the concept of nonviolence ever since Malcolm had been assassinated. Kenny had not, until the murder of Martin. It was the killing of the man of peace that made him now want to pick up the sword.

"So what you say, babe?"

"Well, Kenny, what about school?" Sal had asked lamely.

"School? Aw, girl, you know all I got to do is transfer to a school down there. That ain't even no big deal."

"Well, what about me?" she asked softly.

"What about you? I want you to come with me. You know I wasn't gone leave you up here. It's you and me, babe, hell or high water. That is, if you say yes."

Sal pictured his face, the slow smile, the wide brown eyes glimmering gold. Or tears. She didn't know which. Eyes she wanted to snatch. She hesitated but a moment, trying to imagine life without him.

"When we leavin?"

They left for California three weeks later.

Sal went around to say good-bye to the JGs. She would miss them so much, and leaving the neighborhood would be hard. She had been happy here. Leaving her grandmother was the hardest of all, the one person she had been with all her life.

But she had to answer the call; she had to seize the time. And the time was now.

Sal and Kenny settled in South Central L.A. in a big rambling old house that had been donated by a wealthy sympathizer, which they shared with eight other members of their multicultural movement, commune-style.

Most were students, at least part-time.

Everyone had part-time jobs. Kenny got work parking cars for a local chain, and Sal as a cashier at a neighborhood supermarket. Both registered as part-time students. But both saw their real occupations as revolutionaries, waking the masses, fighting the unjust system in which they lived.

Sal was finally right in the middle of it, not a helpless spectator shouting at the television screen, and it was exciting, no, it was thrilling. Staging "actions" in front of Fortune 500 companies now, taking over entire college campuses, lying down in the middle of busy intersections during rush hour, making known to the world their demands for justice, freedom, and an end to racism as they spoke into the cameras for the six-o'clock news. Speaking truth to power! Right in the middle, right where she wanted to be.

Spending their evenings singing the protest songs of Nina, Odetta, Richie Havens, Fannie Lou Hamer, dancing, getting high off home-made sangria and good hashish. Talking far into the night about everything under the sun.

And the nights. Ahh, the nights. Sex, sex, sex, anywhere, everywhere. Sex in the garden, sex on the stairs, sex in the hammock, sex on picnics, sex on the washing machine. Especially on the washing machine, Sal's ass bumping, banging, sliding around, while Kenny held on tight, tighter, holding her up, her legs around his waist, arms around his neck, pulling him in closer.

Ahh, the nights!

All in all, it was a glorious, radical, romantic time to be young, Black, and freedom loving, and it was too good, just too damned good to last. Sal tried to pin down in her mind exactly when it was that things started to spin out of control, but her memories faded in and out.

It all seemed like a big blur, like some drug-induced hallucination. One minute, they were all happy, productive, and free, and the next, there were guns and bullets and books on bomb making in the house. Oh, there had always been talk at various times during their many late night, open-ended discussions about pulling off some bank heists to finance the revolution, about maybe bombing a few nonoccupied buildings, just to get the government's attention, just to let Washington know they were serious.

But as far as Sally Mae was concerned, that's all it was, idle talk, fed by too much wine and too many Thai sticks. But then came the guns, the dynamite, the late-night visitors, and hasty, whispered meetings to which she, and most of the other women in the house, were not privy.

"We got to leave this place, babe. We got to go." She had confronted Kenny one late night after waiting up for him in their bedroom.

"What you mean, go?" he had protested.

"This is why we came. This is the revolution. What you think we came down here for?"

"Well, I, for one, sure as hell didn't come down here to be makin no damn bombs and shootin people." Sal shook her head. See, Kenny didn't know. He was a city boy, a northerner. She knew about guns.

This wasn't some cowboys and Indians TV show, where people got shot one week and were back the next, walking around like nothing had happened. Sally had walked in the backwoods with her grandfather, had seen him take down squirrel, possum, deer, with one shot. And those suckers stayed down.

They had had this discussion before, but tonight, she meant business.

"Okay, okay, quiet down. Now, baby—" Kenny began, speaking softly, putting his arms around her.

"Uh-uh, don't 'baby' me. I got eyes. You must think I'm either blind or a damn fool, one. I got eyes, Kenny. And I don't like what I'm seein round here." Sal pushed him away, stood up, hands on hips.

"Okay, babe, tell you what. You start lookin for a place. We got a little money saved up. You find something we can afford, and we can move outta here by the end of the month. How's that?"

He grabbed her by the foot, licking the underside of her instep, pulling her back down to the bed. His tongue went down to her toes, pulling each one into his mouth, kissing, pulling, sucking first one, then another, then another. Sally gasped, dropping her head back helplessly.

"End of the month. You promise, Kenny?"

"I promise, babe. End of the month."

His tongue by now had worked its way up her legs, which he now parted. He looked up at her once again, tiger eyes dancing. "Promise."

If only she had insisted that they leave sooner. If only she had taken the lead for once, surely he would have followed. But no. She surrendered, settled down into his arms, and they made mad love till the morning light.

"Well, if it ain't Miss Sally Mae Washington, the Angela Davis of the hood."

Sal peered into the bar's mirror and locked eyes with the large, cognac-colored man standing behind her. She nodded into the mirror.

"Evenin, Tookie." She took another sip of her champagne.

Tookie slid down onto the stool next to Sal's.

"Give her what she drinkin," he yelled to Shirley.

"But, Tookie, she drinkin champagne now, but she been drinkin beer all night, till you came in," Shirley whined.

"I don't need you tellin me bout what she *was* drinkin, damn it! I said, give her what she drinkin."

Shirley switched back down the bar, pouting, working the hips a little harder this time. As she refilled the ice bucket, she glared at Tookie, then at Sal, then back at Tookie again.

Well, I be damned, thought Sally. *She got a thing goin on wit Tookie. Old enough to be her damn daddy! Umph!*

The devil told Sal to play up to Tookie big time then, just to aggravate Shirley, but she decided against it. For one thing, she was too tired, and for another, if she started up with Tookie, she'd probably never get rid of the man. In spite of their being adversaries of late, she knew he liked her. Always had.

"So, Miss Georgia Girl, what brings you into my spot tonight?" he asked, as Shirley banged down the ice bucket in front of Sal.

Sally smiled at her for a second, eyes narrowing, then turned her full attention to Tookie, giving him a dazzling smile and batting her lashes.

"Well, you invited me to stop by anytime, didn't you?" she mur-mured, playing up that syrup-and-honey accent for all it was worth.

As Sal and Tookie laughed and flirted, Shirley stood at the opposite end of the bar, sipping on a bourbon and soda. Clearly, she was furious.

Two hours and three champagne splits later, Sally Mae bolted her front door quietly so as not to wake Doll. She walked straight through her living room, past the kitchen, and down the hallway. The apartment was quiet except for the low buzz of the television playing in her son's bedroom, in the back. Omar's door was open, so she went and peeped in. And there they were, the loves of her life, lying on the bed fast asleep.

Sal smiled, moving in for a closer look at them. Her grandchild, whose actual name was Starlina, had been rechristened "Doll" by Sal when she first laid eyes on her, and Doll was the only name she answered to. Omar was lying on his side, one arm covering Doll and the other cradling her head.

His face, Kenny's face all over again, always seemed younger to her when he slept. He looked so vulnerable, so helpless, all his tough-guy, I'm-the-man defenses down. Sal chuckled to herself, taking Doll from his arms and placing her down in her crib. The baby stirred slightly, then turned onto her stomach and went back to sleep. Sal kissed her cheek lightly and backed out of the room, leaving the door slightly ajar.

She walked back down the hallway to her bedroom, taking off her coat and beret along the way.

Once there, she quickly removed and hung up her clothes, and stepped into her nightgown, all the while humming along to her night table radio, WDAS, playing the oldies.

Stepping into the bathroom, she brushed her teeth, and threw a little water on her face, giggling to herself about Tookie and Bad Tooth Shirley. Shirley had been so mad!

Hmph! Serve the bitch right, always pokin her damn nose into somebody else's business.

Sal was still smirking as she slid into her down-filled-quilt-covered bed, remembering Shirley rolling her eyes and sucking her teeth.

Shirley just didn't know it, but she didn't have a damn thing to worry about from her, mused Sally Mae. The last thing she wanted to do was get involved with anybody in the bar business, or any part of the nightlife scene. She had had her fill of that, and then some.

As she lay warm and snug, listening to the Delfonics' "La La Means I Love You," her thoughts returned to Cali, back to Kenny, back to the night when, without warning, the two of them had been dragged from their bed, thrown against the wall, handcuffed, and arrested, along with everybody else in the big old house.

Even now, almost twenty years later, she could remember how confusing it had been, how fast it all had happened.

"What's the charge, Officer? What's the charge?" Kenny kept yelling as he was dragged along the floor of the bedroom, still in cuffs.

"'What's the charge, Officer? What's the charge?'" a young, cold-eyed white police officer mimicked his words in a high-pitched, feminine voice. "Don't you worry about the fuckin charge. Just move your Black ass outta here, you nappy-headed motherfucker." This from the Black cop who held on tight to Kenny's long, natural hair.

Sally could hear sirens blaring, and the glow from the red-and-white police lights was visible through the bedroom window. She could also hear what sounded like the same scenario being repeated throughout the house. Police yelling, barking orders, her friends screaming. She decided to be very, very quiet.

One police officer had her by the arm. She offered no resistance, and when she asked if she could please put on her sandals, she was allowed to do so.

Once out of the bedroom, she could see that all the house's occupants had been handcuffed and were being led out the door.

They were used to being hassled by the police—it happened all the time—but they had never before been rounded up at home in the middle of the night and taken to jail.

Usually, they were busted for protesting without permits, unlawful assembly, disturbing the peace, all petty misdemeanor offenses, then taken down to the police station, hassled a bit about their pot, their politics, their race mixing, and their hair, and eventually let go.

Sal wondered what kind of trumped-up bullshit this was about. Damn pigs! Must be short making their quota tonight. She remained calm, until they were herded out onto the porch, certain this was really no big deal.

Then she saw the cameras. And the reporters.

She looked around for Kenny, but was blinded by the lights from the cameras. The police made a grand show of securing them all together in groups by linking a long chain through each set of handcuffs. Squinting, Sally could just barely make out police cars, trucks, and what looked like lighting equipment. She could hear people talking everywhere, all at once.

Each group was led down from the porch and into waiting police vans, meat wagons.

Like slaves in a coffle, Sal thought, biting back tears, willing them not to fall. Just before she stepped into the meat wagon, she heard someone, it sounded like a TV or radio news reporter, announcing something to the effect of "conspiracy to bomb" and "harboring known fugitives" and "related charges."

Aw, shit, aw shit. Sal shook her head.

The group spent the night in jail, and were arraigned the next morning. It seemed someone in the house had been an infiltrator, had been working with the police all along. The police had tipped off the media, and now they were big news.

Their legal team, made up of public defenders and liberal lawyers as well as law students, screamed "entrapment" at the tops of their lungs, to no avail.

For some reason, all the women got out on nominal bail. All the men, ostensibly because they were "dangerous radicals with international ties to communist and other radical organizations, and therefore a clear-and-present danger to the community, as well as bad risks" were held on extremely high bail.

"As if only men could be dangerous," Sal sniffed to herself, but kept her mouth shut.

From that point, events had transpired rather quickly. Sally Mae and the other women did not get back home until the next afternoon, when they were finally released. The place looked as though a hurricane had swept through it. Doors had been broken down, windows shattered, closets and drawers emptied out, their contents strewn in heaps on the floors.

It took them weeks to make the place livable again. On top of that, their benefactors, the people who owned the place, regretfully informed the women that they had to be out by the end of the summer. They were constantly harassed by either the police or the press.

Two weeks later, Sally and the women had their preliminary hearing. As there was absolutely no evidence that any of them had known anything about the guns or anything else relating to any conspiracy, all charges against them were promptly dismissed, just as the women figured they would be. They knew and everyone else knew that it was the men the law was after.

Sally and the women left the courtroom surrounded by supporters. Her plan had been to go straight out to the prison to see Kenny and celebrate this minor victory with him. He had seemed so dejected when she had visited him two days before, and she finally had some good news for him. But it was too late in the day. The buses had stopped running. It would have to wait until tomorrow.

So the women had gone straight home, where they cooked a large meal and celebrated their good fortune. Sal, pleading fatigue, had left her housemates and guests at around midnight. She was tired and a little dizzy. She had eaten and drunk too much, too fast, to make up for that morning, when she had been too nervous and on edge to keep anything down.

Sally Mae had been sleeping soundly for about two hours or so when the horror began. Screaming, high-pitched wailing, seemed to be wafting throughout the house. She sat up slowly, leaning to one side, groggily trying to rise. She could hear footsteps running up and down the stairs, doors slamming.

Aw, hell, not another damn raid.

She rose from the bed, fell back, and vomited all over herself, soiling her nude body and the bedsheets. Still the screaming persisted. She rose again, weak and shaky, pulled on a robe, and wobbled on rubbery legs out into the hallway. Holding on to the banister, she made her way down the stairs.

Coming down to the first floor, she saw everyone running, jumping up and down, watching the news on television. The telephone was ringing, but no one bothered to answer it. She was about three steps from the bottom of the landing before she could make out what the news reporter, the same reporter who had stood on their lawn less than a month ago, was broadcasting in his rapid-fire delivery.

"—here at the scene of an apparent attempted jail break. The entire prison is now secured and in lockdown status. The guards have— yes, the guards have again taken control; they are all accounted for and safe. We have confirmed three inmate fatalities: James "Jomo" Barnes, thirty-one, thirty-year-old Kenneth "Kenyatta" Roker, and twenty-nine-year-old Jeffrey—"

Sally Mae collapsed to the floor.

Kenyatta Omar Washington Roker was born six months and one week later. Of course, by that time, his mother, out of practicality and necessity, had completely reinvented herself. Gone was the revolutionary, power-to-the-people Soul Sister Sally.

In her place now walked another incarnation, the Miss Night Life, switchin-in-the-kitchen Sally Mae.

After Kenny's death, Sally had notified his parents in Philadelphia, given them all the information she had, which was the "official story" the police had released, namely, that Kenny and six other would-be revolutionaries had attempted a jailbreak, had taken guards as hostages, and had been overpowered by other guards who had been "required to use deadly force for their own personal safety."

Sal never did find out the truth of what had happened that night. Kenny's parents had arranged to have his body flown back to Philadelphia for the funeral.

Sal had had no money even to buy a plane ticket, and the Roker family did not offer to supply her with one. The stash she and Kenny had been saving had disappeared in the raid. She wouldn't, she just couldn't, ask her grandmother or aunt and uncle for the money.

So on the morning of Kenneth Roker's funeral, while the Roker family sat in Philadelphia with their son's lifeless body, Sally Mae Washington had sat in Los Angeles with the legacy of their son's life growing inside her.

She needed to make some money. She would not consider abortion, no, not Kenny's baby, not the last gift he had left her. Uh-uh. She had one more month before she had to vacate the house. She was three months along, but not showing at all. She had gotten her job back at the supermarket, but it was still only part-time, and it was not enough. She would need more.

So she had hit the streets, and after pounding the pavement for a few days, she was walking along Central Avenue when she had a slight dizzy spell. She grabbed onto the wall of the nearest building on the busy commercial strip. It was a hot, muggy day, and sweat was pouring down her face in thin streams. Her thick hair was heavy on her forehead, around her ears and neck. The ground seemed to be coming up in waves to meet her.

God, help me. Please don't let me pass out here on the street, she prayed quickly.

Just then, a man stepped out of the door of the building she was now leaning against, almost bumping into her. He was at first startled by her presence, then seeing her frightened face, concerned. He took her by the arm, leading her back to the door he had just exited.

"Honey, honey, take it easy. This hot sun too much for you, huh?"

Sal tried to hold back, but she felt too weak to offer much resistance. "I'm—I'm just a lil tired, that's all," she gasped, trying to straighten herself up. It was then that she realized she was standing in front of a bar, or nightclub of some sort. She glanced up, and there in front hung a sign, "The Fox Box."

"The Fox Box?" She grinned at the man, holding one hand over her eyes to block out the sun. Even though she was weak and dizzy, the name "Fox Box" tickled her so much, she got a fit of the giggles.

"That's right, the Fox Box. And I'd like to invite you in to take a load off and have a cool drink—that is, if you can stop laughing at my sign long enough," the man replied in a gruff tone, though his eyes twinkled.

He led Sal into the cool, dark interior of the air-conditioned, clean, and comfortable club. It was about two in the afternoon, so there were only about ten or twelve patrons at the bar. The man helped Sally to a seat, walked behind the bar, and presently sat a large ice-filled glass of orange juice in front of her.

"Thank you," she said shyly, picking up the glass.

"Now, don't be gulpin it all down too fast," the man admonished.

It's nice in here, Sal thought, as she looked around. Her rescuer had disappeared into the back somewhere, and she was left alone to collect her thoughts. After a while, he returned to the main portion of the bar and stood talking and joking with the patrons.

Seems nice, she thought. The place kind of reminded her of the Strip. She was feeling better now, more relaxed. This period was the only time in Sal's life when she didn't seem to have much appetite. She had to start forcing herself to eat in the mornings, even a few crackers. She just couldn't go around having fainting spells in strange neighborhoods. She covered her stomach with both arms.

"Too chilly in here for you?"

The man was back. Shaking her head no and smiling, she took a good look at him. Pecan-tan skin, regular features, medium height and size. Compact and wiry in physique, he had an almost military bearing.

Somewhere about in his midforties. Kind eyes.

"My name is Sally Mae Washington." She extended her hand, still smiling.

"Mine's Choker. And I love the way you talk, Sally Mae." He clasped her hand in his.

"Thanks for the juice. I really needed that. It's just that I didn't eat any breakfast today, and I been out since this morning. You know of any job openings round here, Choker?"

"What can you do?"

"Anything that pays well."

"Can you dance?"

"Dance? Sure, I can dance, but— ah, well—"

He held up his hand, sensing her discomfort.

He thought for a moment. Then his eyes lit up.

"Anybody name Sally Mae *got* to know how to cook." Choker smiled.

"You bet I can cook!"

And that's how Sally Mae got her job cooking in the kitchen of the Fox Box Go-Go Bar and Lounge. Choker had been looking for a cook to replace the woman he now had, who was moving back down South. Sally had been cooking since she was a girl, and being a southern-style cook, could match most women in the kitchen any day.

So while she continued at the supermarket for fifteen hours a week, she now also worked at the Fox Box from Wednesday through Sunday nights, 9:30 until 2:00 A.M.

She loved having the kitchen to herself, loved the music and the tips. Choker owned the entire building, a three-story affair. The second-floor rooms were used as dressing rooms for the dancers, and there were boarders on the third floor.

At the end of the month, Sal joined the residents on the third floor, taking a large, rear room.

The rent was cheap, and it was extremely convenient.

Things went well until she started to show. She had explained her predicament to Choker before she moved in, and he had had no problem with it. It was the folks at the supermarket.

At first the manager, a white man of about fifty, had made clumsy comments about her getting fat. She had ignored him. One day when she was around five months along, he had come right out and asked her about her "condition," as he called it. She confirmed his suspicions, and things went downhill from there.

"Well, I notice on your application form, you checked off the box that says "single."

"That's right."

"So you're still single, then?"

"Right again."

"Well, do you plan on marrying at any time in the near future?"

"No."

"Is there any reason why not?"

"No."

"Well, Miss Washington, this is a family business, after all, and we do have a certain morals code—"

"Excuse me, Mr. Linton, I gotta throw up." Sal clamped her hand over her mouth and darted off to the ladies' room, leaving the manager to deal with the cash register and the customers.

This is deep. She shook her head in the bathroom mirror, as she wiped her face and rinsed her mouth. Incredibly, the supermarket knew nothing about all her recent troubles. On the afternoon following her arrest, she had called in sick, apologizing for not letting them know earlier. In the weeks that had followed, she had called in, telling them she had to resign because of finals, and if there was an opening in the future, she would appreciate being considered. They had bought that, too.

After Kenny's death, she had simply reapplied, and been rehired.

They didn't say shit about her being arrested on conspiracy charges to bomb buildings and overthrow the government, but now they were upset because she was pregnant and unmarried. Deep. She was sure if they'd known, she would never have gotten her job back.

We really must all look alike to these people, she thought, grinning in spite of her still-woozy stomach.

Sal told Darla, one of the other cashiers, that she was ill and was going home. She then punched out on the time clock and ran out into the street, before anyone could stop her. She knew she was definitely going to be fired for this, but she simply had to get out of that place, away from those bright, fluorescent lights, away from Linton's haughty, judgmental eyes.

She walked the six blocks from the supermarket to the Fox Box, her anger slowly replaced by a gnawing fear. What was she going to do now? She really needed that little money from the market. But why was it anybody's business in there whether she was married or not? Especially Linton's, who found every opportunity to pop in and out of the women's locker room, trying to sneak a peek at them undressed.

"Nasty lil creep," Sal muttered under her breath, as she entered the Fox Box.

"What's up, lil mama?"

Topaz, one of the dancers at the club, who was also one of Sally's fellow boarders on the third floor, was sitting at a table, having her customary 3:00 P.M. VO and Coke, along with Vangie, another dancer. Sal waved to both women.

"Come on over and set a spell. You look like somethin the cat dragged in." Topaz gestured to an empty chair. Sally walked behind the bar, poured herself a large orange juice with plenty of ice, and went over to join the women.

It must have been God who had led her to the Fox Box on that hot day, for here, she had found an unofficial family. Choker treated her like a daughter, even though she had never told him the entire story of her circumstances, and the dancers, a few around her age, but most a bit older, fussed over her like mother hens.

Most of them had children, so they were full of advice on how she should take care of herself during her pregnancy, what she should eat, drink, how much sleep she should get, etc.

Sally herself tried hard not to think about the pregnancy at all, even as her stomach grew rounder and larger as the months passed. She lived day to day in a certain kind of denial peculiar to females who find themselves in situations wholly beyond their control, moving forward on faith, praying that somehow, some way, things would work out for the best.

Sal sat, lit up a smoke, and took a big gulp of her orange juice.

"Girl, I done told you bout that smokin. It's not good for the baby," Topaz scolded.

"And what's in that orange juice?"

"Ice, Topaz, just ice. All right?" Sally snapped, irritated. She tried to take the words back as soon as they were out. "I'm sorry, I'm sorry. I didn't mean to yell. It's just one of my bad days, that's all."

Sally Mae grabbed another chair and propped her feet up on it. She then proceeded to tell them what had happened with Linton, the whole story about Kenny (so far, all they knew was that she was pregnant and unmarried), about her refusal to call on her family for help.

As soon as she got to the part about Linton's personal questions, Topaz was pounding on the table. "What? You shoulda told that motherfucka to kiss yo Black ass. Who the hell he think he is?"

"Girl, you don't need to be bothered wit dat shit. You better get you a digit," Vangie said.

"A digit?"

"Yeah, girl, a digit. A check. I was wonderin why you was always workin so hard in yo condition and all, but I figured it wasn't none of my business."

"Chile, you shoulda been gettin you a check a long time ago. Why you wanta put up wit dat bullshit?" Vangie seemed truly puzzled.

"A check? What kinda check?"

Sal looked from Topaz to Vangie. Topaz and Vangie looked at each other, then at Sally Mae, realizing that she really didn't know what they were talking about.

"A digit, a check, a welfare check, stupid." Topaz laughed, spreading her arms in mock exasperation.

The women went on to explain to Sally that she was eligible for welfare, that she could have been getting a check and food stamps, plus free medical care all along, instead of sitting all day on her days off at the Free Clinic for her prenatal care.

Growing up in Philadelphia, Sal was aware that some of her neighbors received what her grandmother had called "relief." About once a month, some of the kids on the block could be seen early in the mornings pulling along their red Radio Flyer wagons, loaded down with government surplus foodstuffs: beans, peanut butter, rice, butter, cheese. The reason they were out so early was most of the kids were hoping none of their friends would see them with the government food. They were ashamed of being on relief. It was something everybody knew but nobody talked about, a sort of unspoken neighborhood agreement not to embarrass the less fortunate, the same way one would not make fun of a person who was blind or who had a limp.

Now, these women talked about getting a "check" or a "digit" as if it were no big deal. They urged Sal to go down to the welfare office first thing in the morning.

"If you get a check, along wit what you makin workin the kitchen, you be set. Just don't tell em bout yo job workin here," Topaz cautioned.

"Why not?"

Topaz and Vangie rolled their eyes.

"Look. Let us tell you what to do, and do what we say, and you'll make out fine. Okay?" Vangie leaned forward.

For the rest of the afternoon, the women schooled Sally Mae about the welfare system and how to play it, what the caseworkers wanted to hear and what papers they wanted to see, what to say and, more important, what to keep to herself.

Two days later, Sally Mae had a digit, food stamps, and a medical card. She was truly grateful for the help, but unhappy about the whole experience. She had hated sitting in the huge, utilitarian welfare office nearly all day long, waiting for her name to be called, along with row after row of poor girls, women with small children, and elderly folks. She had felt like one of a large herd of cattle. Truth was, she felt like a victim.

She needed it, so she took it, but she resolved, sitting in that uncomfortable chair with her feet swelling, while she filled out yet another form, that she would not be a slave to a welfare check for long.

Not this girl.

Sal never went back to the supermarket, even to pick up her last paycheck. She called in, resigned for personal reasons, she told them, and had them mail the check to her. She continued to work in the kitchen straight up till the day her water broke. She was rushed to the hospital by Choker and Topaz, and delivered Omar, all within the space of eight hours.

She spent the first two weeks after his birth just looking at him, drinking him in. The women at the Box had told her all about what to expect in childbirth, about labor pains and so forth. But they hadn't told her that she would fall so in love with him. Her mind had been so focused on working, on saving and making a place for them for the past six months that the first sight of him took her totally by surprise.

He was beautiful. Every finger, every toe, every thick brown hair on his well-shaped head, every nook and cranny on his perfect little body. When she brought him back to the Box from the hospital, Topaz and the girls had brought in a secondhand crib, a playpen, and a stroller, and set them up in her room.

They had already given her a surprise shower two weeks before, so Omar now had all the clothes, diapers, and stuffed animals any newborn could want or need. He also had an adoring surrogate family in the dancers, who ooohed and ahhhed over him constantly and took turns picking him up, holding him, carrying him around. He had everything but a daddy.

"This boy's gone make some woman a good husband one day," said Topaz.

"Anytime a baby boy comes into the world loved and surrounded by so many women, he will always love women."

"Just as long as yall don't turn him into no faggot, kissin him and pettin him up alla time and everything," said Choker, grumpily, but they just laughed at him, knowing he was just jealous, having to share space with the new man in the house. And Omar was definitely the man in the house.

Sally had insisted on going back to work two weeks after his birth. She had had an easy delivery and she felt just fine. She had gotten a small increase in her welfare check. But she knew she would need more. She couldn't stay in this one room forever, with a growing child. She would need more money than what she was making, more than that welfare check, in order to get back to Philly, to get back home again.

She knew she could find a job once there, and Gram would take care of Omar, just as she had taken care of her. But she would need more money. She couldn't go back there, staying in her aunt and uncle's house with a baby and no husband. It had been bad enough before. It wasn't as if they had been mean to her or anything, but still.

So she had started a long letter to her grandmother, along with a snapshot of her and one of Omar, taken at the hospital by Choker, explaining her circumstances. They hadn't heard from her in a while, and she had never told them about being arrested or that she was pregnant. All they knew was Kenny had died in jail, and she had not come home with the body.

Before she could mail it, she got a letter from home, but it was in her aunt Tamar's handwriting. Her grandmother had died of a stroke three days before. Short and sweet, just like her grandfather. Sal's heart felt like someone was squeezing it tight, wringing it out. Her grandmother represented home to her. Wherever Gram was was home.

Now Gram was gone, and Sal, again, had no money to get there. She had never really been close to her aunt and uncle. She had always held the feeling that they were somewhat ashamed of her, that they merely tolerated her presence because of her grandmother, and because it was the decent thing to do.

Sally stayed in her room and cried all night, rocking her baby boy, in mourning for her beloved grandmother, whom she would never see again, and in mourning for Kenny, whom Omar would never see at all.

By morning's first light, she had made some tough decisions. Philly was out. She lifted Omar, looked into his face.

"You and me, babe. We alone in this world now. No mama, no daddy, no sister, no brother. All I got is you, and all you got is me. Home is where I am for you, where you are for me, and anywhere we lay our heads is home. That's just the way it is."

Omar looked up at her, tiger eyes smiling.

And that's the day she decided to become Mustang Sally.

CHAPTER 13

PEACHES

Nineteen fifty-nine. That had been Peaches's first year with Janice and her family. She had arrived on their doorstep late one night, accompanied by Vaa, Ursula, and two policewomen. Jan, already in bed, had heard the telephone ringing, followed by a hasty discussion between her parents, her mother's voice low and urgent. She tiptoed to the top of the stairs and eavesdropped on the conversation.

"The child got to stay somewhere. She can't go into foster care. She is family, for God's sake, Roy."

"I'm not arguin with you, Lila. I'm just wonderin who's gone end up footin her bill. You know Ursula. She probably wasn't even payin Elmo, probably keepin all that child's support money for herself."

"Yeah, and look what happened. That dirty, lowdown dog. The poor chile. I can't even stand to think about what she's been through." Lila shuddered.

"Well, what you gone tell Jan about it? She don't even know about things like that. She just a baby." Roy was clearly worried for his daughter.

"That motherfucker. I guess he's gone be hidin behind his badge and blue socks now. But somebody got to teach that bastard a lesson. Somebody got to take him to school," Roy muttered, almost to himself.

"I'll just tell Jan her cousin is coming to stay with us for a while, that's all," said Lila. "Them two always was tighter than two peas in a pod. There's no reason to tell her anything more. So it's settled, right, Royal?"

When Jan heard her mother call her dad "Royal" in a certain tone of voice, Jan knew she was asking her father for something that meant a great deal to her.

But she didn't have time to think about that now. Peaches was coming! Peaches was coming to stay with her! They would be together all the time. Janice heard her mother's footsteps on the bottom stair and scooted back to her bedroom, scrambling into bed quickly, so excited she had to will herself to be still.

But when the doorbell rang about two hours later, Janice shot down the stairs, almost beating her parents to the front door.

"Get back upstairs, girl. You know it's way past your bedtime," Roy halfheartedly admonished his daughter, knowing full well that she would pay him no mind.

Peach looked so small, clutching a small overnight case, standing on the porch between two no-nonsense Juvenile Aid police officers, Vaa, who had insisted on coming along, and Ursula sheepishly bringing up the rear.

Quite a bunch.

"Yo, Peach."

At the sound of Jan's voice, Peaches dropped her case, and ran past the women into the house and straight into Jan's arms. The two girls hugged tightly.

Peaches burst into tears. Jan did also, although she didn't know why. She could only feel her friend's distress and respond to it.

"Jan, why don't you take Peaches up to your room and you two can get ready for bed? I'll bring yall up a snack in a minute," Lila said softly, after she too had hugged Peaches tightly and welcomed her to their home.

After the two girls had gone up to Jan's room and shut the door, the adults seated themselves in the living room downstairs. Ursula played her pitiful cards, again reciting her sob story like a mantra.

"I'm just a po single mother, tryin to raise my chile all alone. I don't get no help from her daddy, you know. He got his new bitch to take care of, don't have no time for Peach. I been workin and tryin to get a better place for us, and I had to let Peach stay with Elmo and Liddy, cause the school people was on my ass, threatenin to take my baby away from me." She spoke rapidly.

"I didn't know what was goin on at Elmo's. I swear I didn't. I thought that was a good place for Peach to stay while I got myself together, him being a po-lice officer and everything, a respectable person in the community and all."

She cried copious tears, and when she said "po-lice officer," she glared pointedly at the two female cops sitting across from her. Neither responded, although they did shuffle a bit in their seats.

They knew a bullshit story when they heard one, but being Black officers themselves, they felt personally betrayed that Elmo, one of their own, could have done such a thing. The child had been taken to the hospital, examined and cleaned up, and although technically she was still a virgin, Elmo had made her into a woman in every other way. It had taken them awhile to get her to talk, but when she finally did, they had believed her story.

The fact that the child had suffered this horror for so long was almost too much for them to bear.

And now, here was the mother sitting before them, raggedy-ass wig, too-tight, short dress, long, red killer fingernails, FM high heels, far too much makeup, looking for all the world like a sandwich board screaming cheap, cheap, cheap, actually trying to win their sympathy and condemning them for being fellow officers of Elmo at the same time.

Throughout Ursula's tearful defense, Roy just stood at the front window smoking a cigarette, looking out into the street. He would let Lila handle this one.

He knew his wife had always wanted more children. Hell, he had, too. He had wished for a son desperately. But for whatever reason, they had only been blessed with one.

He quietly resolved to hunt down Prez.

Man ought to know what's goin on with his own chile, he reasoned.

At this point, Vaa jumped up and walked over to Ursula, dramatically pointing his finger down at her. "Bitch, I told you not to leave her with that man on day one. I told you, and don't say I didn't."

He whirled around to face Roy and Lila. "I'm Elmo's next-door neighbor. I have known Ursula for years. I consider Peaches my godchild, and I love her like she's my own. If I could take her, I would. But she tells me she loves your daughter very much, and that you are very nice people." Vaa was so angry, he was trembling. "I'm begging you to please look after her. Please. She's been through enough." He said this last sentence with a sob.

Neither Roy nor Lila knew quite what to make of this strange person standing before them, clearly dressed in a woman's bathrobe and pink hair rollers, with a five-o'clock shadow, yet. After all, this was 1959. But even then, the only time Vaa went into anybody's closet was to store his gowns and heels. Lila coughed nervously. Roy raised his left eyebrow, glanced down to Vaa's feet, which were encased in his ever-present slides, then turned back quickly and looked out of the window again.

But they somehow managed to look past his attire and straight into his loving heart. Lila smiled and nodded. She was a realist. She just wanted Peaches. She understood what Ursula was about, she was what she was, but saw no sense in sitting around beating up on her at this late stage.

"If Ursula can't or won't take care of her only child, then I will," she told the policewomen, displaying the same level-headed practicality that Janice would later be noted for.

The police officers, still seething with scorn and yes, a little shame about Elmo, silently decided to use whatever influence they had to make sure this child stayed with Lila. They both knew from experience that the system didn't really give a rat's ass about one more little Black girl and would just as soon place her in foster care as not.

They looked at each other, nodding as they rose to leave. They would make it so.

Meanwhile, Janice and Peach talked deep into the night. When Lila came up later with sandwiches, both girls pretended to be asleep, and only after she was gone did Peaches slowly, haltingly tell the whole story of what had happened to her at Elmo's.

"You promise, Jan, you won't tell anybody?"

"I promise, Peach."

And, in fact, after that first long night of talking, they had never spoken of it again. Ever.

CHAPTER 14

TOO SHORT TO . . .

Elmo had been arrested, charged with child molestation, and held overnight. He had been provided with an attorney from the Fraternal Order of Police, and was released the next morning on bail, his preliminary hearing set for two weeks hence. Vaa couldn't believe his eyes when he looked through his front bedroom window and spotted Elmo, big as day, strolling up the street, not even twenty-four hours later.

Vaa was beside himself; he was furious. He couldn't have known that by allowing Peaches to take a bath the night before, a lot of the evidence the police and the district attorney would need for the preliminary hearing was lost, washed away.

He had been shattered to learn that without this crucial information, saliva, semen, blood, hair specimens, and such, it would boil down to Elmo's word against Peaches's.

Elmo, of course, was a fine, upstanding citizen, a policeman, over twenty years on the force, who knew just about every judge and/or legal mover and shaker in the city. Peaches was the nine-year-old daughter of a known prostitute.

"Oh, no, honey. Oh, hell, no," Vaa spoke out loud, reaching for his well-worn address book. "You think it's over? It ain't hardly over, you sick, perverted bastard," he muttered, dialing the phone and watching Elmo at the same time.

On the day after Peaches arrived at Jan's house, Roy left work early and drove up to North Philly, Prez's neighborhood. First he went to his house. Inez eyeballed him suspiciously, wanting to know what his business was with her "huzban."

"Friend of the family, that's all. Just happened to be in the neighborhood, and thought I would drop by."

"Well, he's not here now, and I don't know where he is, anyway. My huzban ain't in the habit of receivin visitors off the street without even no phone call or nothin," Inez said officiously, jutting her jaw out when she said "huzban."

"Woman, please. I already know whose huzban he is." Roy jutted his jaw out right back at her. "I done told you I'm a friend of the family, and Prez Pearson ain't no more yo huzban than he is mine." Roy turned, grinning at the startled look on her face as he walked back down the steps. He couldn't resist taking people down a peg or two when they got too high on the horse, too hincty.

Roy hit Germantown Avenue and found Prez in the third spot he stopped in, the Cadillac Club.

"Well, I be damn." Prez looked up, smiling, but with a question in his eyes.

"What's happening, man?" Roy slipped onto the bar stool next to Prez. "Look, man, I need to talk to you about some of yo bizness, but I think we better move this conversation over to one of the boots," Roy said in a low voice.

"No problem, man. Let me get you a lil taste. Still drinkin dat Four Roses?" Prez signaled the bartender.

"You know it, boss," Roy responded.

"Solid. Go on back, I be right over."

Roy took a seat in a back booth. Soon Prez followed. The two men talked for about an hour, heads together, voices low.

Two days before his preliminary hearing, Elmo's body was discovered down on the banks of the Schuylkill River, between two abandoned tractor trailers. His throat had been slashed, his pants and underpants removed, and his genitals had been stuffed into his mouth.

Of course, the police did a thorough investigation, Elmo being a police officer and all, but no one was ever arrested or tried for his murder.

Cut too short to shit between two shoes.

About a month later, Prez finally came by to see Peaches. The child hung back at first, holding on to Lila's waist. But Lila wasn't having it.

"He's your daddy, chile. He came to see you, and he's gone see you," she said sternly, disengaging Peaches's thin arms from around her body.

"He can see me from here," Peaches said defiantly. "He ain't been to see me all this time. Why he want to see me now?"

"That's enough with the smart mouth, now."

Lila had then spoken to Peaches in a low, soft voice, stroked her hair, and led her over to the sofa where her father was, taking a seat herself, and pulling Peaches down firmly in the middle.

Lila made chatty conversation with the redheaded father and daughter, praising Peaches for how well she was doing with them, and how much they loved having her. After a little while, she had them eased. She then excused herself, dragging a reluctant Janice with her into the kitchen. "She's gone be just fine, Jan. Leave her alone. Let her get to know her daddy again," Lila scolded Jan lightly. "Now, sit down."

Janice stood at the kitchen door like a guard, ready to run in to Peaches's defense at the slightest hint of trouble. "He ain't gon take her away, is he, Mommy?" Jan asked for about the tenth time. That was the thing both Janice and Peaches had been afraid of ever since Lila had casually announced two days ago that Prez was coming by.

Jan knew Peaches wanted to stay. She no longer wanted to live with either her mother or her father. She felt safe where she was.

"No, Janice, he's not gone take her away. Look like you finally got your wish. You finally got the sister you always wanted." She smiled and hugged her only child.

Lila had always liked Prez. He was hardworking, respectful, and basically intelligent, except when it came to women.

Peaches made up with her father slowly. He came around about once a month to see her. On that first day, he had brought her a beautiful doll, with long curly blond hair.

"I'm too old for dolls now, Daddy. I'm ten years old," Peaches had said in her new, grown-up voice.

"My God, so you are." Prez dropped his gaze away from her accusing stare.

"Besides, don't nobody play wit no white dolls no more. Everybody got colored dolls now."

"Oh, so I'm behind the times now, huh?"

He smiled, loving her so much it hurt almost to look at her. Whenever Prez even thought about what she had suffered at the hands of Elmo, he would quickly put it out of his mind. He looked again into the eyes so like his staring back at him. Gone was the worshipful light that had once made him feel like a king, gone the unconditional love.

"You way behind the times, Daddy. Way, way behind."

Now when he came by, he gave her money. That seemed to satisfy her. She always seemed happy to see him, showing him her schoolwork, her report card, telling him all about the drill team and the latest activities she and Jan had been involved in. But no longer was she his loving, affectionate little girl. She would never forgive him, he realized, for not being there for her. And he would never forgive himself.

As for Peaches, as soon as Prez had left that first night, she had carefully put the doll back into its gift-wrapped box, placed the lid back on the top, then joined Lila and Janice in the kitchen.

"How you doing, honey?" Lila came over to her, put an arm around the child, stroking her hair.

"Fine."

"Everything all right?"

"Everything's fine. As long as I don't have to go nowhere."

"You don't have to go nowhere, baby. You home now, for as long as you want to be."

Lila bent down and kissed Peach on her cheek.

"I want it forever. I want it to be forever."

The remainder of their evening was unremarkable. Peaches seemed okay, although a little subdued. The family had their dinner, the girls did their homework, watched TV with Roy and Lila for a while, (no drill practice today), then went up to bed.

It wasn't until much, much later, when she was sure everyone was asleep, that Peaches crept back downstairs. Picking up the large box containing the doll, she tiptoed to the kitchen, quietly opened the door to the back porch, lifted the lid of the large trash container stationed outside the back door, and guided by the soft yellow light in the doorway which was always left on at night, dropped the box into the trash.

She then tiptoed back to the dining room China closet, and quiet as a mouse, reached into the bottom, and took out a bottle of Roy's Four Roses whiskey.

Fishing a paper cup from her bathrobe pocket, she poured a healthy slug into the cup. Sitting there at the dining room table in the near dark, she sipped the burning brown liquid slowly, as silent tears fell from her wise, woman's eyes.

CHAPTER 15

AFTER THE DANCE

Here they come, here they come, here they come, the Justus Girls," Chicken Wing shouted mockingly, though his eyes glowed every time he looked at Peaches.

It was the fall of '61, the first weekend after the first week at Sawyer Junior High School for the Justus Girls, who now called themselves simply the JGs.

The hit record was "Locking up My Heart" by the Marvelettes, and the JGs walked four abreast down the Strip, all wearing their new Lock-up boots, the latest thing in fashion, on their way to the rock-and-roll show at the Nixon Theater.

But Jan and Peaches had been on the outs ever since the Gaines twins' Labor Day party. The two girls only spoke to each other when absolutely necessary, and then only in stiff, formal tones, dripping with sarcasm.

"I can't believe yall still actin like this. It's been over two weeks now," Sal said impatiently.

"I'm hip, Sally Mae. Yall need to lighten up," Rachael seconded.

"Aw, Roach, you and Sally don't know a damn thing about it," Peaches replied.

Rachael had been playfully nicknamed Roach by Peaches, and the tag stuck. She was now Roach to them all.

"You're the one don't know a damn thing. The whole block is talkin bout you like a dog," said Jan to Peaches disdainfully.

"Aw, they are not. You just tryin to boss me around as usual. You ain't nobody's mother," Peach snapped back.

"And you ain't nobody's grown woman, neither," Jan said harshly, flaring her nostrils, walking directly over to Peaches like she was ready to knock her down.

"All right, now. That's enough of that. Now, yall is gone have to end this shit before we go any further," Sal yelled, stepping in between them quickly.

"You ain't lying. This don't make no sense," Roach agreed.

"Don't make no sense, Roach? She the one don't make no sense. Yall saw her dancing with Chicken Wing at that party, didn't you? Lettin him grind all over her, feelin on her butt and everything. Yall need to be talkin to her, not me," Janice sputtered, still furious at the memory.

"Aw, that's bullshit. He wasn't feelin all over my butt, neither. You just mad cause he asked me to slow drag stead of you," Peaches taunted.

"Look, it's over, okay? It's over," Sally Mae said.

"Now, let's make up, cousins. Come on, come on, now, shake hands," Roach added.

Sal pushed Jan and Roach pushed Peach until the two girls collided, laughing. They continued on to the Nixon, as if nothing had happened.

"But didn't Carlton Hooks look fine?" Roach said, a dreamy look on her face. "I could have danced with him all night."

"He sure did, honey, but not as fine as Reesie Jones. Now, that's what you call too good-looking to even be a boy. Those big eyes, and long curly lashes. *Umph, umph, umph,*" Sal smiled, shaking her head.

"Yeah, yeah. They all right, but neither one is fine as Chicken Wing, and he's the best dancer, too. Did you see us doin that mean cha-cha?" Peaches went straight into a dramatic cha-cha step, ending with a full turn.

"*Hmph,* didn't look like yall was doin no cha-chaing to me," Jan said. "Looked more like the dog. And you was the dog."

Peaches opened her mouth to say something, then closed it again, sighing loudly, and tossing her head.

Naw, it wasn't over. This was only the beginning of a running rift between Janice and Peaches, a crack in the cement of their friendship that would forever widen. It was about boys, of course. Janice thought Peaches was far too fast, too free with her favors when it came to the boys.

She was always flirting. She looked at the boys like they were lunch and she was starving. *Nothing but boys on her mind all the time,* thought Jan.

Peach, on the other hand, thought Janice acted snooty, stuck-up, whenever the boys were around, like she was too good for them. She was also convinced that Janice was jealous because she, Peaches, was so easy around them, found their company so comfortable.

Sally Mae and Roach were somewhere in the middle. They were nowhere near as prudish as Janice, but nowhere near as wild as Peach, and although they tended to side with Jan on this subject, they both kept out of it. They had seen the way Peach had let Wing paw all over her at the party. They had seen his hands grabbing her butt while they did a slow grind up against the wall. And so had everybody else.

Sal and Roach had heard some of the kids whispering about Peaches's behavior and didn't quite know what to make of it themselves. But hey, she was their friend, she was a JG. They kept quiet.

The girls entered the Nixon and after stocking up on popcorn and soda, found seats toward the center of the room. But as they sat, Janice on one end, Sally Mae and Roach in the middle, and Peaches on the aisle, Peaches was thinking about the party. If it was one thing she knew, thanks to Elmo, it was what men wanted. Men, boys, same thing. Made no difference. If they were males, she had their number. She knew she wasn't the smartest, like Janice, who got all As and Bs routinely, and read books voraciously. She wasn't the bravest, like Sally Mae, who would take on anybody who so much as looked at any of them the wrong way, including the boys. And she wasn't the prettiest, like Rachael, whose delicate loveliness sometimes caused grown-ups to stop in the street to stare and smile into her beautiful face.

Nope, she didn't have none of that goin for her, Peaches thought. But she had the boys. She was delighted by her knowledge of and perceived power over the boys. She told herself she'd play their game to get whatever she wanted out of them.

But what she really wanted was simply to have them hold her, kiss her, want her. When she had slow-danced with Wing at the party, when she had felt his youthful hardness pressing into the inside of her thigh, a thrilling rush had shot through her entire body. She was so on fire, her knees were shaking. As he pushed his narrow pelvis into hers, she could not help but respond.

It felt so good, his arms around her, holding her tightly, his warm beer-scented (beer! *oooo!*) breath on her neck. And he was young. And fine. Not like ole Elmo. Sheeit. Goody, goody, smarty-pants Jan don't know a damn thing about this. When it came to the boys, Janice was like a child compared to her. All of them were.

But Jan had slow-danced around the floor a few times herself, and she too had been thrilled at the feeling of her young partner's erection; she had felt that same tingling sensation inside, the tangible proof that boys really were different from girls. But Jan always backed away, instinctively preserving her—her what? Her reputation, that's what.

The years at Sawyer went by in a blur of school, parties, roller-skating, and boys. And the drill team, of course. Roach's brother was drafted into the service and sent to a place called Vietnam to fight in a war no one seemed to know much about. Sally Mae's life with her grandmother, aunt, and uncle went on as usual.

But at the home of Roy and Lila Jackson, two major events took place, one after the other, that would alter the course of Jan's life. The first concerned the unexpected death of Roy. A truck driver, he had been driving his rig over the Ben Franklin Bridge one Friday afternoon on a run to New York, when he suddenly pulled over, in major traffic, to the extreme right lane, telling his startled helper that he had to stop.

"What's up, Roy? What the hell you doing, man?"

But Roy, grim faced, put the gear in park and turned off the ignition. He clutched the wheel for a second, then slumped forward, unconscious. By the time Lila and the girls arrived at Camden's Cooper Hospital, he was dead. Heart attack, they said. Forty-two years old.

Gone.

The family was grief-stricken. But Lila couldn't afford that luxury for long. The house was automatically paid for through their mortgage insurance, but there was nothing else. There was nothing else because Lila had let the life insurance payments lapse for a few months. She had let the payments lapse because she hadn't received anything from Prez for Peaches's care for over four months.

The second event concerned Prez. Lila hadn't received anything from Prez for Peaches because Prez had fallen from a porch roof while painting a house and broken his hip. Being a nonunion worker, he had no accident or disability insurance.

Lila had had to beg, borrow, and steal just to get the money to put her beloved husband in the ground properly.

Having only the money Lila brought in from working at the beauty shop, the Jackson family quickly fell from fairly comfortable to barely scraping by.

CHAPTER 16

ANOTHER TEAM MEETING

All right, ladies, the meeting has come to order." Jan clapped her hands briskly. But Sal and Rasheeda were lost in the sixties, singing along to the Blue Notes' "If You Don't Know Me by Now," which they had turned all the way up on Jan's stereo system.

"I swear, yall are gone blow out my speakers," Jan grumbled, turning the sound down.

But she was pleased. Things had so dramatically improved in her life since their last meeting, she scarcely remembered the scared, broken-spirited person she had been as little as eight weeks ago.

To begin with, on the following Saturday morning after the first JGs meeting at the Oasis, Rasheeda, Sal, and Princess had shown up at her door, bright and early, bearing mops, buckets, cleansers, and baskets of food. They had rung the bell, banged on the front door, yelled, and carried on so loudly that she had had no choice other than to answer it. By the time she had gotten downstairs, she could already hear Sal hollering.

"The fuck you lookin at, ho? Yo newsy ass need to be up on the Strip gittin wit that young girl that's takin all yo man's money!"

Oh, hell. Jan hurriedly opened her door, grabbed Sal and pulled her inside. Rasheeda and Princess followed closely, trying not to laugh out loud.

"I swear to God, Janice. How can you stand livin next door to that newsy, gossipin ole cow? I woulda had to clean her clock a long time ago, I swear. Peepin out the damn window this early in the mornin, tryin to see who alls comin over here. Flea-ridden jackal!"

"I know, I know. I told you how she was. But even if I did kick her ass, with my luck, I would end up in jail, on top of everything else." Jan sighed, shaking her head.

"And got the nerve to be playing religious music all loud, like she's some kind of Christian or something," Rasheeda shook her head in disgust.

"Child, that lady talks about everybody in the neighborhood, what she got, what they ain't got, what they need to get, and everything else. She even threatened to put water on the kids out here last summer for running on her lil two-by-four lawn."

"She did what?" Princess looked astonished. "On whose kids?"

"Oh, yeah, she threatens everybody's kids all the time about that little patch of grass out there," Jan said.

"Well, where else do they have to run and play around here?" Rasheeda asked no one in particular.

"I'm not a violent woman, but if I ever see her spraying water on my kids or anyone else's, her butt is mine."

"Her lawn? Did you see all that mess on her lawn?" Sal laughed out loud. "I swear, I ain't never seen the Baby Jesus, Joseph, and Mary all crowded up beside Santa Claus, the elves, and the damn reindeer, all sittin side by side. I mean, what the hell is up with that? And when is she gone take it down, chile? It's almost February!"

"Well, every year, she adds more stuff to it. It gets more and more crowded. It's too tacky for words, but she thinks that shit looks good!" Jan giggled.

"Hmph! The woman needs reeducating," Rasheeda said, trying to take the discussion to higher ground. "She needs to relearn the true meaning of peace on earth, about loving her neighbor, if she truly calls herself a Christian."

"She need to take that horsehair wig off her bald head and mind her own damn business," said Sally Mae. The JGs dissolved into gales of laughter.

"Enough about her. Let's get down to business," Jan repeated weakly.

They had prepared a week's worth of dinners for her, shushing her feeble protests with hot cups of herbal tea and fresh muffins straight from Rasheeda's shop. Sally Mae had even brought along a six-pack of Miller's.

They had talked as they worked, played music, and ate, joking with her and keeping her spirits high.

And from that Saturday to this, each weekend, either Sal, Rasheeda, or Princess had shown up like clockwork, helping her clean, cook, and throw away the piles of newspapers and junk mail she had accumulated.

But mostly to talk and make plans. Not a week went by that she didn't hear from each of them by phone, gently urging her to do what she had to do, and as a result of such constant care, she could report to them today that things were looking better and better for her.

She had called Malcolm Merritt, the lawyer from Legal Aid, an old friend from her city hall days, and managed to get the sheriff's sale on her house stopped.

She was helping Rasheeda out in the shop now, and eating a more healthful diet. It wasn't much money, but it sure helped. She was working out a bankruptcy plan with her young, handsome lawyer, whereby she could save her house and start all over again.

And most important, she had filed a sexual harassment suit against her former employer. Maybe she couldn't beat city hall, but, as her lawyer suggested, she could give it a hell of a fight. But the most striking change was she had begun to look outside herself to her larger community. Sal had talked her into going down to the rec center one night, and she had been surprised to find that most of the young people hadn't even had typing classes in high school.

"This is a travesty, Sal," Jan had whispered. "If they don't even know the keyboard, how will they master computers?"

The very next day, she was on the phone, trying to round up old typewriters and computers for the rec center. She had found her calling, and was a woman on a mission. Almost, not quite, but almost like the old Janice, large and in charge.

"I'm not there yet, but I'm on my way," she said, beaming at Sal and Rasheeda. "Thanks to you guys."

The JGs high-fived each other. Jan's success was also their own.

"Oh, you'll make it, girl. You'll make it," Rasheeda said. "Never had a doubt in my mind."

"Fuckin A," Sal agreed.

Rasheeda was next. Her problem had to be dealt with, and they did not have the luxury of time.

The Tuesday evening before, Hakim had been arrested and charged with possession of drugs, with intent to sell or distribute. Seems that the police, acting on an anonymous tip, had gone to the location of Oasis 2, their new, as yet unopened shop in North Philly, found the door to the shop conveniently open, and upon entering, they had found displayed on the front counter in plain view, just enough crack and drug paraphernalia to charge Hakim with a felony.

The bust had all the earmarks of a setup, even the cops could see that, but it was Hakim's shop, and that's the way it went down. Rasheeda, of course, had bailed him out of jail, but this, on the heels of the custody case, had not only depleted their savings, but also put the custody case in danger.

"Well, do you think James set him up?" Jan asked.

"I don't know. I don't know what to think. I called him, and he swore he knew nothing about it, but he also threatened to move for immediate custody." Rasheeda was almost crying. "I know how the lawyers and courts can do, and I know James, how single-minded he can be when he wants something. Remember, I was married to him. If they take my boys, I'll die. That's all there is to it. I'll die."

"Now, Roach, ain't nobody doing no dyin round here, cept maybe the bastard that set yall up," Sal said.

"What did you say that judge's name was on the custody case? Califano?"

"Right. Califano."

"All right. Do you have the judge's name for this bust?"

"Yeah, I have it written down at home. Hakim's preliminary hearing is two weeks from now."

"All right. As soon as you get home today, you call me and give me that name. Jan, you and me gotta make a run tomorrow. We gotta go see Red Top."

Janice looked at Sally. She started to say something but stopped when she noticed the determined set of her friend's jaw. "Okay. Red Top. I think I see where you're coming from. No problem."

"Why would yall be going to see her, of all people?" Rasheeda was puzzled. "What's she got to do with us?"

"More than you might think, Roach. And the less you know about it, the better it will be. Don't you agree, Sal?"

"Indeed so, chile. Just trust us. Me and Jan can handle this part. After all, it just wouldn't do for a nice Muslim woman such as yourself to be seen enterin a whorehouse to visit with a madam." Sal smiled, her eyes crinkling mischievously.

"Even on a Sunday."

Red had been expecting them. Or someone. As she got older, she seemed to become more clairvoyant.

Things just happened right around when she thought about them. She had always been a woman of secrets, and secrets can sometimes bestow great powers upon their keepers.

She knew someone would be coming and she knew somehow it

would have something to do with Peaches. But still she was surprised to get the phone call from Sally Mae the night before, asking for her help. Sally Mae, of all people.

Sure, she had responded, come on over tomorrow, around seven. After she had hung up, she almost ran down the steps to tell Daddy Baby that Sally Mae and Janice were coming to pay a call. Damn.

And now, here they all were, Daddy and Red sitting on the living room sofa, Jan and Sal facing them in occasional chairs. After pleasantries were exchanged, the JGs were offered refreshment, beer, wine, champagne.

"Beer for me," Jan answered.

"Same here," Sal echoed.

"What? No champagne? Thought that was yo taste." DB smiled, winking at Sally.

"Yeah, well, beer will do just fine for tonight," she answered shifting her eyes. The man always had given her the creeps, always staring at her whenever he saw her on the street, at the market, in the bar, anyplace.

"Heard anything new about Peaches?" Jan asked hopefully.

"Nothing yet. But I know we gone find out somethin soon. It's goin on four months now. Somethin's gotta shake loose," Red answered.

"Yeah, and when it does, it's gone be taken care of. I watched that chile grow up. She never did nothin bad to nobody." DB spoke softly, almost as if he were talking to himself. "But Red say you havin some problems." He looked from Sal to Jan.

"I told DB you girls were coming by. I hope yall don't mind," Red interrupted.

"I know you were good friends of Peaches. I remember all yall, with your lil drill team and everything. Yall sure was cute. What's that name you used to call yourselves?"

"The Justus Girls," Janice stammered. She was amazed.

"That's it. The Justus Girls. The JGs. Yall was something else." Red laughed. "And I tell you something else. I watched yall grow up around here. Yall know what I'm about, what my business is, and yall always gave me respect, always spoke to me in the street." Red nodded. "I guess it ain't no secret that a few of your lil classmates ended up passin through here, workin for me and Daddy. But not you girls. Not the— what you call it, the Justus Girls. Yall made your way in the world without flatbackin, on your own terms, and I'm glad to see it.

"Maybe if I had been born at a later time, I could have made other choices about how to spend my life. Who knows? But I'm glad to see you girls goin your own way. And Peaches was tryin to do the same thing, God rest her soul." Red's voice trailed off, and for a minute, Sally Mae and Jan thought she was going to cry. "What I'm tryin to say is I'm just proud of yall, that's all."

Sal and Jan looked at each other, now truly baffled. This was Red Top, the legendary madam, talking.

Some of the old-timers still spoke about the days when she wore silks, furs, and diamonds, and drove a pink Cadillac with matching shocking-pink fur interior.

Her and Monsieur Daddy Baby had been two of the most well known players on the Strip. Why would she even have noticed their little ragtag drill team?

Red smiled at their bewilderment.

"Yeah, we saw yall. Me and DB and Ursula used to come to watch yall all the time. You just didn't see us, that's all." Red glanced over at Daddy. "You girls always gave me respect, and that might not seem like much to be grateful for, but I am. All right. So much for that. Now, what can I do for you?"

Sal took a large swallow of her beer to overcome her nervousness and plunged in.

"Well, Miss Red, you know—"

"Oh, no. No 'Miss.' 'Red' is just fine, darlin."

"Well, Miss—I mean, Red, you know last night when I called you, I told you I had got yo number from Tookie, down to the bar. I had been askin aroun bout lawyers and judges and all, cause I, well, my friend was havin some real bad legal problems, and—"

"And what friend would that be? You?" Red glanced at Janice.

"No, not me, Miss Red. Well, yeah, I have had some problems lately, but it's really Rasheeda we're talking about."

Then Sal picked up the ball, pleading the urgency of Rasheeda's case. First, she told them about the ongoing custody suit, then about the drug bust.

"Rasheeda? That's the pretty little Muslim girl got the store?" Daddy asked.

"Yeah, DB. The one they used to call Roach. No need to even ask why she's not here." Red laughed.

Sal laughed with her, ducking her head. She liked this woman.

"Who are the judges in the two cases?" Red asked.

Janice handed her a page from the yellow pad where Sal had written the names. Red studied the paper, smiled, and handed it to Daddy, who glanced at it quickly.

"Califano and Collier, DB." Red grinned.

"Oh, shit." Daddy snickered.

When they had finished laughing and grinning at each other, they assured Jan and Sal that they would see what they could do.

"Give us a few weeks. Leave me your number. I'll get in touch when I have news," directed Red. "Anything else?"

Sal then started pleading Jan's case, like the lawyer she had once dreamed of being. Daddy and Red listened and shook their heads sympathetically. She tactfully left out the passing-out-in-the-bar part.

"Names, we need names, and where he work, his position," Red said, after Sal finished. Jan wrote out the information on a yellow sheet of paper and passed it to Red, who looked at it and frowned. "Name don't ring a bell. You, DB?"

"Can't place it."

"Okay, no sweat, we'll find him. Like I said, I'll get in touch as soon as I have news." Red folded the papers and placed them in her pocket.

"Anything else?"

Sal and Jan looked at each other again. They both shook their heads in the negative. They couldn't think of anything else, yet, Red and Daddy seemed to be expecting more.

"What about you, Miss Sally? Nothing needs fixin in yo life?" DB sat up straight and looked directly into Sally's eyes when he asked the question.

"My life? No, nothing I can think of, thank you," Sal answered.

"I already know yo boy got a baby by that crazy-ass Shirley's crackhead daughter. I know the boy trying to go to college and all," DB said genially, leaning forward on the sofa.

Sally's mouth dropped open, her antennae on full alert. Why was this ole ass pimp getting all up in her business? And why did he keep staring at her like that? Was he trying to recruit her into the life or what?

"Listen, my boy and my grandbaby is my business. We all doing just fine," she replied testily. "I don't hardly need no advice on how to raise my family."

Monsieur Daddy Baby's gaze dropped to his lap, his fingers drumming against the arm of the chair.

Oh, shit, Sal thought. *I done tore it now. Me and my big mouth.*

"DB didn't mean no harm. He's just concerned for all the young folks in the neighborhood, that's all." Red stepped in, saving the day.

"No harm done. I'm sorry to be so short. It's just that Omar and Doll is all I got in the world, and I guess I get a little overprotective sometimes, you know."

Sally Mae wasn't used to eating crow, but this time, for her friends, she would eat it and like it, and smile.

Jan had to suppress a grin, listening to Sal copping out like that, when she knew Sal really wanted to cuss the man out. She really was a hell of a friend, Jan thought to herself, squeezing Sally's hand.

After another beer and more small talk about Peaches, the neighborhood, Rasheeda's Oasis, and Sally's work at the rec center, they politely thanked their hosts and departed. Red watched them from the doorway as they made their way down the path, through the gate, and to Jan's car. As soon as they pulled off, she returned to the parlor.

"Well, what you think? Guess she told you, huh?"

DB shook his head, drained his drink. A small grudging smile stole across his face. "She somethin else, all right. What can I say?" He spread his arms, palms up.

"Huh, not a damn thing. You didn't say nothin then, so don't say nothin now," Red retorted.

"Maybe, maybe not. But you know what they say."

"No. What do they say, DB?"

"That it ain't over till the fat lady sing. And I ain't heard no singin yet."

CHAPTER 17

THE JGs:
THE TEEN YEARS

By the time they began high school, Janice and Peaches were working at a fast-food restaurant to earn money for clothing and other incidentals so important to teenage girls. Makeup, records, and the like. Prez still sent money when he could for Peaches, but his hip had never healed right, and he was fighting to keep from losing his house over unpaid hospital bills. He opened his place up as a little speakeasy on the weekends, running card games and selling liquor and dinners, to make ends meet.

But even with all that, there was still fun for Jan and Peach. Dances, record hops, skating parties, and bus excursions to Atlantic City, Wildwood, and even Coney Island with Bibleway Church filled their weekends, when they could manage to take off work.

The drill team had disbanded with the demise of the Elks home, but the main four JGs still hung tough.

"But did you see Smokey? Did you see him singing right to me? Did yall see that?" Sal screamed over the noise in the subway station, her voice echoing against the tile walls.

"Yeah, yeah, we saw it. We saw it," Jan, Peaches, and Roach nodded in exasperation.

"And he kissed me right here, right on my cheek," Sal went on, holding her right hand to her cheek, sighing.

"But that's all right. I got Marvin's hankie," Peaches said, waving the white square cloth around in the girls' faces. Then she held it to her nose, took a whiff, and closed her eyes, smiling and doing a slow drag pantomine.

"Just let me smell it, Peach," begged Roach, grabbing for the handkerchief.

"Hell, no. You should have gone up on the stage like me and Sal. Maybe you would have got somethin, too." Peach ducked Roach's hand, laughing and waving the handkerchief around.

"But did you see him sing, 'Bad Girl' straight to me? To me." Sal was in her own world now. The JGs were standing in the subway station in downtown Philadelphia, waiting for the El to take them back to West Philly.

"So? How about that time Wilson Pickett pulled me up on the stage to dance?" Jan piped in.

"Dag, Jan, that was six months ago," Roach said.

"So? It still happened," Jan said stubbornly, her eyes alive from the memory.

This was the second of three exchanges they had to take from North Philly's famous Uptown Theater, and they were still riding high, all the way home. The rock-and-roll shows did it to them every time.

The JGs lived for the Uptown shows, where one could catch up to six top acts for only two dollars, tops. They usually went twice, for the shows ran ten days, saving their money and planning their wardrobes around each outing.

The colored lights, the music, the young, wild, and boisterous crowd.

But mostly it was the men. Sexy, smooth-stepping young black men, with shiny skin, hooded eyes with promises peeping out, then, with a wink, settling back, sunken and deep within. Smiles like pearls and voices dripping honey. Looking good enough to eat.

Smokey Robinson. Butterscotch beige bee-stung lips, dancing, diamond green eyes, and a voice as soft and trembly as a teenaged choirboy's.

And Marvin Gaye. That face, that fabulous face. Nobody could beg better than Marvin. When he went down on one knee and started to plead, young girls swooned and old women fainted. Married women threw pieces of paper with their phone numbers hastily scrawled on them onto the stage. The hell with their husbands.

But it was Wilson, the Wicked Pickett, who was truly the wild one. The women might throw their phone numbers up to Marvin, the romantic, but to Pickett, they threw their panties. He was the mad, bad boy their mamas had warned them about. But Mama wasn't here tonight and the Wicked Pickett was, soulful, sexy, and dangerous as a shiny black pistol.

James Brown ruled, of course. He always came to town with his own show. The JGs would start screaming the moment he hit the stage, standing on top of their seats, collapsing into a near faint when he went into "Please, Please, Please," his signature finale.

There was the time the girls had left the Uptown after one such show and were riding the Broad Street C bus. The bus had just stopped in front of the old Chesterfield Hotel at Girard Avenue to take on passengers, when Roach let out a small, excited whoop.

"Look, look out the window, in front of the hotel. It's him. Oh, God, it's him." Roach was madly in love with Eddie Kendricks, the tall, handsome, golden tenor of the Tempting Temptations, who had headlined the show, so when she said "him," they knew who she was talking about.

They turned to look and sure enough, there he was, Eddie Kendricks, big as you please, standing on Broad Street, waving to someone who had just let him out of a long white duece-and-a-quarter, aka, Electra 225.

"Come on." Roach was on her feet, pulling on the bus cord and running down the aisle.

"What the hell? Come back here, girl. Where you think you goin?" Peaches yelled after her.

Sal and Jan looked at each other in disbelief. For quiet, demure Rachael, this was way out of character.

"Come on, yall, hurry up!" Roach called to them, now standing at the bus entrance, blocking the door.

"Now, look. Yall got to either get on or get off. I got a schedule to keep," the bus driver said, turning to look at the girls.

"All right, all right, keep yo drawers on," Peach answered, popping out of her seat. Jan and Sal did the same, and all four girls suddenly found themselves standing on Broad Street, staring at Eddie.

"I swear to God, yall better come on," Roach pleaded.

Eddie spotted them on the way to the lobby and froze, eyeing them warily. Sal, Jan, and Peach looked at Roach. The JGs were on one side of the lobby entrance, Eddie was on the other. Each was about an equal distance from the front door.

Eddie took a step toward the entrance and stopped. Roach took a step and stopped. Eddie took a step backward, Roach took a step forward. Suddenly, Eddie Kendricks pivoted a half turn, and took off running up the street, the JGs in hot pursuit.

He ran up to the corner, turned, and ran down the block, the JGs still behind him. Reaching the back entrance of the hotel, he ducked into a back door. The JGs ducked in behind him. Up the back stairs he ran, followed by Roach, then Peaches, Sally Mae, and Jan. One flight, then two, three, four.

Upon reaching the fifth flight of stairs, he suddenly stopped, totally winded, and slowly turned to face them. Roach, running right on Eddie's tail, tried to brake to a stop, just two steps below the landing on which he stood, but Peaches bumped into her, pushing her straight into Eddie, knocking the man to the floor. Then Sally Mae bumped into Peach, and finally Jan into Sal, looking for all the world like the Three Stooges at their clumsiest.

"Oh, I'm so sorry," Roach said, trying to help Eddie to his feet. He looked terrified.

"We didn't mean it," offered Sally Mae lamely, trying to brush off Eddie's clothes. Jan and Peaches echoed their statements, apologizing profusely, trying to get Eddie up and on his feet again.

"That's all right, girls." He laughed in his soft Alabama accent, the most beautiful sound Roach had ever heard. Eddie fished a pack of smokes from his shirt pocket. The JGs again fell all over themselves trying to light matches for him, falling into him again.

This time he really laughed, now comfortable, realizing these were just a bunch of starstruck teenaged girls. He chatted with them for a few minutes, asking their names, their favorite songs, admonishing them to stay in school and to finish their educations.

The JGs mostly stared at him, mouths open, jaws dropped, nodding their heads up and down, like those little dogs one sees peering from the backs of car windows. He gave each of them an autograph. Then with a wink, a smile, and a soft Alabama good-bye, he was gone.

The JGs floated back down the stairs and out onto the street, acting as if they had been blessed by the pope. They started back around to Broad Street to catch the C again, walking on air.

"Damn. Did you see him?" Roach looked as if she had died and gone to heaven.

"I swear to God, there ought to be a law against a grown man bein that pretty," Sally Mae agreed, shaking her head.

"I know, chile. He was so fine, it hurt to look at him." Peaches beamed.

"Lord have mercy," was all Jan could manage.

That night, the JGs sang "My Girl," at the tops of their lungs on the subway, down the Strip, all the way home.

"To be Young, Gifted and Black," Nina Simone's anthem to their generation, played softly in the background on the radio in Jan and Peaches's bedroom as the JGs took turns posing in the mirror. Ricky West, one of the boys in their crowd, was having a going-away party, but the girls just had to all gather together first to make last-minute repairs before showing on the set.

"This skirt is too damn long." Peaches frowned, pirouetting and studying her reflection in the mirror. "It's almost down to my knees. And it's too big for me, too."

"Oh, girl, please," said Jan. "If it was any tighter, you wouldn't be able to make it down the steps, let alone dance."

"Can't you tease it up higher?" Roach whined, as Sally Mae worked a comb through her fine hair, using so much Spray Net Jan had to open a window so they could breathe.

"Tease it? Chile, I done teased it, squeezed it, whipped it, and dipped it. This is bout as far as it's gone go."

After finally assuring themselves that everybody's hair, nails, makeup, and clothes were just right, that they couldn't possibly look any better, that they now had the highest freestanding Afros in West Philly, the girls set off to walk the two blocks over to Cedar Avenue, where Ricky lived.

As usual, the closer they got to the party, the more excited they became. But tonight, they were also a little sad.

"Ricky West. Damn! One more down. How many more to go?" Roach asked no one in particular, and no one answered. They all knew exactly what she was referring to. It was the monster. The monster called Vietnam.

The JGs lived in a fairly close-knit neighborhood. They had known most of the boys around the way since elementary school, the same boys who had teased them remorselessly when they had formed the drill team.

They had played together and fought together, running in and out of each other's homes. They had teased them, hugged them, and held them tight on the dance floor.

But now, one by one, they were disappearing, snatched away to Vietnam, like some grotesque version of the Ten Little Indians game. Roach's brother Ray Ray, one of the first to go, had stumbled home, walking wounded down the streets, mumbling to himself and screaming like a madman three nights out of seven. He was in and out of the Veterans Hospital, but it didn't seem to do him any good.

Petey, the Gaines twins' brother, was officially listed as missing in action, and Ruthie Bolton's brother Ralph had been sent home in a coffin.

By 1966, it seemed that at least once a month, another one of their boys was gone. A lot of their girlfriends were marrying hastily, just in case the one they loved never made it home again, just in case they were pregnant.

So far, Philadelphia's Edison High School for Boys had the highest rate of Vietnam casualties of any high school in the nation. Black Power was just beginning to bust out all over town, tempered by a burgeoning antiwar movement that shared space with the civil rights movement. People, places, and all things familiar suddenly seemed temporary, almost surreal.

And the crowd partied harder, the JGs and their friends often dancing till dawn, pumping their fists in the air, defiantly defying the god of death, the monster, Vietnam, daring him to come again. But he always did, taking yet one more of their beautiful boys.

They were into the sixties now, the real sixties, and as the world changed, so did they. They were in twelfth grade, and high school had never been like this before: student protests, walkouts, civil rights marches, antiwar marches, protests against ROTC recruiters on the campuses, sex, drugs, rock and roll.

The JGs put in their share of days hookying school, sneaking over to the park to smoke cigarettes and drink beer, sipping a little smuggled-in wine at parties.

They also attended more than a few hastily pulled together shotgun weddings. There was something in the sure knowledge that some of the boys would die halfway across the world that made girls who had sworn they would be virgins on their wedding nights give it up with the quickness, a combination of confusion, loyalty, lust, perhaps even sacrifice. But something.

In these days, it was illegal to get a prescription for birth control pills if one wasn't married, so it was either the condom or nothing at all.

Most of the boys preferred nothing at all. Peaches did, too. Bareback riding, they called it then, and that's what got her into trouble.

"Pregnant?!" Jan echoed, jumping up, moving toward Peaches. Peach jumped up quickly, running behind Sally Mae's chair, using her as a shield.

"You're what? Pregnant? Peach, how could you?" Roach's hand now up to her face in shock.

"How could I? You know damn well how, Roach. You ain't that damned innocent," Peach retorted, defensive as always.

"All right, all right, everybody just calm down now," Janice said. Sal sat, quiet. Roach, spreading her hands, palms down, did the same. The JGs were down in Roach's basement rec room, playing 500 rummy.

Although Peaches had been more quiet than usual lately, they had assumed it was because she missed Chicken Wing, who had been in Nam for about the last month or so. But since she had been going out with Jerome DeLong lately, no one had thought much of it.

"Well, how do you know for sure?" Jan asked in a measured tone, sitting back down at the card table.

They all looked at Peach.

"I know, because I'm late, and you know I'm always regular, Jan." Peach sat crumpled in her chair like a broken doll.

"How late are you?" Roach asked.

"Five weeks."

"Five—oh, shit," Sally Mae groaned.

"Yeah, I'm hip. Oh, 'shit' is right. It's Wing's baby. What am I gone do?" Peach wailed.

"Now, just calm down, girl. We'll figure out somethin," Sal said, reaching across the table and taking Peach's hand into her own.

"Yeah, we'll work it out. What we need is a plan," Jan said with a confidence she didn't feel.

"Don't cry, Peach. Please don't cry. You know I got your back," Roach crooned, leaning over to pat the distraught girl on the shoulder.

The JGs put their heads together and quietly considered possible solutions to Peach's dilemna. Their first idea was that Peaches should have an "accident."

They all watched the soaps, and had seen countless white women miscarry after minor slips or falls.

So in the weeks that followed, Peaches proceeded to trip on air, and fell down in the street. She slipped off of a chair, and fell to the floor. Once she even got the nerve up and threw herself halfway down the living room steps.

All she got for her trouble was bruised knees and elbows. She tried various combinations of over-the-counter preparations: quinine and gin, Triple 6 Pills, Lydia Pinkum's Medicine for Ladies. But she only got sick to her stomach and vomited everything up each time she tried.

She tried a mustard plaster placed directly on the stomach while sitting over a bucket of hot water to "draw the baby out," so the word on the street had it. But she ended up burning the skin on her stomach and almost blistering her thighs and hips.

Finally, Peaches decided the only thing left to do was pay a call on Betty Booker, a neighborhood woman who specialized in helping girls and women "in trouble."

"Yall goin with me, right?" Peaches asked, fear in her voice.

"Of course we're going with you, silly." Roach laughed, though, being Catholic, this was something that was against everything she had been taught to believe in. "Peach, now, you know if this is what you really want to do, I'm here for you. But have you ever thought of maybe just going on and having the baby?" Roach was almost pleading.

"Have it? Have it, and then what? Whose gone take care of it? Whose gone take care of me? My mama? Sheeit!" Peaches rolled her eyes, shaking her head fiercely.

"I wouldn't even have a home myself, if it wasn't for Aunt Lila and Uncle Roy taking me in. Now, you expect me to bring a baby in there? Sheeit, my ass would be out on the street."

"Oh, Peach, you know that's a lie. You know damn well Mom ain't gone hardly throw you out. Don't even set up here lying out your mouth like that." Jan glared at her, her voice harsh. "Ain't nobody tell your lil fast ass to go get knocked up in the first damn place."

"Oh, that's it, huh? You been waitin to say that ever since I told yall. Well, you finally got it in. I hope you feel better now."

Tears were streaming down Peaches's face. Jan hung her head, ashamed. Her mother had always told her to never kick anyone, not even a dog, when they were down.

"I'm sorry. I shouldn't— I shouldn't have said it. I apologize," she mumbled, still looking down at the floor.

"Look, you said it, you apologized, it's over. Now, let's go see bout this Betty Booker woman." Sally Mae said curtly, rising and heading for the door. The JGs filed out silently behind her, Jan's arm around Peach's waist.

Betty Booker, a no-nonsense and crisply formal woman somewhere in her late forties, would let only one more person in her house with Peaches. Peaches asked Jan to accompany her, just like that, as if they had not just argued only minutes ago. Sal and Roach agreed to wait for them in the park.

After seating Jan in the living room, Betty Booker took Peaches upstairs, conducted a quick examination, then brought her back down. "You're two months along now. My fee is three hundred and fifty dollars."

"Three hundred and fifty dollars?" Peach gulped, and looked at Jan despairingly.

The woman might as well have said five thousand dollars. Peaches and Jan brought home twenty dollars per week, respectively, from their fast-food jobs.

"You got four more weeks to get it done, or I won't touch you," Betty Booker said brusquely. They were quickly ushered out. The whole thing had taken about fifteen, twenty minutes.

"Three hundred and fifty dollars! Damn, that's about five whole months' pay." Sally whistled through her teeth when they were all in the park.

"No, no, we can do it. Look, I'll put up ninty-five dollars, you and Roach put up eighty dollar piece. That's two hundred and fifty-five dollars, and, Peach, you can put up the rest," Jan said forcefully. She looked at Sal and Roach. They both nodded.

Peach was crying. Her friends were coming through for her. The JGs sat in the park a while longer, making their plan.

"Now, let's all go home and get some sleep. We got work to do," Jan said.

One evening on the third week before the big day, Jan and Peach were sitting in the dining room finishing their homework, while Lila watched the ten-o'clock news on TV. When they heard the words *Betty Booker* coming from the set, both their heads shot up, Lila let out a "Lord have mercy," and the girls ran into the living room just in time to see Betty Booker unsuccessfully trying to cover her face with her hands while being led down her front steps by two police officers and into a waiting double-parked police car.

"In an early-morning raid today, Booker was arrested and charged with performing illegal abortions on pregnant women, including minors. Police sources tell us Booker has a record going back at least fifteen years on the same and related charges," the newscaster droned on.

"Jesus Christ. I got to call Caroline," Lila exclaimed, talking and dialing her best friend's number on the table-side telephone at the same time. "Caroline? Girl, did you see? I know, honey. I didn't even know she was still in business."

Lila talked on, not noticing the stunned expressions on the girls' faces. Peaches and Jan walked back into the dining room, gathered up their books, and went up to their room, moving as if in a dream.

"Night, Mom."

"Night, night, Mom."

Lila waved at them, not even bothering to look their way, so engrossed in conversation with Caroline was she. The girls willed themselves to walk at a regular pace, as if nothing had happened, as if their plan had not just gone straight to hell in a handbasket.

"What am I gone do now?" Peaches howled, eyes wide with fear, as soon as they were safely in the bedroom with the door closed.

"Calm down. Let me think," Jan said quickly. "Maybe we can find somebody else. I know Betty's not the only one. We'll meet with Sal and Roach tomorrow, do a little asking around. Let's just sleep on it tonight. And, Peach?"

"Huh?" Peach sat on the little stool in front of the dresser, rocking slightly, arms around her stomach, heart in her throat.

"Don't worry bout it tonight. You know us. We'll figure out something. Just be cool and get some sleep."

At 3:30 A.M. that morning, Peaches sat at the dining room table drinking vodka (she had switched to Lila's vodka, remembering that it had no odor). She was smoking a Salem, still slightly rocking, deep in thought. Jan was probably right, she decided. The JGs would figure out something. Betty Booker couldn't be the only one. Because if she was, Peaches knew what she had to do.

She stubbed out her cigarette, took the ashtray and the glass into the kitchen, and quietly replaced the vodka bottle after pouring in just a little water. Then she went upstairs to bed.

But Jan was wrong. The heat was on. Betty Booker's well-publicized arrest had driven the other inner-city abortionists underground. The JGs called all over town. North Philly, South, Germantown, Chester, even Camden, New Jersey. Nothing happening.

It was the sixties, but even so, having babies out of wedlock had not quite become the fashion yet. In a matter of a few short years, it would be a common sight to see unwed young girls strutting down the streets in the neighborhood, swollen bellies boldly poking out in front of them. But not just yet.

This was the time when no full-grown woman, let alone a teenaged girl, would be caught dead out in public with a big stomach and no husband. This was the time when a young girl who suddenly looked a little plump around the middle, or who cut gym one time too many was quickly dispatched by her teacher to the school nurse. If the nurse confirmed the teacher's suspicions, that girl was sent home immediately with a note from the nurse and the principal. A follow-up telephone call and visit from the truant officer came next, just to make sure the parents were aware of the situation. This was before Planned Parenthood, and obtaining birth control was out of the question, unless one was married. Being pregnant and unmarried was the absolute worst thing a girl could do to her family. She would bring shame and disgrace upon them all.

The boys, on the other hand, well, hey, boys would be boys. Wild oats and all that.

So some seven weeks later, the JGs stood together at yet another hastily pulled together wedding ceremony. But this one was different. This was one of their own. As Peaches and Rome exchanged wedding vows, no one was all that surprised that she looked to be at least three, four months along.

She's doing the right thing, one woman whispered.

At least the baby will have a name when it comes into the world, murmured another.

Better late than never, muttered the church ladies.

The JGs held hands, hugged Peach, laughed some, and cried even more. One down.

All in all, it turned out pretty well. Even Ursula and Prez attended and actually got along in the same room together. Then again, Prez was smart enough to come alone, and to leave before Ursula really got started in on some serious drinking. And when Kim was born, she was loved and adored by them all.

And as she got older, well, everybody had eyes.

Everybody could see. The delicate bone structure, the large, long-lashed eyes, the golden skin.

Nobody was stupid here, or blind. But nobody said anything, at least not out loud, not in the presence of Peach or Rome or any of the JGs. Rome was here, alive, in the flesh, a proud and loving young husband and father. And Chicken Wing, sweet, golden boy, was cold in the ground, captured and killed by the monster. Nobody said anything. They'd better not.

CHAPTER 18

MIDNIGHT CALL
FROM GEORGIA

When Sally Mae got in that night, there was a note on the kitchen table from Omar. It was quite late. She and Jan had stopped at the Devil for a while and gotten into various mischief, Sally talking trash and flirting with Tookie, just to make Shirley mad.

"Somebody named Baby or Bay Bay something called long distance from Georgia. Wants you to call her back. Says it's very important," the note read.

He had underlined "important." Underneath that was a phone number. Sal sat down at the table, passing a hand over her eyes. Baby. The only Baby she knew in Georgia was Bay Girl. It had to be her.

All right, all right. I'm in control here, she told herself, although she felt a fluttering sensation in the pit of her stomach. Not allowing herself another thought, she picked up the phone and dialed the number.

It rang three times, four. She glanced up at the wall clock. Oh, Christ. It was 2:30. She should have waited until morning. Just when she was about to hang up, she heard momentary static, then a slow hazy drawl.

"Lo?"

"Hello, Bay? This is Sally Mae. Did you call me tonight? Sally Mae Washington."

"Sal. Oh, wait, let me get up. Hold on a minute." Dead air. Then Bay was back.

"Well, well, Miss Sally Mae Washington. How's life in the big city treatin you?"

The slow, easy Georgia drawl reminded Sal so much of home and her grandparents she felt like crying. She bit her lip, caught up in longing.

"Just fine, Bay, just fine. And you?" Sal replied politely.

"Fair to midlin, fair to midlin. Listen, I won't keep you in suspense. You know, I owe you a favor. Been owing you for years, ever since we was kids about six or seven, right?"

Bay's low chuckle filled Sally's ears.

"Anyways, I'm callin to pay you back. Them people been here lookin for you." Bay's voice was suddenly serious.

"What people, Bay?" Sally's heart had flown up into her throat.

"You know what people, girl. The law is what people. They had a warrant and everythang. They started in California, and they been to New York and they been here, and sooner or later, they be up there."

"Bay, did these people say what they wanted?" Sal was trying to sound casual.

"Oh, girl, who you thank you foolin with that shit? You think we don't know about what happened with that man in California? Sheeit. That was the talk of the town round here some years back. You was like a damn celebrity or somethin." Bay snorted.

Okay. okay, so she knew. All right. Now, what to do? Run? Again? Leave Omar and Doll? Sal rubbed her suddenly damp palms on the thighs of her jeans.

"Well, what you gon do?"

"I don't know, Bay Girl. But I know I'm tired of running. I got a family now, and I don't want to leave them again."

"Sheeit, you been had a family. That shit never stopped you before."

"Yeah, well, that was then. Listen, Bay, I preciate you warnin me. I hate to cut this short, but I got to make some calls, make some plans, and as soon as I can, I'll get back to you."

"Okeydokey. And, Sally Mae? I hope it works out for you. You let me know, you hear?"

Sal was touched. Bay Girl actually sounded concerned. "Okay, Bay. Gotta go. And thanks again."

Sal hurriedly called Jan.

"Look Jan, this is Sal. Listen, can you put me in touch with that Legal Aid lawyer that's handling your case? I gotta talk to a lawyer early in the mornin, and I ain't got one."

Jan gave her the lawyer's name and number, but when she pressed her for details, Sal clammed up, as usual.

"Oh, just a lil humbug from a long time ago. I'll let you know what's up after I talk with the lawyer tomorrow. Okay, thanks. Bye."

Sal hung up before Jan could say anything else.

She lit a cigarette. She had known that sooner or later, she would have to face this moment. Damn, what was it, almost twenty years ago? She was a lot older now, and a lot more tired. The very thought of leaving Omar and Doll now made her weak in the knees. But the thought of facing the alternative made her weak all over.

She was sweating now. She reached in her pocketbook and pulled out her blood pressure pills, popping one without water. She sat drumming her fingers on the surface of the table. Sal sat that way all night, and only moved to the bedroom in the morning when Omar came into the kitchen to fix breakfast for himself and Doll.

At exactly 9:05 A.M., she dialed the lawyer's number. A pleasant, deep masculine voice answered.

"Good morning. Merritt and Brown law offices."

"Uh, good mornin. Can I speak to Mr. Merritt?"

"This is Malcolm Merritt speaking."

"Uh, Mr. Merritt, you don't know me, but my name is Sally Washington, and I'm a friend of Janice Shephard's."

"Oh, of course, Mrs. Shephard. What can I do for you, Mrs. Washington?"

"I'm in big trouble, sir, and I gotta see a lawyer as soon as possible, and Jan gave me your name, and—well, almost twenty years ago, I was accused of a crime down in California, and I ran away, and I just got word last night that there's a warrant out on me, and the law is lookin for me, and, Mr. Merritt, I been runnin ever since then, from place to place, and I'm tired of runnin. I—I want to do the right thing," she stammered, perspiration running down her face, down her underarms, down the cleft between her breasts, like hard rain.

"All right, all right, Ms. Washington, calm down." Mr. Merritt spoke gently.

"First off, when was this crime, and second, what was—"

"The crime was murder." Sal spoke quickly. "A m-man was killed, and they lookin for me."

There was a pause on the other end of the line.

"How soon can you get here?"

"Right away. Give me your address."

Within twenty minutes, Sal was out the door and on her way to the bus stop. As soon as she reached the attorney's office, a secretary as ushered her right in.

"Good morning again, Mrs. Washington." Malcolm Merritt rose from behind his desk and extended his hand. Sal weakly accepted it and sat down.

She felt shaky and unsteady on her feet, a combination of fatigue from no sleep, a headache from hunger, and a rolling stomach from the beer she had consumed the night before. The too-bright morning sun hadn't helped.

But even in such a sorry state, she still couldn't help but notice how fine this young man was: early thirties, maybe, smooth mahogany skin, and flawless smile, mustache, close-cut beard, he moved, pantherlike, with the grace of a young Poitier. Sal was mesmerized by his bald head.

Jesus, help me, she thought, brushing back the stray ends of her braids. I know I'm goin crazy now. Gettin ready to go to jail, and I'm settin up here scoping out a dude. Jesus, please.

"Now, why don't you start from the beginning, and tell me the whole story?" He smiled, taking out a yellow pad and pen.

Sally told it all, starting from the day she first saw Charley Favor, right up to the night of his death. She told him all the whys and wherefores, and everything she had been doing from that day to this. When she had finished, she asked to use the rest room.

There, she emptied her bulging bladder and splashed cold water on her face. When she returned, Malcolm was reading through the copious notes he had been taking throughout her narrative. He had asked her a few questions, but had been otherwise noncommittal.

"Mrs. Washington," he began as she sat back down, "I'll make some calls and find out just what the charges are, if indeed there are any, and then I'll be more able to advise you on a course of action. I'll be in touch in a day or two."

"Meanwhile, Mrs. Shephard called while you were in the rest room. She wants me to tell you not to go home, but to wait until dark and then go straight to someone called Daddy and Red's house. Do you know who she means?"

"Yeah, I know who she means. I just don't know why. But she must have a reason for sendin that message."

"I think maybe she does. I also think you've got a real good friend," Merritt said.

"Tell me about it." Sal nodded.

"So how will I get in touch with you?"

"Just call Jan, give her the message. I'll get it."

Sal stood up, accepted his outstretched hand. "Uh, Mr. Merritt, about the money, I—uh, all I had on me was this two hundred dollars," she stammered, still shaking his hand.

"I'm sure we can work that out later, Mrs. Washington."

"I'll find a way. I got to," Sal half murmured to herself, going toward the door. By the time she had her hand on the doorknob, Merritt had moved from his desk and was standing right behind her.

"Mrs. Washington," he said softly, turning Sal around by her shoulders, to face him. He had the clearest, most reassuring brown eyes. Young eyes.

"Hey, look. I know Jan Shephard is a righteous sister, so I know you are, too. So, you call me tomorrow morning, and I might have some news for you."

Sal tried to swallow the knot in her throat.

He seemed genuinely concerned. She thanked him again and opened the door to go, but he touched her shoulder once more.

"Just for my records, is that Miss or Mrs. Washington?" There they were again, the warm, deep, gentle eyes. Sal couldn't look at them anymore.

"It's Ms.," she tossed over her shoulder, walking quickly out the door and down the hall. When she reached the elevator, she couldn't resist looking back. He was still standing there. Watching her. It had been awhile, but Sal still recognized that look that a man gives a woman when he's interested in her.

What the hell was up with that? she wondered.

The man was young enough to be her son, plus she'd just told him she was involved in a homicide. She shook her head, truly puzzled, and stepped into the waiting elevator.

Malcolm Merritt watched his new client walk down the hallway, watched her ungirdled ass moving in those tight blue jeans, and felt himself getting hard.

"Whoa—down, boy," he murmured, to no avail. "Am I going insane?" He had been with plenty of women in his life, women his age, some younger, some older. But this one, this one who had swept into his office with a telephone call and an air of mystery, this woman nearly old enough to be his mother, with the breathless, southern accent, the dazzling smile, and the braids flying every which way, this woman who might be involved in a murder, had caught him completely off guard.

He continued to watch her as she reached the elevator, glanced back once at him, then was gone.

Malcolm felt light-headed. He didn't know how long he stood there looking down the hallway. All he knew was that at that very second, he would have done anything, gone anywhere, said anything, if he could just get his hands around that big Black ass of hers tonight.

God, I need a cigarette, he thought, shuddering, and finally closing the door.

Sal headed straight to a pay phone. She called Jan. Nobody home. She called Rasheeda. Same thing.

She didn't have Daddy and Red's number with her, so she decided to just follow Mr. Merritt's instructions and wait until dark. So she spent the day hanging out.

She started to go to the movies but nixed that, realizing she wouldn't be able to keep her mind focused on the film. She went to the IHOP and ordered a large pancakes-and-eggs breakfast, but she was so filled with worry that she couldn't manage to get much food down. Still, she started to feel a little better after she had a little food in her stomach. She window-shopped a bit, walking the cold Philadelphia streets, looking at the various faces of passersby, wondering if any of them felt as desperate as she did at this moment.

She started to tense up again, that choking feeling, like the wings of butterflies brushing against the inside of her chest, flying up into her throat, beating against her windpipe, threatening to fly out of her mouth.

Hell, Greyhound was right around the corner.

She could still run. But then she thought of Omar's face, of little Doll's baby-love smile.

She walked for a good part of the day, trying to decide what to do. By the afternoon, she was hungry again. She grabbed a cheese steak and soda from a corner vendor and walked up to the Ben Franklin

Parkway. Spying an empty park bench, she sat and ate, recalling the words her son had spat at her just under a week ago. Sal had been trying to show Omar the correct way to brush Doll's teeth. She thought he was being a little too rough with the child.

"Omar, she just a baby. You can't brush her teeth like you do your own. You have to do it more gently, or the chile's gums will bleed."

"Oh, yeah? How would you know? This is my child, not yours. Mine!" Omar had snapped sharply, grabbing the toothbrush from Sally's hand.

Sal had backed off, throwing her hands out, palms up, in a gesture of peace. She did her best to help Omar with Doll, and she didn't mind one bit. Where had all that come from? She knew how hard it was for him, going to school and trying to be a father. She was extremely proud of her son for taking responsibility for his daughter.

Yet, it seemed the more she tried to do for them, the more he resented her.

"You know what, Omar? I don't know why you givin me such a hard time when you know I'm the only one that's got your back," Sal had said.

"Got my back? Got whose back?" Omar had laughed harshly. "Since when? Where were you when I needed to learn how to brush my teeth? Huh? When I learned to ride a bike? To tie my shoes? Where the hell—"

"Look, boy, don't start with me. That school took good care of you, and so did yo uncle and aunt. You learned, didn't you? Somebody taught you how to do it, cause I damn sure paid em enough money to." Sal was getting mad.

"Yeah, you're right. Somebody did. But it damn sure wasn't you," Omar shot back. He rinsed Doll's mouth out. "I'm taking care of my child a hell of a lot better than you took care of yours, Mom." He spat out the word *Mom* like a curse.

A fresh tear ran down Sally's cheek onto the napkin and the cheese steak. She had wanted to smack him then, to smack those hateful words from his mouth. But she hadn't. He was right. Sal hadn't raised him.

How could she, always on the run. Now, here she was trying to step all into his space, trying to be a mama to an almost-grown man.

At exactly 7 p.m., Sal was standing at Daddy and Red's door. She didn't know what to expect, couldn't imagine why Jan had directed her here. A maid appeared at the door after the first ring, a pleasant-faced woman, maybe early thirties. God, she looked familiar, but Sal just couldn't place her.

"Good evenin, Miss Sally. We been waitin for you."

Sal stepped inside, again silently admiring the ornate baroque furnishings, thick carpeting and crimson walls, seemingly made of a fine, feltlike material.

"I've been told to take you straight up to your rooms." The maid smiled. "Just follow me. We goin up on the third floor."

Rooms? Now, just what in the devil was up here?

"Yo, sis, don't I know you from round the way, somewhere?" Sal asked, trailing behind the woman up the steps.

"Sho, you know me, Miss Sally. I been waitin to see when you was gone recognize me. Member that time you hid me and my kids when my husband was beatin the hell out of me? I know it's been bout five years now. We go back a long way."

"Damn! Nettie, right? How you doin, girl?" Sal grinned, hugging the woman.

Years ago, Sal had been a sort of underground railroad conductor for battered women, finding them places to stay, even putting them up in her own home sometimes until arrangements could be made for more permanent lodging. Nettie had been one of her first families. Now, Sal remembered her, the straight-up-from-the-country girl and her two cute little boys, all looking like frightened animals when she had first met them. They had stayed with her for about a week, until the Women's Shelter had found them an apartment and had gotten Nettie onto welfare and into a training program.

"Computers. I tried, Miss Sally. I really did. But I ain't never been no good at readin in the first place, and if you cain't read, how can you follow the instructions?" Nettie threw her hands up.

"But one thing I knew how to do was clean and take care of a house. So I started doin that. Well, I got me a job taking care o' this old white lady live down on Rittenhouse Square. You know the kind. Got plenty of money, old, sickly, and they families ain't got no time for em. Just waitin for em to croak, so they can get they hands on that money." Nettie shook her head.

"Well, anyhow, the pay wasn't all that hot, but I couldn't afford to quit. I had already lost my welfare digit. I still had a medical card, cause you member my baby boy, Billy, had real bad asthma. But I was stretched to the max, chile."

By this time, they were nearing the third-floor landing. Nettie started talking faster now, trying to get all her story in.

"Anyway, one day I was pushing Miss Adelaide. That was the ole lady's name. I was pushing her in her wheelchair through Rittenhouse Square. They was havin some kind of outdoor art show down there, and out of the blue, here come Miss Red, looking sharp, you hear me? Sharp.

"Well, she walked right up to me and say, 'Hey, don't I know you from the Strip?'

"Well, I said yeah, cause I usta hang up there sometimes after work. I say, 'Yeah, I be on the Strip.'

"Well, she say, 'scuse me' to Miss Adelaide, real nice like, and pulls me to the side. 'How would you like to come work for me?' Miss Red say.

"Well, chile, I just stood there. I was tryin to thank of a nice way to tell her I wasn't no ho, you know, without hurtin her feelins, and I guess she caught on, cause she laughed and say, 'No, no. I want you to be my housekeeper.'

"She say, 'Whatever she payin you, you bring yo last pay stub to me, and I'll double it.'

"Then she put her card into my uniform pocket. She say, 'I just cain't stand to see you, young as you is, pushin that ole bitch around.'"

"Git out." Sal chuckled.

"Sho did, now. Well, Miss Adelaide act like she ain't hear her, but

I know she did. Anyhow, I called Miss Red that night and I been here ever since." Nettie smiled broadly. "And she kept her word. I started at double my pay from when I was working for that ole bitch—I mean, Miss Adelaide."

Nettie and Sal laughed together and high-fived.

"You go, girl." Sal grinned, shaking her head.

By this time, they were standing in front of a large, beautifully polished mahogany door.

"They's all in there waitin for you. We all in yo corner, Sally." Nettie squeezed Sally's hand before knocking on the big wooden door.

"Miss Sally is here, ma'am."

"Bring her on in," a voice from somewhere inside replied.

Nettie opened the door and ushered Sal in.

"Have a chair, Miss Sally." The low, unmistakable voice of DB.

Seated in a smallish living room were Red, Daddy, Jan, and Rasheeda. Sal almost lost it for real then.

Oh, no. Roach was in a fuckin whorehouse!

This was too much. She took the first available seat.

All eyes were on her. DB cleared his throat. "So how you feelin?"

"All right, I guess, under the circumstances," Sally answered warily. She glanced at Jan and Rasheeda for a clue.

She didn't know how much any of them knew, or if they knew anything at all. They returned her look with questioning eyes. She decided to play it safe and give up as little information as possible. She looked over at Red and DB, trying to keep her expression blank.

"Well, look, here's the deal," Monsieur Daddy Baby continued. "We understand you in a lil bit of a jam. There was two bounty hunters by yo house this mornin around ten-thirty, showin yo picture around and everythin, askin for you." He stared pointedly at Sal. Getting no response, he went on.

"We put in a call to Janice here, and she went over there this afternoon and spoke to your boy. Him and the baby are all right. Her and Sister Rasheeda got some of yo clothes and things, and put em in the back bedroom. I told Janice to call the lawyer she sent you to and tell you to come straight over here. This is a separate apartment from the rest of the house. You can stay here for now, and from here, we can send you down to our other place, if necessary." DB gestured around the room. "Won't nobody be lookin for you here."

Sal looked from one face to another. All seemed to be in agreement, even Rasheeda. She was so tired. She longed for sleep.

"But why? Why are you doin all this for me? You don't even know what kind of trouble I'm in. I don't want to bring no heat down on nobody. Why would you do this for me?"

Red Top walked over to Sal and sat on the arm of her chair. "Look, we know you from livin in the community. Everybody know you good people, always doin things to help people out, tryin to fix up the playground and all, tryin to get them damn crack dealers off the corner. "This is just me and DB's way of showin appreciation. Please stay. Get a good night's sleep, and things will be more clear in the mornin." Red Top put her hand on Sally's, patting it gently.

"And my kids are all right?" Sal asked.

"The kids are fine," Jan assured her. "I'm going to watch Doll in the daytime while Omar's at school."

"And when Jan comes to work, she'll bring Doll with her. She can play with my girl," Rasheeda said softly.

Sal shook her head. This was all happening too fast. But she was too beat to think about the whys and wherefores now. She needed sleep.

"Well, if it wouldn't be putting yall out, just till I can make a move." She looked at Daddy and Red.

"Girl, go on in there and lie down," Red said breezily, squeezing her hand again.

"Yeah, come on, Sal. I'll show you where I hung your clothes and things," Jan volunteered, leading Sal to the back bedroom, Rasheeda trailing behind.

And that's how Sally Mae came to stay in a whorehouse for almost a week without doing any flatbacking at all!

CHAPTER 19

SALLY AT DADDY AND RED'S

Is there anything else I can get for yall?"

"No, Net, we're fine. If we need anything else, we'll call you, honey." Red smiled.

Nettie lingered at the door.

"I said we'll call you, Nettie."

Nettie scurried out, shutting the door tightly behind her. Damn, she thought. Must be somethin really big happenin with Sally. All of them up in here, even that Muslim girl. Sho would like to be a fly on that wall.

But Nettie knew better. She had taken a vow of secrecy when she came on board, and she knew she'd better keep it.

Seated around the living room portion of Sally Mae's temporary lodgings were Sal, Janice, and Rasheeda on the large sofa, DB and Red in the two occasional chairs, and Vaa, Puddin, and Gigi in chairs they had brought in from the little kitchen. There was liquor on the coffee table, as well as wine, soda, and juice, chicken wings, and potato salad.

The JGs had no idea why this meeting had been called, but they hoped for the best. Maybe it was news about Peaches. Sally Mae had still not told a soul just what was going on with her, and no one had asked her any more questions. She had been a guest of Daddy and Red's for almost a week now.

She sat stiffly, drumming her fingers on the arm of the sofa, wondering what the hell Puddin and Gigi, Ursula's old running buddies from back in the day, and Vaa, of all people, were doing there. BB King's "I Pay the Cost to Be the Boss" flowed through the room as everyone served themselves and made small talk. After a while, Red cleared her throat.

"Okay, everybody. DB wanted to call this meetin tonight, just so we could make sure everybody's in step."

"First thing"—she now looked directly at the JGs—"we asked Puddin, Gigi, and Vaa to be here, cause we're all still tryin to find out who killed Peach. So we're all workin on that."

The JGs nodded.

"But in the meantime, me and DB was still workin on the other things yall came to us with, and now, we've got this mess with Sally—" Her voice trailed off. Everybody looked at Sally, who sat determinedly watching her own fingers drumming on the sofa arm, her face a blank.

"Well, anyhow," Red continued, "we'll get back to that. Meanwhile, I'm sorry to say there's no news about Peaches. Puddin and Gigi been askin all their ole friends, even some of the tricks." Red lowered her head and blushed slightly.

"I talked to all my girls, and none of em heard a thing. Even DB put the word out on the Strip, offerin a lil something to whoever could turn up the shooter. But, so far, nothing. Nobody's shakin loose."

"Hell, even the po-lice ain't got shit. I been in touch wit my, uh, sources down to the precinct, and they ain't got shit. Not a damn thing. Just keep on buggin them girls of Peach's all the time, draggin em down to the station over and over."

"But that's all right," Puddin broke in. "It's just a matter of time."

"Damn right. We'll find the dog who did it," chimed in Gigi in her high-pitched voice.

"And when we do, I want him first. He's mine," Vaa declared, waving his arms, dropping ashes from his ever-present cigarette holder all over the place.

"But we do have some good news about your judge, Janice. We don't know about the man that robbed you, but we might be able to, ah, get Califano to go the right way." Red smiled, winking at Vaa, Puddin, and Gigi.

"Well, that would be a first, honey. That man's been going the wrong way for years," hooted Vaa.

"What? I don't understand," Jan asked, smiling a little, uncertain what the joke was.

"Well, chile, we ain't gone tell you everything. We just think we might have a way to make him see the light, put it that way." Puddin giggled.

"Oh, you got that right. We'll make him see the light from here, all the way to fuckin China!" Gigi squealed. Even DB joined in the raucous laughter that time.

"Just be cool, honey. We're takin care of it," Red said, laughing and wiping her eyes.

"Oh, man, I need another drink on that one."

She reached over to the coffee table, refilling her glass with ice and Chivas. The JGs sat, smiling politely, totally clueless.

"All right, all right. Now, Sister Rasheeda, my advice for you is to keep on fightin for your boys. Don't give up. You may think you losin the battle, but trust me, you gone win the war." Red winked.

Rasheeda looked around. Daddy, Puddin, Gigi, and Vaa were all nodding in agreement. She didn't know these people well, but she had seen them in the neighborhood and even in the Oasis, and somehow, she trusted them. Believed them. She squeezed Jan's hand, nodding back.

"Now, Miss Sally." Red took a deep breath, "We know you have to go to Los Angeles for the hearing in ten days."

Jan and Rasheeda gasped, turning toward Sally.

"How you know that? Who told you that?" Sal looked alarmed. Hell, she had just found out herself that very morning when she had spoken to Malcolm on the phone. He had made the deal for her to appear for a hearing as a material witness, and since she was not considered a formal suspect at this time, she could come out of hiding. But she had to appear at the hearing.

"Well, ain't that just as bad?" she'd asked him.

"No way," he had answered. "They have never charged you with anything. This is a hearing to determine if they have enough evidence to bring formal charges against you, or anyone else, for murder. The assistant district attorney I talked to explained to me that this is something of a fluke. They have a new D.A. who has apparently decided to clean up all their old cases, since they're converting everything to a new computer system, and when this case jumped out, the bounty hunters just took it and ran with it. Now, I'm not saying there's nothing to worry about here, but in old cases like this, witnesses often die or move away, evidence is lost. It's sometimes difficult for them to make a case."

"So what's your advice, Mr. Merritt?"

"My advice is for you to go to the hearing. I can set up representation for you there with an old law school buddy of mine. You said you were tired of running, didn't you?"

"Yeah, I did. And I am."

"Well, good. Let's get this thing over with. Call me tomorrow. And Sally, you can call me Malcolm. Okay?"

"Okay. Well, I'll talk to you tomorrow, Mr. Merr— uh, Malcolm."

Sally had hung up feeling flustered. And now, here was Red telling everybody all about it already.

"Yeah, well, DB had talked to that lawyer, that Merritt fellow, earlier, before you called him," Red said.

"DB?"

"Yeah. Me."

"I talked to him. The boy sound like he know what he doin. I think you be all right with him." DB sat back, nodding at her, a slight smile, or was it a smirk, playing at the corners of his lips.

Sally returned his look, trying again to figure him out. What did he want from her? If he thought she was going to take up hooking at this late date, he had lost his mind. But she kept quiet.

"So anyhow, that's it for now. When we find out anything else, we'll be in touch," Red jumped in, breaking the silence.

Jan and Rasheeda thanked them all for any help they could, or would provide. Puddin and Gigi waved them away.

"Hey, that's just the way it is for women like us. We got to help each other when we can," Puddin said.

"Damned straight." Gigi nodded.

"You know it, girl," Vaa broke in, "cause women like us got to have each other's back."

Even Sal loosened up at that.

Pretty soon, Puddin, Gigi, and Vaa went out to the elevator and downstairs with DB and Red. Jan and Rasheeda remained firmly in place on the sofa. But just before leaving, DB, leaning on two canes, had walked slowly over to Sally.

"You better call this number before you go to L.A.," he whispered, pressing a slip of paper into her palm. Sal glanced down at the paper.

"Bay Girl? What you doin with Bay Girl's number?"

"Listen, just call the girl, awright? Damn! You been havin an attitude with me since Day One, and you ain't got no time for that shit now. Just take the damn number and call the girl tonight. Ten days be up before you know it." He turned away impatiently and walked out the door.

"What's up, Sal?" Jan walked over. She and Rasheeda had caught the exchange between Sally and DB from the sofa where they sat.

"Damn if I know. That man is so strange. You know, I even offered to pay him and Red for lettin me lie low here, and for helpin me and all, and they wouldn't take a dime. Not a dime." Sal shrugged.

"Well, hey, don't look a gift horse in the mouth. Just thank Allah for his blessings," Rasheeda said cheerfully.

"Yeah, I know. And it's not that I'm not grateful and everything, it's just I can't figure out what he want. He's always starin at me when he think I'm not lookin."

"Maybe you remind him of somebody," Jan said thoughtfully.

"Yeah, well, I hope that's all it is, cause I ain't even tryin to be up in here sellin no snatch at my age for nobody."

"Oh, Sal, I don't think it's about that at all. Has he asked you for anything, or stepped to you the wrong way?" Rasheeda asked.

"Naw, naw, nothin like that. He's been real nice. Matter of fact, tonight is the first time I've seen him since that first night. I don't go downstairs at all."

"Yeah, I can dig it. When we come here, we come up the back way. These walls are definitely soundproof. You'd never even guess you were livin over top a whorehouse at all," said Jan.

"He asked me to smile," Sal said, almost to herself. "He is one strange ole dude."

"Strange, but fine. Still fine after all these years," Jan said, grinning.

The room was quiet for a while, but for the sound of Etta James's "Sunday Kind of Love" moaning soulfully from the stereo. Jan and Rasheeda sat and sighed. And sat and sighed some more, staring pointedly at Sally.

"All right, all right, yall. Get off my tit. I'll tell yall everything, swear to God I will." Sal turned to her friends. "But not tonight, okay? I'm kinda tired, and I got this real important phone call I gotta make."

"Yeah, well, when, Sal? When? Damn! I mean, what is it? You still don't trust us after all this time?" Jan had had it. "Here we are runnin all around doin what we can, I got Doll staying with me, you got Roach sneakin around up here in a whorehouse, and you still don't want to give up the tapes?"

"I know, I know. And I appreciate everything yall doin, swear to God I do. Look, I got to go to Los Angeles next week, I got some runnin round to do and some plans to make. But I swear, before I leave, I'll tell yall everything," Sally Mae begged, pleading for time.

"You tell us when you're ready, sis. Come on, Jan. Let's go." Rasheeda leaned over and squeezed Sal's hand, then rose.

"But I don't see why you can't—"

"Come on, Jan."

As soon as they were gone, Sally Mae poured herself a generous glass of champagne. She sipped slowly, smoking a cigarette and listening to Etta, now singing "Misty." Finishing the drink she poured another, then another. She wished she had a joint. Finally, she fished the slip of paper DB had given her out of her jeans pocket, picked up the receiver, took a deep breath, and dialed Bay Girl's number.

CHAPTER 20

JAYRON

About a week later, ten o'clock in the evening near Malcolm X Park on a cold February night found Janice, stupidly staring up at stars that gleamed like cracked ice in a velvet sky. She had just let Shaft off his leash to run free and was taking her time around the square, picking out the constellations. The sky was black, the moon was new, and Jan was lost in the glow.

So lost was she that she paid no mind to the rustling sound in the nearby bushes. So entranced was she with the beauty of the sky that she barely heard the sound of the sneakers squeaking lightly on the sidewalk, but sensing a presence, she started to turn. It was too late.

"Give it up."

"Wha—" Jan felt something hard in her back, just under her left shoulder.

"Give it up."

Oh, shit. The voice sounded young, quavering, uncertain. But the thing in her back felt hard.

Taking a deep breath to center herself against her rising panic, Janice held both arms out and up.

"Okay, okay. Look, I don't want no trouble. I've got a few dollars in my wallet. I'm going to reach in my left pocket and get it for you. Okay?"

Jan's soft tones belied her fast-beating heart.

"Cut the talk, lady, just give me the money. I ain't got all night."

She felt a sharp poke from the hard thing under her shoulder. Jan reached into her pocket slowly, and removed the wallet. She held her left arm out with the wallet in her hand, still not looking back.

"He—here it is. You can have—"

The wallet was snatched from her hand, the hard thing removed from her back, and the sneakers took off running, all in a flash.

"Shaft! Yo, Shaft! Here, boy!"

Jan pivoted on the spot, and started to chase after her attacker, calling her dog as she ran. Shaft was by her side in a few seconds, then running ahead of her.

"Get him, boy! Get him! Stop, thief! Help!"

If her head hadn't been so full of the moon, she would have realized just how ridiculous she was, a forty-something-year-old woman chasing down a man with a gun in the middle of the night. But she wasn't thinking about that. She was mad. She really needed that little bit of change, and besides, all her ID was in that wallet.

"Get him, Shaft!"

Shaft was by now out of sight, but she could hear him barking. Jan kept on, almost out of breath and knees beginning to ache, but running still.

"*Owwwww! Ahhhh!*"

The sound came from somewhere about a block away, followed by more barking.

"*Owwww!* Lady, you better call off this dog! *Owwww!*"

By this time, the houses on the other side of Pine Street started to light up, and Jan could see people coming out onto their front porches to see what was going on.

"Call the police! Call the police! I've been robbed," Jan screamed, now half running, half staggering toward the source of all the noise.

Shaft was circling an old station wagon parked near the corner, still barking. On top of the wagon cowered a dark, crouched figure. It was so dark that all Jan could really see were a pair of white sneakers.

"Lady, you better get yo damn dog!"

"Or what? What you gone do, punk?" Jan asked, her voice ragged from her unaccustomed sprint.

She knew a bluff when she heard one. She knew he didn't have a gun, or he would have shot Shaft from the jump. "I think you better just keep sittin your ass up there on that car till the cops get here, or you won't have no more ass to sit on."

Shaft had stopped barking, but still circled the car warily, making low growling sounds. Jan couldn't get over her fearless pet. He had never had any training or obedience classes, yet he had instinctively protected her. She looked up again at the new moon and smiled.

"Thanks, Junie."

Presently, two police cars arrived. Most of the neighbors on the block were now outside, but none would venture across the street to where Shaft guarded the person on the car.

"Uh, lady? Is that your dog?"

Jan walked over to one of the police cars, where two patrolmen sat safely inside.

"Yes, it is."

She gave them her name and address and explained what had transpired, and after first making sure she had Shaft back on his leash, they exited their cars and walked over to where the figure still sat crouched on top of the station wagon, guns and nightsticks drawn.

"Okay, buddy, come on down."

"I—I don't know if I can walk," a frightened voice meekly replied.

"Whaddaya mean, you can't walk? You got up there, didn't you?" said one of the officers.

"Yeah, but that was before that damn dog bit me."

"Oh, hell. All right, let's give you a hand." The officer sighed.

Reaching for the suspect's arms, the two cops managed to get him down on the ground between them.

"*Owwww!*"

"Aw, hell, he's just a kid."

Jan walked over and looked straight into the frightened eyes of a child, holding on to a torn, bloody pants leg and staring into the flashlights of the police. The boy, slim and cinnamon colored, nervously bit his lower lip, revealing a gold cap covering one of his front teeth. He studiously avoided her gaze.

A boy! He was just a little boy! Lord have mercy.

"Jack, I'll call for an ambulance," the first officer said to his partner.

"Ma'am, would you like to come to the station with me to make out a report?"

"Oh, definitely. Wait a minute."

She spotted something blue on the ground. It was her wallet. Jan picked it up, counted her money. It was all there.

"Well, being that you got your property back, you really don't have to come down tonight. It can wait till morning."

"Well, what about this kid? What's going to happen to him?"

"Oh, the ambulance will take him down to the hospital and check him out. It doesn't look too serious. Probably just broke the skin, but they'll have to do a rabies test on him, give him a tet shot."

It was true the boy didn't seem to be hurt badly. He was able to limp to the police car with the aid of the other officer.

"And then what?" Jan persisted.

"Well, then he'll probably be taken back to the station and processed, and depending on what they find, he'll go home. Or to juvie."

The officer looked at Janice sharply. He was tired of answering this woman's questions. He was tired, period. After all, she had her wallet back. What was the big deal? And what was she doing out here by the park this time of night in the first place? Hell, kid probably had a record, anyway.

"I think I'd prefer to come down to the station now, tonight," Jan said firmly.

Janice sat on the hard wooden bench at the Eighteenth District drinking nasty coffee from the vending machine. She had driven herself to the station, after first dropping Shaft off back at home. She was tired and cranky. Her butt was hurting from the slats on the hard bench. Finally, she was called in to give her statement to another police officer, who filled out the incident report.

"How's the boy?"

"Huh? Oh, the kid? He's fine. Just a little skin torn. They cleaned it up and gave him a tetanus shot. He's already been released," the officer replied kindly.

"Released? When? Are his parents here? I didn't see nob—"

"Wait, wait, one at a time." The officer grinned, holding up his hands.

"When I said released, I meant released from the hospital. He's in our custody. He's in the back."

"In this building? So what's going to happen to him now?"

"Well, he's being processed, and if he has priors, he's probably going to Juvenile Hall," the officer replied. "He'll probably go to the Youth Study Center, since he's only eleven. He'll stay there till his case comes up in Juvenile Court. You'll be notified when and where to appear to testify. After that, it's all up to the judge."

"I see." Jan nodded.

"Eleven years old. I swear, these folks don't even care about their kids nowadays. You can bet when I was eleven, my parents knew where I was," the cop said.

"Well, so did mine." Jan arched her left eyebrow upward. She wasn't sure what this white man meant by these folks.

"It's a damned shame, but that's the way it is nowadays. They just have em like hens layin eggs, drop em to the ground, and keep on walking," the officer went on, clearly without a clue.

Something about that "hens layin eggs" jumped down hard on Jan's last nerve. She stood up, grabbed her pocketbook, and marched toward the door, but suddenly turned back. "What's this kid's name, anyway? I might know his people."

"Let me see." The baffled officer flipped through the report, wondering just what the hell he had said to tick her off.

"Jaron, Jarod, or something. These crazy names these kids have nowadays, their mothers must just make em up on the spot, I gue—"

"Last name. What's the last name?" Jan asked impatiently, deciding to ignore that last remark.

"Ah, here it is. JayRon. JayRon Wade." The officer smiled up at her.

Wade. JayRon didn't ring a bell, but Wade? "Thanks very much," Jan said tersely to the officer.

As soon as she was in the hallway again, she made a beeline for the public telephone.

"Hakim? Hi, it's Janice. Sorry to be callin so late, but can I speak to Rasheeda? It's real, real important."

"Peace. What's up, Jan?" Rasheeda's voice came sleepily through the line. Jan gave her a quick rundown of the evening's events, finishing with the boy's name.

"What?" Rasheeda was now wide awake. "Oh, Jan! I'll be there as soon as I get some clothes on."

Jan replaced the receiver, walked out to the front entrance and lit a cigarette. How many years ago had it been? Eight? Ten?

Jan had been working in the Family Court then, in a division that handled the placement of children into foster care when their parents had been arrested or convicted, and there was no other relative to care for them. When the file of Doris Wade's three children had first crossed her desk, the name had meant nothing to her.

However, when she had checked out the box marked "next of kin" and had seen "James-brother, NYC," she dropped the file back on the desk.

James? Roach's James? She dimly recalled meeting James's sister at the wedding, but could this be the same woman? Janice had immediately placed a long-distance call to Roach in New York, and read the information to her. Indeed, Roach hadn't known anything about it, but she had caught the first thing smoking, and was in Philadelphia that very night. Just like that.

Back then, it seems Dottie had been a booster, and this being her third conviction for stealing from downtown department stores, she now had a felony conviction and had to serve a twelve-to-eighteen-month jail sentence. James had already been notified, and wanted no part of the children.

Well, Roach wasn't having it. It had taken her and Janice approximately a week to work through the red tape and make a few phone calls to certain politicians, but two weeks later, Rasheeda was on that train back to New York, with twelve-year-old Rhonda, ten-year-old Mickey, and three-year-old baby JayRon, in tow. And just as she had been there all those years ago, here she was tonight.

"Yo, sis." Roach kissed Jan on the cheek, frowning at the cigarette. "Those things are gonna kill you, you know."

"Yeah, yeah, yeah. You pick your poison, and I'll pick mine," Jan said, stubbing out the butt on the ground.

"Chile, you mean Hakim let you come out by yourself this time of night?"

"Sure. Hakim's pretty flexible, and I just called him on my cell phone to let him know I'm here," gesturing toward her large pocketbook. "Now, what's going on? What do I have to do? First of all, are you all right?"

"Yeah, I'm hangin. Not too shabby for an ole lady tryin to be FloJo or somebody out here." Jan laughed. "You should have seen me hoofin it, girl. You woulda died."

"Girl, I don't even want to think about it." Rasheeda passed her hand over her eyes. "This ain't back in no day, Jan. You can't be running around the streets late at night like you're twenty-five no more."

"Ten o'clock? That's late? Give me a break, Roach."

The women argued all the way back into the police station. Jan pulled Rasheeda down onto her old hard bench and recapped everything the police officer had told her.

"You know, Jan, I haven't seen Dottie or those kids since she got out of jail all those years ago, and came to New York and picked them up. They stayed with us for almost two years. And JayRon, you remember, wasn't quite five years old when they left me. She's called a few times over the years, but that's it. You know Mickey got killed?"

"What?"

"Oh, yeah, about a year ago. The only way I learned about it was from James, when he came down for the funeral. And Rhonda's in jail, last I heard."

"Oh, no, Roach. For what?"

"Boosting. Hooking. Who knows what else." Roach shook her head sadly. "Those kids never really had a chance. You know, now that I think about it, it was just after Mickey died that James all of a sudden started fighting me for custody of the boys. I was surprised that he even came down for Mickey's funeral. He never spent any time with Dottie's kids before. Or ours either, for that matter. Too busy chasing money."

"I don't even know where Dottie is, but I know one thing. I know my nephew can't go into nobody's foster care. No way. Look what foster care did to James and Dottie. No way." Rasheeda shook her head vehemently.

"Well, I'm with you on that. Tell you what. We'll go in and see these juvie people. They have to let you see JayRon. You're his aunt. Then we'll find out what we have to do to keep him out of there," Jan suggested.

"I don't know how I'm gonna find room for him, though, and what Hakim's gonna say."

"Well, we'll worry about that bridge when we come to it. I don't want to see him in foster care, either, even though the lil sucka did try to scare me half to death tonight. Come on." Jan rose from the bench.

They walked arm in arm back into the juvenile division. After speaking with the officer and showing some identification, Rasheeda was allowed to go upstairs to see JayRon, while Jan, hind parts aching, again waited on her favorite bench.

It was around 1 A.M. and the station began to come to life as the police force changed its tour of duty. Various cops, detectives, and other personnel filed in and out. Some glanced over at Jan. Some nodded, some didn't. Janice was so tired by now, she felt like stretching out on the bench and going to sleep.

Just as Rasheeda came back down the stairs and started toward her, Jan felt someone staring at her. She looked up, and across the room stood a tall, handsome man. He smiled, revealing a small gap between his front teeth. Jan nodded, puzzled. She was sure she had seen him somewhere before.

"Jan, I talked to JayRon. He's fine. Just scared and ashamed and . . ." Rasheeda's voice trailed off as she followed Jan's gaze across the room to the man. "Well, who is that?"

"I don't know." Jan couldn't seem to tear her eyes away from the man, who was still smiling at her. She felt woozy.

"I know I've seen him somewhere before. I just can't remember where. He looks so familiar. He—"

"He looks a little bit like that movie star, Laurence Fishburne, doesn't he," Rasheeda commented. "Don't you think?"

"Oh, shit! It's him! It's him, Roach," Jan sputtered through clenched teeth.

"It's who? Laurence Fishburne? Oh, yeah, right. Girl, you must be tired." Rasheeda rolled her eyes heavenward.

"No, no. It's the guy from the hospital, the guy that was talking to me when I woke up that night I passed out in the Gold Post. Oh, shit, he's a cop!"

Jan was utterly mortified.

"We've got to get out of here." Still speaking through clenched teeth, she rose, grabbed Rasheeda by the arm, and started dragging her toward the exit, walking quickly, head down.

"Janice, what is the matter with you?" Rasheeda was pulling back.

"I can't face him, Roach. I'm just too embarrassed." Jan was now pulling hard on Rasheeda's arm.

"But Jan, I'm trying to tell you, we have to go back upstairs. They're going to let me take JayRon home tonight." Rasheeda's eyes were shining. She was really enjoying Jan's discomfort. "Come on, this way." Rasheeda did an about-face.

"Okay, okay, let's go. Anywhere but down here." Jan turned around and began pulling Rasheeda again, this time in the opposite direction, head still down. Rasheeda, suppressing a giggle, let herself be led along, sneaking another glance over at the cop. He was still standing there. Grinning.

They had gone up to the Juvenile section, Rasheeda passing Jan off as her sister to the female police officer handling JayRon's case. Being in a different department, the woman had no way of knowing Jan was the same woman who had given the police report on JayRon only two hours before.

The boy was so small. He really was just a child.

JayRon looked up at Jan, then at Rasheeda, shame in his eyes.

"I'm ready to take him home now, Officer," Rasheeda spoke politely. "Is there anything else I need to sign?"

"No, I think we've taken care of everything. He has no priors. We've contacted his mom, and she says it's okay for us to place him in your custody. Your identification checks out as next of kin in Philadelphia. Of course, you understand you'll be responsible for him showing up in Juvenile Court two weeks from now for his court date?"

"Of course," Rasheeda replied, grabbing JayRon by the arm, pulling him out of his seat.

"We'll be there, all right."

JayRon eyed Janice warily, but not knowing what else to do, he went meekly along with his aunt. The three of them left the building in silence. Jan looked around and was relieved to see that that guy, that cop, was no longer standing in the lobby.

Once outside, they walked down the block to Rasheeda's van, slowing down to accommodate JayRon's limp, and it was only when they got to the van that Rasheeda stopped, turned, and grabbed hold of JayRon by the shoulders.

"This is Miss Janice, Jay. She's the woman you tried to rob tonight." Rasheeda's voice betrayed no emotion. "Is there anything you want to say to her?" She turned JayRon around by his shoulders to face Jan.

The boy hemmed and hawed, studying his sneakers intensely. Jan could just make out his soft, unformed features by the light of the street-corner lamp. She tried to look stern and angry.

"Sorry, Miss," he mumbled, jamming his hands down into the pockets of his low-slung jeans.

"What? What did you say, boy? Look at me when you speak to me."

The boy slowly looked up into Jan's eyes.

"I'm sorry, miss. I didn't mean it. It's just that I was out of money and I needed to get back to the shelter and I—"

"Shelter? What shelter?" Jan looked over JayRon's head at Rasheeda.

"It's a long story, girl. I haven't even heard all of it myself. I'm going to call Dottie when we get home tonight and find out what's going on," Rasheeda answered, unlocking the van's doors and letting JayRon in. She turned back to Jan. "I'll fill you in tomorrow soon's I know more."

"That's cool."

"Wait a minute, Jan. Look, I appreciate what you did tonight. I owe you."

"You owe me? Hell, you gave me a job. I owe you."

"Yeah, well, you know what I mean."

The two friends hugged, Rasheeda got into her van, JayRon in the back, and drove home, Jan following closely behind.

"You up?" Roach's voice came through the receiver.

"I am now," Jan mumbled, stretching and looking over at the bedside clock. Damn, it was ten o'clock! She should have been at the Oasis over an hour ago.

"Sorry, Roach. I guess I just forgot to set the alarm."

"Oh, girl, don't even worry about it. I didn't figure you'd be coming in here today, anyway, after what happened last night and all."

"No, I'm coming in. Just give me a lil time to throw some water on my face and brush my teeth."

"Jan, really, you don't have to, if you don't feel up to it," Rasheeda protested weakly.

"Will you stop acting like I'm some fragile lil ole lady? I said I'll be there. See ya in a minute." Jan hung up. She knew Rasheeda was probably swamped, this being a Saturday, with the twins away at their weekly basketball practice. She swung her legs over the side of the bed, feet searching for her slippers. Willing herself to rise, she padded into the bathroom, thinking about the night before.

JayRon! The little bugger. She found herself smiling in spite of herself.

When Jan got to the Oasis at around 11:15, the place was jumping. She pitched in immediately, relieving Rasheeda behind the steam table, freeing her up to wait on the take-out customers. It wasn't until two in the afternoon that they got a break, when the twins arrived from basketball practice, doe-eyed JayRon trailing shyly behind them.

Rasheeda put the boys right to work, while she and Jan finally sat down at one of the back tables.

JayRon also went to work, doing whatever he could to help out. He had spoken to Jan, and every now and then, snuck a glance over at her, as if trying to gauge her mood.

Jan bit back a smile.

"So this is the deal," Rasheeda began, as the two friends sat down to a sandwich, soup, and tea.

"What's the deal?" Sally Mae walked up behind Rasheeda, catching them both by surprise.

"Chile, don't do that! You like to scared me to death." Rasheeda gasped, clutching her chest.

"You ain't lyin, Roach." Jan had jumped, too.

"Well, what in the hell is goin on?" Sal was in a good mood. "Yall know I'm back home now. Free again, at least for now."

"Well, sit down and be quiet, if you want to know what the deal is, cause the Georgia Girl sure missed it last night."

Sally pulled up a chair. Quickly, Jan and Rasheeda filled her in on the events of the evening before, speaking in low voices so the boys wouldn't hear. Every now and then, they would have to stop, shushing Sally Mae's usual salty language, her "no shits" and "git the fuck outta heres."

"And why didn't nobody call me?" she wanted to know when they had finished.

"Well, Sal, it happened so fast, and what with you being underground and all, you know," Jan said.

"I was wonderin where yall was. I called both of yall, and you wasn't home, Jan, and you know Hakim. He wouldn't give up no info whatsoever. Damn!" She turned and looked at JayRon.

"I seen that lil boy when I came in, but I just figured he was one of the twins' lil friends. Damn!"

"Sally, *shhhh!*"

"Okay, okay. So you say you talked to his mama?"

"Yeah, chile. It's deep, deep."

"What's deep, Roach? I've been in suspense all night. What's all this about a shelter? I swear to God, girl, give it up. You know we're dyin to know."

Jan was peppering Rasheeda with rapid-fire questions. Rasheeda kept shaking her head, holding up her hands. She leaned forward.

"No, girl, you ain't dyin. Dottie's the one dyin." She spoke in a whisper.

Sally and Jan looked at each other, then back at Rasheeda.

"Dottie is in a shelter. Well, not a shelter, actually. It's a hospice, a place for women with AIDS with no one to care for them. It's where they go to die."

"Aw, hell." Sally dropped her head.

"Have mercy," Jan whispered.

The JGs were silent. A chill seemed to pass through the room. They were all thinking the same thing.

Another one bites the dust. They had seen so many.

Jan's eyes welled with tears. "Oh, sugar, I'm sorry." She patted Rasheeda's hand. "There's just no nice way to say it. I mean, I really shouldn't be all that surprised, what with Dottie living that kind of lifestyle and all, but still—"

"I can dig it. Still, nobody expects anybody they know to get it, till they get it," Janice completed the sentence.

The JGs fell silent again, turning their eyes to the rail-thin young boy now laughing and joking with his cousins up front, gold cap shining.

"How long she got?" Sally asked presently.

"I don't know. She only told me she's got it, and her and JayRon had to move into the shelter, I mean, hospice, because she's too sick to care for herself and watch him."

"Well, where's the boy's daddy?" Sally asked.

"Sal, please." Rasheeda sucked her teeth. "Dottie never talked about no daddies, not for JayRon, anyway. Not that I remember. By the time he came along, she was deep in The Life. Her husband had been gone a long time ago."

"Yeah, guess so." Sal nodded.

"So are you gonna send him back down to the shelter?" asked Jan.

"He doesn't want to go back there. That's what he was trying to tell us last night," Rasheeda replied.

"The only reason he was down at that park was because he was looking for my place. He had caught three buses from the shelter that day and got off the bus way down at Fifty-second and Elmwood. He had been walking around all day, trying to find me. He got hungry and had spent his carfare on hot dogs on Fifty-second Street. His mother didn't even know where he was."

Oh, Lord." Jan shook her head.

"So what you gone do?" Sally asked.

"I honestly don't know, Sal. We really don't have the room or the budget for one more right now, but how could I turn him away?" Rasheeda's eyes flared suddenly. "That damn James! This is his only sister. He knew she was sick. He's the only other blood relative this boy's got, and he hasn't done a damn thing."

Her tone softened. "I guess I'm gonna have to call him and beg him to do the right thing by the child."

Rasheeda sounded like she would rather drink muddy water and sleep in a hollow log.

"Do me a favor, Roach. Hold off on that for a minute," Janice interrupted. "Just where is this shelter, anyway?"

"All the way up in Germantown. Why?"

"Could we go up there tonight to see Dottie?"

"Well, I guess we could. But why?" Rasheeda said slowly. "I already told Dottie we'd keep him here till we could figure out something."

"All right, this is Saturday. You do that. When I come in on Monday, we'll talk about it again."

Rasheeda nodded and looked over at Sally, who shrugged her shoulders, equally puzzled. Jan obviously had something on her mind, Rasheeda thought.

She just hoped Jan had some kind of solution.

"I swear to God, Jan. You ever seen her wearin sandals in the summertime? I swear, them claws be hangin over the front of them sandals, tappin on the ground. Bunions settin up there like rams' horns. Swear to God."

"Get the hell outta here, Sal."

Janice was laughing so hard, she had to cover her mouth to keep from spitting beer all over the Devil's bar.

It was a week and a half after their meeting at the Oasis, and the two JGs were sitting in the Devil, drinking beer and talking shit. As usual, Sally was busting on Bad Tooth Shirley.

"I swear, Jan, sound like she got steel taps on her sandals, but it ain't no taps. It's them damn dinosaur feet! Bitch be lookin like Barney about the feet and shit, Jan. I ain't lyin."

Jan howled. Shirley cut her eye at them from down at the other end of the bar, but kept on working.

"Sally Mae, you ought to be ashamed of yourself, yall having the same grandchild. You know, you're going to have to get over your hatred of the girl, if only for Doll's sake."

"I know, I know. I'm tryin to, in my mind, Jan. I really am. I just like fuckin wit her, that's all. I even let Omar take Doll over there now sometimes. Well, not that I can *let* him do anything. The boy got his own mind, do anything he want. I'm a just quit tryin to tell him anything."

"Well, that's good. It's a start. Yall heard anything about where Shirley's daughter is these days?"

"Don't nobody know. You think she would at least call to check in on her own chile, but like Dottie say, once that crack got you, it's got you, I guess." Sal shook her head.

"So how's everything workin out so far?" Sally was eager to change the subject.

"It's working," Jan answered.

On the Sunday following the meeting at the Oasis, Jan called Rasheeda and outlined a plan. After she had finished, there was a moment of silence on the line.

"Are you sure, Janice?" Rasheeda finally replied, her voice colored with doubt.

"Well, it wouldn't hurt to check it out, see how things are," said Jan.

"Let me call Sally Mae and run it by her, and we can meet tomorrow at your place again, closing time. I think it could work," she added, sounding more like she was trying to convince herself, rather than Rasheeda.

That Monday evening, the JGs met at seven, talked awhile, and by 9:30, they were at the Germantown Hospice for Women, which was housed in an old former junior high school.

They had expected it to be tough, but Sally and Rasheeda were struck dumb by the sight of these women, about forty of them or so, in various stages of the dreaded disease. Their ages ranged from the youngest, a sixteen-year-old runaway, to the oldest, a fifty-eight-year-old former heroin user.

These women of all ages, all races, shared one thing in common: They were all living with a killer that had invaded their bodies, but nonetheless, still holding on for dear life.

The place was clean and neatly kept, but the heavy odor of anti-septics and disinfectants combined could not mask that smell, that death smell. It seemed to cling to the very walls of the place, seeping in from beneath the floorboards clear on up to the rafters.

Dottie was waiting for them in the lobby, a large living room–like area, painted in bright, cheerful pastels. Small groups of people dotted the large space, parents, relatives, and friends of the residents, even a few husbands and lovers. Children were everywhere.

"Rachael, Rachael! Over here!" Dottie yelled, waving from a sofa on the far side of the room. Rasheeda stood at the entrance for a moment, stunned into silence, remembering the once-robust flygirl with the Coke-bottle figure, until Janice poked her in the ribs.

"Dot." Rasheeda moved forward and crossed the room, gathering Dottie in her arms. They held on to each other for a few moments, and when they separated, both women were crying.

"Sit down, sit down," Dottie gestured, pulling a Kleenex from the pocket of her white terry-cloth bathrobe and wiping her eyes.

"You probably don't remember, but you met Sally Mae and Janice at my wedding." Rasheeda indicated the JGs, as they sat in the comfortable chairs, pulling them into a semicircle around Dottie. Dot nodded and smiled all around.

Jan leaned over and grabbed her by the hand. "Glad to see you again, sista."

She enclosed Dottie's frail, weak hand in both her strong ones. Dot blinked, startled. She had purposely not offered her hand, knowing how paranoid some people still were about contagion from AIDS. The other residents were the same way. All waited first for a hand to be extended to them before they offered theirs. It hurt too much if that offer was rejected, if the person shrank away from their touch.

Sal followed Jan's lead, reaching over to shake Dottie's hand. The women talked awhile. Dottie explained that she had been living with the HIV virus for the last four years, which had then developed into full-blown AIDS two years ago. She told them how she had had a home health worker come to her apartment each day to care for her, but that she herself had grown too ill to care for JayRon.

"He a big boy. You know how boys are when they get that age. I can't run behind him or make sure he go to school or nothin. I was gettin SSI for myself and a welfare check and food stamps for him, but I ain't have no money for no baby-sitter or nothin."

"Well, do you want us to try to contact his father?" Rasheeda asked softly.

Dottie snorted. "His father? Get real. Now, who would that be, Rachael?" Dottie wiped her eyes again. "You know how I was back in the day. Now, I ain't proud to say that, but hey, there it is." She shrugged.

"He hates it here. Hates it. I wrote to James, and he never even answered my letters. Called him and he had got his number changed. It's unlisted now."

She looked down at her hands, gnarled and withered like those of an old woman.

"Rachael, you know my Mickey already dead, and Rhonda doin time, got the same thing. And now, lil JayRon—

"I know I did a lot of wrong in my life, so I guess it's just time for me to pay up for my sins. But my right hand to God, Rachael, I never expected my kids to suffer so bad for what I done."

One tear fell from Dot's dark, thin face, dropped down her cheek and splattered against her hand.

"Well, that's what we came up here to see you about," Jan said. She took a deep breath. "How would you like to come and stay with me? You and JayRon?"

Dottie looked at her, then at Rasheeda, who was nodding and smiling.

"Dot, Janice is one of my oldest and dearest friends. So is Sally here. Jan's got a big old house with plenty of room. I live less than three blocks away from her, so I could come by and see you all the time, and you could have the home health aide come in the daytime."

Rasheeda was talking rapidly, her words rushing together, though she didn't know why. This had been Jan's suggestion, after all. Both she and Sally had tried to reason with her. Did she know what she would be getting herself into, taking in a woman she didn't even really know, a woman dying of AIDS, a woman with a son who had tried to rob her less than a week ago?

Jan had set her jaw stubbornly.

"Listen, I've been thinking and thinking on this, ever since Saturday night. You know, my mom used to say that sometimes in the middle of a crisis, God sends you an opportunity. Just—how long was it, two months ago, I was ready to pack it in. I was actually praying for death. And I might be gone right now, if it wasn't for Peaches. Peaches dying, as bad as that was, brought you two back into my life, and I'm here to tell you, you guys saved my life! Yall came to bat for me, stepped right up to the plate, and swung! Yall saved my life."

Jan swallowed hard.

"Okay, so now here I am, sittin up in that big old house, just me and Shaft, and here it is again. More trouble, more crisis. I can't explain to you why, but somehow, I just know it's my turn now to step to the plate."

Jan's eyes searched Sally's, then Rasheeda's. "I've got to make this leap, yall, on faith. And I know what I'm doing. After all, it's not like it was the first time."

And it was as simple as that. Within a week, Dottie and JayRon were living with Janice. The JGs had gone to work, cutting through the typical red tape, had had the welfare caseworker and SSI people notified to have Dottie's check, medical card, and food stamps sent to Jan's address, and had JayRon registered at Stanton Elementary, their old alma mater. Just like that.

CHAPTER 21

RACHAEL, ROACH, RASHEEDA

Give us one more, Tookie," Sally Mae yelled down the bar.

"Anything for you, Dollface." Tookie, who had replaced Shirley behind the bar, flashed his gold-toothed smile.

"Well, I'm glad to hear everything's workin out for yall, Jan."

"Yeah, well, I'm glad, too. Dottie's really no trouble to take care of, what with the home health aide coming every day, and the Meals-on-Wheels people bringing her lunch. I make breakfast for everybody, and JayRon makes his own sandwiches for lunch.

"I bring her downstairs in the mornings when she's up to it, and sometimes she stays downstairs all day. JayRon's been no problem so far. He's so happy to be out of that shelter and have his mama with him. He really is devoted to her, you know."

"Yeah, I noticed when I was over there how he was runnin around, fetchin stuff for her, and tryin to make her comfortable. That's nice." Sal nodded.

"And you know, Sally, I didn't realize how lonely I was until they came. That woman is so full of stories, girl."

"I'm hip." Sally nodded. "You know, I ain't really expect to like her, to tell you the truth. Now, don't get me wrong. It wasn't the prostitution part. If the only thing you got to sell is yo ass, and times is tight, you sell yo ass, that's all. You feed yo kids."

"It was the drugs, wasn't it?" Jan asked, glancing at Sally Mae through the smoky mirror of the Devil.

"It was the drugs. I just can't see nobody throwin away they whole life for no damn drugs." Sal snorted.

"Ha! Look who's talkin. I suppose that reefer you've been smokin since the sixties ain't drugs, huh?"

"Now, wait a minute. That's different. Marijuana comes straight from the ground, the same ground the food we eat comes from. It's a natural thing," Sally answered defensively.

"Yeah, yeah, yeah, but it's still a drug, Sal. I don't care what you say."

"Yeah, well, it ain't no chemicals in it."

"It's still a drug, and it can lead to stronger things. That's how people get started, you know."

"Oh, come on, Jan. Like you say, I been smokin since the sixties, and you ain't never seen me goin to the stronger stuff."

"Well, I guess people choose their own poison." Jan sighed, looking down at her vodka and orange juice. "Speaking of Dottie, remind me to get her a six-pack of Bud before we leave out of here tonight. I promised her I'd pick it up for her."

"A six-pack? You buyin beer for a sick woman on medication? Janice, are you crazy?"

"No, Sally Mae, I am not crazy. Dottie's not just a sick woman, she's a dying woman, so what the hell difference does it make at this point?"

"Yeah, I guess you right. You know, I can't get over that girl saying she was makin at least seventy-five thousand dollars a year back in the

day, between boostin and flatbackin, before she got on that pipe and
lost every dime choosing to get high. That ain't no chump change.
"Seventy-five thousand dollars! Damn! That's a whole lotta dicks, ain't
it, chile? *Ooooweee!*"

"Girl, you are so crazy," Janice sputtered, almost spitting out her
drink. They were laughing so hard, the other patrons at the Devil
looked over at them, these two attractive forty-something women
who always seemed so deep in conversation.

"Girl, don't tell me that's Juan Jenkins down there on that bar
stool." Janice was staring through the mirror at a tall, emaciated figure
nursing a beer at the far end of the bar.

"Indeed so. Old Fine Wine. Remember when we used to call him
that?" Sally nodded.

"Damn, he used to be one pretty man," said Jan. "Ruthie Bolton used
to be crazy about him, would have died and gone to hell for Fine Wine."

"Sho would, now. It's that her-on done him in. Caught up in the
web, and he can't break free."

Sally and Janice were doing some serious gossiping now.

"Somebody must have told him Ruthie stepped through here the
other night. That's probably why he up in here, hopin he can still
work that old Black magic on girlfriend," Sally said, lowering her
voice. "She layin low. You know her and that Rasta man she so crazy
bout now jumped bail down in New Orleans."

"Jumped bail? Ruthie? Ruthie, the real estate queen? Get the hell
outta here, Sally Mae."

"Swear to God. Her sister say the po-lice come to their place down
there one night wit a search warrant, and they had drugs and guns up
in there. Once she got hooked up wit him, she lost everything, all
them houses she had worked so hard to buy, everything, all chasing
behind that so-called Rasta."

"Well, I can't understand it." Jan shook her head in disbelief. "I
mean, Ruth was always so serious-minded. Always working, saving, buying property, renting it out. How many buildings did she
have?"

"Five or six, at least. She learned how to do that workin for that white man, Stockman, up on Arch Street. Girl had three properties before she was thirty years old. She the one helped me get my place."

"And she lost them all, every one?"

"From what I hear, she did. She stayin over on Baltimore Avenue in an apartment now." Sal shook her head sadly.

"Still with the Rasta man?"

"Yup. You know it, chile."

"Oh, Lord. I just don't get it. The boy wasn't but bout twenty-one, twenty-two when she hooked up with him, right? Ruthie got bout fifteen years on the kid. How could she throw everything away behind some pot smokin, gun-carryin young boy?" asked Jan.

"Well, like she told me, it was that thang." Sal leaned back on her barstool.

"What thang?"

"The sex, girl, the big *O*, or maybe it was the big *D*." Sally laughed. "Now, she ain't come right out and say, 'Sal, it's the sex,' but she let me know in so many words. You know Ruthie been married and divorced, had a few boyfriends, including Fine Wine, but she told me in all them years, she never had nobody satisfy her like that Rasta man. Took the chile damn near forty years to find somebody to lay it on her right. It was that thang, chile. You know how that thang can make you do." Sal snickered.

"Damn! So you think she's a slave to the sex, huh?" Jan asked.

"Slave? I think sistergirl is absolutely, positively, one hundred percent dickwhipped." Sal howled, nudging Janice in the ribs.

This time Jan did spit her drink all over the bar.

"Yeah, guess so. Too bad it's with the wrong man," she replied, trying to clean off the bar with her paper napkin.

"Dig it. But did you notice how fast Roach changed the subject when Dottie was askin her how her and Hakim met?" Sally nudged Jan again.

"I'm hip, I'm hip! Talkin about, 'Oh, we were just old acquaintances. Girl, I had to turn my head away, so Dottie wouldn't see me laughing." Jan grinned.

"You know Roach wasn't bout to give up the tapes to that woman."

"I know it, and you know it, too," agreed Sal.

Rasheeda sure wasn't going to tell Dottie the truth about Hakim. No way. Not that she had anything to be ashamed of, but the truth was just too weird, too unbelievable, the kind of thing that only happened on the *Late, Late Show.*

Rachael had become a Muslim in her heart the day she met the sisters in the maternity ward when her sons were born. She had read all the literature they had left for her, and struck up a friendship with Sister Kareema, her hospital roommate.

By the time she left the hospital with her beautiful twin boys, she had made the decision to learn all she could about this fascinating religion, new to her but old as time. She had tried to explain her feelings to James, and at first he had been indulgent, thinking it was just some sort of phase she was going through.

But it was no phase. As Rachael studied and attended services at the local Masjid, all the spaces that the Catholic religion had left empty in her soul slowly began to fill up. This faith was about her, about people of color, every color, all over the world. No white statues to kneel before, no white God to look up to, but multicultural, many-hued, embracing all who believed. This was the faith of Malcolm, and it filled her heart and soul with light.

As time passed, she knew she could no longer stay with James, whose earlier indulgence had now turned to sneering disdain. They simply could not communicate.

The children had changed her priorities. His world was about money, power, position, and the benefits each could bring.

Hers was about love, family, community, children, and faith.

She couldn't see bringing her boys up in the environment they lived in, where prestige and material things mattered more than anything she held dear. Having her children around people doing drugs and alcohol was too high a price to pay for her. So after eleven years of marriage, she had ended it, ended their life together.

James thought she was crazy.

Rachael, Rasheeda now, had returned to Philadelphia with her boys to live again with her mother. She had already been put in contact with the neighborhood Masjid, and they had begun attending services there.

One Saturday afternoon, about six months after her return, Rasheeda went to a wedding for one of the sisters at the Masjid. As she watched the happy couple at the reception, she felt a pair of eyes on her. She turned shyly and met the brother's steady gaze, and he nodded soberly. She did the same.

Being new to the group, she was, of course, of some interest to the single brothers in the Masjid, and some had already made polite advances. After all, she was still as pretty as ever. But Rasheeda was also still legally married to James, and although the divorce process was in motion, she really didn't desire another man at this point in her life. But there was something about this one, something familiar. Rasheeda turned her head quickly back to the couple, not looking in the man's direction again. As her life began to revolve more and more around her Muslim community, she found herself in the presence of the same brother on a regular basis. She knew his name was Hakim, that he was divorced, and that he owned the Oasis, which at that time was just a small grocery store selling Halal meats and fresh vegetables and juices. He was always the same, always smiled and nodded, but never made a move toward her.

One summer afternoon, she was walking past the Oasis with the boys. Hakim was standing in the doorway.

"Afternoon, Sister Rasheeda," he said, smiling, as she passed.

"Afternoon, Brother Hakim," Rasheeda spoke, passing quickly.

"Rasheeda! Wait up."

Rasheeda turned. She was already about five or six stores past his, but something about the way he called her name made her heart jump.

Hakim ambled up to her.

"You really don't remember me, do you?" he asked. He looked deadly serious, the smile now gone.

"I—I don't know," she answered honestly, studying his face up close now, or as much as she could make out behind a face almost obscured by the heavy beard, the tinted glasses, the mustache, the thick, beautiful dreadlocks winding in all directions. There was something, something about the eyes, the smile—

"I thought you looked familiar when I first saw you in the Masjid, but—"

"I should look familiar." Hakim cut her words off. He bit his lip, cleared his throat. "I almost raped you once," he said softly.

Rasheeda blinked, saying nothing. She grabbed the boys' hands a little tighter.

Hakim took a deep breath, sighed. "Back in the day, a lifetime ago, I used to be known as Danny."

Rasheeda swallowed hard. Her eyes widened.

Why, of course, it was Danny. Same smile, same sparkling eyes. She felt the blood rushing up into her cheeks, thinking back to that long-ago day on the sofa, the music, the vodka. It was as if it had happened yesterday. She struggled for composure.

"Oh" was the only sound that came from her mouth.

"And I want to say I'm sorry."

She looked at him sharply, trying to spot a joke on his face, in his eyes, on his lips, but no. He seemed sincere.

"I've been Muslim now for about twelve years, and a lot of times over those years, I thought about the way I used to treat women, what I was doin with you, among other things. And I'm sorry."

Rasheeda looked into his eyes again, seeing nothing but sorrow and regret. "Yeah, well, we were just kids then, Brother Hakim," she found herself saying." That was then. This is now."

Oh, God, now she sounded like she was being flip, she thought to herself, still trying to digest this information.

But Hakim nodded as if he understood. He then invited her and the boys into the shop for some cold lemonade, showed her around, telling her about his rebirth into Islam, his divorce from his non-Muslim wife, trying to show her how he had turned his life around.

He joked with the boys, treating them to homemade ice cream. Rasheeda took it all in.

Presently when she rose to leave, Hakim grabbed her gently by the arm.

"You always was a nice girl, but even if you wasn't, I shouldn't have tried to take advantage of you like that," he said solemnly.

"Brother Hakim, it's over. You've moved on, and so have I." She smiled at him then for the first time and, gathering up her twins, said good-bye and left.

That's the way it started. The next time Rasheeda attended the Masjid, Hakim offered her a ride home. And the next. Presently, they began to talk about themselves, to open up to each other.

Finally, he persuaded Rasheeda to come and work for him in the Oasis on a part-time basis. And that's the way it went. Exactly one week after Rasheeda's divorce from James was finalized, exactly one year, six months, and three days after their conversation on Fifty-second Street, Rasheeda and Hakim, a.k.a. Rachael and Danny, were married.

Rape? Well, maybe. Maybe not.

Rachel had been every bit as willing as Danny that day. And if it hadn't been for the intervention of Peaches, who knows what would have happened?

All Rasheeda knew was when Jan and Sally Mae had relayed the story about Ruthie Bolton and the Rasta man to her, in an instinctive way, she had understood completely. Ruthie was following behind that thang.

It had been the same for her. Being Muslim, she and Hakim had not had sex until their wedding night. But from the moment he had first leaned over and kissed her in the pickup following their third or fourth real date, that thrill had shot straight through her body, down to her toes, and back up to her hairline, just as it had on their now-legendary day on the sofa.

It was still there; that touch, after all these years, still left her jangly and weak in the knees. He took her breath away.

And on their wedding night, she couldn't help but compare the slender, strong body of the young Danny to the full, hard-muscled masculinity of the now-matured Hakim. The feel, the size, the smell of him. That small, telltale mole, just below the left side of his throat, just as she remembered it. Waiting to be kissed, again and again. And finally, finally, here it was, the big *O!* Just as the JGs had told her it would be, just as she knew it could be. A long-ago promise made by his body to hers, now fulfilled.

Rasheeda felt truly blessed. And though she felt a little sorry for Ruthie Bolton, she understood perfectly why she was so willing to follow that Rasta to the ends of the earth, and well beyond, if necessary. It was that thang!

Rape? Maybe. Maybe not.

CHAPTER 22

MUSTANG SALLY

Okay, now's the time, Ms. Washington. Now's the time." Jan clinked her spoon against her glass.

"What time?" Sally squirmed uncomfortably in her seat. She turned and looked around. The JGs were seated around Jan's kitchen table.

"Aw, don't even be looking around. Dottie and JayRon are upstairs watching TV, and I've got the stereo on. Nobody can hear us."

"Yeah, Sal. Give it up. Give up the tapes," Rasheeda added. "Nobody here but us chickens."

The JGs were having their last meeting before Sally Mae's departure to California for her hearing. They had already spoken to Red and done everything they could about Jan's and Rasheeda's cases.

Now, they sat, Great Western Champagne and Martinelli's Cider on the table before them, waiting to hear an explanation from Sal, who sat drumming her fingers on the table.

"Oh, all right, all right! Damn," she finally responded.

"This is the deal." Sal pulled up her chair.

She began her story in fits and starts, but after a couple of more champagnes with peaches, her tongue began to loosen up. She told them all about when she and Kenny had gone to Cali, how they had lived happily for almost five years before falling in with the revolutionaries and Kenny's death, which they already knew about, anyway.

"Okay, okay, stop." Jan raised her hands. "First, how come you didn't come up here for Kenny's funeral?"

Sal lit another cigarette, took a deep drag. "Cause I couldn't afford to. I was pregnant, and I ain't have no money. That's why," she answered curtly.

"What about your aunt and uncle? What about Kenny's people?" Rasheeda pressed. This was something Sally never talked about, and they had never pushed the issue. But now, they wanted the whole story, not the bits and pieces they usually got from Sal.

"Don't you think I asked them, Roach? My aunt and uncle never gave me no extra money, never. Yall know that. Yall remember how hard I had to work just for school clothes and every lil extra I ever wanted. Hell, they really didn't even want me around. They had to take me in, cause I came with my grandmother. And Kenny's people disapproved of him bein wit me from the jump. Thought I was too Black, too nappy headed, and definitely too country for they high-toned, high-yella family," Sally fairly shouted, blinking rapidly.

Rasheeda, fair skinned herself, winced when Sal said "high-toned, high-yella." She knew her friend wasn't directing these hateful words toward her.

But still.

"Don't you think I wanted to be here? I didn't get back here for two whole years! Yall remember! And when I finally got back, the first thing I had to do was call them mothafuckas up to find out where my own goddamn man was buried."

Sal stopped, poured herself another glass of wine, mixed in the canned peaches.

"And when I went to Kenny's grave out there in Mount Lawn, don't you know I wanted to lie down on that grave, girl, swear to God, lie down and catch that dirt up in my fingers. I wanted to bury my face in it, smell it, taste it, try to squeeze Kenny up from outta that damn ground and take him home with me."

Tears were now streaming down Sally's face unchecked, as she continued. "You think you the only one that lost somebody, Jan? You think you the only one that would have made a deal with the devil himself, if only he could bring yo man back to life? You think I didn't want us to grow old together, with kids and dogs and flowers and herbs in my garden? Even now, I still dream about that sometimes, me and Kenny, old and gray with our teeth in a glass jar, rockin side by side, with our kids and grandkids all around us. Even now. So you ain't got no premium on grief, Miss Girl. You ain't even special."

Sal stood up from the table, pointing to her chest. "And to this day, Kenny is the only man I have ever truly loved, the only one. You know, he would be forty-four years old now. I met him when I was eighteen, and I still love him just as much today as I did then. You ain't even the only one. But I couldn't afford to set around grievin. I was gettin ready to have a baby, and I would have to take care of that baby, me, nobody else. My gramma, my only real family, was gone, and my husband's family didn't even want to accept me, much less my chile, as they own. Seem like they blamed me for the whole thing, us leavin town, Kenny's death, everything."

Sally Mae was pacing the kitchen floor now, back and forth, back and forth, furiously smoking. "So I went on welfare, just till I had the baby. But that didn't work for me. Too lil money and too much humiliation. Then I started cookin in the bar. Still not enough for two people to live on."

"Why didn't you call us, Sal?" Rasheeda asked softly.

"Oh, I don't know, Roach. I mean, there I was halfway cross the country, and we had lost touch and all, and well, I really didn't know what to do. I know I never felt so alone in my life," Sal made a help-less gesture.

"Well, what did you do then?"

Sal stopped pacing. She placed both hands on her hips and chuckled. "What did I do then? Well, then I became Mustang Sally." She grinned through her tear-streaked face.

Jan and Rasheeda looked at Sal, at each other, then back to Sal again.

"Yeah, yeah, just like the song. I took up dancin for money. Now, yall know I always could dance my ass off. Well, I was cookin at the Fox Box and livin in a lil room over top of—"

"Wait a minute, wait a minute. The what?" Jan was trying not to laugh.

"Fuck you, Janice. The Fox Box, okay? That was the name of—"

She was interrupted by gales of laughter from Jan and Rasheeda, and despite herself, she soon joined in.

"Well, I guess they had to call it somethin. Anyway, as I was sayin, I was already livin and workin at . . . the bar, so I seen where I could make three, sometimes four times as much money dancin on the stage than what they was payin me to cook in that lil hot-ass kitchen."

Jan and Rasheeda exchanged glances again, but did not interrupt. Sally Mae, the liberated women's-rights champion, dancing in a bar?

"I know what yall thinkin, but I'm a tell you somethin. Dancin paid me the best money I ever made in my life, and gave me the most independence. When you been livin poor for a while, and you finally start makin yo own money, good money, you ain't got to take no shit from nobody. Not no landlord, not no welfare worker, not no half-steppin man. Nobody."

Sal glared at Jan and Rasheeda, daring them with her eyes to disagree. They said nothing.

"Sheeit, if I'd a stayed wit the dancin, I'd a done all right. Me and Omar would have been just fine. But nooo, I had to get greedy. I tell yall, it was greed. Greed is what got me in the mess I'm in now."

"Greed? Greed for what?" Rasheeda asked.

"For money. For things. Fine cars, beautiful clothes, nice houses," Sally Mae said, shaking her head.

"But, Sally, out of all of us, you never seemed to care that much about material things," Jan responded.

"Yeah, well, that was before I had a child to raise all by myself. Kids change things in a big way, you know."

"Touché." Rasheeda nodded.

"I had been workin steady at the Fox Box—yeah, I know, go head and laugh. Anyway, I was pullin down some good bread and tips, bankin almost every dime, cause me and Omar was still livin in that room over top the bar, and even though everybody was real nice to us and all the other dancers spoiled him rotten, I wanted us to have a place of our own."

"Well, that doesn't sound so greedy to me, wanting a place for your baby and—"

"Naw, I ain't talkin bout that. That came later. Anyway, Omar had just started walkin, and I was scared to death he might wander out in the hallway and fall down the steps. So I was steady savin my dollars. I was even thinkin bout goin back to school. Just around the time I had saved enough to start lookin for a decent place in a decent neighborhood, I met Charley Favor."

"Charley Favor?" Jan frowned. The name sounded familiar.

"Yeah, you might remember him from way back. He played pro football here and in California and a coupla other places."

"*Ahh,* yes. Used to be up on the Strip, used to hang out at Mr. Silk's." Jan nodded.

"Yeah, but didn't he get—"

"Killed? Yeah, that's the one," Sal answered, sitting back down.

"He used to come in the Fox Box, too, when I was dancin there. I knew the man had eyes for me and all, always stuffin big bills down my G-string, gettin all up in my boobs and all, but so did a lot of guys. I ain't pay the man no mind."

"G-string? Oh, no, Sally." Rasheeda laughed, trying to picture Sally Mae as a go-go girl.

"Oh, hell, yeah." Sal beamed, in spite of herself. "I was da bomb. I was a star, honey. Had the mens' jaws droppin, and they eyes poppin."

"Lord, have mercy." Jan looked heavenward.

"Anyway, like I say, Charley used to come in the Fox Box and flirt with me alla time. He'd walk in dressed like a million bucks, flashin a lotta gold, fannin his money in front of him on the bar and shit. All the girls played up to him. Like I said, he was a big tipper. I still ain't pay him no mind. He seemed like a clown to me, dressed up in all that ole Superfly shit. I mean, I was workin as a dancer shakin my butt and all, but I was still me. I still read books, still kept up wit what was goin down politically. I was not impressed by a bunch of shiny stuff. Them gold chains looked like slave shackles to me.

"As far as I was concerned, I was there to make money, as a means to an end. I planned on gettin out of that lifestyle as soon as I had enough money for me and my boy.

"Now, I swear, I wasn't tryin to play the dude. Well, not at first. But for some reason, the less attention I paid to him, the more he paid to me. He started tippin me bigger and bigger, started sendin me champagne, which you know I just turned right around and sold back to the bar later on."

Jan and Rasheeda nodded. It was an old barmaid's trick, and it worked for two reasons: one, you stayed sober, and two, you made a little extra money to put in your pocket.

"Finally, he asked me out. I turned him down. He asked again, and again. The other dancers started tellin me I was a fool not to go out wit him, you know? 'Girl, you still young and fine. You better use it now while you still got it, cause it don't last all that long,' as Topaz used to say."

"Topaz?" Rasheeda queried.

"Yeah, Topaz. She was one of the older dancers at the Box. I swear to God, yall, forty-five years old and could give any twenty-year-old a run for they money. Mama was all that. Anyhow, I told her the man just wasn't my type. Besides, I was in there tryin to make some money to take me and my boy outta there. I wasn't even lookin at no man, what with Kenny barely cold in the ground.

"Topaz say 'Sheeit! Ain't yo type? You ain't got no husband, no man, and a baby to raise. Girl, you cain't *afford* to have no fuckin type. Yo type ought to be whoever got the money to pay.'

"But I was makin money my own self, and I told her that.

"She say, 'Sheeit! That man spends more in tips in one night than what it take you a whole week to make. You say you want a nice place fo you and yo boy to stay, you want to go back to school, you want to spend time wit Omar? That nigga live out in the Valley, got a swimmin pool, got a maid, everything.'

"She was right. Everybody knew Charley had it goin on. But still. Then Topaz say, 'If you play it just right, you and yo boy could be livin good. You could go back to school, send your kid to a good school and everything.'

"Well, that time I really listened to Topaz. I thought hard about my situation. Workin and savin alla damn time, never goin no damn where, never havin any real life outside the bar. And for what? Even if I got us a nice apartment, then I'd have to hire a baby-sitter to stay wit Omar while I worked. And if I went back to school, I'd have practically no time at all to spend wit my son. I thought about the way Charley threw money round the bar like it was water, and that's when the greed first started to kick in. Hell, why shouldn't I have some of that money, since the fool obviously wanted to give it away so bad?

"I decided to follow Topaz's advice and play this fool for all I could get. Yeah, fool. That's the way I saw him. He was too loud, too overdressed, too country, even more country than me, had gold teeth wit big ole diamonds in em, wearin fur coats and them big ole hats wit feathers on em and shit. Fur coats in Cali! Chile, it was too much.

"Now, I'm not tryin to make excuses for myself, but I swear, it was almost like he was beggin me to take him off, showin up night after night with flowers and lil gifts, just dyin to get wit me. So I played him, played him like monopoly. I ain't lyin. The more I resisted him, the more he came after me. The more unimpressed I acted with the places he took me, the more he tried to impress me.

"He begged me to quit workin and come live wit him. I refused. He paid for me to get my teeth fixed, paid for an expensive nursery school for Omar. I showed just a lil bit of appreciation. Hell, I was still dancin, still makin good money at the Box, and he knew it. Then he took to buyin me some real expensive stuff.

"Girl, that man bought me a white mink fur, a ruby ring, and finally, a candy-apple-red Mustang. Pretty soon I was ridin around Cali in my white fur coat with the top down. That's when I really became Mustang Sally."

"Get outta here, Sally." Rasheeda laughed, waving her hand. This was too much.

"You don't believe me? Hold up, hold up." Sal raised her hand. She got up, went into Jan's living room, and returned with a large plastic bag, from which she extricated a photo album. She sat back down, opened the book, and began flipping through it.

"There," Sal said, pointing triumphantly. "That's Mustang Sally."

Jan and Rasheeda inched closer to her and looked down at the album. There, on page after page, was Sal, although this was an entirely different woman from the Sal they knew.

"Oh, no," whispered Rasheeda.

"Mercy," said Jan.

It was Sally, lying across the hood of a red Mustang convertible, wearing a short, tight, red dress.

One leg was crossed over the other at the knee, with a shiny red-patent high-heel shoe dangling from the end of her foot. Fanning out underneath her body was a luxurious white fur coat, covering the hood of the car.

There was a shot of Mustang Sally onstage, a long Tina Turner wig framing her face, her body in full movement. She was wearing nothing but a silver-and-red G-string and matching pasties on her high, full breasts, and black patent-leather boots.

There was another of her straddling the head of a man who appeared to be seated at a bar, still another of her swinging around a pole, Tina-hair flying wild, paper bills stuck into her G-string like an oversized green money belt.

Jan and Rasheeda flipped through all the pages.

There were shots of some of the other dancers, some of Sally holding a smiling baby Omar up to the camera, and a some of her alone. In a few of the snapshots, Sally was accompanied by a tall, large chocolate brown man wearing a smile with red diamonds shining in the centers of his gold front teeth.

"See? Told you," Sal crowed.

Janice and Rasheeda were simply astounded.

"Chile, I was da bomb."

After Jan had poured herself a full glass of wine and refilled Rasheeda's cider, they both took large gulps, then looked at Sally Mae again, as if seeing their friend for the first time.

"You know, Sal, I'm almost afraid to ask, but what happened next?" Rasheeda asked.

Sal downed her pagne and poured another, mixing in the peaches and syrup slowly. She lit another smoke.

"What happened was I let Charley and greed win me over, and me and Omar moved in wit him. It was that red Mustang that done it." Sal shrugged. "That tore it. Like I told yall, it was the greed."

"Okay, okay, we got your point. And then what?" Jan asked impatiently.

"And then—then he got killed."

The JGs talked far into the night, as Sal finally gave up the tapes, told it all, bared her soul to a shocked and shaken Jan and Rasheeda.

The next morning, Sally Mae sat at the window seat on the train, waving good-bye to Omar.

"Seems like you've been doing this all my life," he had said, just before she boarded Amtrak.

It was true. She had been leaving him one place after another since he was five years old. But this time, it was him and Doll.

"But I always come back, don't I?" She had tried to smile and tickle the cleft in his chin, so like Kenny's.

This time, he was having none of it. His eyes, brown and blazing, held sadness, and something else, a sharp glint of anger, of accusation. Sally turned away quickly, mentally running through the checklist of events that had occurred the evening before.

After she had confessed all to the JGs, they had surprised her.

"We thought you might be needing a lil something, so we—" Rasheeda had stammered, handing Sal a roll of bills.

"Aw, come on, yall. I can't—"

"Oh, girl, take the damn money and shut the hell up," Jan had clucked impatiently.

After hugging and thanking them profusely, she had slipped back home to call Malcolm Merritt once more. "I think I'm ready to go, Malcolm," Sal said, when he picked up the receiver.

"About time you called back," he scolded. "I've been waiting all afternoon. You are one mysterious lady."

They talked for a while, discussing the case, who Sally was to see when she arrived in Los Angeles, their legal strategy, and she assured him she would call him to let him know where she was staying as soon as she got to California.

"I just don't understand why you have to leave on a Friday morning, when your hearing isn't until next Tuesday," he said.

Sal said nothing.

"And you're not going to tell me, either, are you?"

Still nothing.

"All right, all right. I guess you know what you're doing." Malcolm gave up.

"I hope so," Sal spoke at last. "I'll check in with you again the day before the hearing."

"You can check in with me anytime you want, Sally Mae. I'm always available. For you."

"Uh, yeah, well—okay." There it was again. Was this brother giving out signals or what?

Sally Mae willed herself not to think of him, of that bald head and slow smile, of the eyes that had made her swoon. She didn't have time to think about it now. She was too busy pondering the odd conversation she had had the night before. She had already taken time off from her job at the rec center, and reluctantly packed some of Doll's little clothes and toys so she could stay with Shirley during the days, while Sally Mae was gone.

"And just how long do you spect that to be?" Bad Tooth had asked in her irritating manner.

Sally had hemmed and hedged her answer. She really had no idea.

"Oh, a few days, a week, maybe," she had said breezily, not letting her fear color her voice.

"Family emergency, huh?" Shirley pressed.

Nosy-ass bitch.

"Yeah, somethin like that."

Sal hung up as soon as she could and had just finished packing her own suitcase, when the phone rang.

"Sally Mae? It's Red."

"Oh, hi, Miss Red," she answered, puzzled. Now what?

"Girl, I done told you bout that Miss stuff. Anyway, we know you leavin in the mornin, and uh, DB want to talk to you fore you go."

"Well, Mi—Red, I'm kinda busy wit my packin now. What he want?"

"He just want to talk to you, chile," Red said softly.

"Okay, put him on."

"No. He don't want to talk over the phone. He want you to come over to the house."

Sally had reluctantly agreed to be there in an hour.

The whole thing was getting weirder and weirder. First, there was the second call last week where Bay Girl asked Sal to please, please come down to see her on the Friday before the hearing.

"If you don't have the money, I'll wire it to you," Bay had said.

"But why," Sal had asked. She hadn't even thought to ask Bay Girl how she even knew the hearing date.

"Because, like I said, I owe you one, and the payback is long overdue," Bay had answered cryptically.

Sally Mae had promised to try.

"Naw, naw, you got to do mo than try. You got to come on down."

Bay Girl wouldn't hang up until Sally definitely committed to meeting with her that Friday night.

The next morning, Western Union was on the phone, with news that the money had arrived from Georgia.

Well, Sal thought, she couldn't back out of it now.

She knew she had to go. Something, she didn't know what, but something was pulling her back home.

And now, here was Monsieur Daddy Baby, wanting to see her. Just what did he know, and how did he know it? Sal mused, as she grabbed her coat and bag on the way out the door.

"Ah, Miss Sally Mae. Set down and have a drink. Champagne?"

DB was all smiles as he gestured toward a chair across from where he was already seated. Sal nodded, sat.

Nettie had shown her right in, and they were on the first floor, seated in what appeared to be a den. Red Top was nowhere in sight.

DB watched Sally pour a healthy glass of pagne, mixing it with OJ and ice. He shook his head, smiling.

Sal took a long swallow, lit a cigarette, then sat back and returned his gaze. Those eyes, something about those eyes. She had to break the stare.

"What's this all about, Daddy Baby?" She spoke quickly, trying to focus on anything but his eyes, because whenever she looked at them, she seemed to hear singing.

Monsieur Daddy Baby cleared his throat, drumming his fingers on the arm of the chair. "I just wanted to make sure you had everything you needed for yo trip," he said pleasantly.

"Yes, I think I do, thank you," Sal nodded, her damp hands slipping around her glass.

"Cause if you need any money, or anything—" He spread his hands.

"No, I think I got enough."

Between what the JGs had given her and what Bay Girl had sent through the wire, together with what she already had, she figured she ought to make out all right.

"*Uhm-hmn*. An you leavin tomorrow mornin, huh?"

"Yes, sir. Omar's drivin me to the Thirtieth Street Station in the van."

"Omar, huh? That's a fine boy you got there, Miss Sally. Ain't too many young boys that would take on the responsibility of raisin they chile alone."

"Thank you. I know he is. He's willful and stubborn, but he's intelligent. And he's not alone. He's got me," Sally said proudly. She didn't know what she had done right in this life to be blessed with a child like Omar, but she thanked God for him every day.

"Oh, I know he do. I didn't mean it that way. I meant raisin the chile without no mama, that's all. Boy goin to college, workin, and everything. You should be right proud."

Monsieur Daddy Baby was beaming at her now, eyes twinkling like stars. The singing started again, just around the far corners of her mind.

"Oh, I am proud of him. But I know you ain't call me over here just to talk about my boy." Sal looked away, took another swig of pagne.

"No, no. I just wanted to make sure you was really gone catch that train to Georgia first." Monsieur Daddy Baby caught her eyes and held them in his, searching.

For what? What the fuck this ole man want to hear from her? She decided to play it straight. "Yes, sir. I should be in Georgia by tomorrow night, God willing."

Monsieur Daddy Baby leaned back in his chair, nodding. "Good."

"Is that all you wanted to know?"

"That's all I wanted to know."

Sal drained her glass, thanked him for his hospitality, determined not to give him the satisfaction of seeing the bewilderment she felt showing on her face.

She rose to leave. He waved.

"And, Sally Mae?"

Sal paused and looked at him again.

"Just keep in mind two things: Everybody makes mistakes, especially when they young. You, me, everybody." Monsieur Daddy Baby shrugged. This time, it was he who looked away.

"And?"

"And what?"

"You said two things. What's the other one?"

The singing now filled the room.

"And sometimes, it's better late than never. Trust me."

CHAPTER 23

JAN: THROWDOWN
NUMBER 1

ain't like you. I don't spend my time in the past, worshippin dead people an moonin over what might have been. If only this, if only that. Fuck that shit." Peaches spat the words out defiantly.

"An I don't give a damn about what's gone happen tomorrow, neither. What's happenin now, that's what I'm about, what's happenin today. And today, tonight, I'm in love with a sweet, sweet man, and I don't care who don't like it. I'm a hold on to it tight, with both hands."

This had been Jan's last conversation with Peaches. It had taken place about four months before Peaches's death, and it had gone very badly.

Peach had called Jan one afternoon, all excited, insisting Jan come over right away. Janice at the time had been sinking deeper and deeper into depression, and hadn't seen Peaches but once or twice since June Bug's funeral, but the urgency in her cousin's voice won over her curiosity.

When Jan arrived at Peach's apartment, Peaches hurriedly pulled her back into her bedroom, away from the children and grandchildren.

"What? What is it?" Jan asked.

"Guess what? I'm gettin married." Peach was literally jumping up and down with joy. She grabbed Jan by the hands and started spinning her around the room, as they had done when they were girls.

"Married? To who? When?" Jan sputtered.

"You'll never guess, not in a million years." Peach beamed, her eyes spinning in her head.

"Girl, I ain't got all day for this Twenty Questions shit. Come on. Who?"

"Griff," Peaches whispered, putting a finger to her mouth.

"Griff? I know you ain't talkin bout Griffin Hart?"

"Chill, Janice, not so loud," Peach shushed her, jerking her head toward the living room. "You know how thin these damn walls are."

"Peach, look at me," Jan spoke quietly.

"You ain't tryin to tell me you're marryin Griffin Hart, are you?"

Peach nodded her head up and down, a secret smile on her face. She held her left hand out, so Janice could see the small diamond ring on her finger.

"Girl, you done lost your mind. You've gone too far this time." Jan sat down on the bed.

"See, I knew you was gone say that, but I don't give a shit. I love him, and he loves me. He's good to me, do for me, gives me whenever he can. He's the best thing I had in a long, long time." Peach placed her hands on her hips. "And the sex be poppin, too." She laughed.

Jan dropped her head into the palm of her hand, closing her eyes. She looked up at Peach.

"I know you think I'm stupid, Jan. You always did. But I don't care."

Jan still said nothing. She was annoyed by the shine in Peaches's eyes, irritated by her girlish giggling.

Peaches had left Rome after years of physical abuse that had begun

early in their marriage, spurred on by the rumors that he was not
Kim's natural father. She had hung in there a long time, trying to keep
together the only real family she ever had, the one she had made for
herself. And there was the guilt, of course, from letting him think that
Chicken Wing's baby was his at the time of the marriage.

How could she still be so naive, Jan thought, incredulous. She'd
been battered, bruised, busted up, and yet, she still believed some man
was going to save her.

"You know you makin a fool outta yourself, now, don't you, actin
like some sixteen-year-old love-struck, schoolgirl?" Jan snapped
harshly, throwing the words at Peach like punches.

"How can you live to be this damn old and still actin like an ass-
hole? And you know what everybody's gone say about you and
Griff."

Jan took silent, smug satisfaction in the way her words wounded
Peaches, in wiping that silly grin off her face.

"You jealous," Peaches said quietly, after she had recovered.
"Always was."

"Jealous? Hah! Jealous of Griff? I know you're crazy now," Jan
said, snorting.

"No, not Griff. Me. Cause I got a life, and I got a man, and all you
got is death and memories," Peach retorted, empowered by love.
"Least I got that. Least I got my babies, my grands. I didn't kill my
babies. I had em, whether I could afford to or not," Peach sneered.

Jan recoiled. They were almost close enough now to touch noses,
this time without Sally Mae or Roach to referee. They stood toe-to-
toe, engaged in a serious stare-down contest for a few seconds. Jan
lost.

Secrets, secrets so shameful, buried so deep down in the soul that
even a second's thought, a whiff of memory, was like touching a hot
stove. Eyes filling with tears, she blinked rapidly, turned away, and
bolted for the door.

How could she? How could she say this to me?

That was the last time Janice had seen Peaches alive, and it had taken her a long time to admit that Peach had been right on the money.

She had been jealous of Peach's new love. Not of Griff, per se, but of Peach's courage, of the very fact that she still had it in her, that no matter how many times she got knocked down, Peach could still pick herself up, dust herself off, and fly out again, arms and heart wide open, to even the possibility of a new love, could still run out in the middle of the night to meet some man. Like a lovesick schoolgirl. Like a cat in heat. Like a woman in love.

Jan, on the other hand, had shut herself up tight as a drum. The remark about the babies had particularly hurt Jan. Only Peach had known that Jan, finding herself pregnant while June Bug was in Vietnam, and worried about helping her mother pay the bills and keeping her "good government job," had had an abortion, which she had regretted for the rest of her life. (In those days, unmarried pregnant girls were fired on the spot.)

She had never conceived again.

Peaches had been right about a lot of things, thought Jan, suddenly filled with a newfound respect, and yes, even a grudging admiration, for her friend. Now.

But not then. Oh, no. And the next time she had seen Peaches walking down the Strip, arm in arm with Griff, the father of the late Chicken Wing, the boy with the laughing eyes and delicate features, she had turned away and walked in another direction.

"*Hmph*," she had snorted derisively, sounding for all the world like the same old church ladies who had passed judgment on Peach when she was a young girl with a bulging belly.

"Look at em. Well, at least they got something in common."

All these thoughts and others rushed through Jan's mind as she sat in Courtroom 308 that Monday morning, accompanied by Rasheeda. They hadn't heard anything from Sal since she had left town, but Omar reported that she had been in touch, so they were cautiously optimistic.

Jan had already spoken with Malcolm, who was also handling her case, and after quickly scanning the sheaf of papers she had brought along with her, work records, satisfactory performance evaluations, and so on, she had returned to her seat beside Rasheeda to wait for her case to be called.

She had seen Milligan when they first walked in. He refused even to look her way, but sat smiling in a confident manner with the attorneys representing the city. About five minutes before Judge Califano was scheduled to take the bench, Rasheeda hunched her.

"Look in the back, look in the back, turn around," Roach stage-whispered. Jan turned.

And there they were, sitting in the very last row: Puddin, Gigi, Red Top, who smiled and winked, and even Nettie, the maid, looking very excited. Sitting next to Red was a strikingly beautiful woman who looked to be about somewhere in her fifties. She looked Asian, or maybe Afro-Asian. Decked out to the nines in a tomato red wool suit of conservative cut, she stood and waved at them.

"I didn't know they were coming," Rasheeda whispered again.

"Me neither."

"Who is that woman waving at us?"

"I think that's China Doll. She's one of Ursula's old roadies. Remember her from the funeral?"

"Oh, yeah." Rasheeda nodded, but before she could think of anything else, the bailiff stood up at the front of the courtroom.

"All rise, all rise. The Honorable Dominic Califano presiding."

Everyone rose as the judge entered and was seated. Califano, a man of about sixty, looked quickly around the courtroom, his eyes stopping when he got to the back. Jan knew she was number five on the court calendar list of cases to be heard that day, so she was surprised when her case was called first.

She rose, squeezed Rasheeda's hand, and walked to the front of the courtroom to stand beside Malcolm.

It was over in less than ten minutes. Califano scanned through the documents Jan and Malcolm had presented for a few minutes, glanced toward the rear of the courtroom once, twice, then called the attorneys from each side up to the bench for an off-the-record sidebar conference. All the while, Jan tried to get Milligan's attention, but he steadfastly refused to look her way.

Malcolm returned to her side, a huge grin on his face. "Here's the deal," he spoke rapidly. "The judge has persuaded them that it would be in their best interest to settle. They are offering you—let me see." He whipped out his calculator.

"Two years of the amount on the face of your last contract, plus first dibs on the contract, when it comes up for bidding for next year."

"Two years? How much—" Jan stuttered.

"Your last contract with them was for ninty thousand dollars. That's one hundred eighty thousand dollars," Malcolm answered, grinning again.

"One hundred eighty thousand dollars? I'll take it, I'll take it!" Jan reached over, hugging Malcolm effusively, and knocking his glasses off. Her eyes darted quickly toward Milligan's table. Gone was the smug confidence, replaced by a stunned, dead-eyed stare of disbelief.

Once he had readjusted his clothing and eyeglasses, Malcolm had Janice sign off on the various documents agreeing to the settlement, and their business was done. He shook Jan's hand as she prepared to leave the courtroom.

"They're going to cut you a check by the end of the business day, so by the end of the week or so, you should have it. Ms. Shephard, I don't know what it is, but you must have some angels working your corner. I've never seen Califano settle a case this quickly."

Jan laughed out loud, turning toward the back of the courtroom, and giving a discreet victory sign.

"Angels? Well, yeah, I guess you could call em that."

Later that day, when they were all seated at the Oasis having lunch, courtesy of Rasheeda and Hakim, she had the little group rolling with laughter when she recounted Malcolm's remark about "angels working her corner."

China Doll had laughed the loudest.

"Well, we might be angels. But we sure don't work no corners anymore, do we, girls?"

The entire group erupted.

"But don't worry. I'll make it all worth his while." China winked at Red, who winked back.

There are sometimes strange sights to be seen on the Strip, and only on the Strip would one find this little party, which consisted of three ex-hookers, one madam, a maid, and an unemployed secretary, having lunch together in a Muslim establishment, all to celebrate the victory of the secretary, which had been brought about by the mere appearance in the courtroom of the ten-year kept mistress of the judge hearing the case.

Angels? Hey. Why the hell not?

CHAPTER 24

RASHEEDA: THROWDOWN NUMBER 2

When Janice finally got home that night, the house was quiet.

"JayRon?" No answer. Shaft was whimpering to be fed, as usual. Jan walked into the kitchen, opened a can of food for the dog, and gave him fresh water. She poured herself a glass of juice from the fridge, still euphoric from the unexpected outcome of the hearing, and was about to go up to check on Dottie when she spotted the note on the kitchen table.

"Dear Jan. Me and JayRon went to take care of some business. We should be back in a day or two. It is very important. Please do not worry about us. Love, Dot."

What the hell? Jan walked back into the dining room and looked into the corner. The wheelchair was gone. Aw, shit. She didn't want to even think that Dottie had gone out to score drugs and had taken that child with her. But experience had taught her to expect just that.

She dialed Rasheeda's number, and related the facts.

"Oh, Jan, no. You don't think she—"

"I don't want to think that, Roach. But you know how it is."

"Yeah. Well, I know she didn't go back to that shelter. She hated that place. You and her had been getting along all right, right? No problems or anything?"

"Sure. Just fine. No problems that I know of."

They talked a while longer and then hung up, each mystified. Jan sat down at the kitchen table. She couldn't figure it out. Dottie and JayRon had been with her less than two months, and they were like old friends.

Dot had shared secrets with her that she probably hadn't told another living soul. That's the way it was with people when they knew they were dying. That's the way it had been with Junie.

James "June Bug" Shephard had been a firefighter with the city of Philadelphia. He had rescued people from burning buildings, carried children to safety, delivered four babies, won numerous awards and citations. June had been splattered in the face with blood, squirted in the eyes with blood, had worked right in it, for the fifteen years he had been so employed.

He had always been in good physical shape, daily performing the same exercises he had learned to do in the Army. So when he first began to feel a little stiffness, a little pain in the joints, he attributed it to simply getting old. After a while, though, when the symptoms persisted, accompanied by chronic fatigue and difficulties in concentration, Jan had insisted he visit a doctor. So June went to the department doctors, was administered a battery of tests, and went home to await the results.

"Hepatitis?" June couldn't believe it, and neither could Janice. June Bug had smoked a little weed back in the day, they all had, but being secretly afraid of needles, had never gone any further than that. The worst part of it was that his disease had been termed "non–job related" by the department.

The Philadelphia Fire Department had not issued plastic gloves or protective masks to its employees until 1990, not realizing that such diseases as Acquired Immune Deficiency Syndrome, as well as Hepatitis C, could be transferred through blood and blood products. It wouldn't be until years after 1990 that they would begin to make the connection between the lack of protective gear and the growing number of firefighters and paramedics suffering with AIDS and Hepatitis C in Philadelphia.

So Jan had watched most of their medical insurance go down the drain for June's care. And they had clung together tightly, backs to the wall, as June grew weaker and Jan stronger. As Jan bathed him, cleaned him, lotioned, and clothed him, she had come to know her husband better in those last years than she ever had.

And she had never loved him more. Jan knew about dying people, all right.

At that very moment, Dottie was sitting on a large sofa next to her wheelchair, in a tastefully and expensively appointed living room on New York's Upper East Side. Across from her sat James, her baby brother.

"Are you sure you don't want to lie down, DotDot?" asked James for about the sixth time, referring to Dot by her childhood nickname.

Consumed with guilt and still a little afraid of his big sister, despite her frail appearance, he had already sent out for Chinese, having nothing prepared to serve to these unexpected guests. He was shocked at her appearance. Now, he sat, a scotch-rocks in his hand, trying to mask his shock at her appearance. JayRon was in the den, watching videos.

"Naw, Jimmy. I'll lay down when I need to." Dot waved his concern away. "I can lay down anytime, and before long, I'll be layin down for good. But just now, I wanna talk."

Dottie fished a pack of Kools from her handbag and lit up. James was at her side with an ashtray in an instant. She smiled up at him.

Dot was tired. She had been on the go all day.

As soon as Jan had left that morning, she had gotten JayRon to help her get dressed. From Jan's, they had caught a hack to the bank, where she had cashed her check. In her large pocketbook, she carried just enough medication to last for a couple of days.

On the way to Thirtieth Street Station, Dot had told the hack to make a little run up to North Philly, where, leaving JayRon in the car with the driver, she had walked slowly and painfully into a boarded-up, seemingly abandoned house and copped three days' worth of Methadone, taking a dose while still inside the house.

Just in case.

Once they had arrived at the train station, Dot had given JayRon the money for two round-trip tickets to New York City. After settling down on the train, she had sent the boy to get them something to eat from the snack bar, and when he returned, she had turned over the remainder of the money from her check to him. So easy.

Yet, for her, so hard.

They reached Penn Station and caught a cab to James's address. Thank God he hadn't moved. Dot and JayRon stepped into the dimly familiar lobby, where she had announced herself to the person at the front desk. A very surprised James had come downstairs almost immediately and escorted them up to his apartment.

And now, here they were. She had taken another dose of her Methadone, plus the pills she was taking for her medical condition. She was comfortable, and now, it was time to talk. And talk they did. Dot informed James of Peaches's death first. Yes, he nodded. Of course, he remembered her. She had been one of Rachael's bridesmaids.

"I'm sorry to hear about Peaches, but what's that got to do with you?" James seemed puzzled.

"Well, in a roundabout way, that's one of the reasons I ended up here today. See, Jimmy, you turned your back on me, and maybe I understand why. I know what you think of me."

James started to cut her off, but Dot held up one weak hand.

"Now, now, I said I'm a talk, and when I get finished, it will be your turn."

"Fair enough."

"Naw, it ain't fair. It ain't fair at all, but I ain't got no time to be holdin no grudges against you or nobody else. See, you don't know everything, Jimmy, even wit yo lil fancy-schmancy college degree and fancy job and everything."

Dottie hesitated, took a deep drag from her cigarette. She looked over at James. "You don't member all what happened when we was kids, do you? I know you don't, cause you was too little. You member our daddy?"

"Of course, I do. He was a Merchant Marine," James answered somewhat impatiently, wondering where his sister was going with this.

"Yeah. Uh-huh. Member he used to come home and bring us presents and stuff alla time?"

James nodded, smiling.

"Yeah, well, guess what? That wasn't our daddy. That man we called daddy, Earl? That was mama's boyfriend."

"What?" James sounded as if he had had the wind knocked out of him.

"Yeah. That's right. See, I member our real daddy." Dot smiled weakly, going into her pocketbook and pulling out an old-time metal frame, handing it over.

"That's our daddy."

James peered at the photo, at the face of a man who looked just like him about twenty years ago, smiling back at him.

"I know. Look just like you, don't he?" Dot grinned.

James could not stop staring at the picture. "Where is he?" He asked in a low voice.

"Don't know." Dot shrugged. "Might be dead, for all I know. He just never came back. That's all I know. Anyhow—" Dot stopped. She could see James was struggling to digest all this information at once. "Anyway, Earl, the man you thought was our daddy, that's the one who killed Mama."

James put his hand over his eyes. That thudding sound of her head, of his mother's head, DotDot screaming, the blood, it all swirled around like a bad movie inside his head.

"Yeah, he killed her. But the reason why he killed her was cause she walked in on him tryin to rape me." Dot spoke in a strangely detached voice, as if she were talking about someone else, some other little girl.

"DotDot, no."

"Oh, yeah. It happened. And it had been happenin for a long time. He just went too far that time, that's all," she continued in the same dull monotone.

"What do you mean, a long time? You were a little girl."

"I mean, I had been puttin up wit his shit for a long time, not sayin nothin cause he treated Mama nice and he bought us all that stuff and bought food for the house and all."

"You're not trying to say Mama knew about it?"

"No. I don't really think she knew. I'm sayin she should have known. I know she loved us. All I'm sayin is she should have taken better care of us. That's all."

"Well, look who's talking! You got one kid dead, one in jail. You didn't do such a bang-up job yourself, did you?" James snapped, his eyes flashing.

"Yeah, you right, you right. But who did I learn to be a mama from? Who taught me, Jimmy? Huh?"

James sat, silent.

"Jimmy," Dot said softly, after a minute or two had passed. "I ain't tryin to make no excuses for myself, and I sure ain't tryin to blame Mama for what went down. Shit happens, you know? I'm just tryin to get you to understand that our family wasn't really no kind of—what you call em, role models? I was dyin in a damn shelter, me and JayRon. I called for the only brother I got in the world, and you turned your back."

James looked away.

"Naw, none of that. I didn't come all the way up here to put you through no guilt trip about me, and I ain't tryin to make you feel bad. I'm tellin you all this to say that we don't know no better, you and me. Who taught us any better? Foster homes? Grown men feelin up and grindin on my body?"

James said nothing. Dottie went on.

"When I was dyin in that shelter, I called out for you, and you didn't come. But Rachael did. Just like the time I got busted. She came down to Philly and got my babies and brought em back up here. And it's because of Roach, excuse me, Rasheeda, that I got a nice place to stay at today, a comfortable place for me and my boy." Dottie took out a tissue and wiped her brow. She was beginning to perspire.

"You mean to tell me they still call her Roach, after all these years?" James stifled a smile.

"Yeah, well, you know the JGs. They got they own thing goin on."

"Yeah, right, the Justus Girls. Tell me about it." James nodded.

"Anyway, I know you think I came up here to try to hit you up for some money, or somethin like that. But you can rest easy on that one, bro. Ain't nothin you got that I can use now."

She started to cough uncontrollably. James moved to plump up the cushions around her, but JayRon beat him to it. At the first sound of Dot's distress, he was at her side like a shot.

"That's all right, Jay. Mommy's fine," Dottie assured her son after the coughing fit had subsided.

After making sure his mom was indeed all right, JayRon returned to the den. James's eyes followed the boy. "He's a good kid, huh? He really takes care of his mama." He smiled.

"He's the best. More than I deserve."

"So, you were saying—" pressed James.

"Oh, yeah. Me and JayRon's stayin with Janice, another one of Rasheeda's friends."

"Yeah, I know Jan," James said.

"Anyhow, like I was sayin, Rasheeda, soon as she learned where I was, her and Jan and Sally came down and got me and JayRon outta that shelter. Now, this girl ain't no blood kin to me, yall been divorced for years. That didn't make one bit of difference. As far as she was concerned, me and the kids was family, and that was all there was to it. And her and Jan and Sally have been just like family to me, me and JayRon. And they do for each other, too, help each other out and all,"

Dot continued. "If only we woulda had somebody like them when we was kids, Jimmy."

"All right, all right, Dot. I'm grateful for what Rachael and her friends have done for you and JayRon. I really am. Now, what is it you want me to do?"

Okay, Dot thought to herself. *This Negro was gone bottom-line her, no matter what. All right. Time to play the trump.*

"Jimmy, you know if Rasheeda hadn't come down and gotten my kids that time, they would have gone into foster care, don't you?"

"Yeah, I know."

"And the way I was livin then, I probably never would have seen em again. You know that, don't you?"

"Yeah."

"I never forgot that, never. See, our mama was taken away from us, and kids need to be wit they mama. Baby Bro, that girl lives for her family. And that's why I'm here tonight, beggin you not to take her kids away. I've seen em. They real happy, they doin just fine. And if you really want to do somethin for yo poor ole big sis, then leave them boys right where they are. Leave em wit they mama."

James's jaw tightened.

"Dottie, do you know I gave Rachael everything, anything she wanted? She didn't tell you that, did she?" James said bitterly.

"Jimmy, she ain't tell me nothing, nothing bout why you and her broke up, and I ain't blamin either of you. If it's over, it's over. Now, I ain't no marriage counselor or nothin, but it seem to me from the looks of things you was spendin yo life chasin money, while she was spendin hers chasin love. So no, you ain't give her everything, or she woulda never left you."

James said nothing.

"I might be readin that wrong, I don't know. I'm just askin you to hear me out."

So they talked on into the night, sister to brother, laughing, crying, finally together again.

•   •   •

Two evenings later, a private ambulance bearing New York plates pulled up in front of Jan's house. JayRon jumped out, racing ahead to ring the bell.

"Aunt Jan! Aunt Jan! Come on out," he cried excitedly. "We back!"

Janice ran to the door to see what all the commotion was. When she got there, she was greeted with the sight of two ambulance attendants dressed in white, one weighted down with an armful of boxes, the other pushing Dottie in her wheelchair.

JayRon ran back to the ambulance and retrieved another armful of bags and boxes. Jan stood dumbstruck, holding the door open as the little caravan passed through.

"Yo, kiddo," said Dottie, winking at Jan and reaching down to pat Shaft simultaneously.

"Brought you somethin from Bloomingdale's."

Jan closed the door and wordlessly followed them into the living room.

Two days later, Janice picked up the receiver on the third ring.

"Jan?" It was Rasheeda. "Jan, you'll never believe this. We just got papers from James's New York lawyer, hand-delivered. Jan, he's dropping the custody petition," Rasheeda squealed.

"Get out, girl."

"I know, I know. Isn't it incredible? Just like that. All he wants to do is work out some kind of arrangement where the boys can stay with him during the summers and on holidays, and since we don't celebrate Christmas and Easter holidays, anyway, that is not a problem, no problem at all." Rasheeda's words were rushing together.

"I'm so glad for you, Roach."

"I know. I can't believe this is happening. I guess people really can change sometimes, huh?"

"Guess so, girlfriend."

"Anyway, how are Dottie and JayRon?"

"Great, everybody's great."

"She ever tell you where she was when she disappeared those two days?"

"Well, yeah, she did, but she's sworn me to secrecy," Jan replied, winking over at Dot, who was sitting on the sofa, finger to her lips.

Jan knew she would eventually tell Rasheeda the whole story, just not now. Not yet.

Red Top and Daddy Baby were also delighted when Rasheeda called them with the news that the custody battle was over.

"That's just wonderful, sweetheart," Red responded.

"Thank you. But, Miss Red, did you and your—uh, husband have anything to do with this?"

"Not us, chile. Swear fore God. Not a thing. Sometimes people just come round and finally do the right thing on they own, you know."

"Yes, ma'am, I do know that. And I never stopped praying to Allah on it."

"Well, prayer always helps, honey."

Yeah. Prayer, a baby brother's guilt, and a dying sister's last wish. Old James didn't stand a chance.

CHAPTER 25

SALLY GOES HOME

Sal found herself standing in the dark, at a deserted little depot, illuminated by one pitiful electric light. She had expected it to be small, but when the bus driver had pulled over to let her out, she was sorely tempted to stay on the bus.

Blinking her eyes, she peered out into the night, but all she could see was blackness. She had just begun to root around in her handbag for Bay Girl's phone number when she heard a rumble in the distance.

Presently, a dusty, ancient pickup pulled up to the depot. An equally dusty and ancient little man exited the truck.

"Miss Sally Mae! Well, how do." He greeted her like an old friend.

"Uh, hi," Sal answered, wondering who he was.

"I know you don't member me, but I'm Rafe. I knowed you when you was just a lil bitty thing." The old man smiled, revealing a full set of sparkling white dentures.

"Sho nuff?" Sal said, slipping back into down-home slang, just from the sound of Rafe's honey-toned voice. After years and years of short, staccato city-talk, it sounded like music to her.

"Sho nuff. Knowed all yo peoples, too. Yo granddaddy, granma, even yo mama. I come to carry you to yo sistah house."

Rafe picked up Sally's suitcase and carryall and started for his truck. Uncharacteristically at a loss for words, Sal followed the old man silently.

The words "Yo sistah house" had caught her completely off guard. Sal knew Bay was her half-sister, had always known it. But still.

As they rode along down the open country roads, she was only half listening to Rafe's cheerful chatter. The smell of the pine trees, the earth, the very air, brought back such a strong flood of memory, she was afraid she was going to cry.

She vaguely remembered seeing Bay from time to time when her grandmother took her into town. Bay Girl would be walking along with her mama, and Sal's grandmother would hastily pull her along, while Bay's mama did the same to Bay.

Sal would steal a glance back over her shoulder and find the girl looking back at her, almost like looking in a mirror, their similar faces filled with curiosity.

"Come on, chile." Gram would pull her again, muttering to herself about "that no-good polecat what drove yo mama crazy."

What could she want with me? Sal wondered. *And why now?*

Sal willed the pickup to go faster, faster. She wanted to be there now, get whatever this mess was over with, and move on.

The smiling woman who answered the door still looked the same. Older, of course, and she had always been a little heavier than Sally, a little shorter, her skin a shade or two lighter. But still the same face, same eyes, same smile, a smile like—like looking into a mirror.

"Welcome, welcome." The woman now grabbed Sally Mae to her, pulling her close. Puzzled, Sal awkwardly let herself be embraced.

"Come on in. You must be tired. And hungry."

Bay Girl was nervous, too. She was moving and chattering rapidly at the same time. Sally relaxed a bit. She was hungry. Starving, in fact. She could smell the smothered chicken and greens the minute Bay Girl opened the door, and now, she was actually salivating.

"Have a seat."

Sally Mae first thanked Rafe for the ride and tried to pay him, but he refused to take her money.

"Naw, thank you, honey. Glad to do it," the old man said, tipping his worn straw hat.

"Well, Mr. Rafe, I know you gone take a lil supper wit us, ain't you?" Bay smiled at him.

"Well, I believe I will, Bay, if it ain't puttin you out none."

By this time, a tall, very slender, and very handsome man bounded down the steps and put an arm around Bay.

"Oh, 'scuse my manners, Sal. This my huzban Leon. Leon, this Sally Mae. I know you was jus dyin to get down here so you could get a look at her," Bay Girl beamed. Leon extended a hand, which Sally grasped, and as he shook her hand, Leon looked from Sally to his wife, then back to Sally. His face broke out into a dazzling smile.

"Damn," was all he said.

"I know. Ain't it somethin?" Rafe piped in.

Bay laughed, and after a few more pleasantries were exchanged, How was the trip? How's the weather up there in Philly? and so on and so forth, Bay showed Sal upstairs to the guest room, where to put her things, and where to freshen up for dinner.

As Sal listened to Bay Girl, she glanced at the woman out of the side of her eye.

"I know you waitin for me to explain why I asked you down here. And I'm a tell you directly. But first, I gotta feed my huzban and git him on his way. He's drivin down to Florida tonight to spend the weekend with our boy. They goin fishin."

Her boy. Of course. Sal had seen the pictures on the mantel of the smiling teenager, dressed in cap and gown, when she was downstairs.

"Now, git yoself freshened up and come on down, so we can eat. Don't worry. We got plenty of time. Plenty."

Bay smiled again and left the room. Sal did as she was told.

Over a dinner of chicken, greens, potato salad, corn bread, and peach cobbler, Sally began to relax. She liked these people. They were plainspoken and unpretentious, just as her grandparents had been. Leon, Jr., called Lonnie, was a sophomore at Florida A&M, where he was studying architecture. He was only a year older than Omar.

When Sal fished out the wallet-sized high-school graduation photo of Omar that she carried everywhere and held it next to Lonnie's larger picture, everyone was struck by their strong resemblance.

"I swear fore God, them boys looks like brothers," Rafe exclaimed.

And they did. Sal looked around the table slowly, from one face to another, finally stopping at Bay's. *She is my sister! She really is my kin,* she thought to herself, wonderingly.

Meanwhile, while the diners filled their bellies with the tasty, rich food, Rafe filled their minds with stories about the old days when her grandfather had kept a whiskey still back in the deep part of the woods.

"Swear fore God, the man could break down and set up a still faster than anybody I ever seen." Leon teased her and Bay Girl, declaring he couldn't figure out which of them had the bigger appetite. Sal ate like a horse, no matter what the situation, and Bay seemed to be matching her, forkful for forkful.

They talked some more about the weather, the crops, the neighbors. Everything but the real reason for Sally's visit. Finally, dinner was over, and Leon went upstairs, emerging with an armload of fishing attire: hat, hip boots, vests, and such. He said a few more pleasant words to Sally, kissed his wife, and left, along with Rafe, who promised to see her again when she left.

Bay Girl, after seeing the men off, came back into the kitchen and switched on a small radio. Blues filled the room. As she began to clear the table, Sal rose to help.

"Naw, naw, set down. You the guest."

After she finished wiping down the table, Bay sat a generic bottle filled with a clear liquid before them, two glasses, and a bowl of ice.

"Care for a lil drank?"

"Well, yeah, all right. But what is it, vodka?"

"Sheeit. This ain't hardly no vodka. You wont a chaser?"

"Chaser? I don't even know what you got here."

Sal laughed. She was so glad to see Bay Girl light up a cigarette, she was almost beside herself with joy. Nervous though she was, she would never have presumed to pull out a cigarette in a nonsmoker's home.

"Chile, you know what I got. I got the real thing. I got the same thing yo granddaddy had. I got the corn."

"Oh, damn, that's corn liquor? Wow. I ain't seen none of this since I left the South."

"Go on. You mean you, the granddaughter of the best moonshiner in the county, and you don't drank no corn? Get out." Bay seemed truly surprised.

"Nope. Never touched the stuff. Well, not less you count the time I snuck into granddaddy's stock one time when I was a lil girl, and got sick as a dawg," Sally confessed.

"Well, you ain't no lil girl no mo, and you gone have the real thing tonight." Bay laughed.

She walked to the refrigerator and took out a bottle of soda and a carton of orange juice, which she set out on the table.

"Awright, now. We got everything we need. You can try it straight, on the rocks, with soda, water, orange juice, whichever way you like it."

Koko Taylor's "I'm a Woman" settled across the room.

Sally took a deep breath, picked up the shot glass Bay had filled to the brim, and downed its entire contents in one swig.

"*Ahhhhh! Ahh, ahh, ahhhh!*" Her throat was on fire. Her eyes filled with tears, her nose began to run. She looked over at Bay and tried to speak, but began to cough instead. Bay, who was laughing so hard she could hardly stand, slid around the table and patted Sal on the back.

"Girl, don't you know you cain't down no corn like that? This stuff is pure, straight from the ground. This ain't none of that ole big-city processed sheeit."

Sal grabbed the jug of water, poured a large glass and gobbled it down, wiping tears from her eyes.

"I'm a Woman" played on as the big sister taught the little sister the fine art of drinking corn.

Bay allowed Sal one more shot, heavily mixed with orange juice, before she capped the bottle, rose abruptly, and cleared the table again.

"Okay, let's go."

"Go? Go where?" A warm feeling was beginning to steal over Sally's mind and body, and that blues was sounding real good. "Thought we was gonna have a talk?"

"We kin talk while I work." Bay started out the back door. Sal had no choice but to follow the woman. Out in the yard was a maroon-colored van.

"Let's go." Bay Girl jumped in on the driver's side and motioned Sal around to the passenger side.

"Go where? Work where?" Sal climbed hastily into the van.

"I got my deliveries to make. This Friday night. That's why I had to send Rafe to get you. Leon had to load up the van." Bay turned over the ignition and pulled out onto the road.

"What kind of deliveries? You ain't talkin bout no drugs, now, are you?" Sal began to get tense again.

"Drugs? Hell, no, girl." Bay chuckled, keeping her eyes on the road.

"You know that corn you just drank in the kitchen? That's what I'm deliverin. That's our business. We kinda picked up where yo granddaddy left off."

"Get the hell outta here."

"Hell, yeah. We do all right, too. Friday is our busiest night," Bay said proudly. Sal shrugged her shoulders. This was going to be an interesting trip.

Their first stop was at a little white brick roadhouse, with no sign on the front.

"You just gotta know bout it, that's all," Bay said in answer to Sally's baffled expression. Bay pulled around to the rear and backed the van up almost to the back door.

"Come on." The women walked around to the front and went in. Bay directed Sal through a crowd of dancers to a seat at the bar, while she went off to schmooze with someone in the back. A short while later, she returned and took a seat beside Sally. They each ordered a beer, which they got on the house.

"This shit is way deep," Sal murmured under her breath, as she turned to watch the dancers twirling across the floor.

"Like I say, grown straight from the ground. Good to you and good for you." Bay clicked her glass against Sal's. Sal finished her beer and was about to order another, but Bay placed a hand on her arm.

"Not now. We got a long night ahead. Let's go." She drained her glass, stood up, and started for the door. Sal followed.

They made about eight or nine more stops that evening, mostly at bars and clubs, a few at private residences.

"We go everywhere. We got as many white customers as we got Black." Bay Girl grinned. They had at least half a beer at each business they stopped in.

Sal could see why Bay had stopped her from reordering at that first spot. The woman was all business, slipping in, making small talk with the owners, giving them a little play, and slipping back out, all in under twenty minutes.

As Bay drove, she talked. She told Sally that Leon and she owned their property and their land, and that they also sold vegetables that she grew in her own garden.

"Yeah, a lil veggies, a lil herbs, a lil magic, you know. This and that."

"'Magic' what? 'This and that'?" *Oh, Lord,* she thought. *Please don't tell me this woman got reefer growin out there in her backyard.*

"Just thangs, that's all. Nothin fo you to worry bout. Just a lil this and that." Bay smiled cryptically, but said no more about the subject. She talked as she drove. She was happy, she told Sally. She had a man she loved, who loved her back, a beautiful child, and they owned the land they lived on. "I feel blessed, Sally Mae. Deed I do."

Sal, in turn, talked about Omar and Doll, about her job as a community outreach worker at the Rec Center, about Omar being a part-time college student. Nothing more.

When they completed their last delivery and got back to the house, Sal made a beeline for the bathroom.

"When you through, come on back down to the kitchen," Bay yelled up the stairs.

Sal, splashing water on her face, could hear the strains of Etta James singing "Trust in Me." She was tired, but nothing could have kept her from going back down those stairs. The corn, the bars, the music, the midnight deliveries. Damn, what next?

And Bay Girl. Sal shook her head. It felt as if she had known her all her life. They had talked and joked like old, dear friends. At every stop they made, people had commented on their resemblance to each other. Maybe it was the liquor talking, or the fatigue, but Sally felt a strong emotional pull toward this woman.

When she walked back into the kitchen, Etta James was wailing through the house.

"Oh, so you dig Etta, too?" Sal smiled.

"Oh, hell, yeah. Etta is the one, the true queen of rock and roll, blues, jazz, and soul. Etta is the goddess." Bay nodded, snapping her fingers to the music.

After comparing their favorite recording artists for a while, Sal realized that Bay Girl seemed to be content to talk about music all night long. So she got to the point.

"Okay, Bay Girl. What you want? What you want with me?"

Bay, already seated, had laid out some cold chicken and potato salad, along with the soda, OJ, ice, and, of course, more corn. She had also lit two large red candles, and Sal could smell incense coming from somewhere.

"Yeah, yeah, okay. But first things first. Eat." She gestured as she prepared a small plate for herself.

Well, she didn't have to tell Sal twice. They ate quickly, making more small talk about the night's events, and when they were through, Bay again jumped up and cleared the dishes and food away. This time, she returned to the table with a small, smoky blue crystal decanter and two more glasses.

"I want you to try somethin." She filled the glasses with a honey-colored liquid from the decanter.

"Well, what's this?" Sal took the glass Bay offered, but eyed it suspiciously.

"Oh, girl, damn! What you thank, I'm tryin to poison you or somethin?" Bay took a sip from her glass.

Sal sniffed hers. It had a fruity, almost perfumelike smell.

"What is it?"

"Drank it, Sally Mae. Slowly."

"All right, all right." Sal took a small sip.

It was thick, syrupy, and delicious. She took a little more.

"Uh-huh. Thought you'd like it. The Irish calls it mead. We make it ourselves, and we just calls it honey wine. It's supposed to bring clarity and insight. I make it myself, and I only serve it on special occasions. And I'd say this is a special occasion. Wouldn't you?"

Bay had hunched forward, and was now looking directly into Sally's eyes. She took another sip. "I owe you, and I want to pay up. Thangs got to be set right."

"Owe me? You keep on sayin that. What you owe me for?"

"Well"—Bay spoke slowly, savoring the taste of the mead in her mouth—"it ain't so much that I owe you, personally. It's my mama's debt, and I got to pay it," she said matter-of-factly.

"Yo mama? I never even knew yo ma—"

"I owe you for what my mama did to yo mama." Bay sat back, rubbing her eyes with her fingers. "It's a long story, and I'm a tell it to you. But before I do, I want you to tell me yo story, all of it, no half-ass, and I want you to tell me the truth."

She leaned forward in her chair again, her eyes pulling Sally's like magnets. The air was very still, and there was no sound except for

Etta's growling voice, Etta, wailing, "I'd Rather Go Blind Than to See You Walk Away."

Sal could see the red candles flickering from the corners of her eyes, and the incense was flaring her nostrils, but other than that, the room seemed to go dark, darker, to finally fall away, till there was nothing left but Etta, the firelight, and Bay Girl's eyes.

Is she hypnotizing me? What in the hell is goin on here? Sal willed her eyes to close, and the room began to spin. Yet she did not feel drunk at all. She opened them again to stop the spinning, and they were pulled straight back to Bay Girl's.

"Okay." She sighed slowly.

Sal found herself telling Bay everything, starting with her and Kenny moving to Cali, to Kenny's death, Omar's birth, all the way up to Mustang Sally. On and on she talked, all the way up to Charley Favor's death, her escape, all the way to this very moment.

Bay nodded throughout Sal's narrative, her face impassive, asking a question occasionally, refilling their glasses once or twice. Or was it more than that?

"And this Charley Favor, they thank you killed this man?"

"I'm not sure what they think. I just know I'm tired of sleepin with one eye open."

"Uh-huh. And did you?"

"Did I what?"

"Don't mess wit me, girl. Did you kill him?"

"See, it wasn't like you thi—"

"Sally Mae. Did you kill that man?"

Sal sighed, speaking in a barely audible voice. "I killed him. Yeah, I did."

Bay sat very still, her face benign, waiting for the explanation she knew would follow.

So Sal pushed on, explaining how Charley's major league football career was on the downswing just around the time they had hooked up, that when his contract was not renewed, he couldn't seem to adjust to life without football.

"See, he was used to bein a big star, bein the center of attention, of always, always havin a pocketful of money. He had never really bothered to invest any of it or save it, so when he got a knee injury, and they let him go, he didn't want to give up that lifestyle he was used to." Sal spoke as if in a trance, caught up in the tragedy of the man whose life she had brought to an end. She seemed unaware of the slow tears descending down her cheeks.

"I went back to dancin, and he took to hangin out down to the Fox Box all the damn time. All of a sudden, he was jealous of every man in the place."

She wiped her face unconsciously.

"I tried to hang in there wit him, but it was gettin harder and harder. Then one night, when I was home, it was my night off, he came in actin all kinda crazy. Now, don't get me wrong. I seen Charley drunk before. But this was somethin else. I mean, he was like some kinda wild man."

Bay reached over and refilled Sal's glass with the mead. Sal took a swig, lit a smoke.

"I don't know if he was messin wit drugs or what, but he came in and woke me up bout one in the mornin, pulled me up out the bed and started yellin bout I betta fry him some fish."

"Wait a minute, Sal." Bay Girl held up a hand. "Now, you say the only reason you got wit this man was cause he was this big-time football star, spendin all this big money. If his career was fixin to go down the drain, why did you move in wit him in the first place?"

"Cause I didn't know! Swear to God I didn't. I didn't know a damn thing bout no football. Still don't. I mean, I knew he had hurt his knee some time back, and they had him on the bench a lot, but honest to God, I didn't know they was gone cut him from the team.

"And Charley was deep in denial. He was spendin money like everything was all right, so I figured everything was all right. I know I was cold bout the way I was playin him, but I swear, if I had known he was bout to lose his job and all, I'd a never been there in the first damn place. I mean, I sho nuff never loved the man, but I didn't hate him, neither. I tried to hang in there with him. I tried—"

"All right, all right, settle down. Anyways, he got you up out the bed to fry him some fish. Then what?"

Sal pushed her braids back out of her face. "Anyhow, I had fixed some spaghetti earlier that night, and I tried to tell him I could warm up a plate for him. Next thing I knew, I was on the floor. He hit me so hard, he knocked me into the wall, and I bounced off the wall down to the floor."

Sally Mae began to rock gently back and forth, back and forth.

"Sally? Sally Mae! Jus calm yoself and finish tellin it. You got to tell it."

"If he woulda just left it alone then, just left it alone, that woulda been the end of it. I'd a just gone back to bed, and got outta there the next day. But then, he pulled me up by my arm and marched me into the kitchen."

"Now, I had already defrosted the fish to cook for breakfast the next day. Charley grabbed the fish from out the refrigerator and pulled me by my hair over to the stove. He was talkin all kinda shit bout how he knew I was plannin on leavin him, and how I had some dude down to the Fox Box and all, and how if I tried to leave, he was gone fuck me up so bad that nobody would want my Black ass and—"

"And was you?"

"What? Was I plannin on leavin him? Hell, naw. I told you, I didn't even realize just how bad the situation was. He had me convinced that he was gone be picked up by another team any day now. No, I was hangin on in there."

"Um-hmn. Then what happened?"

"Anyhow, my nose was bleedin so much, I thought it was broken. But I put on a fryin pan, put the Crisco in there, and lit the stove. I took the fish and started breadin it, all the while wit him sittin at the table, watchin me, callin me all kinds of whores and sluts and everything."

Sal took a deep breath, let out a small sigh.

"While I was waitin for the grease to get hot, I went back in the refrigerator, got out some ice, and was wrappin it in a towel to put on my nose. Charley, the whole time, callin me all kinds of bitches and all."

"But why did he thank you was messin round on him, if you wasn't?"

"I don't know, Bay. Hell, why would I? Sheeit, I had it made. I was a happy camper. Had a nice home, nice car, swimming pool. Met a lot of important people, sports stars, politicians. Even met a couple of movie stars. My boy was bein taken care of. I had it goin on.

"But the one thing he kept sayin over and over was, 'You don't love me. You never loved me.' Over and over again. And he was right. I never loved him, never told him I did. Well, maybe a few times when we was havin sex, but you know how that is. That's just sex. You tell a man what they wanna hear. That's all that was."

She stubbed out her cigarette.

"I was there for what he could provide for me and my chile, right from the jump. He knew the deal. So I guess he figured now he was cut from the team, no more big paychecks, I'd find myself another meal ticket."

"And would you? I mean, was he right about that, too?"

"Bay, I honestly don't know. Maybe, eventually. Maybe not. But I wasn't out there lookin for nobody else at that time. I was tryin to hold it together. That's why I went back to work in the first place. See, Charley really loved me. I mean, he really did. And I loved Charley's money, and everything it brought me. That's the way that thing went.

"Anyway, as I was wrappin up the ice in the towel, Omar came runnin in. He was bout two then. Charley had woke him up wit all that screamin and mess. As soon as Omar saw my bloody face, he started hollerin up a storm. I tried to grab him up in my arms, but before I could get to him, Charley reared up and kicked him clear into the living room.

"Omar rolled like a bowling ball all the way into the front room and crashed into the brick fireplace. He had a large gash on his head. My baby's head was covered in blood, and I swear, Bay Girl, before I even thought about it, I picked up that cast-iron fryin pan, hot grease and all, and I busted him cross the head wit it as hard as I could. Just once. He looked kinda shocked, then fell over to the floor, like a sack of potatoes or somethin. He twitched a few times, and that was it. He was dead."

Sal slumped back in her seat, covering her face with both hands. There. She had finally told it, all of it. She felt somehow relieved, and strangely tired, weary.

"Damn. Then what you do?"

"Then I called Topaz, one of the girls from the Box, packed up me and Omar's stuff, as much as I could carry wit me, and everything I could find wit my name on it, and got the hell outta there. What you think I was gone do? Who you think woulda believed me, a damn go-go girl? Charley Favor still had a name, he was still Somebody, and me, I was Nobody."

Bay nodded slowly.

"Anyhow, first Topaz took me and Omar over to see a doctor who used to do abortions and patch up criminals and all, cause I was scared to take him to a hospital. So he treated me, and checked Omar. My boy seemed all right. There was a large bruise on his head, and he had a cut, but the bleeding had stopped. The doctor patched it, gave him a shot, and told me to keep an eye on him, and if he started actin funny or anything, to get him to a hospital right away. But he was fine. Boy got a hard head, just like his mama." Sal allowed herself a flicker of a smile.

"Well, what about your nose?"

"Ah, that was another story. My nose wasn't broken, but it was fractured. He had to pack it wit gauze and everything. I told him I was just passin through, so he gave me some prescriptions, and told me to check in somewhere and have it looked at, when I got where I was goin. We had to lie low for a couple of days. I called in a few favors, and before the week was out, me and Omar was in New York."

"New York! Yeah, we heard you was up there."

"Hold on, Bay. You told me on the phone that you heard these people was lookin for me in New York. Now, you sayin you heard I was up there. Where you gettin your information from? I sure ain't tell nobody down here where I was. This was the last place I was gone come to. I figured this would be the first place they would look for me, here or Philly."

"Yeah, well, you know how it is. Word gits around. Somebody knew it, that's all. Anyways, go on wit yo story," Bay pressed.

"Well, yeah, that's where I was for a long time. See, I worked the Deuce, and everything was—"

"The what?"

"The Deuce, Forty-second Street. Used to be plenty of bust-out joints and bars all round there, and a good dancer could make some decent money. Everything was goin fine. I worked nights, and I would leave Omar across the hall at my neighbor's at night, and in the mornings, I would get him, and watch her lil girl durin the day.

"But once he got to be school age, my neighbor moved away, and I was havin trouble findin somebody reliable to keep him nights, so when he turned five, I sent him to Philly to stay with Aunt Tamar and Uncle Buddy. I hated to do it, but when I contacted Kenny's parents, they told me they only had my word for it that Omar was their grandson. Oh, yeah. That's how they was. Long story.

"So anyhow, I danced in New York, in Chicago, Detroit, anywhere and everywhere but Cali or Philly. I knew the po-lice was lookin for me. They had been to my job in Cali, and to my aunt and uncle's in Philly.

"So I worked and saved. I sent Omar to a private school all the way through high school. And when I found out I was about to become a grandmother, I went on back to Philly and bought a little duplex, cash money. I was thinkin I would stay in one apartment and lay low, just for a lil while to help out, and maybe Omar, Doll, and Star, the baby's mama, could stay in the other one. But it didn't work out that way. Star's a crackhead. Omar loved that girl so much. I think he would still be out there tryin to save her even now, if she hadn't disappeared with the baby one night."

"Lord have mercy." Bay shook her head slowly.

"Oh, yeah," Sal nodded. "Nobody could find her. We searched everywhere: hospitals, po-lice stations, even the morgue. I thought my son was gone lose his mind. I finally got a call three nights later, some man on the phone tellin me that that girl had my grandbaby up in some crackhouse! In a crackhouse! Well, I just went right up in there, three o'clock in the mornin, and I brought Doll home. And she been wit me and Omar ever since."

"I know."

"You know about the crackhouse?"

Bay smiled. "And about the phone call."

Sal decided to lay that one to the side for now, and think about it later.

"And now, my boy, who should be somewhere away in college, like yo son is, is a single father, tryin to work, go to school, and take care of a baby girl. I just couldn't leave him this time. Not him and Doll. So I've been there ever since. Got me a lil job at the rec center. And now, here this mess come up again." Sal sat back, exhausted.

"Well," Bay drawled finally. "My mama always said ain't nothin like a cast-iron number-nine fryin pan to make a wrong man go right."

Sally looked startled, then saw the twinkle in Bay's eye, and dissolved in helpless giggles, joined by Bay. They laughed like wild women. Finally, they were silent again. Sal settled back and poured another glass of mead. "Okay, that's my story. Now, what's yours?"

It was now Bay's turn to pour.

"You member when we was in the bar earlier tonight, and I told you that my mama been dead ten years now, and my daddy was up north somewhere?"

"Yeah."

"What I didn't tell you is I know exactly where my daddy is. He lives in Philadelphia. His name is Herbert Wendell Ward."

Sal nodded blankly. The name didn't ring a bell. Besides, after all that confessing, her eyes were getting heavier and heavier. She tried to focus on what Bay Girl was saying.

"Sally Mae, he the one sent you down here to me tonight."

Sal couldn't keep her eyes open any longer. The room started to spin. She felt as if she was riding on a merry-go-round.

"My daddy go by what they call a 'street name.' Up in Philly, they calls him Monsieur Daddy Baby."

Sally Mae slumped over in her chair, passed out cold.

She awoke to the sound of Sam Cooke singing "a change is gonna come." She opened her eyes, sat up, and looked around, disoriented for a moment. Then, remembering where she was, she looked over at the clock on the night table. Eleven-thirty. Damn, almost noon!

Monsieur Daddy Baby is your father.

The thought knocked her back down onto her pillow.

Bay Girl gotta be lyin. No fuckin way, Sal thought, shaking her head. But she knew in her heart it was true.

Everything began to fall into place. The way he always stared at her, the inordinate amount of interest he displayed in her and Omar's life, the way he seemed to know what was going on, even before she did.

Sal stumbled into the bathroom, brushed her teeth, and took a shower. She had called down to Bay Girl, but got no answer. She seemed to be alone in the house, so she ran herself a glass of water, got back into bed, and took her blood pressure medicine and two Excedrins.

Just before she drifted back to sleep, Sal thought of Omar, her handsome, too-mature son. Lord have mercy. The poor boy's great granddaddy was a moonshiner, his grandma was crazy, his daddy was a revolutionary, his mama's a murderer, and his granddaddy's a damn pimp!

Hell of a family tree.

"So tell me more. I want to know everything," Sally Mae demanded. It was late afternoon, and the sisters were again sitting at the kitchen table. Bay Girl had awakened her earlier and forced her to drink some kind of homemade hangover concoction. Sal had protested, but whatever it was, it had worked. After a brunch of steak, eggs, toast, and tea, she felt like her old self again.

"Well, I can tell you that Daddy, yeah, Daddy—that's what I call him." Bay Girl grinned.

"Hell, that's what they call him in the hood, too," Sal hooted.

"Anyways, the land me and Leon lives on, this house, Daddy bought it for me, free and clear."

"Well, that's nice. Least he did somethin for one of us," Sal replied sarcastically.

"Sheeit, what you talkin bout, girl? That land over there over the bridge what you grandma and grandpa usta live on, he bought that, too. Bought it in yo name, a long time ago."

"What?"

"Damn right, he did. Bought that land and sent money up to yo aunt and uncle every month while you was growin up, and while yo boy was there."

Overwhelmed, Sal shook her head, staring at Bay disbelievingly.

"Damn right. If you don't believe me, ask them. That's why when you was talkin bout you had to go on welfare and live in that lil room over top the bar in California and all, I was lookin at you so funny. You always had a home, Sally Mae. You coulda come on home and staked yo claim anytime you wanted to."

"Swear to God, Bay, this is the first I ever heard of it. They never, ever talked bout my father, not my grandma, not my uncle and aunt. Nobody. And they sho nuff never told me bout nobody sendin no money."

"Well, they was gittin them money orders all them years, and Daddy been rentin out that land and puttin that money in an account for you and yo boy all these years, ever since he bought it."

"Get the hell outta here." Sal couldn't digest it all at once. "I coulda gone to Kenny's funeral. I coulda brought my boy back to Philly, or even down here. The whole Fox Box thing woulda never happened, I woulda never even met Charley in the first place—"

These revelations were stacking up in her brain, one by one, each one crowding out the next.

"Bay," she said slowly, "it didn't have to be like it was at all."

"Ha! Tell me about it. Daddy just thought you ain't want nothin to do wit it, or wit him, neither. He figured yo mama's people had just poisoned yo mind against him." They sat for a few minutes, Bay letting Sally get her emotional wind back.

"Come on, git yo clothes on," she said directly. "We got work to do."

Bay was in a hurry this night. They only stopped twice for beers. Sal, her mind filled with visions of a tall, dark, handsome, young man lifting her up in his arms, holding her close and singing softly in her ear, was lost in thought.

—I'd give you a million dollars—

At the last bar they delivered to, the women sat and had a beer. Sal looked at the jukebox and played some Ray Charles, while Bay went in the back to get paid.

"Okay, drink up. We got to go." Bay was looking at her watch.

"Now? I thought this was our last stop." Sal wanted to kick back awhile. The music was sounding good, and she had plenty more questions to ask.

"Naw, we got one mo stop to make. And we cain't be late for this one."

They were tooling rapidly down the dark road into the night, a Motown tape playing on the deck, when suddenly, Bay pulled off the road and drove deep into what looked like the woods to Sally, whose now-citified eyes couldn't see anything but black.

"Where we goin, Bay?" Aw shit, what now?

"Magic time, Baby Sis, magic time." Bay Girl laughed, braking the van and checking her watch again by the light on the dash. Or was it by the light of the moon?

"Damn, it's a quarter of. I ain't got much time. It's almost midnight, and there's blood on the moon tonight. You stay here."

Bay reached over and patted Sal's arm, then exited the van quickly, leaving Sally alone in the dark, with nothing but the sound of crickets for company.

The short hairs on the back of Sally's neck were standing up. What the fuck was she doin out here in the dark in the middle of the night?

She lit a cigarette, smoked it, then lit another, and just as she began to stub out the second butt, Bay suddenly appeared at the window of the van, carrying a large paper bag. Funny, Sal hadn't noticed it before.

"Let's go," was all Bay said, though she was still laughing like a lunatic as she switched the ignition on and nosed the van down the incline and back onto the main road.

"I'm sorry, Sally Mae. You just look so scared. I guess I shoulda warned you. I tole you I do a lil this and that on the side, you know?" She reached over and patted Sal's arm again. "I'll explain it all when we get to the house. But now, we gotta hurry. I got work to do."

It wasn't until they were actually on the road itself that Sal looked up and read the sign that she had only glanced at on their way in.

"Peaceful Pines Cemetery."

Aw, hell.

Back at the house, Bay ran straight up the stairs. Sal could hear her running water in the bathroom. What the hell now? She had been truly shaken by the graveyard experience. She had felt ridiculous, but for the life of her, she couldn't get the image of Mantan Moreland, the Black actor from the old forties movies, bucking his eyes and yelling, "Feets, don't fail me now" out of her head. She went out into the kitchen and popped a blood pressure pill, chasing it with a beer she snatched from the fridge.

When Bay came down, she first went straight to the stereo, and soon Etta's *Live from the Vine Street Grill* began to move through the house. She then came back into the kitchen, lit the two large red candles, plus a white one, then put on a pot of water, throwing in a mixture of herbs and roots and God knows what else.

Soon the kitchen was permeated with an aroma sweet and familiar, yet unidentifiable to Sally. Then Bay sat directly across from Sal again.

"See, my mama taught me how to do magic when I was a lil bitty girl. Now, the way the story go, she put some bad shit on yo mama to drive her crazy, cause yo mama was runnin round wit my daddy. Course, you know like I know that every generation got they secrets, so we will never know what really went down tween them three. All we know is whatever happened, here we are."

Bay was filling glasses as she spoke, two of mead, two of corn. She took a sip of the corn, motioned for Sal to do the same.

"Now, what she did was wrong, no matter what went down wit yo mama and my daddy. Bad magic is always wrong. So now, I got to pay for that. Cause the way the thang go, if I don't try to pay up for what she done wrong, one of mine is gone have to. Somebody always got to pay. Nothin in this life is free. Same as if you do right by somebody, it might not come back to you, but somewhere on down the line, might not even be in yo lifetime, one of yourn will reap the benefit of that kindness you did.

"Are you wit me so far?" Bay cocked her head at Sal, who slowly nodded.

"That's jus the way it go. See, I don't do no bad magic, cause don't no good come out of it."

Sally was struggling to keep up with Bay. Good magic, bad magic?

"Take you and me, for example. My mama probably thought she was doin right to fix yourn that way, keep her away from her man. But in the end, they both ended up losin they man, and we ended up losin our father."

"Father." Sal tasted the word on her tongue. She had a father. She knew who he was, what he looked like.

She felt like flying.

"And look at our father. Who knows what mighta happened if he'd a stayed down here, and faced the music?"

"True, he mighta gone the same way, anyways. But without them roots workin him, he might have never left. How many womens did he mess up, how many did he turn the wrong way, all cause of some bad magic? See, you cain't fuck wit people's minds that way. It never benefits you, or nobody else in the end. That shit has a way of comin back on you."

Bay Girl leaned over and grabbed Sally's hand, held it in her own. "Don't be too hard on him, sis," she said softly. "After all," she said, snickering, you look just like the man."

"Me? Hmph, you mean you look just like him," Sally protested, laughing and squeezing Bay's hand. "Lord have mercy." Sal blinked back tears and tried to swallow the lump in her throat.

"Anyhow, Daddy, our daddy called this mornin, say you got to be in L.A. tomorrow. Now, drank up, then come on upstairs so you can take this special bath I made up for you."

"Special bath? Now, look, Bay, I don't know bout all these roots and old wives' tales and shit." Sally shook her head stubbornly, braids flying.

"You know, if I was you, I'd take any help I could get at this point. And don't be so fast to knock so-called old wives' tales. How do you thank we got to be old wives in the first place? Those who know, don't tell, and those who tell, don't know. And we know. Now, drank that shit up and git yo hind parts upstairs. I still got to get packed."

"You got to get packed?"

"You ain't thank we was gone let you go there by yoself, did you? Daddy wouldn't hear of it." Bay grinned. "Now, git up there, take them clothes off, and git in that tub."

Sally meekly obeyed.

CHAPTER 26

SALLY: THROWDOWN
NUMBER 3

In Cali sixteen hours later, Sally and Bay girl sat at a small table in the old Fox Box, now rechristened the Show and Tell Gentlemen's Club.

Sal had hooted. Gentlemen's Club, her ass.

"Get the hell outta here! They done turned the Box into a damn titty bar," she had exclaimed to Bay as they exited the cab in front of the place. The front windows of the bar were plastered with pictures of very nearly naked ladies, posed in extremely suggestive positions.

Bay Girl just stood in front of the window like a hick, gawking in openmouthed wonder. "Sally Mae! You mean to tell me this is what you was doin out here for a livin?"

"Hell, no." Sally laughed, secretly enjoying Bay's discomfort. She might know all about roots and all, but this was Sal's old turf. "Back in the day, we didn't have to do no shit like this. I never took all my

clothes off, and I never stripped down that much." Sal shook her head
at the photos.

"And if any motherfucka so much as laid a finger, one finger on
me, those bouncers woulda hauled they ass outta there wit the quickness. They didn't play that touchy-feely shit back then. The Liquor
Control Board would have shut the joint down in a minute. Damn,
shit sure changes up on you. I never had to pose like that, and I was
a headliner!"

Bay was still staring.

"Oh, come on, girl. Are we goin in or what?" Sal grabbed her sister by the arm.

"Oh, yeah, we goin in, all right." Bay recomposed herself, and
into the Show and Tell they went.

Choker, the old owner, was still there. He had shaken Bay's hand
and hugged Sal effusively. After seating the women, he had brought
over a magnum of champagne (good champagne!) and three chilled
glasses, then took a seat.

Sal was lost in the seventies, gazing around the room, old times,
old loves, old life rushing down on her like heat in the night.

"So, Miss Mustang Sally, it takes something like this to get you
back down here to see me, huh?"

Choker grinned as he poured, teeth glowing in the afternoon light.
"Want some orange juice?" he teased.

"Naw, not today. Today, champagne is fine."

"I just know you got some pictures of that lil spoiled brat of yourn
to show me."

"Little? Ha! Boy six feet tall now," Sal said, preening, pulling out
her ever-ready snapshots of Omar and Doll from her wallet.

"Git outta here! He got the nerve to have a baby?"

"Hey, you know what Topaz said. The boy do love women." Sally
laughed, remembering Choker's predictions that Omar would be gay
because of too much mothering.

Sal and Choker shot the breeze for a while as he filled her in on
how everyone was, what the old girls were up to these days, while

Bay tried to pretend that sitting in titty bars in the middle of the afternoon was something she did regularly.

"Yeah, girl, Topaz married, a grandmother, goin to church and everything. Tryin to make up for all the wild shit she did, I guess," Choker said.

"I got to look her up," Sal mused. A true friend.

The club wasn't open yet, and they were the only people there, but Bay could just imagine what went on in there at night. Ropes and swings were hanging from the ceiling, a long, brass fireman's-type pole jutted up from the floor of the stage. Bay Girl tried to picture Sal swinging around that pole, and had to look down at her watch to keep from laughing out loud.

Presently, the three of them looked up at the sound of the front door opening. A middle-aged, medium-brown-skinned man in work clothes walked in, waved over at them and took a seat at one of the large bars.

"That's him. Excuse me," Choker said quickly, leaving the sisters at the table. He went over to the other side of the bar, said a few words to the man, then poured him a drink. Esther Phillips's "Cherry Red" soared throughout the club.

"That's who? Who we supposed to be meetin here, Bay?"

But Bay shook her head, leaning back in her chair, singing along with Esther. She had been acting mysteriously ever since that strange bath ritual she had performed on Sal the night before. But right in the middle of it, right when the warm water was pouring through her scalp and down Sal's naked body, she had grabbed Sal by the hand and looked right into her eyes.

"You gone have to trust me, Sally Mae. I know you don't really know me yet, but still, you have to let go, give it up, put yo trust in me. Otherwise, it won't work," she said, and somehow, Sally knew it was true, same as she knew everything else she had learned on this magical night was true.

Right then and there, she decided to put herself in the hands of her sister.

And now, here they were. Rafe, in his decrepit truck, had picked them up early that morning and taken them to the airport. When they reached LAX, they had hopped a cab to a small motel just outside of Los Angeles, checked in, and hung up their things. Bay had immediately sent Sal out to the hotel's restaurant for food, and after first making sure she was alone, headed straight for the telephone and began dialing.

"Hey."

"Hey, yoself. Yall there already?"

"We's here."

"How she holdin up?"

"So far, all right."

"She ain't hungover from none of yo ole paint thinner corn, is she?"

"No, she ain't. I made sure she didn't have too much to drink last night."

"Cool. Well, you got the numbers, you know who to call. And give me yall's number there."

Bay talked a little longer, then hung up, made another quick call, then another. She was just hanging up when Sally came back with nothing but two salads, complaining about the food at the hotel.

"No problem. We goin to South Central. We can get somethin on the way. You know, I always did want to try that chicken and waffles Daddy used to talk about. You ever hear of a place called Roscoe's?"

And now, here they were in the Show and Tell. And Bay still hadn't given up any info.

"Them chicken and waffles was all right, wasn't they?" Bay smiled.

Sal sucked her teeth, settling back to listen to Bill Doggett's "Honky Tonk."

"Bay?" Choker was motioning Bay over to the bar.

"You stay here," she admonished, leaving Sal at the table.

Bay Girl sat talking with Choker and the mystery man for about five minutes, shaking her head, then came back over to Sally.

"Okay, we gone have one more, then we gotta roll on out."

Sal knew better than to even ask where. Back at the motel, the sisters rested and talked, picking through the cold salads Sal had bought earlier, Bay grumbling about some of the New Age shops they had passed on the cab ride back.

"Assholes. They don't know what they doin. *Hmph!* Mess round here and call up a demon, they don't watch it. All this talk bout angels. Don't these fools know you cain't have one without the other? It just don't work that way."

At around 10:30, Sal was ready to suggest going out for a late dinner, when Bay jumped up. "Ten-thirty! Aw, hell. Time to get ready."

She pulled the two large suitcases she had brought along up onto the bed, opened them, and started pulling out clothes.

"Okay, Sally Mae, we got one last run. Which one you wanna wear?" She was holding up two wigs.

"Bay, what the hell—"

"Look, I want you to put on these clothes and one of these here wigs, and don't give me no shit now. Our ride be here by eleven."

At precisely 11:00 P.M., a beat-up-looking Chevy station wagon pulled up to the door of a certain motel just outside of Los Angeles. Two gray-haired women of uncertain age, wearing baggy, nondescript dresses and worn-looking slides and carrying two large plastic bags apiece, exited one of the rooms and stepped into the car.

"Evenin, ladies." It was the mystery man from the Fox Box, still wearing his tan work uniform.

The Chevy drove straight into downtown L.A. to the criminal courthouse, where the driver pulled around to the back, and let the women out. Seconds later, one of the back doors of the courthouse opened, and someone motioned the women inside.

Once in, they were each given a cart containing cleaning equipment: mops, brooms, disinfectant, and two large hard plastic trash containers, which the women promptly dumped their large bags into. Silently they followed the man who had let them in onto a back elevator and up to a certain courtroom.

The man unlocked the door, then left them alone, with instructions that he would be standing watch just outside in the hallway.

"It's eleven-forty. Be back out here by twelve," one of the women told him. The man nodded and left.

The women worked quickly. First, they went into the judge's adjoining chambers, where they emptied the contents of the plastic bags they had brought with them and a number of smaller bags and boxes onto the judge's desk.

Then, one following the lead of the other, they set about placing the contents of these various containers in hidden, unobtrusive places all over the room: a little black dirt placed here, a little colored water sprinkled there, a few bright red and white feathers under here, a bit of red Georgia clay over there.

Finishing their work in chambers, they proceeded into the courtroom, up onto the judge's bench, and repeated their actions, dressing the chair and the area around it liberally with the same-colored water, clay, dirt, and feathers.

"Give me that earring," whispered one of the women.

"What?"

"Yo earring, chile. I need something belong to you, somethin wit yo sweat on it, yo scent. I need that earring."

The other woman wordlessly handed the jewelry over.

When they were done with the bench, they went back to the chambers, packed up their things, and started toward the door.

"Wait a minute."

One of the women turned back, removed a small spray bottle, and proceeded to give the bench a quick going-over.

"Okay, let's go. Nothin like Georgia Pine to hide the smell of them spirits," she said as they walked out into the hall where the man waited for them, scratching his head.

Back at the motel, Bay insisted Sally take the special bath again. By now, the up-until-yesterday practical-minded Sal was convinced she was living in some kind of parallel universe, and offered no resistance at all.

The next day, bright and early, Sal and Bay showed up at the criminal courthouse and met with Jamie Sweet, Malcolm's friend, who would be representing Sal. Sweet was big-time. Sally knew of his reputation, even all the way over on the East Coast. He had defended celebrities as well as mobsters. No way could she have afforded him.

But she had learned not to ask questions about anything anymore.

She sat, silently praying and holding on to Bay Girl's hand. Too late to run this time. She had tried to reach Jan and Roach earlier by phone, but had gotten no answer, couldn't get either one on the phone. She had talked to Omar last, telling him she loved him, how proud she was of him, and how sorry she was for leaving him when he was a child.

"Our Father, who art in heaven—" Sal mouthed the words to herself. When her name was called, she squeezed Bay's hand one more time, then took her seat beside Sweet.

"*Psst!* Sally Mae!"

Sal felt Bay hunching her from behind. She ignored her.

"Turn around, turn around!"

"All rise! The Honorable Wilson Waymon presiding," the bailiff announced. The judge was now stepping up to the bench.

Sal felt her knees go watery. She leaned against Sweet for support.

"Turn around, turn around," Bay stage-whispered.

This time she did, her quick glance following the direction of Bay Girl's jerking head motion. And there they were, the JGs, or at least what remained of them. Janice in her finest businesswoman's attire, and Rasheeda swathed in full Muslim regalia, waving discreetly. Sal wanted to cry.

The hearing itself was over in less than an hour. Choker took the witness stand and swore that Sal had been dancing at the Fox Box on the night Charley Favor was reportedly found dead.

Topaz, her old dancing buddy, went up next and swore that Sally and Omar had moved out of Charley's house and in with her at least a week or two before the night in question.

It was an old case. Evidence was lost, police officers who had worked the original investigation had retired, some had moved away, some were deceased.

Throughout the testimony, the judge, a brother somewhere in his sixties, though still quite handsome and distinguished-looking, couldn't seem to take his eyes off Sally Mae.

And when it was over, he banged his gavel and said the word, the one word Sal was waiting to hear.

"Dismissed! Lack of evidence. Next case. You are free to go, Ms. Washington."

All Sal could hear was free, free, free! She jumped up.

"Oh, thank you, Your Honor. Thank you so much." She flashed him a giant smile. Eyes filling with tears, she hugged Jamie Sweet, then turned and hugged Bay Girl even harder.

"Come on. Let's get the hell outta here," Bay stage-whispered, grabbing Sally by the arm and pulling her up the aisle.

"I know you didn't think we'd let you go through this without us, did you?" Jan almost lifted Sally off her feet, she was hugging her so hard.

"I just know you didn't." Roach beamed, grabbing Sal's hand. Sally was too full of feeling to speak. But she turned back once and smiled up at the judge as they left.

As the judge watched the sisters walk toward the women in the back of the courtroom, he could swear he heard singing coming from somewhere. His eyes glazed over as he leaned back in his chair, dazzled by those million-dollar smiles.

Those who tell, don't know. Those who know—

"Now, you know you got to pay."

"Huh? Pay? Pay who?" Sally blinked at Bay Girl quizzically. Oh, so now, here it was. She'd have to grease somebody's palm. Sal knew it was too good to be true. So far, except for out-of-pocket expenses, this whole throwdown hadn't cost her a dime.

"Pay who, and how much?" Sal asked resignedly, reaching over to retrieve her pocketbook from the night table.

The sisters were back in the motel, propped up on their respective beds. Jan and Rasheeda had said good night and retired to their room next door. The television was playing BET Midnight Love videos, but neither woman was really paying much attention.

"Hey, Sally Mae." Bay turned to face Sal. "Forget about yo money. I ain't talkin bout no money." Bay shook her head, got up, and walked over to Sal's bed and sat down. "Sally Mae, a man died, and yo hands and heart are still bleedin from his death. You got to pay," Bay said quietly.

"Pay how?" Sal jumped up from the bed and started pacing. "He dead, all right? And I'm sorry, but there's nothin I can do about it. I can't bring the man back to life."

"No, you cain't. But you can ask God to walk you through this. You can trust somebody, lean on somebody sides yoself for a change. You can ask for help from a higher power, you know."

"God? Who you think been walkin me through this all along, Bay? This and everything else?" Sal stopped pacing and stared straight at her sister. "You know how they say that God watches out for babies and fools? Well, I sure as hell ain't nobody's baby, and if it wasn't for God, this fool wouldn't be here to tell you the story. It was him or me. Don't you get it, Bay? Him or me. And God spared me."

"Whoa, whoa. Who you so mad at, Sally?" Bay held out both hands in a gesture of peace.

"I'm mad at you, tellin me I got to pay. What else can I do? Would you rather I had died stead of Charley?"

"Oh, come on, girl. Ain't nobody talkin bout nobody else dyin round here. And I ain't blamin you for doin what you did. You had good enough reason. I woulda killed for my chile, too. But like I told you about magic, I'm tellin you now, you got to pay for that man's life, or sure as the sun gone rise tomorrow, it will come back on you or one of yourn, one." Bay Girl grabbed both of Sal's hands and held them tightly. "You want to know what you can do? Well, for one thing, you can begin to forgive," she said softly.

"Forgive? Forgive who?"

"Oh, I don't know. Whoever you so mad at. You talk about you want yo chile to forgive you for leavin him. But who haven't you for-given, Sally? Who hurt you so bad that you bricked up yo heart, stayed to yoself all these years, hidin out like some wounded animal, never reaching out to nobody? Who haven't you forgiven? Who you so mad at, right now, tonight?"

Sal froze. She closed her eyes, swaying. One after another, faces of people began to pop up in her mind, like stills from an old-time movie projector.

Kenny, for leaving her. Her mother, her grandmother, for leaving her. Her father, for not being around in the first place. Tamar and Buddy, for treating her like a poor relation. Even Bad Tooth Shirley, for shouting out those ugly truths about her that long-ago day at Stanton schoolyard.

But, most of all, herself. She had never forgiven Sally Mae Washington for selling herself to the highest bidder, for placing her life and the life of her child in harm's way, all for money, for fancy clothes, for a candy-colored car. For shiny stuff.

The tears flowed then, followed by racking sobs that shook her whole body. Bay Girl pulled her closer, leading her back over to the bed. She rocked Sally gently, as one would a child.

"Forgiveness, sis. That's the way it go. I know it's hard, but it's the only way. You must ask forgiveness for Charley's sake, and you must forgive for your own. Thangs got to be set right."

CHAPTER 27

LAST NIGHT AT THE DEVIL

So he's not scared of Shaft anymore, huh?" Rasheeda grinned, watching JayRon and the German shepherd frolicking on the floor in Jan's living room.

"Oh, no, they're best buds now. It took awhile, but now Jay walks Shaft every day after school, when I'm still at the rec center. Now, if only I could convince him to lose that damned gold tooth."

The JGs laughed as they wrapped up their meeting. Seated around the dining room table this evening in addition to Jan, Sally Mae, and Rasheeda were Dottie, and also Bay Girl, up from Georgia to attend the historic Million Woman March, which would be taking place the next morning.

"I swear, yall JGs got some shit wit yall." Dottie had shaken her head admiringly, as the Justus Girls went through a rundown of old business, old problems, new solutions, and new business.

For the last few months, Dot had been treated under a new regimen of the latest protease, HIV-fighting drugs, and the results were clearly visible. Gone were the dark circles under her eyes, she had gained weight, and her skin was beginning to return to the rich cocoa brown that Rasheeda remembered. Dottie and Bay had sat in rapt amazement, listening to all the things the JGs had managed to accomplish since their first meeting less than a year ago.

Rasheeda and James had agreed to shared custody of the twins, and best of all, James would pay for them to continue in an Islamic private school, straight up through high school graduation. The phony drug case against Hakim had been dropped, due to "disappeared evidence," and Hakim and Rasheeda were now busy with the opening of Oasis 2 in North Philly. All was as it had been before.

After paying off her mortgage and delinquent bills, Jan was working full time with Sally Mae at the rec center, teaching office administration and computer skills. It was now her dream to one day open a combination day-care and after-school program for children, along with a training program for adults, and she had already committed a portion of her settlement toward that goal.

And Sally, well, Sal was still at the rec with Jan, doing outreach work in the community, and now that she was no longer a fugitive, giving the downtown politicians hell. She and Bay Girl had grown even closer, constantly on the telephone every weekend. She had taken Omar and Doll down to visit for two weeks during the summer, where she had had a chance to survey the land she owned, had owned all along.

Everything her sister had told her was true. The money from the rental was there in the bank, in her and Omar's names. Sal had immediately withdrawn enough to send Omar, along with Princess (for Peach), to Temple University full-time, so her son could now study in the evenings and also be with his daughter.

And she was making her peace with her father.

As she suspected, her aunt and uncle had been spending the money all along. But that was water under the bridge; she let it go. She now had real family.

So as they left Jan's house on this windy October night, Jan, Sal, Roach, and Bay, Dottie stuck her head out the door. "Now, don't yall do nothin I wouldn't do!"

They fell all over each other laughing.

"Hell, that's everything!" Sal yelled back.

The JGs plus one strolled down the Strip to Rasheeda's Oasis.

"Look at Hakim up there, lookin out the window, waitin for you," Sal whispered, hunching Roach and motioning her head up toward the second-floor front window above the Oasis. Sure enough, the curtain moved slightly.

"Girl, you better not be keepin that good brother waitin," Jan teased.

"Oh, trust me, I won't." Rasheeda winked, unlocking her door and waving good night. "Now, don't yall be hanging out down at that bar all night, because you know we've got to be up early in the morning," she admonished, just before closing the door.

"Yeah, yeah, yeah. We'll be ready."

The three women now continued along Fifty-second, and they were about a block from the Devil when they spotted a small group of young people on the corner of Locust.

"Lord, have mercy, it's Star. It's Doll's mama, Bay. Star! Yo, Star!"

As soon as the girl turned and saw Sally, she started walking quickly in the opposite direction. Sal stepped forward.

"Star! Don't run! I ain't gone bother you."

Star stopped and turned. She was pitifully thin, wearing nothing but a cheap cotton miniskirt, a too-tight pullover, and a thin fake-leather jacket. Her little bird legs wobbled on a pair of plastic high-heeled wedgies. She had a cheap, homemade-looking braided do that was matted and dingy.

"Oh, hi, Miss Sally Mae." Star looked as if she expected to be struck. There was a smear of blackberry lipstick across her mouth, and when she spoke, it was evident that she was missing a front tooth.

Oh, God, Sal thought, but she forced a smile.

"Hiya. Don't you wanna know how yo baby girl is? Don't you wanna know about Doll?"

"Uh—yes, ma'am. How she doin?" Star asked shyly, puzzled by Sal's sudden friendliness.

Sally quickly pulled out her array of snaps, impulsively taking one photo out of the wallet and handing it to the girl. "Star, you know you welcome to come by anytime you want to see her."

Star's eyes lit up in surprise.

"Yeah? Well, I—uh, how's Omi?"

"He just fine. They both fine. Why don't you go on by right now? They both home."

Star took a few steps toward Sally Mae, arms outstretched, eyes misting, then she suddenly stopped, shook her head no, and the best of the young girl who loved her baby, the best of Shirley's pride and Omar's heart backed away, backed away, and ran off into the night.

Sally watched for a moment, then turned to Bay, a helpless expression on her face. "Well, I tried. You see what happened."

"Yeah, you did. Next time, try a little harder, sis."

Jan watched this whole exchange unfold in something akin to shock. Sal, being friendly to Star?

Deep.

"It's about forgiveness," was all Bay would say.

The crowd was jumping that evening at the White Devil, and the women barely managed to secure a small table in the back. No sooner were they seated than Tookie himself appeared, carrying a tray bearing a magnum of chilled champagne, ice bucket, and glasses.

"Compliments of the house, ladies." He grinned, but his eyes traveled past Sal and Jan, straight to Bay Girl.

Sally thanked him and introduced her sister.

"Course, I knowed she was yo sister the minute I laid eyes on her." Tookie reached over, shaking Bay's hand. "And how is yo daddy?" He looked from Sal to Bay, then back to Sal, still grinning.

"Uh—fine, thank you," Bay mumbled, glancing over at Sal, who said nothing.

He knew! Probably always had. Sal sucked her teeth. Damn! Did the whole bar know, the whole damn neighborhood?

"Now, don't even start to poutin, chile. Like Red Top say, every generation got they secrets," Bay whispered, as Tookie walked away.

"Now, what's up with this forgiveness Bay was talking about outside? I remember the time when you would have taken Star's head off on sight," Jan asked, eyes twinkling as she sipped the cold champagne.

"Long story. Tell you later."

"Well, does it include Shirley, too?" Jan pushed on, stifling a chuckle.

Sally looked around the bar, and there she was, Shirley, scratching her head underneath her wig and rolling her eyes at them. As usual.

"Don't push it, Jan. One at a time, okay?"

Jan laughed, also looking around. "Sally, isn't that Inez's husband over there with that young girl?"

"Yup. Same one. Told you. Look at the ole fool grinnin up in that chile's face wit only two teeth left in his whole head. Tryin to wear them tight pants like he twenty-five or somethin. Speakin of twenty-five, whatever happened to their son? I haven't seen him since I got back home."

"I don't know where that ole waterhead boy is, girl. *Hmph!* Probably workin in a carnival somewhere, showin off that big-ass dome."

"*Oooo,* girl, stop it," Sally howled, joined by Jan and Bay.

"I swanee, I'm wit Dottie. Yall got some shit wit yall," Bay Girl said, when she could catch her breath again.

"Huh, you think we somethin? You shoulda known Peaches. Now, that girl was really something." Sal smiled.

"Oh, yeah, honey. Remember when she used to fly down the Strip in that old Chevy she had, screaming at the top of her lungs?" Jan nudged Sally. "I ride my mens like I ride my cars," Sal responded, hands on hips, in imitation of Peaches.

"HARD AND FAST!!!" Jan and Sal yelled in unison.

"Oh, Lord. Sal, remember that night Rome had the nerve to bring that woman in here during Peaches's shift?"

"Oh, Lordy, don't remind me." Sally almost choked on her champagne. She turned to Bay Girl to explain.

"See, one night, Peaches's husband brought this hincty woman in here and had the nerve to set right up there at the bar wit her. Now, Peach was cool at first, served em both what they was drankin and all. Then the girl leaned over and kissed Rome, right in front of Peach!"

"Lord, what the woman want to do that for?" Jan squealed, nodding.

"Well," Sally picked up the story, "Peach reached cross that bar and snatched that bitch's wig right off her head!"

"Git out! Right in here, at this bar?" exclaimed Bay.

"Oh, yeah. But that wasn't enough. She took that cow's tail hair and threw it right in the dishwater!"

"Yes, she did," Jan piped in. "Poor Rome had to tie his handkerchief around the woman's head and get her outta here wit the quickness."

"Well, like Peach say, Rome was still her husband, separated or no. What he expect? And that's what she told Tookie."

"What Tookie say?" Bay asked.

"Tookie ain't say shit, not to Peach, anyway. And she didn't get fired, neither. Rome was wrong to bring the cow up in here in the first damn place. He knew Peach. He knew how she do."

Jan and Sal nodded in unison.

"What are yall sayin about my mom?"

The women looked up into Princess's smiling face.

"Don't worry bout it. Grown folks' talk, that's all. It's all good. What you doin in here, anyway?" Sal scooted over so Princess could sit.

"No, that's all right, Aunt Sally. I was just lookin for Kim. I've been baby-sitting since this afternoon, and me and Omi are supposed to be going to a rally downtown tonight."

"You left the ki—"

"No, Aunt Jan, they're not by themselves. They're with Sheila Brewster, next door."

"Oh." Janice relaxed.

"So if yall see her, would you tell her to please bring her butt on home?"

Princess waved and left, assured that Kim would certainly get the message if they saw her.

"A rally, huh? Her and Omi," Jan mimicked, batting her eyes. "What's up with that?"

"I'm hip." Sal grinned. "I think he got a lil crush on Princess. Calls her 'Aretha,' you know?"

"Aretha? Oh, yeah. Sometimes I forget Princess's real name is Aretha. Well, it's only fitting. After all, the child was named for a queen."

All three women nodded soberly.

"But don't you think she kinda old for my boy? I mean, Princess got bout five or six years on him."

"Ha! Look who's talking! Your sister tell you about that fine young lawyer she's been keeping company with these days, Bay?" Jan said, smirking.

"Aw, hell, yeah. Over and over and over again." Bay Girl laughed. "And I can tell you she's got quite a bit more than five or six years on him."

"Go to hell, Jan."

"You, know, I wouldn't be sellin no wolf tickets if I were you. You need to be takin your blood pressure medicine and savin your strength," Jan said.

"I don't take blood pressure medicine no more, for yo information. Haven't taken it for months. I've been takin a lil somethin Bay fixed up for me, and now, my pressure is lower than it's been in years." Sally Mae beamed.

"Well, now, of course, not havin to look over yo shoulder and sleep wit one eye open no more might have a lot to do wit it, too. I can't take all the credit," Bay said modestly.

"Not to mention, having someone beautiful to sleep with. You know, I'm the one that got them together in the first place," Jan bragged.

"Yeah, Sally Mae told me all about it. So how is it goin wit you two? I can't wait to meet him."

"You'll meet him tomorrow night, after the march. And it's goin, you know, all right. But what about you, Miss Professional Black Widow?" Sally asked, changing the subject.

"What's up wit you and this cop? Bay, remember I told you bout Jan runnin all over the po-lice station from this guy?" Sally laughed.

"Oh, yeah, I remember." Bay Girl nodded.

"Detective, thank you very much. Detective Duke Wilson. And it's going just fine." Jan smiled inside herself, thinking of Duke's eyes, eyes the color of good whiskey, eyes that turned amber when the sun hit them just right. Of Duke's lips—of, funny, she hadn't dreamed of Junie since the night she first kissed Duke.

Hmm.

What was she going to do with this man, who walked straight and strong, without a crutch or any other means of emotional support? Not visible ones, anyway.

This man wanted to hold her, protect her, take care of her. Could she possibly change, switch positions, this late in life? She thought of those eyes again, those lips, and knew she damn sure was going to try. She smiled again, this time on the outside, her eyes lighting up like lanterns.

Meanwhile, Sal talked on, telling Bay about her out-of-character sexual fantasies concerning Malcolm the first time she met him.

"And Jan never said nothin about him bein so fine and all. I was shocked. I seen that bald head shinin, and all I wanted to do was lick it."

The women screamed.

"And did you?" Bay asked.

"Did I what?"

"Did you lick that bald head, girl?" Jan demanded.

"Now, what you think?" Sally shot back.

"This the one look like Wesley Snipes?" Bay asked.

"Naw, chile. This one look like Denzel. Don't he, Jan? Don't you think Malcolm look like Denzel, Jan?"

"Wellll, maybe if I was squinting and really, really drunk—"

"Go to hell, Janice. Anyway, Jan got the one look like Laurence Fishburne."

"Chile, them's young boys. Wesley, Laurence, Denzel. Them boys make you stroke outta here. Now, if it was somebody like Morgan Freeman, or Billy Dee, I'd give yall a run for yo money." Bay Girl grinned.

"Honey, if it was Morgan, I wouldn't be sittin up in here wit yall cows tonight." Sal laughed. Shirley looked over at them again, sucking her teeth. Sal started to say something, but was stopped by Bay.

"Think about Star, Sally Mae. That is her chile, and she got her own cross to bear. Remember, forgiveness."

"All right, all right. Get off my tit."

"So what about you, Bay? How have you been making out?" Jan changed the subject.

"Better than ever. My huzban's fine, my boy's doin well in school, my daddy's okay, and look like my sister's finally on the right track. So I'm a happy woman." Bay sat back, a satisfied smile on her face. "Matter of fact, me and Sally Mae even thinkin bout doin a lil business up here in Philly."

"Business? What kind of business?" Jan looked puzzled.

"Family business." Bay winked over at Sally.

"Oh, you mean pimping?"

"Fuck you, Jan. We thinking bout havin me market some of the, uh, products up here that Bay sells down in Georgia."

"Products?" Jan turned to Bay. "I didn't know you were an entrepreneur, Bay Girl. What types of products do you sell?"

"Oh, a lil bit of herbs, a lil bit of roots, a lil something for the spirits. You know, this and that."

"Oh, yeah, she's a real enterper—, entrapra—, you know. What you said. Girl got her own home-based business." Sally winked at Bay, then had to turn her head away to keep from laughing at Jan's obvious puzzlement. She'd tell her about that later.

Sal talked about Omar and Doll, and how Monsieur Daddy Baby had offered to help with anything they needed.

"So how did Omar take the news about Monsieur Daddy Baby being his grandfather and everything?" Jan asked.

"Well, you know, when I first told him, he didn't say nothin, nothin at all. Then I took him over there to meet Mon—to meet my father, and they spent some time together. Now, they gettin to be like old buddies. It's way deep." Sal lowered her voice, suddenly serious.

"You know, I think it's a man thing. Like with Omar. Now, yall know I'd die and go to hell doin the tango for my chile. And I know he loves me, too. He might be pissed off at me half the time, but I know he loves his mama.

"And yet, now that he's becoming a man, hell, he is a man, there's a part of him that I just can't touch, can't reach, no matter what. Not the way Kenny coulda done it. Not the way my—my father can.

"It's just a guy thing. I mean, all men, sometimes they go where we just can't touch em. Same as us. It's somethin about women that men, no matter how much they might love us, will never understand.

"Specially women like us."

CHAPTER 28

TOUGH LOVE, ROUGH JUSTICE

It was you."

"What? What are you talking abou—"

"Don't play wit me, girl. It was you, and you know you got to go, don't you? You can't come back here. You know that, don't you?"

Red Top was sitting across from the girl at a table in Amazonia's, a waterfront Philadelphia restaurant she had expressly chosen for this meeting, because it was far away from the hood.

"What you mean, I can't come back?" the girl retorted sullenly, fingering and eyeing the money in the thick envelope Red had just pushed across the table.

Red Top slammed her own hand down quickly on the girl's, holding on to it.

"Just what I said."

"You mean I got to get up and just get on a train and leave here today?"

"That's just what I'd do, if I was you."

"So you gone tell em, huh?" The girl sucked her teeth.

"You damn right, I'm gone tell em, all of em. I'm lettin you know right now."

"You gone tell my sister and my grandmother, and the aunties, too?" The girl, half-ass slick still, searched Red's face as if she were looking for the punch line of a dirty joke.

"Especially them. Soon's I get yo lil narrow ass on that train, my first call is gone be to the aunties. And Puddin, and Gigi, and China, and Vaa. And you know I'm gone tell DB. So like I say, if I was you—" She turned her hand over, gesturing toward the envelope, palm up.

It was nearly two weeks after Sally's triumphant return to Philly, when the detectives started coming around to question people in the neighborhood about Peaches again. They had done this periodically, but so far, nothing had come of it.

One of the detectives assigned to the case was the very same young rookie policewoman who had rescued Peach some thirty years ago from Elmo's house of pain. Now a veteran, she had never forgotten the frightened and battered little girl. She was convinced that Ursula, Peaches's mother, had done it, and had been badgering her mercilessly.

But Red Top didn't believe it, not after talking with big-mouth Sheila Brewster, Peach's neighbor, a few weeks after the murder.

"Never seen nothin like it," Sheila had stated soberly. "Miss Ursula was pullin Peach up from the floor, screamin at the paramedics to fix her chile, to please fix her chile, yellin, 'she ain't dead, she ain't dead. Peach just playin around,' though anybody could see that Peaches was gone. I mean, she had a great big hole in the side of her head, and blood spurting out all over the place."

Sheila had shuddered and wrapped her arms about her.

"And all the while, Miss Ursula kept draggin Peaches back and forth across that porch, yellin for the paramedics to please fix her, make her like she was, until the people had to pull Miss Ursula away. She kept yelling for her to 'come on, Peach, walk, walk for Mommy.' I swear, it was as if she was tryin to walk Peaches back to life."

Nah, it wasn't Ursula.

So Red had called down to Georgia and asked Bay Girl to pray on it for her. Bay had sent her some herbal tea Overnight Express with specific instructions for its use. Red had followed the instructions, drunk the tea, and gone to sleep, and the next morning, she knew.

Simply knew.

And now this child had the nerve to be sitting across from her, rolling her eyes. Jesus.

"I told you, Aunt Red, it was a accident. She found out about us and was wavin that gun around and she was drunk, and I tried to stop her, and it just went off. It was a accident."

The girl's face twisted out of shape, her lip quivered, but her eyes were clear as spring, and not a single tear was seen by Red.

"Shut up, shut up, I don't wanna hear that bullshit." Red Top was struggling against the impulse to reach over and choke her. "Accident, my ass! It's a accident that you was runnin round wit the man yo mama was gone marry? That's a accident, too?" Red's voice was low now, her anger under control.

"Marry? Sheeit," Kim sneered, looking and sounding so much like Peach that Red had to turn her head away.

"He wasn't hardly gone marry her. It's me he woulda married. See, yall think yall knew my mother, but you didn't. Yall just didn't know." Kim spread her hands in a helpless gesture.

"Didn't know what, Kim? Didn't know how hard she struggled to keep yall together? Didn't know how she worked at one lil piss-ass barmaid job after the other, when she coulda made big bucks workin for me, because she wanted to set a good example for yall? You just tell me what we didn't know."

Kim narrowed her eyes. "Yall didn't know how fuckin weak she was, how stupid she was. Just had to have a man, any man, just like my grandmother. She mighta started out playin them, but in the end, every one of em played her like a violin." The girl was sneering again. "Dickwhipped by every one of em, includin my father, includin Griff."

"You know what, Kim? You think you know everything, but you don't. If you live to be as old as me, you gone find out that every generation got they secrets. Right or wrong. You don't know it all."

"Yeah, well, I know one thing. I know I ain't gone wind up like neither one of em, my mother or my grandmother. Old, no damn money, and still chasin down the dicks. Hell, I wish she would have gone to work for you. Least she woulda been gettin paid.

"And I don't really give a shit bout no damn Griff, neither. That old man can't do a damn thing for me but help me get to where I got to go. See, it's all about the Benjamins wit me, all day, all the way, 24-7-365." Kim snorted, grabbing up the money-filled envelope quickly and stuffing it into her pocketbook.

"The what?"

"The mon-ey, Aunt Red, the cash, the scratch," Kim rolled her eyes skyward.

"Oh, yeah? Well, now you got you some Benjamins to get you to where you got to go. And you got to go the hell out of Philly. Now. Today. Or I can't protect you."

Red leaned forward and again put her hand on Kim's. "I'm beggin you, baby. I already made some calls to D.C., and my friends down there are gone give you a place to stay, help you get settled. I'll call you in a couple of days and check in on you. Kim, I'm beggin you."

Kim cocked her head, looking at the older woman. Something in her voice and expression told her she'd better do as she was told. She nodded.

"Just call the number in the envelope when you get there. You a smart girl. You can probably make a lot of mon— uh, Benjamins out there."

Red rose to leave, but Kim put out an arm and stopped her. "Aunt Red, why are you doin this for me?"

"Come on, chile. We don't have time for all that."

"Well, thank you, anyway. And I want you to know it really was a accident."

Red Top nodded and the two women left the restaurant, walked to a nearby garage, and retrieved Red's shiny black Cadillac. They drove straight to the Thirtieth Street Station in silence. Red parked the car, opened the trunk, and handed Kim a small suitcase.

"Picked up a few things for you, till you can get yoself something."

Kim wordlessly accepted the suitcase, and they walked into the station and down the ramp. Red stayed right there until the train came, just in case the kid got any ideas about pulling anything slick.

Just before Kim boarded the train, she leaned over and quickly hugged Red, sobbing wildly. "I didn't mean it, I swear, Aunt Red." Red pulled the girl's arm away, pushing her onto the train, and as she watched it ride off down the track, she couldn't figure out why she was helping this girl out any more than Kim could.

Maybe it was because she sensed something in Kim that reminded her a lot of herself when she was a young girl, a coldness around the heart, a way of sizing up men as dollar signs and nothing more. When she was young. Well, maybe not. Look at how she had carried on, crying real tears and all. Maybe it had been an accident.

But as Red made her way back out to the street, it did strike her as odd that this young girl, who had a father she had never known, who had killed her own mother after being caught in bed with her paternal grandfather, who was now hightailing it out of town, away from everyone close to her, had never said a single word about her own two children.

As Red Top pulled out into the Market Street traffic, she wondered how she would explain her part in all this to the JGs, to DB and them when the shit hit the fan. And everything had been going so well. Damn! Now this. Another mess.

Well, she thought, what else was new? Same shit, different day. This was their life, celebrating small victories, while keeping an eye out for the next crisis. And there was always another crisis. Oh, yeah.

That's just the way it was for women like her.
That's the way it was for the Justus Girls.
For women like us.

"You know, you know, you know, you know, we are.
    Oh, yeah."

CHAPTER 29

IS THERE ANYTHING WE CAN'T DO?

Women, women, women everywhere, and all in shades of Black. Lemonade lemons, buttery yellows, cinnamon tans, copper penny reds, tawny golds, Cherokee browns, indigo blues, and licorice blacks. Bunches and bunches of black-eyed Susans, African violets, as far as the eye could see. Beautiful, each one. Radiant faces framed in pageboys, dressed in dreads, beaded in braids, coiffed in cornrows, coiled in multicolored Kente. Daughters of Isis, of Cleo, of Nzinga, of Sapphire, of Coretta, and Betty, and Fannie Lou.

The JGs were surrounded by sisterhood and love as they walked through the crowds at the Million Woman March. Everyone was talking, smiling, laughing at once, it seemed. They could hear Spanish accents, German, French, Caribbean. Tongues foreign but faces familiar, all sharing the connection to the Motherland.

Sally Mae had set her alarm for 6:30 A.M., but her phone had rung at 6:15.

"Girl, do you see all that rain out there?" It was Jan.

Sal got up, went over to the window, and looked out. She groaned. The rain was roaring down in sheets. "Oh, no. They ain't comin in all this mess, Jan." Hell, even she didn't feel like going out, and she lived in Philadelphia. "Did you call Roach?"

"She just called me. We figure we'll wait another hour or so, see how it is."

"Cool. Cause you know we got to go. If it's just ten of us that show up, we'll be the four out of ten," Sal said, though the thought of standing outside in all that rain didn't thrill her in the least.

"You know it." Jan hung up, Sal rolled over, and went back to sleep. An hour later, her phone rang again.

"Girl, get up, get up! Turn on Channel Three."

Jan was yelling into her ear. Sal reached over and clicked on the set, still half asleep.

"And with this terrible weather," the TV news guy was saying, "we really didn't expect much of a turn out for the so-called Million Woman March. But it appears they are starting to come in."

As he spoke, Sally watched the visual and saw what Jan was shouting about.

They were coming! Riding in with the rain!

Buses, vans, trucks, cars, SUVs, all packed to the hilt with Black women. License plates from New York, Maryland, D.C., Maine, Texas, Georgia, (Georgia! Sal screamed), South Carolina, Michigan, Maine. On and on, they came.

"*Awwww,* shit! Here they come, here they come, here they come! Look, Jan, look at them Georgia plates!"

"I know, I know! It's on now!"

There was a click on Jan's line, and soon, the JGs were having a three-way conversation. Well, scream-fest was more like it.

"Do you see them?" Rasheeda was squealing. "And guess what?

The mayor says all the downtown hotels have been booked solid. We sold out Philadelphia! Sold it out."

As the women whooped and hollered, they simultaneously watched their TV screens, where the news guy was now speaking with nine sisters from Chicago, who had jumped out of the back of a windowless U-Haul moving van.

"Welcome to Philadelphia," he greeted them. "Sorry about all this rain."

"What rain?" responded a twenty-something young daughter dressed in jeans, sweats, and a backward baseball cap. "I don't see no rain. All I see is the sun, and it's shinin so bright, I gotta put on my shades!"

The other women laughed at the white newsman's obvious loss for words.

"You tell him, daughter!" yelled Sally Mae.

Jan, Rasheeda, and by now Bay Girl, who had come in from the guest room to see what all the fuss was about, were screaming again.

The JGs made plans to meet at Rasheeda's in an hour for breakfast, and from there, they would proceed downtown to the march. They hung up, and Bay went to the bathroom to get ready.

Sally sat for a few minutes more, transfixed by the sound of drums and the sight of Black women marching up Market Street, wearing bright smiles and waving banners, splashing and singing, damn the weather.

"Thank you, God, for letting me live to be a part of this," she prayed out loud, tears streaming down her face. At the same time, Rasheeda and Jan were doing the exact same thing, giving thanks to God for this woman-made miracle in the rain. Nothing could have kept them away.

They had decided to take public transportation that morning, seeing all the out-of-town traffic, and now they were glad they had. Parking would have been impossible. By the time they reached Benjamin Franklin Parkway, the site of the march, the rain had stopped, the sun was peeping out from the clouds, and the air was charged with electricity.

The city fathers had greatly underestimated the turnout, and there were nowhere near enough bathroom facilities and food stalls available. (Silly rabbits. Didn't they know these were Black women, and if they said they'd be there, they'd be there?)

But the march went on as planned, without incident, sisters pulling together, working it out so everybody got fed and relieved. There were no attitudes, no prima donnas, no divas. (They must have been afraid they'd get their hair wet.)

The JGs cheered each speaker, particularly the young raptivist Sista Souljah, the equally captivating daughter actress Jada Pinkett, and the compelling Muslim Sister Khadijah. The were delighted to see female Fruit of Islam bodyguards flanking the stage, and thrilled by singer Faith Evans's a cappella rendition of "Lift Every Voice and Sing."

They were awestruck by the presence of the wondrous Winnie Mandela, who they understood had had particular difficulties in obtaining a visa to be there, but the organizers had made a few phone calls, cut through a little red tape, and here she was, straight from the Motherland. Awesome!

They had mourned along with their sisters the recent and untimely death of Sister Betty Shabazz, who had also been scheduled to speak.

But when the Royale Steppers walked out on that stage and began their presentation, the JGs were struck speechless. They could only shake their heads in rapt admiration as the adult female drill team, swathed in loose, white, flowing garments, heads crowned in high white turbans trimmed in gold, glided across the stage, moving like queens. These sisters rocked the house, stole the show, took it home!

Just like you-know-who!

The JGs found themselves pressed into service as unofficial ambassadors of Philadelphia, and of the Million Woman March itself, giving directions, recommending restaurants and nightlife, and patiently explaining over and over how the Million Woman March had been the brainchild of two local sisters, Asia Coney and Phila Chineseu, that the whole thing had been a strictly grass-roots, word-of-mouth affair, with all the information circulated through local Black radio stations, BET's Tavis Smiley Show, the Black press, and the Internet, that no, there were no underwriters, no cigarette, no sneaker or liquor companies involved, that the sisters, and each sister there, had virtually pulled this off by themselves, for themselves.

No sponsor, no coach.

(Just like you-know-who.)

Conservative estimates put the number of attendees at one million. Moderates said one million, five. The Million Woman March's figure was two million plus, and that was the figure the JGs left with that day.

The bottom line was two-million-plus Black women spent approximately four million dollars in Philadelphia on one rainy October weekend. The mayor wanted the Million Woman March to come back to Philly every year. Now.

At around nine that night, the Justus Girls, tired, feet hurting, and hungry, but happy, made their way toward the subway-surface trolley cars. The buses were letting everyone ride for free that day, for some odd reason.

"All aboard, sistas! Love, peace, and plenty hair grease!" shouted the driver, a young brother of about twenty-five.

"They know they better ack like they know. They don't even want to get a whole bunch of Black women mad out here tonight," Sally Mae said, chuckling.

"Got that right, sis," shouted a sixty-something-year-old grandmother from the front of the crowd.

"You know how we do."

And that declarative and most thrilling statement set the tone for the day, as well as the ride back to West Philly, to South Chicago, to East St. Louis, West Kansas, California, to England, to Russia, to

France, to Brazil, and everywhere else, all the way back to Africa. That statement, that feeling, that joy, followed them all the way home.

The JGs walked down the Strip in high spirits, laughing and singing. When they reached the Stanton School, their old alma mater, Jan suddenly pulled to a halt. She looked at Sal and Roach, grinning.

"JGs, fall in!" she commanded, breaking away and running off into the school yard. It only took Sal and Roach a second to follow their old captain's lead.

"You know, you know, you know, you know, we are, oh, yeah," Jan started off.

"The Justus Girls, oh yeah," Sal and Roach, now by her side, chimed in. And the JGs marched again, chanting and pumping their arms, loud and strong. Bay Girl watched this impromptu spectacle in wonder. Anyone passing by and seeing three forty-something-year-old women marching around and shouting in the schoolyard in the dark must have wondered what the hell was going on.

When they were done, the JGs collapsed against one another, laughing, hugging, and high-fiving.

Bay started toward them, then stopped cold, looking around.

"What was that?"

"What was what?" Sal replied. The JGs looked at each other.

Bay stood still and listened again. Silence.

"Oh, nothin. I thought I heard somebody laughin. Guess it was just the wind."

The Justus Girls shrugged, linked arms with Bay Girls, and calmly left the schoolyard. They continued on up the Strip, chattering excitedly again about the Million Woman March, dancing in the rain.

Only if they had been forced, only if they had been on their very deathbeds that evening, would Jan, Sal, and Roach have confessed that yes, they had heard the laughter, too. The wild, sweet laughter of a long-legged little girl with hair of many colors, but mostly red.

WOMAN FOUND DEAD AT AMTRAK STATION

by Shonda Payne,
Staff Writer

Washington, D.C., police are baffled by the discovery of the body of a woman in the ladies' rest room at the downtown Amtrak train station.

The body, carrying no form of identification, and discovered early Tuesday morning by an Amtrak rest-room attendant in one of the bathroom stalls, was described as that of an African-American female, approximately 25–30 years of age, with no distinguishing marks or scars. A small suitcase was found alongside the body, containing all new clothing, most with the price tags still attached.

The woman appeared to have died of a gunshot wound to the left temple, although police are withholding an official cause of death pending autopsy.